CW00322329

A BEDTIME STORY

A BEDTIME STORY

John Hole

Hodder & Stoughton

Copyright © 1995 by John Hole

First published in Great Britain in 1995
by Hodder and Stoughton
A division of Hodder Headline PLC

The right of John Hole to be identified as the Author of
the Work has been asserted by him in accordance with the
Copyright, Designs and Patents Act 1988.

10 9 8 7 6 5 4 3 2 1

All rights reserved. No part of this publication may be
reproduced, stored in a retrieval system, or transmitted,
in any form or by any means without the prior written
permission of the publisher, nor be otherwise circulated
in any form of binding or cover other than that in which
it is published and without a similar condition being
imposed on the subsequent purchaser.

All characters in this publication are fictitious
and any resemblance to real persons, living or dead,
is purely coincidental.

British Library Cataloguing in Publication Data
Hole, John
Bedtime Story
I. Title
823 [F]

ISBN 0–340–63757–9

Typeset by Hewer Text Composition Services, Edinburgh
Printed and bound in Great Britain by
Mackays of Chatham PLC, Chatham, Kent

Hodder and Stoughton
A division of Hodder Headline PLC
338 Euston Road
London NW1 3BH

For Chrissie,
Peter, Abigail, Ginnie,
Morag, Joe, Jenny & Ron,
Ben, and George with love
and thanks.

STARTING IT

The little boy had fallen asleep. Harriet thankfully closed *In Which Piglet Is Entirely Surrounded By Water* and gazed blankly out of the nursery bedroom window. Below her, the evening sunlight glowed on the lawn. There was nothing for it, she thought, she had better become a whore.

Her son Timothy's thick eyelashes lay still at last, fringing his pale freckled cheekbones. When Jonty wanted to get at his baby brother, he would call them pouffy-girl's-lashes. Harriet loved those delicate hairs so much it hurt. Timbo had been a very scared four-year-old today. His whole life had been falling apart – in some totally unfathomable way. He had watched her with such frightened eyes. But he was sleeping at last. Everything might feel better in the morning. God, she certainly hoped so.

She went downstairs to the kitchen and put the kettle on. The idea was absurd, unthinkable, horrible. But it was what people said, wasn't it? – 'I'll have to go out and walk the streets.' They didn't, of course. They didn't mean it. It was just a wry joke that you said in conversation, when things were tough. As a fact, it would be an abhorrent idea. But what in hell's name were they going to do? What had happened today had truly felt like the end of the world.

She stood motionless by the kitchen French windows that gave out onto the lawn. She was so immersed in her thoughts that she hardly saw Starfire, the wretched family dog, alone by the pond, doing unspeakable things to the marigolds. She eventually roused herself and thought about baked potatoes. They were absolutely all they had. Perhaps, this evening, she could throw caution to the winds and splash out on one whole complete family sized tin of baked beans to go with them. That would make Jonty and his father sit up and take notice.

She was still feeling shaky from what had happened that morning. She couldn't keep her rotten tears at bay for more than half an hour

1

at a time. The house looked so naked where they had removed their precious belongings. She felt so abused by it all.

Upstairs she heard her husband, Peter, switch on the telly in the office. The telly so recently retrieved, with wry family cheering, from its hiding place in the loft. Yes, it was The News. It made her irrationally angry. But after all, newspapers had been his life. It was only natural that he should want to keep up with the day-to-day shenanigans of his rather more successful erstwhile colleagues. But with each day Peter became more and more morose, less and less able to turn his flickering word-processing screen into their salvation. And they desperately needed it now. There were times, she knew, when all he could do was sit around in his den, doing nothing, avoiding their puzzled and questioning faces downstairs. Harriet couldn't see, if he really loved them, why he ever stopped working for one single solitary moment. Why didn't he just work every minute of the day? After all, their ex-accountant Michael Johnston reckoned the house would have to go next – in six weeks or so. What an impossible, terrible, frantic mess it all was.

Well, here's a joke – this afternoon, I found myself kneeling grossly on the floor of the back loo, eyes shut tight, praying! Given my basic lack of trust in any kind of religion, that really was a touch rich. But, during the last three days, I've been about as close to the bloody bottom as I think I ever remember. Feeling absolutely crucified, in the privacy of the back loo felt just momentarily as if it might be some kind of helpful release. It wasn't, of course, but at least it was private, and I can't possibly let H. know how defeated I feel and, of course, I'm trying to hide what's going on from the kids as much as possible, however little they really understand.

So I've started to pour my pitiful minuscule soul on to this computer screen. Yesterday I whinged away on it for about fifteen hundred words, covering poverty, life, poverty, guilt, poverty, my marriage, poverty and other allied topics of note, before consigning it all to oblivion with the off-switch. Today, I might just begin to keep some of this diary (safe and secure behind a locking code-word). Well, it could finally become the raw material for something or other. The world's longest suicide note probably. Anyway, giving vent to this stream of consciousness about my lot, here, is presumably somewhat preferable to wasting away, on bruised knees and with over-strained face muscles, in the back loo.

Today the bailiffs came. I knew it was going to be soon. I'd sold the Saab to get us through to the end of May. And, of course, it wasn't mine to sell – I think we owned about half the radiator and the windscreen wipers. The entire remainder of the thing belonged, lock, stock and battery, to the finance company. In April, I had thought selling it would just be a temporary measure, fairly easily retrieved. I reckoned I'd be able to sort it all out by the end of May, at the very least.

They didn't get a lot of stuff. We'd hidden the tellies, the word-processor – even some of H.'s clothes.

It was absolute shit.

Called Graham at the paper, as he'd suggested way back in May. Nothing doing. He just didn't seem to want to know. And I had to be really cool and pretend it didn't matter at all. I did it reasonably well, given the various pressures I was under. It's me who should have been an actor, rather than Harriet. He asked me how things were going. I almost blurted out the truth, but managed to limit myself to: 'Pretty good, actually. Could be better, but it's fine. So good to be your own boss. Not to have to arse-lick our Lord and Master. Fabulous not to have to commute.' Good old Graham – he's not such a bastard really – giggled like the clown he is, and said: 'Good luck, old son!' And rang off. And I gave him his sodding job.

The funny thing about freelancing is that you don't know you're actually in the doggy-poo and well and truly unemployed until a good few months after it's happened. You keep on thinking, Micawber-like, that something'll turn up – that the phone'll ring. Only takes one phone call, for God's sake, doesn't it? And then you'd be away again. Finally the phone does ring and, of course, it's someone wanting money! They're all chasing unpaid bills.

I'm afraid I've got to face it, Harri was right. She said we were all washed up work-wise about four months ago – late March. I had been banking on my neat, slightly bland markets series for the Indie Mag. And then Hawtry goes and has his coronary! Just my luck. His too, I suppose. Oh it's a great life in the comics.

Harriet was so busy thinking, that she managed to burn the baked potatoes. It takes real genuine culinary talent to burn baked potatoes. But Harriet had a lot to think about.

The bailiffs had arrived at six-thirty, early that morning. Timmy had soaked his bed and she had got up, as usual, to strip off his sheets

3

and she had seen this guy through the window. A little military man with a turned-up moustache and a turned-up trilby and a trench coat, standing on the middle of their front lawn looking up at the house. A paper in his hand.

She had gone back into the bedroom. Peter went from fast asleep to mad staring eyes in two split seconds.

'We're not here. Hide. Keep the kids silent.' He wrapped his dressing gown inadequately around his square frame and went and stood in the doorway to the bathroom. Harriet squinted sideways out of the window on the stairs to see what the bloke was doing.

'Don't let him see you!' hissed her husband.

'He can't, through the net.'

'He might.'

'Peter, what's he want? You know, don't you?'

'Bailiff, I expect.' That one bleak word made her feel like she had died. This was just so completely awful. Timmy was sitting on his pot in the nursery bedroom – even at his present great age of four he still used the pot at night. He scraped the whole thing noisily towards her, across the floor of the landing, innocent, cheerful, loving and unaware. Jonty stumbled past his brother, bleary eyed with sleep, already vaguely conscious that something was wrong. She held out her arms silently towards her eldest and the two of them sank together in a sweaty embrace lying on the carpet of the landing. 'It's a hide-and-seek game,' she whispered to the boys. 'Prizes for who can be the quietest. Sssh!'

There was a hefty knocking at the front door and then there was a long, long silence. After a while the little military man beat out his menacing tattoo once again. A solemn pattern of knocks echoed through the house. The clock-radio alarm clicked quietly on in the bedroom and Harriet heard Peter curse under his breath from his place by the bathroom. They heard the presenter whispering away to the empty bedroom about hospital closures.

There was another long silence. Jonty pulled back from her embrace and searched her face for some sign of what this extra-ordinary behaviour was all about. They waited and waited. Timothy, determined not to be left out, left his pot and joined them, slightly clammily, clad only in his pyjama top. Next they heard knocking round at the back, at the kitchen door. Harriet lay down on the hard floor with her cheek pressed to the carpet, stretched out, with her arms clutched around each of her boys, hushing them gently. It felt like the Blitz. They seemed to lie there forever. Timothy obligingly went sweatily to sleep, breathing his odd raucous breathing, looking very pink about the cheeks. Jonty was frightened now and kept whispering, 'What's the matter? What's happening, Mummy?' She didn't really know.

It had felt like they were about to be fire-bombed. It felt like there was a marauder out there, a rapist, a serial killer, circling their home. Where was he now? Was he still in their back-garden? Was he peering in through the kitchen windows, with his hand up to the glass? It was so silent. Then she thought she heard the man's shoes scraping on the concrete by the side of the house. The side-gate latch clicked. He seemed to be making friendly noises to the dog. He was a really brilliant guard-dog, Starfire. He'd lick Hannibal Lecter welcomingly on the nose, given half a chance. The boys' big tin Mickey Mouse alarm clock ticked away mercilessly in their bedroom. Radio Four muttered on about the Test match. Peter cleared his throat in the bathroom. No one moved.

After what was probably only about half an hour, they heard the sound of the man walking away from the house. He got into his car and drove away. He and his cavalry twill trousers. She hated little men. How had they allowed a little squirt like him in the army? If he had been in the army.

As soon as he had gone, Peter started a positive whirlwind of activity: 'They'll be back. We've got to hide some of the stuff.'

'Where?'

'In the loft. Come on. Quick.'

'What things?'

'Expensive things.'

To the astonishment of the two boys, their parents, each in a flapping dressing gown, tore about the house, unplugging equipment and humping it up the stairs to the square white panel in the bathroom ceiling that gave access to the roof space. Peter fetched the step ladder from the empty garage and Harriet climbed into the stuffy warm loft to receive the televisions, the camcorder, the video and a lot of the equipment from Peter's office. He even unplugged the phones and, wrapping their wires around them, brought them up the ladder to her. The boys got quite into this new game too and presented her with teddies and various toy cars and a box of assorted ancient Lego. These offerings she placed with equal care behind the loft water-storage tanks, stepping carefully from beam to beam in the dust, feeling her way in the dark, frightened that she was going to fall through the plaster-board into the bedrooms below.

Both she and Peter were hot, dirty and out-of-breath when she suddenly thought of her wardrobe.

'My clothes!' she yelped at him.

'Oh, God, don't worry about them, H. There's no time for that.'

But she took no notice. At eight o'clock in the morning, had Marianne Webb, next door, bothered to look out of the back of her house at their two parallel back-gardens she would have seen her neighbour, Harriet Holloway, clad in her Liberty's dressing gown and not much else, fighting her garden shed door as she manoeuvred numerous black plastic bags into it. There, she hid them behind the garden mowers with the bags of lawn fertiliser that they had never got around to spreading.

By half past nine, all they could do was done. Harriet had got dressed and was trying, with the careful use of Pledge and a duster, to hide away some of the more obvious gaps in the house where their precious belongings had, until so very recently, resided.

Then she found herself in the kitchen, making toast for the boys' breakfast. Bread and marge was all she had to offer. In a funny kind of way it had been almost exhilarating, charging about their lovely house, working breathlessly shoulder to shoulder with her husband, as a team. Godawful too, but it had had a nice feeling of 'us-against-them', for a few moments. She and Peter doing something together.

It gave her a sudden flash of a memory – a cold spring day, oh, years and years ago, squatting on top of the slate kitchen roof of a cottage in Wales. Peter squatting hugely on the other end of the roof, where the beams could support his weight. It had been freezing and precarious up there, buffeted by the wind funnelling up the valley. They had, once again, borrowed Peter's best friend Toby's cottage in the Llanberis Pass for a week's holiday, only to discover, on their arrival, that someone had broken the skylight in the kitchen roof in an abortive burglary. Peter and she had mended the roof by way of good neighbourliness and as payment in kind for their week's holiday.

Toby Lydell–Smith, whom everyone referred to as TLS, was Peter's best mate since university days. The two of them, from the most diverse of backgrounds, had forged a lasting friendship through countless rock-climbing holidays based at that cottage. Later the place had featured in each of their early married lives – first with Toby and his wife Barbara and then ten years later with Peter and Harriet.

That year, when Harriet had found herself trying to help Peter mend the roof, had been a time when she had first suspected her husband of having a sort of fling with some girl or other on the Insight team. She had spent two months being, mutely, so sad for herself and him – and resolutely refusing to be undermined by his flimsy lies and prevarications. It had been about the time Jonty was three – well before Timothy was born. Peter had been in his mid-thirties. It was what happened sometimes at that stage in a man's life, she told herself bleakly. You could read about it in *Cosmo*. If she didn't allow herself to mind, it wouldn't get in the way of their reasonably happy marriage.

Up there, on the roof, in the fiercely cold wind that spring, determined to be robust and helpful, holding the sheet of corrugated PVC in place with numbed hands, scared she might get blown off, frightened Peter would think she was chicken, Harriet had felt such a rush of renewed affection for their marriage. She had felt suddenly, thankfully, so close and warm again towards her grimly concentrating husband. There he squatted, on the other end of the pitched roof, silhouetted against the grey green of the hillside, grunting with the effort of his screwdriver. Peter and Harriet, together up there, on the roof of the world, getting it done. She could still recall that puzzling flood of warmth for her flawed over-weight old fella. Peter would always be there for her, for their children, whatever other stupid macho games he might have to get up to. As far as he was concerned, she would always be what finally mattered for him.

It had been the same today, the day of the bailiffs, with him lugging coat-hangers off their rails, ripping electric cable from the edge of the fitted carpets, both of them dashing about like headless chickens, tripping over the kids. All this wasn't his fault. He was doing his best. It was as much her fault, her brother Julian's fault, as it was his. She did really love Peter. Perhaps even more in failure than in success.

Later he came down dressed, and told her he thought it was probably about the fact that he had sold the car. And not much of it had been theirs to sell. It was such a careless, inadequate thing to have done that Harriet felt a great wave of fury build up within her. But Jonty and Timothy were looking on wide-eyed with wonder and fear. Their whole world seemed to be crumbling. She took herself off, steaming with rage, to dress and to do her face instead.

As she dragged on her jeans and a sweater, Harriet wished she could do something to make her boys feel safe. But she felt so powerless. She felt like a passenger in a car that had suddenly plunged across the motorway reservation towards the oncoming traffic. What could they possibly do? Sell the house? They would still owe the building society a ton of money. Get a job? What was she qualified to do?

Harriet had never really worked – a year of Thursdays in the Blackheath Oxfam shop didn't count. After Jonty was born she had done a few weeks in a boutique in Tranquil Vale that her friend Nell had run, but she guessed that Peter, in spite of himself, had always rather disapproved, and she had packed it in after that Christmas. At drama college they had always said that Harriet McGee really did have what it took. As an actress, if she had stayed with it, she could have earned her crust. But she hadn't, had she? Acting was history now. All those years ago, just when it was all going to happen for her, Peter had come along. With such mature good-nature, he had charmed the pants off her, radically adjusted her life, got her pregnant and, in a flood of love and tears, she had written off a career. Well, anyway, she had declined the season they had offered her at Dundee Rep. She had exchanged ambition for a pretty opulent feathered nest – and two brilliant, adorable, darling sons.

Was there really nothing that she was fit for now? Had she really spent the last ten years hiding herself away behind the show of being a just about-good-enough mum and a passable wife? Because most of the time it had felt a little like a ruse. She always sort of felt that one day she would be found out. She had looked at Peter's colleagues' articulate intelligent, smartly attentive wives and felt like a pale shadow, a sham. Did they know that she hadn't the foggiest (and didn't really care) about the Public Sector Borrowing Requirement, or GATT, or the Euro-sceptics, or the impending reshuffle, or the World Cup, or who was bonking who at Windsor Castle last August? Did they know that her kitchen management resembled scenes from *Roger Rabbit*, or that her ability to keep abreast of the ironing had only been made possible by the kind offices of Turners' Laundry of Blackheath Village.

For three years, at Arts Educational College, she had felt the warm well-being of a round peg in a round hole. Since then, well, it had been OK. She had had the very great joy of those boys, pride in her husband's place in the world, the comfort of untold trips, outings, holidays, luxuries and endless, endless shopping. But, apart from a reasonable ability to look pretty preposessing when occasion demanded, this had all been underpinned by a sneaky feeling that she was probably not very good at not very much. And often a bit bored. And certainly of no earning potential.

So now, here it was – a major, stinking, horrible crisis and she could contribute nothing. No special skills. No resources. She had leaned on the steady rock of her husband Peter for ten years. Her prop seemed suddenly to have given way and she could do nothing to help.

At eleven o'clock the little man returned.

It was just as Peter had thought. They wanted the car back – or, anyway, what they reckoned they were owed. It was thousands. The man had a High Court Writ for Distraint of Goods. He said his name was Barnett. He came from a company called Stacey & Ennerdale, members of the Certificated Bailiff Association from an address in Lee Green, just down the road. Harriet had never thought of there being bailiffs so close to the protected security of Blackheath Park. He now had a large Budget Luton Rentavan parked outside on Blackheath Drive and a young man in a suit called Clive who hovered uncertainly about on the front lawn looking like a petrified tree. With a bit of luck Starfire would go and pee on him.

Barnett was very dapper and matter-of-fact in what was, presumably, his regimental tie and, Harriet supposed, mercifully uncensorious. The gist of it was that Peter had received countless demands for repayments which he had ignored as they had had no means of paying. The finance company had eventually gone to court. Peter had got to a stage, he confessed, when he had begun to throw demand letters away without even bothering to open the envelopes. From the day he left college, eighteen years before, he had never had to face any more trying financial crisis than a late payment of his American Express account. For a bright man, Harriet thought, he could be singularly inept.

It had only been a matter of time apparently before this invasion,

9

or something like it, was bound to happen. She wished to God Peter would tell what the hell was going on in their lives. Not knowing made her feel such a fool. She made the boys promise not to say a word about it while they were at Marianne's next door and where they would, thank goodness, get some lunch with the Webb kids, Pippa and Sam.

She wondered what she and Peter owned that would be worth a few grand or so. The antique and antique repro furniture, she supposed. She stood in the living room and tried to assess the value of the five lovely pieces that they had in there. The room reeked of her activity with the Pledge and her duster. She watched Peter study the paperwork that Barnett had given him. She didn't get the impression that his dour and careful study of the legal phraseology was going to make all that much difference in the long run.

'Our usual practice in these circumstances, Mr Holloway,' the man explained absurdly deferentially standing with his back to Harriet's dried flowers in the open fireplace, 'is to commandeer material goods to a value that we estimate will match, in resale, the outstanding debt which, as you will see, is five thousand two hundred and nineteen pounds, ninety-three pence, including costs and V.A.T. We will inventorise the items distrained and report to you on the outcome. I take it that what we see belongs to your family, Mr Holloway? You can, of course, point us in the direction of those items that might be of value which could pay off this debt without too much embarrassment. Has Mrs Holloway any particular jewellery, for example?'

'That's all gone now,' said Peter wearily.

'All right. Yes. All right, let's see.' And the man walked about the living room as if it was an episode of the Antiques Road Show. 'I have to say to you, Sir and Madam, by way of warning, that I usually find that folk tend to be somewhat alarmed by the sale prices that we are obliged to surmise. It is usual for people to overestimate the kind of return that we can achieve on items at auction. Forced sale is never the best way to realise capital, as I am sure you understand. But I have to say that I usually find I am fairly accurate in my assessments. Almost ten years' experience, I suppose.'

'Lovely job,' Peter murmured.

'Not particularly. Not a particularly lovely job. There's a lot of pain and unhappiness involved. I can't say that I like that. But, well, I hesitate to resort to cliché, but, as I always say, it is a job and I suppose that somebody has to do it. I sometimes wish that it didn't have to be me. But there it is. I try to do it reasonably clinically. And, truth to tell, if a company is soft on its creditors, it is possible, in the long run, for the company itself to go under, and there can then be considerable pain and unhappiness at that end. Just because money is owed to a large-scale company doesn't mean that it doesn't matter, believe you me.'

'Oh, yes, I can just imagine First National Radstock bloody going under because they've lost the residual value of that old Saab! It's a pittance!'

'Peter!'

'Well.'

Barnett didn't reply. He called Clive in and, with some care, they began to assemble furniture in the hall, labelling each piece with nasty gummy labels – the Rosewood book-rack (William IV, £210), the eighteenth-century Serpentine Burrwood chest that her father had found for her in a St Stephen's Street sale in Edinburgh, the year they had got married (£900), the Kyoto jardinière that Peter had given her for Christmas two years before (£450). The hallway began to look cluttered.

Peter sat at the kitchen table, pretending that he wasn't there at all and made much of reading an old copy of the *Independent*. Harriet followed the men around like a shadow. Barnett went upstairs and peered around there – at their unmade bed, at Timmy's smelly bundle of sheets waiting for the wash on the nursery floor, at the step ladder incongruously leaning against the wall in the spare bedroom. She hated him looking in her chest-of-drawers, at her silks and underwear and stores of tampons. She went downstairs and began to unload the contents of the sideboard because they thought that they would need to take it.

Then Barnett came downstairs, and sat in the kitchen while Harriet made them all cups of black coffee. How appallingly civilised could anyone be? There was no milk, of course, and not more than a scraping of sugar, but she did seem to have bucketfuls of artificial sweeteners. Barnett tapped away at his calculator and the house got more and more denuded of well-loved bits and pieces. A side-table, to which she had never given much thought, suddenly seemed to shriek at her with the memory of being a wedding present from fellow students at Arts Ed.; the oil painting over the stairwell, which she hardly ever bothered to glance at, now awakened a cryptic

11

memory of purchase one Easter, in Ilkley, at the annual local art exhibition, when she and Peter were driving up to Edinburgh to see her parents. They had stopped off to have tea at Betty's Tearooms. It was when they were rampantly in love. Ten years later and it was going to pass into Mr Barnett's inexorable care.

It didn't take all that long. By one-thirty the man was ready for Peter to sign his inventory. The house now felt as if it was hardly furnished. It was funny what small value the things seemed to have. The boys came back from Marianne, just as the hapless Clive came through to the kitchen holding Jonty's Nintendo. Jonty saw it and went even more white-faced.

'That's Jonty's,' she snapped. 'You can't have that.'

Clive looked at the man Barnett, who seemed to nod. 'That'd just about do it. Mop up the remaining deficit, Ma'am. Sorry, old chap.'

'It's Jonty's,' she repeated grimly.

'Yes, I realise that. What else should we put in instead?' The boys watched the four of them, astonished. To them the house must have looked as if some sort of hurricane had passed through it, removing parts of its very soul.

'It's Jonty's. It's Jonty's,' she said again. The boy looked at her with such gratitude. She found she had taken hold of part of the vastly expensive plastic gadget that was in Clive's hands and for a moment they both held it between them, their arms outstretched. So silly, it was only a time-consuming, mindless game. Clive let go and Harriet cradled it to her chest.

'There's no telly monitor screen for it, Mrs Holloway,' Barnett said softly.

'There's a remote control in the sitting room,' the Clive man contributed. There was a silence as everyone in the room weighed up this fact.

'Well there's a thing,' Barnett murmured. Silence filled the kitchen. 'But no TV screen,' he continued. 'So it would be quite a sensible contribution. The lad can't use it without a screen, can he?'

Harriet was filled with the alarming idea that Timothy might say the telly was in the loft. Peter obviously felt the same: 'Listen, Harri, they've taken my golf-clubs, sweetheart. It'll have to go. Sorry, Jonty. Sacrifices all round. Then we're done. Then they can go.'

'No!' she said most terribly firmly.

'Harri!'

'Oh bugger you, bugger you, bugger you, you bastard!' Now she was off and shouting. And then, almost immediately, she was crying. It seemed to her they all cried. Jonty hung on to her legs and buried his sobbing head in her belly. Timothy wandered bemusedly off into their starkly empty living room dragging behind him Pippa Webb's old ragdoll. Peter sighed deeply, came over to her, gave her a squeeze and then took the boy's game from her. He put it on the kitchen sideboard in front of Barnett, where the microwave had stood until half an hour before.

In a while, Peter signed various bits of paper and the men drove the van away with all their lovely things inside it. Harriet just felt she wanted to die.

'Harri! Harri, let me in!' Peter tapped the bathroom door and called quietly to her for the hundredth time, his mouth close to the door-jamb. She had been there for a long time. This was being so very tough on the kids. She sat on the edge of the bath and scrubbed at her face very hard with the dry flannel. She felt better when she hurt herself. 'Come on, Harri, for God's sake. Look, I'm sorry, you know that. What more can I say? I can't do anything about it.'

She had finished, after the bailiffs had gone, by slinging a colander at Peter. Not really at him, just across the kitchen. Not very constructive behaviour. But she had come to the end of her tether. She hated him. Peter had never been easy but when he had been successful, he had, at least, been pretty charming most of the time. And the money had helped to oil the wheels of their relationship. Now he was there with her all the time, filling up the house, lying to her about their dire situation, pretending it was going to be all right, when it wasn't.

'Harri, for God's sake let me in! Please. Come on, Trinket.'

'Leave me alone, Peter.' She was still choked up from the crying, and short of breath. Her eyes hurt. The salt stung. She didn't look like a trinket these days. She must look like a little old lady. A little old lady of twenty-eight. 'I can't do this any more.'

'None of us can do this any more, H. But it'll be OK. I spoke to Graham today. There's something in the pipeline. I'll sort it. Believe you me. But come on, let me in. Come on, Harri. Listen, lovely, I love you. You're a brave old lady.'

She sat on the edge of their magnificent bath, in their ridiculously

13

palatial bathroom with the floor-length window that looked out on to their professionally designed and landscaped back-garden. Good thing you couldn't take landscaping away in a Luton van. The golden sun, outside there today, made her feel such an extra emptiness that she had more than half a mind to reach down for the Sainsbury's bleach and gulp the whole lot down in one. Outside, the trees swayed around their now neglected lawn. Each year they used to give their annual media garden party in July, out there. One of the sought-after invitations of the summer that had been – Andrew Neil had dropped by last year. Three years or so ago Cap'n Bob had stayed for a whole half an hour.

And now, here she was, Harriet Holloway, the once apparently attractive, mother-and-newspaper-hostess-of-the-year, the famed 'child-bride' of the once stupendously high-flying Pete Holloway, done for, finished, over. Life over at twenty-eight. What a sick, horrible, pathetic joke!

Her dear buttoned-up father had once muttered to her, standing tall and wiry as a beanpole, in his garden by his runner beans, that he was worried that it might all turn out like this. She had thought then, so scornfully, how much Peter's position in the world totally eclipsed the life and security of Dr McGee and family. Peter Holloway had been the marital catch of the century, surely? But her father had never really warmed to him. Her father had always had a touch of the good old Scots Calvinist about him. Today, now, looking back, she knew exactly what her father had meant. Indeed she was of similar mind. Worse, she wasn't just vaguely bothered about her husband – she couldn't bear him!

'Harri.' Again the urgent whisper, his mouth at the crack of the door.

'Go and see to Timothy, he's crying.'

'Are you OK?'

'I'll come out soon.'

'You OK?'

'No, I'm not OK, Peter, but I'm not going to do anything radical to your aftershaves.'

'That's my girl.'

'I'm not, actually.'

'What?'

'Your girl. I don't feel very much like your girl. I feel like you're someone I know ever so vaguely.' She gave a mighty sigh. She would

14

cope a while longer yet. 'I feel I'm someone *I* know ever so vaguely.' She sniffed and gulped and wrenched air down into her lungs – and gave herself a wry little nod in the mirror to acknowledge her weary attempt at flippancy. 'Oh, I don't know,' she muttered more to herself than anything. 'Peter, you seem like somebody who kindly gave me a ride or something in their car and then went and had a fucking pile-up. I feel like my face has been smashed in.'

'What do you think *I* feel like?' His voice was still muffled, close to the door. He hadn't gone to see to Timothy.

'I don't much care what you feel like any more. I've spent six months caring about what you felt like, Peter. I've run out of energy, caring about what you feel like.' It was getting to be absurd, muttering angrily through the locked door. 'Go and see to Timmy. I'll come out in a bit.' At last, she could hear him going slowly away to the nursery.

Harriet stood up and scraped at her hair. She looked suspiciously at herself in the vast mirror over the bath. She had let herself get into such a state. There was a time – yes, she used to look pretty good. That's why big successful Peter Holloway had had such a passion for her. Ten years ago, anyway. When he was cock of the walk and so proud to be giving it to this teenage would-be actress. When he had been this acute, clever, go-getting, wonderfully charming guy. For her, a positively ancient guy who had triumphed over his well-displayed beginnings with his dear old mum in darkest unfavoured Peckham and who was already doing it all. Now, here she was, locked in an ornate bathroom surrounded by extravagant rubber plants, two kids later, a stone and a half overweight. Housewife and mum. Beaten. Bailiffs battering at the door. And look at her hair! And that pallid tear-soaked face. Oh dear, oh dear.

But she'd always been tall. She was lucky, she had her dad's long thighs. At Arts Ed., they always used to say that the quantity and the quality of the centimetres from her sharp knee to her hip bone would make her her fortune.

She had better get back to it. Deep breath. She unloosed the bathroom catch. She caught a moment of herself reflected in the mirror, illuminated by the light from the garden. Her boobs were still good. Lucky, that.

But, it was just a lunatic idea. Wasn't it?

*   *   *

15

I've always flown by the seat of my pants, and in times gone by it seemed to work a treat, but my much vaunted God-given instinct seems to have atrophied or something in the last couple of years. My gut feelings have just blown up in my face. Like at *The Chronicle* – all right, the Dorcas Leaftree libel wasn't my fault at all. Duncan's advice, that grim night, was that the story would stand up, no problem. There's no point in having a bloody legal eagle watching the paper go to bed unless you take their advice on the tricky stuff, for God's sake, is there?

Two weeks later, it turns out Duncan had been wrong. Counsel's advice was that the libel would stand up in court and the paper would get bloody caned. And that I shouldn't have taken the risk – our evidence of their corruption was based, at best, on misunderstood information.

Duncan Berry's written defence of his advice that night was such a massive exercise of elaborate obfuscation. It was a damned lie – he never ever said, that night, his famous 'rather you than I'. But he had covered his back with his notes. Certainly better than I had. I was stupidly concentrating on extra-conjugals with Mrs Ellen Herbert and didn't give myself enough time to think it through. So it was the Holloway fingers that got burnt.

Settling out of court cost us a lot of money. And, of course, advanced my reputation rather less than zero per cent.

Mrs Ellen Herbert. Why the hell did I do that? Every time, I would wake up afterwards covered with her juices, wondering why, in shrieking fulminating heaven's name, I was there. Why did I chase after it with such lunatic passionate energy? All, finally, when you get down to it, for about six and a half minutes of very questionable ecstasy. Followed by twenty-four hours of torrid self-loathing. I must be totally mad. Why do I do these things? Why?

It's like 'Alternative Options'! Why did I do that? How could I possibly have invested all the redundancy money in Julian's shitty deceitful operation? Nine months ago, astonishingly enough, after Julian had disappeared and all the money had evaporated paying off his creditors, H. and I used to giggle away rather shamefacedly at the ghastliness of it all. Anyway, I was going to be in gilt-edged copper-bottomed employment shortly, wasn't I? No problem. Well, we're well and truly over that phase now. H. is just really depressed all the time and I constantly feel like I'm losing all touch with reality. I've never felt so extraordinarily incapable. I suppose both of us feel this Load Of Guilt. Me, because I entrusted everything to Julian without really checking it out as properly as I ought to have done (but then he was my bloody brother-in-law). And H., because Julian *is* her bloody brother. Sod him.

So I'm sitting here. Absolutely desperate. Brain dead. Christ knows what's going to happen. Mortgage not paid since February. The building society's giving me such grief. And I couldn't face telling her about the court order. So she had no idea about the possibility of them sequestering the furniture. I simply couldn't face dumping any more inadequacy and misery on her. So I'd stopped talking about it. Stopped thinking about it.

Not true. I think about it all the wretched time. Interestingly enough, I've discovered that I'm a lot less courageous than I thought. You discover it's fairly easy being robust as deputy editor on forty-seven grand a year with hacks to yell at and bags of status and respect about the place.

On top of the mortgage there's the bloody bank, of course – spent up to the limit – down four and half grand. Access screaming for my card – down almost three, Amex the same – they're real toughies, that lot! And Visa. Shit knows what I'm going to do. So, I suppose it's not really entirely surprising that I found myself crouched on the floor of the loo yesterday, embracing the lavatory pan as if my life depended on it, eyes screwed up tight, begging for, praying for, the bloody phone to ring. Not exactly a very practical or dignified way of going about my business. If I had a business. And it didn't work either. God (or the toilet) denied my pleas. What I'd give for a scotch. Two scotches. A bottle. Two bottles.

H. thinks she may be able to tie up a loan at her bank. I'm not very confident, but she says they sounded positive.

And you know, to be bluntly honest, and this I know is a pretty appalling confession, what scatters my wits to the four winds isn't actually not being able to feed the kids. Well I'm sure in the end, we'll find some kind of a way to keep them fed. It isn't dealing with the humiliation of Stacey & Ennerdale ripping off all our belongings, however grotesque and bloody hysterical that was. It wasn't having to sell the Saab. It's not even the fact that everyone I ever knew, except TLS, refuses to admit I exist. The thing I feel worst about is that I don't have any place, any position, any say-so, no power, nothing. Oh yes, I know this is pure hundred per cent egotistical garbage, but – God only knows, it's pathetic and sick and horribly

true – I find I can't bear the incognito nothingness. I do not exist.
There is no such person as Pete Holloway any more. The phone will
never ring. Nothing is ever going to happen. I am dead.

And I do miss knowing what's going on. I miss the banter too.
You can't banter much with a four-year-old, or with H. who's just
stony-faced all day when she isn't yelling. I've always suspected
her sense of humour was a style accessory and now, of course,
it's entirely absent without leave.

The day after the bailiffs wasn't much better than the Day Of
The Bailiffs. There was no food and no money. Nothing. And this
strangely empty and bereft house. You can't make an evening meal
for four out of one pot of antique pesto, five half-empty bottles of
mixed herbs, and a packet of Beecham's Hot Honey and Lemon
cold remedy. We had two pounds twenty-three pence between us.
That's all. Absolutely totally all.

I borrowed half a packet of very ancient pasta from Marianne.
The boys thought it dreary as hell and wouldn't allow very much
of it to sully their prissy lips. And all this in spite of H.'s manic
persuasion techniques: 'Ve hev vays of making you eat. Heh heh!'
H. was deeply pissed off with me too, as I wasn't exactly a shining
example myself. Does me no harm to starve a little – I need the
weight-loss. And how.

Escaped up here, claiming I had work. Couldn't switch on the
box as H. would have heard. Amused myself writing nonsense verse
adventures for the kids. The least naff one begins: 'Timmy 4, and
Jonty 8, get their dad in such a bate – ' It turned out to be a jolly
adventure about life in a pasta paradise facing imminent invasion
from some vicious fascist Tories called the Rizz Ottos. I got quite
into it. It'd be a darn sight better than reading that Tintin – their
present fave – the bald fourteen-year-old Belgian detective and his
yelping, wryly-knowing hound. Timmy can't follow Tintin anyway
– unless he squirms on to your lap with the concomitant ramming
of sharp little heels in crotch, to scan all the pictures.

H. and I finished up in bed – getting there together at the same
time, for once. And there we are, both of us lying rigid listening to
the rain on the empty garage roof. We sort of made peace, and I
held her hand, both of us on our backs, three miles apart. I guessed
she was building up to say something, but I didn't fancy another
run-down of my more basic overall failings, so I determinedly set
about getting to sleep. Harriet ummed and aahed and generally

thrashed about and then, blow me, she comes up with this really batty notion – she'll go and walk the streets for us all! I was almost able to remember what it was like to laugh. Kind of broke the tension though, and we both got to sleep quite quickly after that.

Still very hot in spite of the rain. England followed on in the Test match.

'Peter?' She spoke very quietly, her voice feeble against the sound of the rain. Was he asleep? Probably. It was easier to say out loud if no one was actually listening: 'This is just – this is a – oh, I don't know. It's, oh, bugger . . .'

'Hmm? Yeah?' Oh God, he actually was awake. It was one of his slightly weary sighs.

'Nothing.'

'Go on.' Properly awake now. Resigned to having to listen to her.

'I expect this is just such a really stupid idea. No, it's crazy . . .'

'What is?'

'Peterkins, I think we're close – sorry, I've got to talk about it – we're close to the end, aren't we? I can't see how we can get through. I've been thinking – couldn't I go out and earn some – I might be able to earn some money. I've been getting obsessed by this crazy idea. I know it's stupid, but I've been obsessed with this kind of crazy idea that I could – '

'Do what?' Not really listening. Why did he always assume that she was useless, that she couldn't do anything? That if there were problems, it was always down to him to sort them out? Was it always the man who had to fix things? Maybe she *was* useless. Maybe all she was fit for was shopping and smiling at dinner parties. And being a goodish mum? And sex.

She whispered the appalling idea out loud for the very first time: 'Sort of – I don't know – sell my companionship. Evenings out, that sort of thing. People do. Women, I mean. You always read about it, in the magazines.' He snorted quietly, derisively and turned away from her, his broad shoulders dragging the duvet. She ploughed on, whispering urgently, her throat dry with saying it out loud: 'Yeah, I know, it sounds awful. But . . . I could. I think we're done for otherwise. I couldn't bear to lose all this – the house and everything. I do so love it here – Blackheath. I couldn't bear to lose our life. And I think we will pretty shortly. I couldn't take another visit from those

19

dreadful men. It was so awful. I felt like they were going to take me to jail.' She blundered on, saying each thing straight out as it came into her head. Whispering against the sound of the summer rain. 'It's so silly, one of the things I dread most is, one day, having to tell Daddy what's happening.'

'Oh, this is just about disappointing Alasdair, is it?' he muttered, face down in his pillow. But he was listening.

'No, no it's nothing to do with Daddy. Not really. I've just got obsessed by this idea. I can't stop thinking about it. It's awful but it seems possible too. People do, don't they? I can't stop thinking about it. I think I may have gone mad. But I mean it. I'm sure I mean it. I think so, anyway.'

'And I suppose I should hawk me bloody bum down St Martin's Lane, eh?' He let out a shout of laughter. 'The pink pound. That'd do the trick.'

'Don't be silly,' she said quietly.

With an eruption of the covers, he turned back to her: 'Me being silly? Me being silly? Don't be such a fucking stupid cow, H.! You're going to walk the streets, are you girl? Up King's Cross? Come on!' He was actually laughing at her now, but in an almost kindly way. 'Look, Harri, I know this is all bloody tough and we're having a rotten time, but I'll sort something out. I promise. Now go to sleep, there's a love, get some kip.' He'd turned away again. 'You'll see.' He laughed limply: 'As I always say: "It'll look better in the morning."' Silently, she joined with him, mouthing the last six words in unison, as they had a thousand million times over the past four months.

'It never has though, Peter – looked better in the morning. However much you promise. It just stinks. It stinks.' And, oh God, she was weeping again. 'It bloody stinks!' Her voice was a tiny little gasp into the collar of her nightie clenched tight in her fist.

He hadn't heard it. He was asleep, breathing firmly. She would listen to that steady breathing again for another long night. He always seemed to be able to sleep OK.

She lay there listening to the South London rain and thought about her mad obsession. The wet would be good for the grass.

Mrs E. V. Richardson, Harriet's bank manager, became deeply involved in the corner of her office with the business of serving them both coffee. Harriet's heart, which had been rising and falling all morning like a yo-yo, sank to the bottom of the ocean. Elaborate hospitality was always going to be the sign of a woman about to tell another woman that the news was bad. They weren't going to do it.

Harriet thought that she had heard that the 'E' in 'E. V.' stood for Eleanor. Could she dare address her bank manager by her Christian name? A bit of female bonding might not come amiss. It would not be a very good move if she was wrong. Eleanor Richardson, if this was indeed her name, was only about five years older than Harriet herself – thirty-three or four or so. Something of a success to be bank manager to the denizens of well-heeled, power-brokered Blackheath. Actually, she was fairly mumsy underneath the blouse and the straight skirt of the trade. She would have looked more at home serving in a bakery really. She would probably be on around twenty-two grand. And married. How had she managed to put all that together? Hard graft and application probably. She wondered what the Mr Richardson did for a living? They'd have the odd penny or two, wouldn't they, the two of them, on two middle incomes? No bailiffs in their neck of the woods. More and more, with each day, Harriet found her mind crawling with shameful, disgusting, sick-making envy.

'Well,' said Mrs Richardson, when finally she had found the coloured coffee granules and had got herself settled enough to pick up the Harriet Holloway computer read-out and file. She had been putting it off. 'I'm afraid things are much harder than they used to be. We're in a completely different climate nowadays. It seems absurd: five years ago I wouldn't even have had to get any kind of clearance for this kind of extension on a mortgage. I'm really very sorry, Mrs Holloway, but it does seem that they won't wear it. I must say, as I said to you when you first came in to see me, I thought that with your husband's track record and reputation plus your own steady management of the account, we were in with a chance.' She laughed almost gaily, and ploughed doggedly on.

It was disastrous. Harriet just wanted to walk out then and there. She had heard enough. But you have to go through the whole painful rigmarole, don't you?

'But how wrong can you be, Mrs Holloway? It's all a question of establishing guaranteed income. And that seems to be very tricky to do, just at the moment. I really am so very sorry but I don't think we're going to be able to be of much help.'

'They're going to cut off the electricity.'

'Oh, my dear. Oh dear. How awful. Are they really?'

'Yes. Yes, apparently so.' She must *must* not cry in front of this woman.

'I don't know what to suggest. You could talk to the electricity board. They're quite sympathetic, once you get into communication with them. They'll let you arrange to pay so much each month, even a little bit each week.'

'We've absolutely no money.'

'Well. When is Mr Holloway expecting his next payment? Do you know?'

'It doesn't exist.' Harriet felt very grim. 'There isn't a next payment,' she said hopelessly. 'That was a lie. There's nothing expected. We're broke. Skint. We've already had the bailiffs in, the day before yesterday. They took our furniture. They even took away my son's Nintendo game.' Harriet swallowed and fought with her throat to continue: 'It was so awful.' Her treacherous eyes let her down. She scrabbled in her handbag for a tissue. Would she never be able to stop this crying? It had to stop. She must get a hold of herself. It was so limp and pathetic. Mrs Richardson came around the desk and squatted by her side and gave her a squeeze. And a proper linen handkerchief. Harriet mopped up. Probably Eleanor Richardson dealt with more situations like this each day than you might suppose. It was possible that, if only you knew, a good eighty per cent of apparently favoured Blackheath was, in reality, on its knees. The recession was clobbering everyone – even Thatcher's children.

'You'll have to go to the DHSS, Mrs Holloway. They move pretty quickly sometimes, when there's real hardship. They may even be able to help you with interest payments on the mortgage. You'll just have to come out and tell them you're in a bit of a hole at the moment. You've no savings?'

'I told you we hadn't.' It came out rather more snappily than she would have liked.

'Yes, you did. Yes, you did. Well, you can sell the house, can't you? With two children you'd have a very good number of points. You could well be lucky with the council. And they've got some really excellent places now – Abbeywood, Thamesmead. Not far.' She tailed off. They both knew that Thamesmead was decidedly not paradise. But, then, paradise wasn't on the agenda any more, was it?

It had been, for ten long fat years, and Harriet had hardly noticed. Harriet had taken it all for granted.

'I'm going to have to tell Jonty that he won't be going back to Goldings. It's so funny, I couldn't imagine loving boarding school at all. But he so adored it.'

'Yes.'

'I don't know what to do.'

'I think what you need to do, Mrs Holloway, is you need to review the whole position again. Cards-on-the-table time.'

'Yes.'

'We have a financial advisor: Mr Shastri. I could arrange for you to see him, perhaps with your husband as well. He may have some ideas that you haven't considered. I mean, you're both shrewd, successful people who are a little bit down on your luck, just at the moment. It may be, for a while, that you'll have to operate from rather more modest circumstances. And you must get Mr Holloway to go and talk to the DHSS. As soon as possible.' He'd die, Harriet thought. That really would be throwing in the sponge, as far as Peter was concerned. She could imagine it: 'What did you do when you were employed, Mr Holloway?' 'Oh, nothing special, I was Deputy Editor of *The Daily Chronicle*.' 'And you're looking for income support?'

'Jonty will have to go to James Brookfields,' is what Harriet said.

'It will depend where you are living. James Brookfields is not a bad school. At all.'

'Yes.' Instantly Harriet knew that she had sounded unconvinced. But then she had heard innumerable Blackheath mums going on and on about the iniquities of James Brookfields Junior School.

'No, it really is,' Mrs Richardson affirmed vigorously. 'It's very good. I think. Just as good as many a private school.' She got up and went and sat behind her desk again. Harriet had got it wrong. Her lack of enthusiasm for the school suddenly seemed almost fatal. In her head, all she could see was the scuffed concrete playground with the battered wire-netting fencing, on the fringes of an enormous, depressed, high-rise housing estate. She could hear the raucous noise of the kids and she imagined Jonty standing uncertainly by the wall, near the prefabricated buildings. Mrs Richardson continued resolutely: 'It's fine. My own children go there.'

'Right.' Harriet felt a cloud of depression settle in the room. Mrs Richardson had stopped liking her. Her bank manager changed the subject: 'I'm sure this is horrible. But there are ways out. You've got a sizable slab of property up there in Blackheath Drive to start with, haven't you? *Nil desperandum.* Believe you me, there are a lot of people I see across this desk in a very far worse state than you are in. Single-parent mums with three kids living in bed and breakfast accommodation whose Giro hasn't arrived – '

Harriet interrupted her: 'I know, I know. I said I'm sorry. That's all tragic, awful. But what's happening to us feels pretty tragic too.'

But she'd lost Eleanor Richardson's sympathy. All right, Harriet's family had started to go under from much further up on the pile, but it still did hurt her very much indeed. Yesterday, out of the blue, Mrs Stoner and her son Giles had come around from number 21. Having a bit of a spy, Peter had said. They asked if Jonty and Timothy wanted to go to Alton Towers in July. A whole weekend away. Harriet had muttered about being very busy and her two sons, looking white-faced with yearning at the idea, kept such a courageous wretched silence, not even allowing their eyes to say: 'Please.' Mrs Stoner made her exit from the kitchen – they hadn't been able to take her into the acres of empty lounge – with lots and lots to tell neighbouring members of the Townswomen's Guild. When the going gets tough, the dirt starts flowing.

'You could get yourself a job, Mrs Holloway,' continued her bank manager.

'I'm not sure there's anything I'm fit for. I really don't know what I could do – that could be all that worthwhile. I certainly couldn't be an actress now.'

'You've had the training. You should try to put that to use.'

'I was never even a member of Equity.'

She left the bank a failure, wearily untied the dog and walked distractedly up the hill. Starfire, as usual, was pulling his cord every which way in order to see if he could pee on the greengrocer's display. Starfire – at present the best fed of the Holloways – was the least liked, gloomiest, most bedraggled family dog ever to come out of Battersea Dogs' Home. But, having been assured, by countless car window stickers, that a dog was not just for Christmas, Harriet continued to struggle to try to give it care in the community. And while you could hardly say it thrived, it didn't exactly run away.

She yanked at his lead but was hardly aware of Starfire's activities.

Nintendo games and Alton Towers – was that all that this was about? She really ought to be ashamed of herself. She was.

She met Peter, as agreed, by the bus shelter in front of the concert halls, at the top of the hill. He had brought Timmy along. The boy was sitting on one of the tip-up seats, swinging his legs so energetically that his feet kicked the shelter side. Irritatingly. Peter immediately saw from her face that it hadn't worked.

Harriet thought that, to outside eyes, the four of them would appear to be such a delightful, fortunate family group – attractively turned out parents, both wearing their sunglasses, deep in close conversation. Young child at the fullest extension of his security wrist-strap lovingly grasped by his father, family dog at about the furthest end of his extending lead in another direction. Family dog fouling the pavement. Timmy yelped: 'Mummy, look at Starfire!' and then stopped, startled by the sight of the tears pouring down his mother's cheeks.

I pretended that I didn't really hear last night, but Harriet had this lunatic crazy idea that she'd go on the game or something. It was a sort of cry of despair, I suppose. She never meant it literally. The idea, in reality, is so awful. The thought of it! Yeah, it's something a randy old sod like myself might toy with, as a slightly kinky secret fantasy. I mean, I suppose I have very occasionally entertained myself with the idea of her doing it with somebody else. It's something that blokes occasionally think about, isn't it? No more than a somewhat pathetic masturbatory fantasy. Reality is so bloody different. She's absolutely no idea of what kind of a world there is out there in the wondrous 1990s. It's not her fault, the width of her experience is bounded (*was* bounded) by the fabrics department of John Lewis, the centre court on Men's Finals day, the Sainsbury's Deli Counter and Val d'Isere. After all, that's what I tried to give her over the last decade. Pretty successfully, actually.

In fact, it's not as if she is a very sexy lady any more anyway. Yep, when we first met she was a totally delectable, enrapturing eighteen-year-old rut. For ten months I couldn't keep my hands out of her knickers at all! Funny, I think I must have stopped feeling randy for H. about the moment we were spliced and were coming out of the Kirk together. It's such a bugger that it all fades away. And in its place you get Marriage and Being Responsible, and The Boys. Life takes on the heavy, non-scratch veneer of the eternally mundane. We became pretty damn excellent at the mundane – professional at it! Wall-to-wall Nativity plays in Mixed Infants. Endless days of gritty family holidays on the Costa del Sangria. Oh, and the garden – the endless toil to keep the lawn looking trimmer than everyone else's. Actually, I suppose we both rather enjoyed doing the garden. It was one of our best bits, together.

Existence just trickles through your fingers and melts away. It disappears in a sea of trains to catch, and deadlines to meet, and the aroma of baby burps on the girl's shoulder, and teething and schooling and muling and puking. I saw this kid's T-shirt in the Village today: 'Birth, School, Work, Death', it said.

Yeah.

So that must be the reason why pathetic old mid-crisis lifers like me turn their fanatical energies and concentration on to their work and on to smart little numbers like Ellen. Or, bugger it all, on to just one of those two. And finish up hating themselves and screwing up all round. Men – we're all daft eight-year-olds really – like Jonty. Eight-year-olds who want absolutely everything in the toy-shop window. Now.

Ellen Herbert seemed to be libidinousness supreme. Someone else's woman. Someone else's woman, looking for it. All that. I can't ever remember the word going round a building as fast as it did the Monday Mrs Herbert joined *The Chronicle*. Bets were laid, possibilities sized up, guesses were scoffed at, boasts aired, assessments contradicted and passes eventually were duly delivered. It took me about three months. Far as I can make out I was the only winner. Then we really made up for lost time. Completely pathetic stuff. I'd wake up, loathing it – afterwards. But, I suppose it added a touch of salt to the Potato Soup of Life. For about six months. Just enough time to get myself the push. Six months. And all that for what? After all, Mrs Herbert's a self-seeking egotistical bundle of French knickers, when you get down to it.

All I now know is that I'd almost entirely stopped thinking properly about the paper. For a lot of the time, anyway, I'd gone on to automatic – I was just going through the motions. Thought I could do it without thinking. Madness! My main concern each day was: would it be one in which I might tempt that nice Mrs Herbert to another zipper dinner. That's why, finally, I tripped up on the Dorcas Leaftree libel. If I'd been thinking straight I'd've seen bloody Duncan Berry had got it wrong.

*   *   *

'Dad.' She knew she sounded more Scottish immediately.

'Hullo, my dear. How very lovely to hear from you. How are you doing?' He sounded preoccupied. Was there a queue of summer-time colds in reception?

'Fine.'

'And the boys?'

'Getting bigger every day.'

'What can I do for you?' As she'd rung the surgery, he knew that it wasn't just a social call.

'We've got a bit of a cash-flow problem.'

'Again?'

'It takes forever to get paid. Peter's got lots of stuff outstanding. It just hasn't arrived yet.'

'You and your brother – hopeless managers.'

'Well, Julian *is* part of the problem.'

'Yes, I know, I know, hen. Don't tell me. All right. How much? I'll send you a cheque.'

'A cheque's no good, Daddy. I'm sorry. Any chance of cash or, I don't know, a banker's draft or something?'

'That bad, eh? Are you all right?'

'Yes, yes.' She laughed gaily.

'Sounds terrible. Do you want to bring the boys up here for a while. I could send you the rail tickets.' It sounded a heavenly idea. They could escape for the summer. Play in the hills. Eat her mother's great big Scottish breakfasts. Fiddle about getting the bones out of Arbroath smokies. No sauceless pasta ever again. But Peter wouldn't be able to get away to Edinburgh. And how the hell would he manage to survive on his own? Go and live with that Ellen Herbert?

'No, no. Thanks all the same. Love to. But there's so much to do for the boys in London in the summer.'

'Well the invitation is always open. Your mother would love it. Don't get in a pickle, pickle.' He trotted out his well-worn, well-loved aphorism.

'I'm sorry. I think we are a bit.' If she wasn't careful she would say too much. But she felt beaten by it today. Get back, dull tears! 'No, it's all right, but if you could let me have a loan of a couple of hundred pounds – I'll get it back to you pretty soonish.'

'I don't mind about getting it back, but it's adding up to something of a sum now. Isn't there anything at all that Peter can do to speed things up? I mean, they must know he's got a family to support, mustn't they? God, I feel so impotent, all the way up here. I feel like ringing some of these people up, you know, who owe you money, and telling them to get their finger out!' Strong words for Dr McGee.

'I know just what you feel like, Daddy! God, you don't have to tell me! Peter's doing his best. It's all so slow.' It was horrible, lying to her father.

'You'd better come up here with the boys. Much easier.'

'No!'

'Well you're going to have to do something. I'm not going to let you down, my darling, but I'm really not a bottomless pit, as I'm sure you know! I'll go down to Bridge Street before the bank closes and see what I can sort out with Mr Fraser.' He sounded solemn.

'Thanks, Dad.'

'I must get on, my dear. Listen, get Peter to ring me perhaps. You've got to get something sorted out.'

'That's right, Daddy. Thank you.' He put the phone down. He'd been fed up with her at the end – with Peter really. She had a sudden memory picture of her father, presumably younger then than Peter was now. All of them, on the beach at Filey, Julian about nine years old, herself five. Her father wearing a Panama hat, looking absurdly rakish and out of place, with white socks on, and the whole family devouring big greasy Yorkshire Harry Ramsden-type chips. Lovely. She wished she could afford even one portion – 'with, please; leave them open'.

What to do? What to do?

There must be a network of intelligent, attractive, discreet, sexy, well-dressed young women who serviced the rich and authoritative. Since the beginning of time, it had been expected, hadn't it, that in return for the pressures and the stress, in recompense for the toil and the risk they generously undertook on behalf of society, they could have the use of beauteous hand-maidens? You saw them all the time. Yes, there was such a network. You could see it in the pages of *Hello*! magazine and in the *Tatler* and in the gossip columns of the *Daily Mail* and the *Standard* – anywhere where there was conspicuous surplus cash. She had glimpsed it on opening nights and around catwalks and in the restaurants that Peter used to take her to, in the old days. Those women might very well not be directly in a cash-payment scenario but they were, at the end of the day, making sure they got paid – in holidays, and in rent, and in marriage, and in mistresshood and in a thousand other invisible valuable ways. They were trading in their muscle-tone and their tans and their flat tummies and their Gianni Versace silk waistcoats and their Gucci handbags, by providing their masters with delectable morsels of youth and beauty.

But how, in heavens name, did a girl of no experience – a rank amateur – get a slice of that business? Presumably you didn't comb the Creative & Media advertising pages of the *Guardian* newspaper? She could just imagine the idea of it: 'Community & Social Wanker required for The Elderly Rich. Spunky Gorgeous Woman with Time On Her Hands and a Generous Spirit needed to Boost Flagging Male Egos.'

But there had to be a way?

OK, that's it – Harriet, the light of my life, has taken leave of her senses! She's started this manic regime of charging off across the Heath on the bike and throwing herself around the gym at the pools in Greenwich. Every single solitary day. Talk about displacement therapy!

So I'm stuck here with the boys, while she goes and ruins her hair with Greenwich Council's chlorine. She used to live down there, when I first met her, when she was at Arts Ed. She's presumably creeping back into her childhood to escape. She's got absolutely tunnel-visioned about it. She spends all day in a deeply grungy tracksuit. And you can catch her at it, back here, doing bending and stretching and – what do they call them? – extensions. All over the kitchen anyhow. Conversation is now limited to numbers of lengths swum, and poundage of weights lifted, and distance of miles run.

Some of this is just acute jealousy, I suppose. Because me, I'm built like a double pillar-box. My dad was too. That's what finally killed him, poor old sod. I've just got a big frame. Big bones, I always say, offhand, as if it doesn't matter. You can hide it away pretty well in a decently cut suit. But the bloody weight does get out of hand P.D.Q. I've tried to do just about everything to combat it. I used to go to Charlot's Gym in Holborn twice a week and pedal away on his insufferably boring machines – I'd take a book along to read. And I'd play squash – quite often really – well, twice a year. I found it so difficult to find the time. I gave up bread, cakes, potatoes, sandwiches, cunnilingus. And beer. And wine (well, not much). Ate polystyrene crispboard for weeks. Mark you, I'm not totally unfit, I can still walk up the hills reasonably OK. But my God, I only have to be in the same county as a plate of country chips and I instantly need a larger belt size. Grim.

I suppose Harriet's new hyper-thyroidism is a whole heap better than her moping around the house all day here, pretending she's not looking at me with her this-is-all-your-fault-and-what-the-hell-are-you-going-to-do-about-it eyes. But it's a funny old reversal of roles. She pedals off each morning on her, no doubt short-lived, new passion, leaving me to do the ever-loving child-nurturing. She must have got herself some sort of extra sub from her father. There was a letter with an Edinburgh post mark. Land of the one-pound note. Maybe he sent her a few. Wrapped up in a lecture about my sterling incompetence and, correctly predicted, no-hopefulness.

Jonty is being a right little bastard to me just at the moment. He's turning out a real toffee-nosed pain and winding me up something rotten, as they say in the properer class of prints. Good God, it's not as if any of this is to my taste either.

Timothy on the other hand is fine. You'd hardly know anything had happened. No, that's not exactly true. He came into my office this morning, and announced he was going to sell flowers. Seemed like a nice enough idea for a morning – playing shops. Half an hour later, I'd gone up to the loo and I spied our Timothy, on the pavement of Blackheath Drive, clutching a fairly nondescript bunch of tired lupins and other stuff, torn from the back-garden, wrapped in a few sheets of kitchen roll. He was soliciting sales from just about anyone who ventured down the road. I had to charge off out there and pull back our somewhat crestfallen flower-sales-staff. To his understandable confusion, bless his heart! I had to inform the lad that I didn't think it was quite the thing for this particular class of neighbourhood. Told this, he, fairly reasonably, challenged me as to why I thought he'd asked me if he could go out and do it in the first place? Why had I said 'Yeah, OK' when, in fact, I'd meant: 'No, absolutely not!'? Life's so often a real puzzle for your average four-year-old. As a result of this, he immersed himself in this massive deaf, dumb and blind sulk, set to rival that of his brother. It took me a good fifty minutes to coax him back down to earth: 'Timmy, can you hear me?'

But, however I play it, Jonty won't. Hear me, that is. I get this total wall of silence. He sits in the dark, in his bedroom playing with Pippa Webb's Sega. He won't go and spend time with her next door, however much I try to bribe him, or offer him juicily tempting descriptions of Marianne's ten-year-old, hunched over the Junior Trivial Pursuit board. And I've got virtually nothing to bribe him with. Naught compares with Sonic the Hedgehog – the nineties *Lord of the Rings*. Poor old J. no smiles, no zap, no spring. Hopeless. Bugger him.

Got a sort of tickle from Graham. So that was good. But I'm not allowing myself even to think about it very much. And any fees I get now will be months in arriving.

I suppose I could go out thieving. I have actually spent some of the morning thinking about the realities of going out and stealing something and selling it. Yes, I genuinely did – I was considering robbery! The practical ins-and-outs of your fair-to-middling bank raid. Well, breaking and entering, actually. You can't help it crossing your mind, can you?

At least they'd feed you in prison. I sometimes fancy myself sitting in the quiet of the prison-library of some half-civilised Open Prison in the depths of rural Kent, writing a book perhaps – 'Armed Robbery For The Redundant White Collar Worker'. It might be a sight better than rattling around in this desperate house with its desert of fitted carpet.

Then Toby Lydell-Smith rang. That was a treat. He invited us over to dinner on Saturday in Dulwich, so at least we'll get fed at the weekend. I was so touched by that. TLS is about the only mate who continues to treat me as if all is hunky-dory. What a really good bloke he is. But then he likes H.

Slip-slap, one-two, one-two, splish-splash. Harriet was running through the Greenwich Park in the pouring rain, heading towards the General Wolfe statue by the Observatory. She had given up using her brother Julian's wonky old bicycle and had taken to running the interminable two miles from home to the gym and back. Aaron, the sports worker who usually presided over the torture chamber at the bottom of the hill, boasted he knew exactly how to firm up her good bits and whittle away her bad bits without piling on lots of excessive muscle. He reckoned she was doing just ace. 'Ace' meant that Harriet felt like limp bits of string for the whole of the rest of each day.

Splitt-splatt, splott-splott. No-Pain-No-Gain. Bish-Bish, Bash-Bash. Harriet, daily, almost hourly, watched the progress of her tummy, and of her thighs, and of her cheekbones like an anxious gardener tending his seedlings in the spring. She was astonished how quickly the geography could change.

And it made her feel a lot better about herself. When it was all over for the day and she could fall into the tub at home, she would lie there half-conscious and sometimes feel oddly powerful. At least she was doing something. Catching sudden sight of one of her flexing biceps or smelling the waft of chlorine on her skin sometimes even made her feel a wee bit randy.

Harriet got to the top of the hill and stopped by the General Wolfe statue, hands on hips, to catch her breath in the drizzle, as she looked down at the misty river below.

Her companion, Starfire, sniffed about, over by the Observatory, selecting a hundred and six places to pee on the Meridian line before getting on with his traditional Greenwich Park chore. This was the God-given right to get his fat, dull head deep into the Royal Park rubbish bins in order to scatter their vaguely edible contents liberally about the damp grass.

Harriet stood there looking across at the whole of London stretching away below her in the grey muggy morning. The Great Wen. In all its bizarre variation – scaffolding-clad Gothic, hidden Wren copulas, Canary Wharf phalluses. Harriet was thinking about sex. As a function. Doing it. With strangers.

It was a pretty awful idea, wasn't it? If you thought about it honestly. And she needed to start thinking about it honestly. It might be a sizable chunk of the possible shape of things to come. Thus far, she had banished the sex part of her mad plan to the back of her, perhaps somewhat muddled, brain. She had concentrated on what kind of a life it might be that she was obsessively envisaging. How did people get to know about it? How did it work? Above all and, most important, how much money did it earn? And how dangerous was it?

Now, at last, she was facing the question: what on earth might it be like, doing it?

She had what she knew was a crazy Hollywood notion of the kind of trade it might be – a sort of mixture of the good bits of Cathy Tyson in *Mona Lisa*, Jane Fonda in *Klute* and Julia Roberts in *Pretty Woman*. Not that she'd ever see herself as on the streets, for

God's sake. No, she vaguely saw herself as travelling in limousines, and wearing the very latest Donna Karan could offer and getting to kiss Richard Gere. She would be the tops – a sort of amalgam of Christine Keeler, Carmen, Nell Gwynne and Sally Bowles. Her fantasy cunningly morphed all those splendid ladies together, in their masculinely invented lives, and edited them down into one person, at a point in their histories well before the going ever got rough.

But the reality of the sex had to be faced. All those horny male-made films tended tactfully to skirt around the brutal fact of the matter. And that was, that the crucial, all-important financial killing was made, in the end, by taking your knickers off and doing the business. Those film-fantasy hookers didn't seem to have to do very much of that at all. Or if they did, it all happened in soft focus with a thousand flickering candles burning about the place. They'd get to snog the fella, paw lasciviously at his fly-zip for a few saxophone-filled moments, and then, well I never, the camera would decide that it was much more fun to zoom out of the bedroom window, to look at some passing inoffensive cloud. And, well, of course, the girls'd usually do a bit of falling-in-love with the richest, most photogenic, most charming of the clients. Certainly, they didn't seem to go in for much of your actual nitty-gritty. There were never any soiled underpants or having to go to the loo or smelling his breath. Or being hurt. And there were certainly no condoms. Well, not out of their packets. As far as Hollywood was concerned, prostitution added up to a lot of rude talk and a reasonably sexy film poster or two.

Not that Harriet Holloway could speak. In the last decade, she had concentrated totally exclusively on Peter, as far as sexual congress went. She astonished herself sometimes but, for ten years, she had been entirely a one-man woman. Before Peter? Well, first off there had been dreadfully embarrassing fumblings with Eddie Waller in his mother's flat in Joppa, when they were all in the sixth form. That had been the start. Twice had it been? Three times. No protection. Lunatic. She had imagined herself pregnant all summer long. Then, on the pill, with Brandon just after she'd met Peter but before anything physical had happened with her husband-to-be.

Brandon had been a nice boy. Probably still was. He was at the Manchester Royal Exchange recently. She'd seen his name mentioned on the arts pages of some newspaper. Playing big parts. It had been her second term and all of a sudden he had made

London seem a slightly less ominous and crowded place. He had been two years older than her, but she had never thought of him being enormously knowing as far as girls had been concerned. They had done a lot of hand-holding and snogging before anything worthy of pill-taking had taken place.

And that was probably the reason why the positively middle-aged, twenty-eight-year-old, dreamy, wildly raunchy and vastly successful journalist called Pete Holloway had been so desperately attractive when he had turned up at college, out of the blue, in his bright yellow shiny Triumph Spitfire.

Then her real sexual education had begun. Peter had had most of Fleet Street that had high heels. Or so he'd have you believe. Certainly he really did do the things that you read about in books. All that moist scrutiny of the works of Jackie Collins – which had been Harriet's main source of education in these matters – proved, at last, to have been worthwhile. It was the early eighties, AIDS hadn't been invented and, to start with, her womb had been switched off. In 1984, about the time that Jonty was big within her, she, now Harriet Holloway, felt she knew just about everything there was to know. About that. She thought.

Didn't she?

Who could tell? She didn't feel so confident about it any more. Two years of it being her only hobby had been followed by eight years when shopping got to be sexier and sexier, and sex got to be, well, rather more like a quick trip round the local Tescos. When the stork flies in through the window, it feels as if your bonking licence has been endorsed. There's suddenly absolutely no time, no space and no very wonderful motivation for it any more. Obviously they went through the traditional tumble-dry every week or so. Timothy was proof of that.

Harriet called to the reluctant dog and began to jog squelchingly down the hill towards the gym, with sodden shoulders.

It could well be that a lack of interest in sex was the ideal mental condition for the line of business that she had become obsessed with. And 'obsessed' was right. It was as though she had excavated some dread ambition from the back of her black soul and she couldn't leave it alone for a moment. It was like a soothless itch and she needed to massage at the visions that swam in her head all the time. She could never stop thinking about it during the day. And she tossed and turned as tactfully as possible most of each night, turning it over and over in her mind. And she undertook all this completely on her own. She was aware of becoming more and more abstracted by the day. She became divorced from reality, a kind of Sony-Walkman of her fantasy, blotting out the actuality of her life. But the whole household was like that these days, even the boys. The times had made them all terribly withdrawn and uncommunicative.

And every so often, inside Harriet's reverie, there arose an astonishing scandalised fascination that she was barely able to acknowledge, even to herself. There were these funny lurking moments when she knew that she was more than quite interested in the idea of it. The idea of a number of men. Anonymous men.

Her madness bubbled over again on their way over to Dulwich in Marianne's faithful old BMW. They were going to dinner with Toby Lydell-Smith and Barbara, his wife. On the face of it, Peter's reaction, grim-faced as he ploughed through the Saturday evening Old Kent Road traffic, was much as she would have predicted:

'Crap!'

'What do you mean, "crap"?'

'Harri, darling, it's just a crap idea, that's all. You don't know what you're talking about. Think about it, dumdum, why do you think the adjective from the word "vice" is "vicious"? It's a crazy, dangerous, frightening world out there. You know nothing about it, pet. You forget, I've seen the police reports, the filthy things men do to women. Most prostitutes wind up dead! And there's AIDS. I mean, what are you thinking of, woman? You're a great little housewife superstar, Harriet. Stick to that. Don't be ridiculous.'

End of subject.

'I'm not talking about prostitution, Peter. I'm not talking about prostitution, at all. Nothing like that. Oh God, no. I'm talking about glamour-escorts, that sort of thing. I'm talking about really up-market stuff, Peter. Smart, well-dressed, sophisticated, intelligent, top-drawer servicing, darling. You know what I mean. Companionship, glamour, ego-massaging.'

'Ego-massaging! What kind of trashy novels have you been reading, eh? Top-drawer knobs are just the same as back-alley knobs. They stick them into you. And there are thoroughly sicked-up brains attached to them at every level. It doesn't make any odds what their AmEx credit rating is. Blokes are blokes – period. There are fellas out there, my sweet, who get their rocks off hurting women, getting their revenge on their mothers, buggering their surrogate sisters, cutting up their stand-in wives. Do I have to say "Peter Sutcliffe", Harriet. Just forget it. Stop talking about it. I don't want to hear any more about it.' He gripped the wheel like his life depended upon it.

'I can't stop thinking about it. We need this. We're done for otherwise – you, me, the boys. It's a chance I've got to try and take.'

'Shut up, Harri. For God's sake, put a sock in it. I can't bear even to think about it. Something'll turn up soon, you'll see. Graham says there's a sniff of a job.'

'I'm sure there is, Peter, there always is, but these things take forever. And I reckon Malcolm Nicholls would have something pretty positive to say about nuclear annihilation, if you asked him.' They had reached the outer extremities of opulent tree-lined Dulwich. 'Peter, I'm sure you'll get back on your feet soon, my love. But at the moment, at this precise moment, we need to find something that will keep us afloat, now. Or we'll lose everything we've ever had and have to head for Thamesmead. Or it's back to your mum in the back-streets of Peckham. Do you want that? You've fought hard enough to get away from all that. Don't let's lose it all. You've worked too hard, Peterkins, to lose everything you've earned. This just could be it. It's just escort work, I'm talking about. For top people. For cash.'

'There's no such thing as "just escort work", Harri. You know that.'

'Well, yes,' She was silent for a moment as the car slid past Lordship Lane. 'Yes. Well of course not. I know that. I expect it would include sex. But is that such a big deal? You used to say that sex was no big deal. It was just a good experience between people. Like having a good dinner. Or opening a decent bottle of wine. Anyway, what else is there? It'd just be footling me going off and working in a wee dress shop or something, wouldn't it? It's too late for that now. At this moment we need some pretty vast quantities of cash.'

'For Christ's sake, Harri, do you really think I'd ever be able to stand you going off to bonk sick guys who have to pay to get their ends away? You must be joking. I couldn't stand it. You couldn't stand it. Think about it, think about it, woman! I can't believe we're having this conversation.'

'I'm sorry. But, well we are. What else is there, Peter? Tell me that, eh? What else? I didn't want us to have got to this. But we have. We're finished otherwise. You know that.'

'You mean it's all my fault – Julian's crash?'

'No. No, it's not your fault. No, Peter, it's not. You've done everything you can. You've been heroic. It just hasn't worked, just at the moment. Listen, it seems to me, it's become a totally different world. Someone's thrown the rules away, that's all. We're not the only ones. There are loads of people like us now. It's desperate times.' She tested him out gently, slowly thinking herself through what she had to say: 'It's just a matter of who there is who might be prepared to take advantage of there being no rules. It could be a possible way. I think it's pretty sick and ghastly and frightening but I don't think I'm going to be able to stand the alternative.'

'You sound like you're really into this. Are you just getting a blast out of talking about it? Does it kind of turn you on or something?'

'Fuck off, Peter. Of course it doesn't. Quite the reverse, in fact. It's sordid, shitty stuff. Of course it is.'

'Well, there you are.'

'But you can just think of it as a job, Peter. A kind of acting job. A job that I think I could do. I would probably have to pretend to be someone completely different in order to be able to do it. But it is something that I think I could possibly do. If we could find out about how it works. And I guess we could earn a bit of serious money. As I say, what else is there? Robbing a bank?'

'Yeah, I've thought of that.'

'Oh, great.'

'No, Harri, but I have actually thought about – oh I don't know, it's crazy too, but I've thought about burglary, breaking into people's houses!'

She laughed: 'Really?'

'Well, no not really, I suppose. But I thought about it. I actually did imagine myself jemmying into people's back doors the other end of Blackheath Park. Stealing their videos and stuff. Nicking their jewellery. It's all bloody insured, isn't it? Yeah, crazy – completely cuckoo! Like this preposterous idea of yours.'

'Well, this would be better than getting done for stealing from the neighbours. It's a proper job. You get paid for providing a service – businessmen, Arabs, people like that.'

'It's fucking illegal too, H.'

'Not escort.'

'Well, we're not just talking about escort, are we? We're talking about doing it.'

'You sometimes used to say you had a fantasy about seeing me do it with someone else.'

'That was just a fantasy, lovey, something you giggle about in bed, when you're feeling turned on.'

'You didn't mean it?'

'I shouldn't think so. Look, you're a wife, my wife, for God's sake. And a mum.'

'So that means what?'

'You know exactly what it means. God! We're talking about doing the most deeply intimate, personal, private, secret, loving thing to – well – just anybody. Anybody with money! Harri, grow up!'

'Look, I've thought about this. It wouldn't be making love. It wouldn't be having an affair. It wouldn't be fucking with my soul. It would be providing a slightly specialised service. Therapy.'

'Listen to yourself, H. Get a life! You're just lying to yourself.'

'Nurses take guys' clothes off every day and wash them and put them on the loo. All that—'

'Harriet.' They paused at the lights. They watched an old man walking with pitifully slow steps across the road in front of the car. 'Nurses don't have smelly desperate old bastards putting their fat pricks in their mouths!' He was almost shouting. She couldn't reply. They had reached Dulwich village. Outside of the car, the town sparkled unchanged and eternal in the glorious summer evening sunshine. With its stately green trees and mature gardens and well-heeled late Edwardian homes, Dulwich reeked with comfort and privilege. This is where the 'haves' lived. That was the trouble, thought Harriet, she and Peter had liked being among the 'haves' altogether too much. It was more than she could do to contemplate giving it all up. They both needed to hang on to their very last finger nail. It had all been too seductive, for too long.

They drew up at Toby's extraordinarily beautiful, ivy-clad mansion.

'How the hell would you explain to the residents of Blackheath Drive that you work all night and turn up pre-school break-fast time each day in full slap and an evening dress, eh?' He switched off the car. He gave her one of his off-handed crooked grins. She knew those. It seemed to her that he had suddenly stopped saying no. She suddenly wished that she'd never thought of it.

Peter's very best friend, Toby was already in his drive hollering at them. Toby Lydell-Smith was larger than life. It always seemed to Harriet that he shut out the sun.

'There you are! Welcome, welcome! Where have you been, Pete, you old wanker? Put it there! Too long time, no see, dear boy.'

'Tobias Riddle-me-ree, I never thought I'd see the day you'd wear your spectacles round your neck on a chain! You are so camp.' The men hugged each other like elderly bears on heat. Toby always came over like a foolish nineteen-thirties swashbuckler. And he infected Peter with his style almost instantly. Toby's noise was reputed to camouflage an extraordinarily agile and determined mind. Pretty successfully, thought Harriet, who could never fathom the rumours.

'Harriet, my darling,' he continued to shout, 'you look good enough to eat whole in one paradisiacal mouthful. What, in heaven's name, have you done with yourself? You look as sexy as the very devil.'

Harriet had been thrilled, that afternoon, to discover she could slide back into a mauve silk trouser suit from Flyte Ostell that she had bought for a holiday at the end of the eighties. It set off her shoulder length charcoal hair a real treat, she knew. Aaron's work was beginning to prove itself too. After a deal of thought and much testing in front of her mirror, she had dispensed with even the most delicate of her bras. She felt like a twenty-two-year-old again. Well, that was good, at least.

Toby and Barbara's house was a beautifully converted mansion, dripping with boldly colourful abstract art and large pieces of three-dimensional sculpture. Harriet, who knew she was fairly easy to impress, loved the majesty of it all. I mean, how many people do you know who have a Froebl 'Family at Prayer' on a plinth at the end of what they call their library? She was particularly fond of the splendid curling staircase that flowed down to the polished mahogany of the floor in the hall. And she was always surprised, too, to find herself in a living room that had, at the last count, at least four sofas in it.

Peter had become friends with Toby quite by chance while they were both at Oxford, but at rather different establishments. They had actually originally stumbled across each other while burning baked beans for supper in the communal kitchen of the Glen Brittle memorial climbing-hut, on the Isle of Skye. From there on, they had commenced a rock-climbing partnership built around Peter's always nimble climbing leadership and Toby Lydell-Smith's various eccentric but reasonably reliable motor vehicles.

It was only at the beginning of the following Michaelmas term it emerged that Peter Holloway was at the Polytechnic, on Headington Hill on the outskirts of Oxford, while Toby was living in Dicey, in Balliol College at the university. But inspite of their exceedingly different backgrounds, Toby evidently took to Peter Holloway. Over the next dozen or so years they had yelled incoherently at each other up various rainswept and sheerly rocky chimneys and slabs in the Lakes and in Scotland and in Wales. Indeed, it was in Wales where they had tackled most of Joe Brown's routes around Cenotaph Corner in the Llanberis Pass, above where Toby later bought his very own cottage.

Over the years, they had found themselves opposite each other at Guildhall dinners, next to each other, in full formal attire, by the picnic basket, on the lawns of Glyndebourne and often enough in Toby's company box at Lord's. In the end, Toby had fulfilled the office of Peter's Best Man at their wedding.

Harriet knew that her husband was always slightly bemused that Toby had so adopted him, and had so continued to foster their friendship, particularly later on when their marriages and careers had sent them off in totally different directions. After all, Toby Lydell-Smith had always been, very much, 'old money' and Pete Holloway, in contrast, had always been irredeemably 'of the media', hadn't he? But the duo continued to thrive. They were often together. Often in each other's houses – these two uniquely enormous men – Toby as tall as a lighthouse and Peter so broad. And, all their lives, they watched each other with enormous sympathy, a wicked almost sibling rivalry hidden away in apparent unconcern, as they each fought their way through the rocky climbs and suspect belaying points of their subsequent careers.

Toby had a laugh that could shatter glass at thirty paces. Physically, he looked as if he was more likely to be a farmer or a professional rugby player than the high-flying financier that he had become. His only deference to his trade seemed to be his adherence to a spindly pair of half-moon spectacles that for-ever decorated his famous nose. 'Hearty' was too inadequate a word with which to describe him. And he favoured bilious bow-ties.

His wife, Barbara, was much quieter but jolly big too. A Trojan toiler in the vineyards of local and national charities and an inveterate gardener. They had two young skyscraper sons of fifteen and seventeen who had the disturbing habit of drifting silently in and out of social events at their home, as if they were not occurring and as if no one else was present.

The evening was to begin in the back-garden, on the lawn that sloped down to what Harriet could only describe as a small lake, although the Lydell-Smiths referred to it disparagingly as 'the pond'.

Over the past ten years, Harriet had got used to evenings with Toby falling into a usual routine. They would start with the four of them sitting out on the Yorkshire-stone clad terrace contemplating the evening shadows as they crept over the lawn. The pair of ducks confined to the pond by the simple strategy of deftly clipped wings, would bustle about their evening ways and the Lydell-Smith sons would flit in and out like strapping great moths, filching all the pre-meal goodies. It felt downright privileged to sit in such style and comfort, discussing improvements to the garden and new ways of tending the lawn, while the hum of London's traffic seemed like a distant unimportant swarm of bees. For a couple on Life's Scrap-Heap, Harriet reckoned she and Peter were going out in considerable style.

In a while it would get chillier and the fruity tang of the modest little Chablis would begin to pall and they would move indoors to sit at the big Lydell–Smith dining-room table, still in touch with the darkening sky outside, through the open French windows. It was a reminder of a world now gone, sitting there, four faces illuminated by the dozen golden candles immersed in Barbara's latest table decoration. A meal with flavours of the Mediterranean would appear from her kitchen as if by magic. Provençal vegetable soup in a great treacle-coloured rustic pottery vat, followed by delectable fish pie. Strangely enough, Harriet and Peter's stomachs had shrunk and they found they could only eat sparingly. Above them in the flickering yellow light, watching their chatter, the baleful eyes of one of Dale Riddlesden's American canvases would keep solicitous witness. And Peter and Toby would perform for their audience of two loyal and attentive wives, and each other.

Barbara and Harriet would interject their own occasional morsels of wit and information and the party would move inexorably towards the caramelised oranges. And the coffees and the ports and the brandies. By the time Toby had reached his beloved Havanas, the vocabulary would have got fruitier, as the gentlemen of the party began to emphasise their points with the additional colouring of not a few well-chosen Anglo-Saxonisms.

Harriet, resting her weary back thankfully in her chair in Toby's gorgeous dining room, watched these traditional customs in a slightly disengaged way. She felt tired a lot of the time now, thanks to the daily lash of Aaron's rod. Funnily enough, in spite of this, she felt far better than she remembered feeling for a very long time. She was probably kidding herself, but, of all of them there, she felt that she alone might be capable of doing something revolutionary. Perhaps she was just proud of her progress. Certainly her body felt somehow hard and more together and that seemed subtly to inform her brain. All she knew, sitting there, was that she felt pleased to feel so delightfully naked under the 'nothing' silk of her skimpy floating finery.

Later, although Barbara protested that Marcella would come in and clear up the pots in the morning, they all four carried debris from the table through to the kitchen with its dried flowers and shelves of herbs and coloured glass bottles.

At the end, while Peter went to the loo and Barbara went to her 'office' to find some papers for him about her voluntary work for ActionAid, Harriet found herself momentarily at the open French windows watching the dying light from the sky reflected on the surface of the water at the bottom of the lawn. Suddenly, for Toby and herself, they were enclosed in another world. A world to which she was going to have to say goodbye, unless she could screw her courage to the sticking point. Her host collected some last glasses that had been left forgotten out on the terrace. One of the two boys had a CD of some aching rock guitar playing in the dusk from an upstairs bedroom window. Toby stumbled slightly and stopped, out there in the dark, each of his great hands bunched around a clutch of glasses.

They stood and regarded each other happily enough, she in the yellow lamplight of the room, he, in his garden, with an almost full moon behind his shoulder, in the pale white of the night sky. They had run out of things to say. He brushed past her and put his gleanings on the table. He went out again on to the terrace. Peter could be heard exchanging laughter with Barbara at the kitchen door. Harriet was happy to hear her husband laugh. She hadn't heard him laugh genuinely for about three months.

Toby was standing at her shoulder looking towards the ducks that he kept so easily controlled in his garden. His voice was suddenly, throatily private as he looked down at her: 'With the light behind you, I have to tell you, Harriet my dear, you leave nothing to the imagination, in your, er, delightful pyjamas.'

Harriet blushed and involuntarily ducked sideways. She laughed, feeling foolish. Toby stayed where he was and stood regarding her unhurriedly with his hands still full of plates and things. 'You are such a delight,' he said quietly and then he let fly a single shout of his particular brand of laughter. 'Lucky, lucky bastard, old Peterkins, eh?' Toby normally used to terrify her. But now she seemed to be able to look him in the eye. And they did look each other in the eye. Probably the moment lasted a mite too long for comfort. She reached up and kissed him minutely on the cheek and went off to help Barbara in the kitchen.

LEARNING IT

I had another gargantuan row with H. tonight, when she'd finished reading the kids their bedtime stories. I coped with it even less well than usual, banging around the kitchen in a fairly evil temper and finally, by complete mistake, breaking Jonty's 'I am Nine' mug. This was not a helpful thing to do at that particular stage.

The kernel of this banshee-heaven was that Harriet has become absolutely determined that I should go out and explore the trade of the professional escort. And report back. And I demurred. All I know is that we finished up with Harriet, her face wild, blotchy and soaked with tears, screaming at me: 'And when I think that, at the *Sunday Times*, you used to be Harry Evans' blue-eyed boy! Do it! Do it! For fuck's sake, just go and do it! Don't you care about us at all?'

It's a completely manic obsession that has taken hold of the woman and this seeking out the ways and means is all part of it. Presumably daily sweat-management at the Greenwich Leisure Centre, getting her body into shape, is yet one more part of the same bloody lunacy.

Anyway, she's a radically changed person. I suppose, to be fair, she used to be entirely shored up by the life we had, by the money and by the privilege. What has happened in the last six months seems to have slightly unhinged her. Well, it hasn't done much for any of our self-esteems! In her case, it seems to have made her incredibly hard-faced and withdrawn and solitary. And accusing. Not a very nice person to be around at all. But then, perhaps, neither am I. She's certainly never had to put up with me being around the house all day and all night before. She's never had to deal with yours truly, when not everything is going dead smooth. I feel quite sorry for her. But then, I feel quite sorry for me, too.

But I do try very hard not to whinge out loud – except to you, little screen. Apart from that, I'm not sure I, myself, have changed all that much. To my cost, perhaps. Maybe it's different for me, having crawled out of the so-called back-streets of Peckham. The Miss Brodies of Bonnyrigg High School may not have prepared their wee charges all that adequately for coping with a life of disappointment and sudden grinding poverty.

In the end, H. and I heard the boys creeping about looking white-faced in the hall; we ran out of steam and the disagreement fell into disrepair. The best way through for me here seems to be to work up some of the blessed research she thinks she needs as a story, and then use the result to write a piece. It shouldn't be too difficult to sell. Every time circulations dip, editors the world over shake the dust off their favourite vice piece to claw back a few thousand readers by pandering to basic human lechery. Annie White did a thing, I remember, in the 'Life' section of the *Observer* a couple of weeks ago. I'll ring her and see what she's got. She'll have some leads. Might get me out of the house.

In the shower, Harriet let the hot water drill on to her scalp for much too long, beating comfortingly through the black slick of her hair. The rods of water felt like some kind of releasing Chinese torture – nice and nasty. And very hot. She felt at about two removes from reality. She so regretted losing control with Peter in the kitchen. It was dreadful for the boys – particularly with Jonty being so down.

They were never going to be able to afford to pay for all this hot water.

Clearly, Peter's *amour propre* must be under considerable threat. What would she, Harriet, have felt about their relationship, if it had been Peter who had announced, out of the blue, that he proposed that he trade his body, on all their behalves, with various aging paramours. Perhaps nothing startling, she thought to herself, wryly. It might not have been new news. Although his last so-called secret paramour, a year ago – horrid, mean-mouthed Ellen Herbert – hadn't exactly been aging. Pretty old, that's all.

Peter might just have to lump it. There were presumably appetites out there in every office and drawing room that needed feeding. That created a market and, as Peter used to be only too fond of saying, if a nation is in irretrievable moral decline, you might as well get down there at the very bottom, ahead of the pack.

She was aware that she was grimly contemplating the same business as those sad students and single-parent mums who took their clothes off, lunchtimes, in the William the Fourth. She could see the hand-painted notice in the pub window as she jogged her way down the hill into Greenwich. But although she saw herself as working in the basement of the appetites, she hoped that in her case she might be able to offer a fantasy of some extra special class. She was going to go for quality. Was she just kidding herself? She had this vague notion of it being a nicely distancing, acted performance. And not just an acting job, but a whole production. She was going to have to be designer, writer, director and leading actress of a unique one-woman show. The punters would, in theory, get a star. And hopefully pay through the nose for it. She would try to offer them a dripping erotic archetypical dream. She would be a sort of Nineties Robyn Hood – the only difference being that she would steal from the rich and keep the lot.

But, to start with, she would need a fair bit of cash to set it all up. Where the devil was that going to come from? She couldn't ask her father for any more. And yet she couldn't begin to plan it unless it was properly financed. Without the protection of a sizable pile of cash, she'd probably get into this desperate trade at the wrong level and could finish up being clubbed to death in some back alley around King's Cross.

She had had a really breath-taking idea about the money.

She would also need a lot of leads and information about how it all worked. She had better make friends with her husband again. Then perhaps he could set about discovering how best his wife could become a hooker.

Damn, Annie White is in New York for ten days. I took a deep breath and, trying not to think too much about the phone bill, tried to find her there. It was not a success and if there's no Annie White, there are no easy leads on this vice piece. So I tried Charles Edgar at BSkyB. He always has his nose to the gutter. If you want to know what the rumour really is, or what the tapes actually say, or which of them is really a dyke, Chuck is your man. Either he wasn't there or he wouldn't take my call. Holloway is not exactly a name that conjures up an instant response these days. I got the kind of blank that I got while researching when I was up for the job on *Today*. Oh, it's a whole evil shrinking world now (or, where it's not shrinking, it's being taken over by the thirty-year-olds – the Burchills and Targets of this benighted business). And, yep, of course, no one thinks of me as a writer in any case. Editors don't write.

I sometimes find myself thinking that perhaps I would have been wiser to have abandoned ambition at the outset and put down long roots at *The Surrey Advertiser*, all those happy years ago in Guildford in the seventies. It feels, now, like that was a golden time – magistrates' courts Wednesday and Thursday, picking over road smashes on the A3 Monday and Friday, reviewing plays at the Arnaud on Monday night, first flat, first car, first love and first-class expenses (although we didn't know that then!) – halcyon days.

Harriet has managed to get Jonty to go on the great daily swimathon with her at last. Timbo was next door with Marianne Webb, so I had a modicum of freedom. As it felt like I was flogging a dead horse on the phone, I forgot to give the dog his walk, and, with one bound, I took myself off to the Land of the Travelcard. To have a bit of a root about.

So I found myself once again in blessed Soho. Our roving reporter goes shop-lifting. What a lovely crazy place it still is. Grace 'n' Grot. That brilliant mix of Italian small-town dellies, gnarled Sicilian-type hoodery, camp lovey-dovey theatricality and the flash, showy, stab-in-the-back of the movie-go-round. It doesn't even smell like London. It certainly doesn't sound like London – even the kids, in Great Pulteney Street Junior School, yell like they've been trained by Lee Strasburg to play Neapoliteenies.

I mooched about fairly indecisively, actually, keeping a wide berth of the Groucho Club. Truth to tell, I'm humouring H. I was just so glad to be able to get out. Glad to have something to do. I wondered if I shouldn't be in Shepherd's Market. That's where the whores hang out, isn't it? Around the Mayfair hotels.

I seemed to remember that there used to be some anonymous looking escort contact magazines in the top racks of the newsagents in Soho. Blowed if they were there now. Every foreign magazine under the sun – *Oggi* and *Holla*! and Deutsche this and Deutsche that. And every foreign language edition of *Playboy* you could ever conceive of, but nothing usefully squalid.

Then, just off Brewer Street in the vilest, dampest, old newsagent's I'd ever had the displeasure of visiting, I homed in successfully on two likely looking little numbers. Both tightly wrapped in cellophane. And both obscenely expensive for what they were. *Capital Contacts* (£5 – FIVE pounds!): 'The biggest Contact mag in the South!! Contains: Home phone Nos, personal details, sexual preferences and explicit photos of advertisers living in London & the South of England. ADULT SALE ONLY.' And *Golden Circle* (£3.95): 'Executive Limited Edition – not for sale to persons under the age of eighteen years.' I bought the *Standard* and 'borrowed' the two aforesaid items. I carried them off and read them in the relative privacy of the gentlemen's cloakroom in Charing Cross station. It was about the right ambiance for what they contained.

I suppose, over the years, I've seen a lot of shit and death and foul play and I reckon I'm reasonably well seasoned as to the blacker sides of man and his nature. Woman and her nature too, for that matter. If you're a newspaper man that's par for the course, comes with the pay-cheque. Same as if you work for the police or in hospital A & E. But nothing had really prepared me for these sad, sorry sagas, for the down-right depression of these two handsome little numbers. Oh dear, no.

Each tawdrily unattractive booklet, under each tawdrily unattractive full-colour card cover, ran three columns of small ads, sandwiched between the larger ads for the usual routine sex-talk lines, for the usual love bondage kits, and for your average international rubber and leather catalogues. Ads, of course, amply illustrated by the most unappealing amateur snaps of the advertisers themselves in various states of crude, crotch-revealing undress. This catalogue of pictures of on the whole deeply unattractive women (and some limp-looking, equally deeply unattractive young men) were casually cropped, presumably in order to accommodate the three column format of the mag. This meant that various arms, heads and limbs were lopped off in the most random take-it-or-leave-it way, making the women appear more like slabs of meat, more like sawn-up torsos than people. Most of the women's faces had either been blanked off with what looked like torn Sellotape or scribbled out on the surface of the photographs with nervy Biro – presumably to preserve anonymity.

The range of age, shape and lewdness of the bodies illustrated was so sad. Each picture told a just comprehensible tale of sad suburban desperation. The clues were all there for the asking – the edges of chipboard veneer coffee tables, the portions of unmade G-plan beds, the glimpses of open airing cupboard doors, the blank white radiators, the electric plug sockets, and, everywhere, floors covered with the absolute ultimate in swirling-migraine carpet design.

49

The photos had one particular common denominator – they were all completely and uniquely unappealing.

And the words matched the photographs – but then who can be sophisticated in a two cm single column? 'ILFORD. Lovely, adventurous, ac/dc slut, 6'1" in stilettos. Sex mad, tarty, early 40's seeks very W/E men, big girls, bizarre unusual invitations. Visiting service and master available if required. I am an "O" level specialist.' etcetera, etcetera, bloody etcetera.

Most of the ads seemed to offer 'discretion', and 'cleanliness'. They tended to suggest they would provide 'O' as a speciality. They were looking for 'TV's' and 'W/E' men. They were 'AC/DC' or they were 'DIY' and they claimed 'ALA' if you sent them a 'SAE'. I tell you, I reckon you needed a GSOH to read even a tenth of the ads. They offered to send you their worn undies, or a 'long sexy letter'. They were 'into video' and they required 'no fees'. A large proportion offered 'husband to watch'. There would be 'no rushing', or alternatively 'exquisite cruelty, exacting positions', and 'unflinching obedience' would be the order of the day.

After a page or so, the appeals got so similar, so inarticulate and so direct they became incredibly dull. I'd never felt so little turned on. It was exactly the sad grimly obsessed trade that I suppose I'd always assumed it to be. I tucked the booklets behind the pedestal in the loo and left them there. It was the right place for them. I think I might be a prude after all.

Went off to call Ellen. She said she could get out to see me at seven for a quick half. Rang H. to say I'd be late – felt just like the old days. She said Jonty'd swum OK. Didn't know he could. Must have learned at Goldings. Never tells me anything, that boy.

Hung around all afternoon in St James's Park. Felt rather like one of the homeless. Hadn't a bean. Nowhere to go. Found, sat and read the *Standard* and the back of a crisp packet. Did the Quick Crossword. Extraordinarily edifying.

Then walked very very slowly to Holborn through the Inns of Court. Sat and waited for her in the Duke's Head without having to buy a beer. As it was still early for the Dukie's clientele, the place seemed huge and echoing and almost woebegon. Ellen came in forty minutes late. Afternoon excitement about interest rates. The city in a tizz. The usual thing.

Ellen looked pretty good, I must say. I'd almost forgotten how really petite she is. And bright – mind like a Volvo. Her hair very red and much longer than it used to be. Big welcoming smile on her neat small mouth – but the usual dead-cool, private, appraising eyes.

We fenced about awkwardly for a little while. We'd never (no, I suppose that should read: 'I'd never') actually finished off the relationship (or whatever it was) properly. I'd got sickened with myself, and with it, and with her, so that I'd allowed there to be a sort of uncomfortable quick fade when I left the paper. That's apart from some rather desperate mute clawing at each other in Anthony's Brussels apartment for one incredibly mistaken night just before Julian McGee upped and did his runner with all our money.

But suddenly there we were and it felt, uncannily, just like before – me, enraptured by those great, watchful, russet, come-to-bed eyes. They seemed to scour their way down to the very depths of my shitty soul. It's really remarkable how quickly wicked alchemical magic gets blurred in the old memory-data-bank, only to jump fully fledged and throbbing into life once you're sitting across a pint from it. The only difference now is that you know that, along with the instant, sheer, ecstatic bliss of it, afterwards, all we could be sure of dishing out to each other would be more of the lies, the guilt, the anger and a cart-load of mutual self-despisal. After all, why did I ever need to do any of that? Why couldn't I be content with Harriet and the boys? Harriet's still a very attractive woman. And she herself would never ever dream of going to bed with another man. Oh, I can't bear it if it all just boils down to your everyday archetypical masculine mid-life bloody crisis – I mean, that's such a thunderingly prosaic, pathetic explanation.

In spite of her lazer-sharp analytical gaze, Mrs Herbert did try not to be too curious about the whereabouts of my livelihood. But then, that's one of life's bonny old ironies – it actually makes me laugh out loud sometimes – everyone thinks I left *The Chron.* absolutely loaded.

She did the decent independent woman thing and fetched us a round. God knows, it was absurdly good to have my hand around a pint of Four X. It went straight to my head – I hadn't eaten since I don't know when.

Then, in the midst of grinding the usual street-of-shame rumour-mill, she gets suddenly confidential and shamelessly pleased with herself in a girly sort of way. And drops a load of dung on my head. She's seeing Michael Stainton. No wonder she's so bloody sorted and is not the slightest bit miffed with me disappearing on her. That's just so like our Ellen – she always has someone on the go. Presumably I was just the one she had on the go, before the one she has on the go now.

And old Michael Stainton's into his second or third marriage himself, isn't he? He's got at least six kids scattered around the home counties. Well, four or five anyway. She's got no scruples, has Ellen. I wonder why she sticks with Andrew. Doesn't he know she's always riding the range with various guys in various anonymous European hotel beds? Andrew Herbert must know, mustn't he? Maybe he gets off on other people screwing his wife. Could be. Reminds me of: 'husband to watch'. God, I can't really imagine it, myself. If that's the truth of it, what a sick, sad character he must be.

And yet, and yet . . . I have to say, secretly, that in the blacker depths of my corrupted soul, that universal little green god of jealousy seems always to have to battle away for a place inside my unseemly head, with that wicked, wanton witch that they call voyeurism. So, yes, as far as Ellen was concerned, I did tend to tuck my keening, excluded envy of her latest dallying away. I obscured it very effectively behind a wretched fantasy of the lustful lady groaning orgiastically in old Stainton's ear with her ankles up around his neck. In fact I got marginally turned on by it and wanted her to tell me more. I may be just a tiny bit cracked myself!

But she managed to keep most of those intimacies to herself, and instead came up with some information for my so-called 'piece about the escort business that I've been asked to do'. She said there are a stack of ads in the back pages of that old warhorse *What's On*, of all places. And there are. A whole full page. Good God. I'd never thought of looking at that tired old thing. I'd gawped at the back of *Time Out*, of course. Astonishingly enough, there's absolutely no joy on the escort front to be found there.

And as well as *What's On*, there are fifty-six agencies in the *Yellow Pages*! Even a cub-reporter might have thought of looking there. I was tickled by one of the agencies called: 'Cinderella'. A little bit of poetry.

Ellen went back to work. As soon as she had left the pub I realised again just how little she meant for me, had ever really meant. Once she was out of sight, I even remembered her, within seconds, as being less attractive, less fun and more trouble. It was just seeing her again and being able to smell her that killed me.

I hauled my way down the streets to the river and walked the sixty-seven and a half miles back to Charing Cross Station. I caught the train to Blackheath again.

Not before I half-inched this *What's On* from Smith's. Ye Gods, I'm beginning to be a shop-lifter supreme. Well, 'A' level standard, anyway. It has a whole page entitled: 'Escorts'. Eighty ads. About a quarter of them in Arabic. About half of them advertising the services of agencies – '24 hours', 'Credit cards'. There's a whole barrelful of worlds going on out there in Londontown that you never know about, until you root about.

Fifteen words in *What's On* cost £16 including V.A.T. There were some fifteen ads or so that seemed, on the face of them, to be from private advertisers. They all had names like Lorena, Sable, Sandi and Exotica. I picked a priapic Pamela who claimed to be 'an elegant, warm and utterly discreet companion. For those special evenings.' I will ring her tomorrow and find out what she can tell me. We'll have to see. In fact it smells like a good story. I'll ring Frances Kinnear of the *Guardian* Saturday Mag. She might take a bite. Please God.

Spent *no* money today. Ticketless, both ways, on the train. Oh, yes, I bought a *Standard* 30p. Lovely life. Another perfect day in penury.

Harriet wondered what the 'K' and the 'Y' in the name 'K-Y Jelly' stood for. She lay on her big double-bed putting altogether too much of the funny sticky stuff up her fanny. She had got it all over the duvet cover too.

Around her on the bed lay the fruit of various efforts with condoms. Harriet had never ever had to use a condom *hors de combat* before. At school, her friend Morag had produced two which they had giggled over and blown up while sitting under the beech trees behind the local petrol station. After she had had the boys, she had been on the pill. Then, two years ago, because she had had a series of headaches, she had got a cap fitted. She had liked it. Even the smell of it on her fingers. It meant she was in charge of that bit of her. At least.

But now she was going to have to learn about handling these things. She had used some of her father's money to buy the K-Y and a goodly selection of rubber johnnies. Mr Traders, at the Village chemists, must have been startled by the quantities she seemed suddenly to need, but if he was he didn't show any sign of it. Peter was in town doing the research she had demanded, the boys were out to a valuably sustaining tea with the inquisitive Mrs Stoner and her horrible child. Harriet was alone in the house on her personal research project, dripping with her very own 'sterile, greaseless, transparent water-soluble non-irritating jelly'. The dog had got tired of throwing itself bodily at her steadfastly closed bedroom door. Harriet could, at last, concentrate. She was practising how best to maintain an everyday – or perhaps every-night – *savoir-faire* while extracting condoms out of their extraordinarily impenetrable foil packets. There must be some world-wide pro-life conspiracy that made the things so stolidly inaccessible.

She then spent the best part of half an hour seeing if she could unroll them on to the end of the brush-pan handle. In various ways. Sexily. Mostly, ludicrously. This was as much as anything because it was difficult to hold the brush really firmly between her knees. She was, indeed, very bad at it to start with. She was pretty bad at it, to finish with too. But then, there are so many things that it is very difficult for a girl to do with her one hand while lying spreadeagled on a bed – she had always found masturbating Peter with her right hand, for example, an extremely painful process as it gave her a horrid crick in her shoulder every time such activity seemed to be called for. She used to find it almost impossible to combine the busy physical activity of her wrist with the painful catch in her shoulder blade, while, all the while, keeping up a good selection of appreciatively sexy moaning.

This learning was testing stuff. But each day she reckoned she felt fitter and looked better. Even Peter, with all his preoccupations, noticed the welcome liberation of her cheekbones. Where on earth had they been lurking all these years? The slight puffiness of her cheeks, that she had decided to live her life with forever, had fallen away. In their place there appeared taut, positively shadowy hollows that, at the age of twenty-two she would gladly have killed for. Her hours in the gym were paying off magnificently. But then, not having anything substantial to eat must be helping too.

There were times when, in spite of her palpitating fears, she began to see herself as a primed rocket about to blast into the unknown. She now had to prepare the inside of her head for take-off. Time was short; this short life was not for just check-in time and mooching around in Duty-free, it was for flying, and probably for taking things off.

She was quite clear about one thing: the only way that she was going to be able to keep out of the gutter, hold on to her self-respect and earn the big bucks was to keep totally, classily, in control. If she was mad, brave or pushed enough actually to do it, she would be naughty but extremely proper.

If she was actually really going to do this job, she would do it as someone called Natasha Ivanov. She had always had romantic notions about being called Natasha – it sounded Russian and romantic and flecked with snow and leather knee-boots and an accent you could crack a whip with. And Ivanov? At Arts Ed. she had performed in the play of that name – Chekhov's first full length play – a gloomy study of a bitter marriage which had originated out of a brief youthful infatuation. That autumn term, Harriet had been one of three year students who played the role of the wife, in tandem, not terribly well. But the play continued to plague her with funny resonances even now. 'Natasha Ivanov' – it had an innocent but mysterious ring to it – haughty and, just possibly, naughty.

Right, Natasha's grandfather, an exiled Russian Jew, had come over from Berlin at the beginning of the war. He had been an excellent tailor for thirty years in Spitalfields. Was that too archetypical? Not really. Well perhaps it was.

Natasha's father was a school inspector. Yes. Good and Dull and rather Prim. That sounded more like it – a whore who had a school inspector for a dad – almost a turn-on in itself? Perhaps he could be a lay preacher too. And her mother had been a nun. No, no. Now concentrate – her mother had been an excellent housewife and cook but she had died in childbirth. Natasha had been an only child, brought up by her slightly austere father – the grim school inspector. And a maiden aunt. No. His mistress? No. No, just a single-parent upbringing. That was OK. Josef Ivanov and daughter, alone against the world.

Natasha would have faintly foreign accented speech – to disguise her ringing Edinburgh tones. Why? Well, because she did. No, because she had au paired in Paris for five or six years after school. Didn't sound very likely but it might do. A whisper of an accent – the faintest throaty roll of her 'r's and a few archly mispronounced vowel sounds – would always help to keep Natasha, slut, a completely separate entity from Harriet, purest mother and wife.

Natasha was going to be only twenty-three. Birthday in August. A Leo. She lived on her own, in an apartment, somewhere vaguely north of the Columbia Road Sunday Flower market that Harriet had adored going to, in the old days, on Sunday mornings. Close enough to Spitalfields and to Natasha's roots. A slummy, untidy street with pubs emptying out late in the evening with discord and noise. She had a third-, no, fourth-floor flat under the eaves. Inside, it was gorgeous – fairly big, with sunlight streaming in from the back on good days. Full of dried flowers and pot pourri in pottery bowls – a bit like Barbara Lydell-Smith's kitchen.

And her job was escorting men. She would need some sort of face-saving ambition? Yes, she was putting money by with which to buy herself a house in the country – somewhere like Harriet's own father's house, but in – well where? – the New Forest? Too far from town. Natasha needed to be turned on by the big late-night London scene. Farnham? Canterbury was lovely. Cambridge – yes, all those fresh-faced hormone-filled Public School boys. And you could get down the M11 to London in what Peter called two flaps of a bum's rush. Yes, Natasha Ivanov hoped to finish up with a house just off the Backs. With a punt moored at the bottom of her lawn. And young men drifting in and out of her sitting room, in white flannels and long blond hair. In blazers. So, in the meantime, Natasha was saving up.

Natasha Ivanov was going to be an icon. She would realise that endlessly sought-after image – vital rapaciousness held just in check by modest grave formality. Natasha would be perfectly attired, in that demurely sexy way that only the rich English have. She would have the butter–wouldn't-melt-in-her-mouth, battened down sexuality that Princess Diana embodied so archetypically. Her stride would be slightly longer than you would expect. When she walked, she would lead by her collarbones, looking the world slap bang in the eye. There would be no head-ducked, careful examination of the cunning arrangement of the paving stones for her, when Natasha passed people by.

Natasha should look like a walking female Aston Martin. If you could find the 'on' switch, Ms Ivanov would hit bedtime abandon from nought to a hundred and fifty miles an hour in ten seconds not so flat. She would need to broadcast that kind of reserved sensual vibe that provokes in men a hopeless yearning to want to give her what Peter would call a good seeing to. Of course, you'd never ever be able to guess from her demeanour or public behaviour that what she did for a living was so unusually intimate or so very commercial. Even so, to public gaze, she would look as if she knew what she was about.

The question was, could Harriet be Natasha? In a funny kind of way, it might be a lot easier to be this fictional inamorata than to conduct herself as herself, as the woolly-headed would-be-good Harriet Holloway. If you are playing a part, it is always possible to lose your more vulnerable self in it. It is astonishing what a metamorphosis even a reasonably timid person can undergo while playing a role. As Natasha, Harriet could see herself as having an up-front clarity and control that she could never achieve in her own personal life. Harriet could already see herself as getting to be quite jealous of how easy Natasha would be in her skin. Well, that was the idea, anyway.

And Ms Ivanov's appearance would match her self-knowledge. Her hair would always be a touch more elaborate than you might normally expect. Her make-up would be subtlety and specialness incarnate. She would smell different. Natasha would wear *Gio* from Georgio Armani, whereas Harriet always wore her eternally favoured *Caleche*. She would always have perfect, sheer, unsplashed nylons, very very slightly higher heels than girls usually went for – but, you see, she never walked far, Natasha always used cabs. She might be famous for her very showy but really classy earrings, for her perfect, well-clipped, modest finger-nails, for the way she sat and the way she stood, for the firmness of her handshake. She would be bloody brilliant. For the way Natasha 'was' would be her vocation, her job, her very identity. Natasha would be woman as commodity. How disgraceful.

The bloke who had invested in her time would be quietly, maturely, prep-schoolboy-cock-a-hoop that he had Natasha Ivanov's light touch on his sleeve, as he caught the Maître D's eye, or entered the hotel lobby. And Natasha would listen to all his stories, to each of his highs and lows, to his problems and his delights with a warmly intelligent interest. She would remember, for that evening anyway, the names of people he told her about, as she sat with superbly crossed legs, smiling with understanding concern. And when Natasha's turn came she would reveal a broad unchallenging knowledge of a wide variety of urbane and amusing topics. Harriet was going to have to do some real homework here. She would have to read the dreaded newssheets, listen to 'The World at One', get a handle on events. And then, every so often, when the occasion warranted it, Natasha Ivanov would whisper surprisingly dirty things into her escort's astonished ear.

In fact, she would be such extraordinarily ideal man-fodder that, at times, if you were a woman of spirit, you very well might want to throttle her!

Well, that was the theory of it, anyway.

Because she had her doubts too. As she began, with every new day, to accumulate all the parts of Ms Ivanov – her way of moving, her way of talking, her terminology, her make-up, her pride in herself – she would also have to face echoing roomfuls of uncertainties. Not just fear for her safety and everyday ordinary boring stage fright but real concern about the morals of it. Not the morals of sex-life, but the morals of gender. Here she was inventing the ultimate sex-object, the woman as plaything, the woman as recreation facilitator. Could she even think about being able to look herself in the eye over this?

She had never seen herself as a fully-paid-up thinking feminist, but she often grieved over the Lot of Womankind. Occasionally when she would venture into that slough of despond – the concrete shopping-bunker of neighbouring Lewisham (one of the capitals of 'Essex' – awash with shell suits, anklets and deodorant that would kill at thirty paces) and she saw the second-class citizenry about their toils in support of their all-powerful menfolk – she would promise herself that she ought to do more on behalf of their lot.

Well, Ms Ivanov was to be no victim. She would be entirely in charge of her own destiny. She would make the choices, where choices needed to be made. It was one of the main things that made Harriet dry mouthed with apprehensive excitement as she thought the whole thing through. She was going to take her life very much into her own hands. And finally, she didn't seem to have a vast amount of choice any more. As Peter was always fond of saying, before it really meant anything serious: 'needs must when the debit drives'.

So Harriet would have to stomach the hoodwinking of loving wives, the betrayal of families, the deception of trusting children that her *doppel-gänger*, Natasha, would be party to. She had little trust in the idea that men playing away from home tended to help keep the home more secure. But Natasha would be nobody's mistress.

Natasha would be a one-off. Harriet had this idea that, in any case, the kind of men that she guessed at being her customers could still genuinely care for their wives and children and be reluctant to involve themselves in home-threatening activity with a real 'friend'.

The more mature men that Harriet saw around her in the nineties seemed more and more exhausted by the idea of trying to work at relationships. They seemed to want a language in which the term 'date-rape' did not exist, and a situation in which the answer to their most urgent question was always certain to be 'yes'. They were ever in search of that holy grail – the zipless fuck – the Torrid Sexual Experience unattached to any personal or emotional strings. It would be the T.S.E. in which all the work, and all the management, and all the required precautionary health measures were guaranteed and undertaken by the 'catering company' that they had engaged. And, in return, obviously, such professionalism would cost them. Short-term possession of her arms and legs, and all that they contained, would, of course, cost them something more than an arm and a leg.

It was expensive professionalism and commitment that she hoped would keep her out of the gutter. She had a memory, years ago in the dear dead days of the eighties, when she and Peter had been in Phoenix, Arizona, on some working/holiday freebie. He had persuaded her that it would be educational for them to go and see what had been recommended as a quality high-gloss piece of strip-theatre. It had been all the rage with the media people of Phoenix that season.

It turned out to be a smartly glittery downtown cabaret theatre, all gilt chandeliers and cut mirror-glass. Twelve or ten awesomely tall girls, she had reckoned. Legs up to their earlobes. A virtual breast-implant catalogue. And throughout the whole show, however carefully she watched, however searchingly she examined their faces, she had seen not so much as a passing flicker, no intimation of irony, no suspicion of boredom. They must have performed at least twelve shows a week and yet they all of them persuaded her that this show was the only show – the only show in the whole of their weekly schedule that really mattered to them. They were all, every tapering limb of each of them, every skilfully tweaked lock of luxuriant hair of them, thrilled to be there, doing it for Peter and Harriet that evening – then, there, on that Thursday or on that

Tuesday or whenever it was. They were only there for Harriet and for Peter and, presumably, for the forty or fifty other folk who were along for the ride on that evening. It seemed as if it was only the formalities and conventions of the theatre performance space that stopped them from happily ravishing every man in the audience and, perhaps, not a few of the women as well.

Harriet had scrutinised the innermost secrets of their eyes with such attention throughout the ninety minutes, as the women had stroked their way lasciviously out of their improbable ruffles and sparkles. As they finally presented each private personal inch of their powdered, honed bodies to that ad hoc bunch of strangers, Harriet had not seen one single moment of deprecation, of regret or of second-class citizenry. The only humiliation in the room might have hovered around the shoulders of the men, there, as they sat silently sipping their Margaritas and revealing themselves almost incapable of responding in any way to the performances. At the end of each classily choreographed idea, the audience roused itself into such a pathetic, feeble, splattering of applause. And, in spite of much humour in the show there was not a single laugh in the house all night. Arousal was obviously a deadly serious business.

Harriet would liked to have laughed at the humour. At the same time she would liked to have roared with undisguised delight at the astonishing prowess with which those young women performed. She realised what a pride they had in what they did, and how their unflinching commitment gave them a perfect shelter behind which to hide any personal uncertainties that might float around in their minds as they sucked their fingers and squeezed their nipples and toyed with their vaginas. They were magnificent and she had loved them, their courage and their arrogance. Natasha Ivanov was of their mould. Maybe that was where the idea of her had been born.

I rang this Pamela – the escort whose advert I'd read in the back of *What's On*. Very Chelsea – I was surprised. She sounded like she was in some kind of a flat-share. Telly on, in the background. So I lied a little: 'Hullo. I'm Pete Holloway. At *Chronicle Newspapers*. We're doing an article for the paper on escorts. I wondered if I could meet with you to have a chat – an interview?'

'Another article?' she said quite cheerfully 'I was hoping this was a job. I seem to spend my whole life doing interviews for newspaper articles. What's the world coming to? Unfortunately there's not much money in interviews. Except, maybe, for the journalists.'

'I'd just like to meet you and ask you a few questions. How you're affected by the recession, what kind of men use the service, that sort of thing.'

'*The Chronicle*, did you say?' There was a touch, a touch only, of Dublin about her voice.

'Yes.'

'You're not interested in the recession. All you eager gentlemen of the press want to know is what we do in bed with the clients. Whoops, are you recording this?'

'No, no, of course not.'

'Then you are!'

'No, I'm not. I'm just arranging to try to meet with you. A half-hour's chat. I'm working up an in-depth story. This would be for background. I think there could be a very interesting story here. And it would be in confidence, of course. You wouldn't be identified.'

'Oh deary deary dear. Sorry, I'm not interested.' She laughed: 'The words "in-depth" and *The Chronicle* don't usually exist in the same sentence, do they? Sorry, I'd love to meet you – but for business, not for articles. You see, my time is money.'

'Well, I could pay you for your time.' Mentally crossing my fingers, but she had almost rung off.

'Well, there's a thing!' There was a silence as she considered this development. 'OK, now you're talking. When would you want to meet?'

'Tomorrow evening? I could meet you in the West End.'

'What about the Royal Palace Hotel? They've got what they like to call their American bar. What time, do you think?'

'Seven–thirty?'

'All right. I'll see you there. What about fifty pounds for a couple of hours, Mr Holloway?' She was very quick with my name. Part of the job, I suppose. I said I thought it was a bit steep. She said she was offering me bargain basement terms – but that it was that time of the year. I guessed that she might be about to hang up on me, so I said I thought that it would be all right. It wasn't, of course. I haven't had fifty quid about my person for months.

She asked me what colour tie I'd wear. I don't wear ties a lot these days. She suggested – still jolly, but fairly matter-of-fact –

that I should perhaps carry a *Financial Times*. A touch traditional, I thought. Rather fancied carrying a copy of *Knitting Today*, but I kept this notion to myself.

Well, she wasn't going to get the fifty nicker, I fear. I would have to pass her a rubber cheque if it came to that. I had to have something to buy her a drink with, however. Harri and I searched the house high and low for coinage – every pocket in every trouser in every cupboard, down the back of the sofa and all the vases and ornaments that were left – big row when I tried to liberate the kids' ancient Noddy-In-Toyland mini-bank. The row was actually of no fixed avail as, when I got there, the mini-bank was bare. Final haul – a lorra lira (actually an astonishing amount of Italian tin coins as they normally have the grubbiest old notes for the smallest possible values), ein paar Deutsche Mark, bitte, and (yippee!) a two thousand peseta note. Took this off to town to change them prior to Pamela. Nine pounds seventy-two p. after commission. Sterling coins accumulated during this fine-toothcomb operation amounted to a priceless, princely sixty-eight pence. Rather good, eh? And Harriet still seems to have some paternal cash stashed by, wherewith to purchase meagre fare for the kids for tomorrow.

Incidentally, I found an empty Durex packet on the floor behind the back of the bedside table! Well, that threw me. For a moment I had the most violent flash of husbandly suspicion. And then, thank God, I remembered that, when H. and I were in the Caribbean, Julian stayed here with that yachtswoman, Francesca, he was dead keen on then. I was brought short, instantly, by how that whole instinctive jealousy number can so quickly be swamped, for me anyway, by a wave of unaccountable and pretty unacceptable lust. I really loathed the momentary fleeting idea of H. up to some tricks, however far-fetched that might have been, and, at the same time, I know that I quite liked the idea of it too. Of course, I know that it wouldn't be like that, in reality. End of story. Funny, though.

Anyway, thus it was, that I found myself clutching a bedraggled copy of the *FT*, and mooching about, feeling decidedly naff, in the considerably chromed confines of the American Bar of the Royal Palace Hotel, on the Strand. The place wasn't all that full and I hoped against hope that none of the appalling women present, when I arrived, was going to be this Pamela. There was a light sprinkling of sepia skinned, iron-grey American matrons scattered about the place, accompanied, only rarely, by those few of their menfolk who hadn't yet cholesteroled and pegged it.

They weren't. Priapic Pamela arrived a quarter of an hour late. Strong face and body, firm handshake, sort of square with broadish shoulders and big tits, short smart dyed blonde hair. She looked like a cross between a well-loved infants' teacher and a professional tennis player. Quite possible. Quite likable. Charcoal grey, shirtwaister dress. She could have been a reasonably elegant local authority planning officer up for a committee meeting. She wanted cash.

I pushed my old *Chronicle* business card at her and got them to bring us some drinks. She had a Coke. We fenced around a while, about her fee.

'I'm very sorry,' said she, 'I just have this one rule and that is that I don't hang around if there's any difficulty about the money, Mr Holloway. Life is just too short. You wicked gentlemen will always try a little blarney when it's time to pay. Arab gentlemen particularly, I find. Quick with the fly, as they say, slow with the wallet.'

'It is actually your rules that I'm interested in. This isn't an escort job tonight, Pamela, it's just background for an article.' But she was on the verge of going. 'Listen,' I said smiling hard, 'I'll feed you. We'll have something decent to eat.' She had virtually gone. She hadn't even touched the Coke. Evidently a woman of principle.

'Now, Mr Holloway, nice Mr Holloway, you promised me you'd pay me when we spoke on the phone. You have to understand my position. I could be out there somewhere earning my living at this very moment. You jolly newspapermen are all the same, aren't you? A meal doesn't pay the rent, does it? I have community charges to cover and washing-machines to fix and the milk bill to sort out like everybody else. And, after all, when all's said and done, it's not exactly as if we're talking cheque-book journalism here, are we? Forgive me, I thought you gentlemen of the press were always splendidly endowed with expenses.'

'Not since Wapping. It's all changed.' I didn't sound very convincing. She wasn't very convinced: 'Oh well.' She sighed. And she gave me what my mother would have termed an old-fashioned look: 'Sorry, Mr Holloway.' And she got up to go: 'Anyway, nice to meet you.' It didn't sound as if it had been. 'OK, OK'. I pulled out my cheque book. 'It'll have to be a cheque – I'll make it seventy-five.

How's that?' I was suddenly generous with my bouncing signature. She stood there, looked me over and then slowly she sat back down, suddenly much more relaxed. She picked up and tinkled the ice in the Coke. I gave her the cheque, duly signed: 'But, OK, no meal.' I said, 'We'll just stay here and I'll ask you a few questions. It won't take long.'

She took the cheque and read every word of it, very carefully, and then, charmingly, folded it, and put it into the top of her dress. I imagine into the top of her bra. I wrote at the top of the first page of my notebook: 'Rule 1. Don't fuck about, get the money or bugger off.' She smiled at me and almost visibly settled down to give me an hour or two of her time.

The curtain had gone up. It was as if she had suddenly allowed herself to become someone else. Someone a lot pleasanter. It struck me that at the beginning, when she first arrived, unlike usual first meetings with women when they do their utmost to make good first impressions, Pamela didn't feel the need. We both knew why we were there. There was no need for dissembling. Now that I'd bought her, she hit the 'friendly' button. But not before she added: 'If that cheque's not honoured, Peter, I'll come round to *The Chronicle* and tell all your sub-editors and tea-ladies that you can't get it up!' We laughed together merrily, oh, very adult and worldly wise.

She was a mature student at the LSE. Second year. No grant. The life gave her a just about bearable living. Busy before Christmas, and in the spring. Summer holiday time, like now, was pretty bloody – no conferences, no big international exhibitions and all the men off on their summer hols trying to remember how to screw their wives. Once she'd got started, she sounded a lot more Irish and talked very readily.

'There are the escort agencies, and quite a lot of the girls think they give you at least a modicum of security. I have me doots, Peter, myself. And, of course, they cream off a booking fee of, well, at least thirty per cent, more, some of them. V.A.T. as well. And you're up against the rest of the portfolio. So you're directly compared with the competition, which isn't always the best idea. I'm freelance, me. Always have been. The only good thing, I suppose, about an agency is that the guys can go down to Bayswater or Victoria or Dolphin Square and pick a girl from the catalogue and at least they know what they're getting, which can save you embarrassment. Though it feels like choosing a wallpaper in Sandersons, I always think.

'But that's what we are, I suppose, at the end of the day – physical wallpaper – that's all. Chewing-gum for the testosterone glands and for endomorphic rushes.' I suppose I looked at her with some respect and she laughed. 'Oh, I know my stuff, Peter. Yes, it's working women like myself who, er, hold back the swelling tide of loneliness in the big city: isn't that what they call it? That, and the fact that my gentlemen find that a date with me can be something usefully macho to sound off about to their boardroom cronies or their gentlemen's club chums. I give them a chance to live out a fantasy or two – imagine that they've lived a little. Work out a few gentle, or even not so gentle, kinks. What is it with you men, present company excepted, of course – that you want such odd stuff? I don't believe women want half that infantilism and cruelty and role-playing and tying up and smacking. The nanny condition of the English, it's amazing to behold.'

'That's what they want?'

'Almost universally. When they're prepared to be honest about it.'

'Why, do you think?'

'Well, first off, I reckon the English upper middle-class parent is the most abusive in the world. He packs his son off to boarding school as soon as he turns eight, for Christ's sake. No wonder the poor kid flips when he's grown up. Looking for mummy. And, of course, on the whole, men are just so very repressed, so incredibly unwilling to express themselves in any honest way, with sex. Very very shy, really. No wonder Englishmen are the worst lovers in the world.'

'Yes?'

'Oh yes. By far. They can't ask for anything. Not like English women. Women anywhere really. You meet women who've got themselves in hand and they can really go with the flow. You know what I mean? I mean they can cry, and do, and be generous enough to reach out and meet someone else halfway. And that means that they don't have a backlog of dark urges that they need to keep scraped back and well hidden under their particular carpet. It's like dancing – you think: most English women will bop about, given half a chance and a bit of a beat – they'll offer themselves up to the music – boogie on down – let it touch their psyche, just a bit. You ever see English men dance? Just for fun, not for trying to pull? English men over thirty? Not a chance. It's the same with

fucking, Peter. So often, they can't manage. The English man – he's
the original wham-bang-thank-you-mam merchant. "Whoops. Oh,
I'm so sorry, love, I came. Sorry, I didn't mean to." Two minutes
in. Extraordinary. Not that it doesn't make my job a lot easier. Well,
quicker, anyway.'

'So you sleep with your clients?'

'Does the Pope play with himself? Peter, I cost a ton and a half
for four hours as an escort. That doesn't even begin to keep me in
continuous stationery. So – what's an innocent student to do? Yes,
if I want to, I go duvet-diving. I'm rather good at it, Peter. Could
you get a sample on *Chronicle* expenses?'

'What do you charge, then.'

'For you?'

'No, not for me, Pamela – in the general run of things.'

'Anything. Everything. Anything I reckon I can get. You have
to make an educated guess at the guy's resources. This job's just
character analysis – the whole thing is about making informed
instinctive guesses about johns. Anyway, never less than the same
again, at the very very least. In fact I feel a bit soiled if I find myself
in a bedroom for less than three hundred. Normally it's two fifty or
so on top of the initial layout. Last Christmas I picked up two and a
half grand for jumping some Kuwaiti and his son together one night.
The whole thing was done and I was out in ninety minutes. And lo,
there was a profit in the land.' She laughed and sipped delicately at
her drink.

'I tell them "all night". But it isn't normally. Normally it's a quick
unedifying squelch with the Johnsons and they're happy for me to
be off in half an hour. Instantly, Madame Guilt comes stalking down
the corridor and into their ejaculated psyches and they want to ring
home or whatever and tell their lady-wives that they love them, to
remember them to the children – the usual story. Of course, every so
often there are guys who want a fuckfest for their money and then I
have to work for my living.'

'Do you mind the sex?'

'Good God, no. Well, not usually. I don't hang about where I
think it would disgust me. It's my choice. Well, it is if I'm not
feeling too hard-pressed financially. It's OK. I mean, Peter, I don't
get off on it or anything. It's work, that's all. In the end it's just a
job like anyone else's – you don't get the opportunity to select the
better bits from the badder bits. Actually I like some of the johns.

Yeah, there are times when I enjoy myself, I suppose. I have a few serial johns – repeats. Mark you a lot of them are just pathetic. On the whole they're quite pleased. I do it well, I leave them happy in the main. "Leave them laughing"'s my motto. And I do it all fairly tactfully. Oh Mary Mother of God, they love my tact and decorum. That's the English way, of course, you know – keep it tucked away under the duvet. They're usually pretty frightened and shy beneath the blather. As I say, you have to make judgments all the time in this business. How far to go. What they might like. They don't often tell you. Very often they haven't got a lot of English anyway. In that case, very often, the meal is a darn sight harder work than the wanking.'

'Who are the best, then?'

'What do you mean: "the best"?'

'Lovers.'

'None of them are lovers.'

'Well, the best nation. If the English are so crap.'

'Danes. By infinite miles. They're all so damn sensitive, they're almost feminine. And they go on forever. Which can be something of a drag. Sometimes.'

'What about your private sex-life?'

'What private sex-life? Who's been talking? Well. My private life's my private life.'

'Sorry.'

'No. I don't suppose I've got much of a private life. I don't get out much, except for work. I don't really have a social life. I avoid it. You can't often tell people about what a very hard day you've had at the office, when you've spent midnight to 2 a.m. in the Dorchester, sitting astride some inert old Rabbi whose name escapes you, can you? I've an eleven-year-old son. Sean. Single parent. It's OK. He's my social life. And there's my dissertation. I'm always behind on that.'

'Are you gay?'

'No, I just look like this.'

'Sorry, it's just what you said about women.'

'Well, it's true. All you men used to be so masterly at quelling the natives and forcing civilisation down the reluctant throats of various perfectly happy indigenous nations, but, sad to say, in the process you threw sensitivity and romance and tenderness and giving, out the window.' She grinned ruefully: 'Sorry, it's my soap-box. I've come to the somewhat banal conclusion that it's women who are where it's at. If women governed the world, Peter, it'd be a whole different ballgame. Perhaps that isn't exactly the phrase. But, no, I don't get excited by the taste of wet pussy – apart from my own.'

'What are the punters looking for?'

'Nineteen-year-olds.' She looked crestfallen. By restaurant candle-light I claim I'm twenty-five. Lying down, by the light of a digital clock radio, my tits are a twenty-two-year-old's.'

'Is it dangerous?'

Pamela looked at me with such a withering look: 'Of course it's dangerous. And you work for *The Chronicle*? There are some bloody maniacs out there, my friend. I don't know any girls who haven't had a few fairly frightening experiences. And there are always some girls that you completely lose track of. That frightens me. I always tell myself that they've got out. A lot have got a habit and it's that what gets them in the end. Not me, thank Christ. Thanks to Sean, really. I wonder what happens sometimes. Things get hushed up pretty quick. This is a cloak-and-dagger world – there's a lot of madnesses and reputations and happy families at stake out there, that could get blown away so very easily, given the wrong word in the wrong ear. It's not all two-thousand-pounds-to-keep-mum, passed to you in a brown paper envelope in Victoria Station, believe you me. So you have to keep your wits about you all the time. Write this down in your little book, Peter: Rule two. "With a john, you have to get out early better than late, just as soon as it ever gets dodgy." I used to know a working girl called Mandi, she'd always say, of the bent guys: "You stay and talk, you'll stay and squawk." On the whole the girls are pretty wised up. We might all look like ice-wouldn't-melt-in-our-fannies but, in your head, you have to be well–watchful all the time, and tougher than whipped steel.' She thought for a moment: 'Actually the real danger is staff at the mansions.'

'The mansions?'

'Hotels to you. They always kid on that hotels turn a blind eye. Some do but most don't, you know. You can't trust hotel staff, however friendly they seem. Well I suppose they can't afford for their blessed mansion to get the reputation as a number one knocking shop – in spite of the fact that they all are. There's more sexual activity in hotels than anywhere else in the land. Anyway, you can take it from me, they catch you going home, they'll turn you in.

You have to be virtually invisible – I know every single fire exit and escape route from just about every hotel inside the M25! Any woman can walk into a hotel with a fella, it's the getting out afterwards that's difficult. And it's worse if they're like the head porter at the Royal Yorkshire – Norman. Whatever he says, you can't trust him, he's only looking for a free ride. End of the day, they're all men. And where they're women, they're worse. Don't expect sisterhood. We disgust them. They'd like to see us all garrotted. And then, on the other hand, just when you've got used to running that gauntlet, you find there are some of them on the take.'

'Commission?'

'You could call it that. I know at least two working girls who do a regular number of hotel drops every month. They reckon it's worth their while – they feel safer and pick up a fair bit of trade in return. But then the porter is in control, isn't he? And I mean if you want a pimp, you might as well get a pimp. You cut them in and they're in the know. They're always in a position to turn you in if they want to lean on you, if they want to get you into line. Bugger that for a laugh.'

'You have trouble with the police?'

'If you haven't got a police record, you aren't a professional. This business is like cannabis. It's fairly harmless but it's against the law. In fact, you could see it as social work. But the Mary Whitehouses of this world are determined to make us into these evil criminals. The johns are never the guilty ones. Funny that. Is it to do with newspapers like yours being run by the chauvinist majority, I wonder? Is it to do with the fact that everything is run by the chauvinist majority? Yeah, could be. Anyway, I'll tell you something: working-girls like us help to keep the world turning calmly. We keep various lacklustre parents together in terminal wedlock, and numerous maniacs from cutting people's throats. We aren't on Social Security. We pay our Council taxes and keep the Inland Revenue happy. Would you believe, I'm registered as a self-employed cabaret artiste? We're brighter about our health than most kids giving it away on the common. We add to the gaiety of nations. And we risk personal life and limb to keep the world's pecker up. I can't see what harm we do. We should get awards for industry – upholders of the market and private enterprise – very Baroness Thatcher.' She glanced almost invisibly at her watch. 'In actual fact, Peter, legally it's extremely hard to pin me down. My advertising doesn't suggest sex in any way, of course. I don't work at home, so they can't get me under the 1751 Disorderly Houses Act. Occasionally the odd working-girl gets threatened with something called the 1861 Offences Against The Person Act – they can get you for assault, for God's sake, even though all the parties discovered in attendance at the time of the crime have consented to be there and have, astonishingly, removed all their clothing of their own free will.'

'What about health?'

'I don't do much penetration now.' She held out her right hand towards me with her fingers outstretched. 'I'm wizard with me fingers, Peter. That and a few wanton noises and you've done the business. When I have to, well, you have to be careful and do it right. They all say: "Oh, go on, for me. Let's not use one." They must be mad. You just have to be sexy with it, that's all. It's getting easier, that. They expect it more now. AIDS has, at least, helped that. Certain middle-eastern countries, where anyway there just aren't any alternative forms of contraception, they're pretty used to it, so it's no big deal.'

I couldn't ever remember being in a situation where I found myself talking turkey, straight off, so frankly with anyone like that before. It was so unusual to sit there in that quiet hotel lounge, chatting so blithely, about the sexual function, with an attractive woman, who did it as her job. There she was, smiling and chatting and vivaciously thinking through her life with her hands on her knees, for all the world like a youthful, pretty, maiden aunt, crunching the ice from the Coke between her teeth. Later, I suggested she had a G & T, which she did, slightly reluctantly. I was gently, pleasantly, turned on by the conversation. There was a familiar warmth about the solar plexus and a comfortable thickening of the old equipment.

'How do you get the work?'

'Where did *you* find me? I advertise. God, I spend some thirty quid a week advertising. People pass my card around. I get recommendations – it's more boasting than anything, but it does the trick. These geezers, they think: "If it was all right for Head of Sales (Europe), it might be a laugh." That's what I am, a bit of a laugh. Something to remember. "I was in London and this would-be graduate sucked me off." So many of them have got wives at home who have forgotten what it's all about – haven't sucked cock since they were doing domestic science at college. But then so many of my gentlemen haven't got much of an idea themselves. If they had, they wouldn't be pushing fifty nicker notes into my knickers.' She looked at her watch. 'Time, gentle man, please. Have you got enough in your nice little notebook now, Mr Peter Holloway?'

'I think so. Yes.' I peered myopically at my scrawling. 'Yes. I think so.' She stopped and watched me: 'You going home now, Peter?' she asked.

'Yes, I think so.'

'You're quite a "yes, I think so" sort of person, eh?' She laughed. 'Interview over, or are we going to do some more?' She continued to watch me. 'Or what?' She did it extremely well and with a great deal of spirited charm. Feeling like I felt at that precise moment, if I had genuinely had the wherewithal, I probably would have been rogering her rigid in a suite upstairs within a twinkling of a flexing of plastic. But I didn't. So we didn't.

'Um. No,' I said.

'Don't look so mortified, Peter. I've got a lot of vacation reading to catch up on. And an essay – "Capitalism, the Market and the countries of the Eastern Block" or something. And I've got to sort out Sean's socks. He's going camping with the neighbours tomorrow. I think. Or maybe it's the day after tomorrow. I can't say I'm not disappointed, but there it is.'

'I'd love to actually. But I can't, I'm afraid.'

'You're a dear good splendid man and, if I could, I'd give you a note of commendation for your wife.'

'How do you know I'm married?'

'Men are. Bye-bye.' We both stood and she shook me by the hand and then she laughed and kissed my cheek: 'Lucky woman,' she said in my ear and she went. She had made me feel terrific. For the first time for ages too. I sat down and wrote on the page: 'Professionalism means making the man feel that he, out of the hundreds that have gone before, is unique and special and the kind of treat that the girl has been looking for since time began. Professionalism means doing that every time.'

Harriet spent a good fifteen minutes hovering adjacent to the phone in the bedroom. She sat on the bed and looked at it. She went and cleaned the bath. She returned and sat on the floor by the bedside table and looked at it again. Then she decided it was time to go and comb the chewing-gum out of the fur of Timothy's big teddy bear. Then, she felt it might be a possible idea after all, and she went back into the bedroom and picked up the receiver. But she put it down and thought she ought to go and take a paracetamol and perhaps try to tackle the scaling in the shower rose – the water in south-east London was incredibly hard. Then she dragged herself determinedly back to the bedroom and stood there, her heart doing overtime.

'Start now,' she said out loud to herself. 'Start now. Start now.'

Well it had to begin somewhere. She couldn't put it off any longer. This lengthy, probably rather indulgent, period of preparation had been all very well, but Harriet had lives to save. She must take her little bit of courage in both hands and do it. She had a budget to raise, capital to establish. The time had finally come when she must begin. Or had all this been so much la-di-da, pie in the sky – just games? It was the end of the hottest July of their lives. She had to make the first all-important phone-call. Even if she made this call, she reminded herself, she didn't have to go on with it if she didn't want. But it was a first step. Only.

'Harriet,' she intoned to herself, grimly like the man on *Gladiators*, 'you will start on my first whistle.'

Unfortunately for this initial frightening episode she could not hide behind the shelter of her newly invented character: Natasha Ivanov. Or at least not entirely. As her quarry knew Harriet Holloway only too well, she was not going to be able to lurk behind comfortable anonymity. Given the circumstances, there was going to be no way in which she could pretend to be anyone other than who she was. Or at the very least, an edited version of who she was.

'Do it,' she said to the empty bedroom.

And eventually, with a thumping pulse and a severe shortness of breath, she made the call. It was her first proper step out into the world of her possible new enterprise, the first time that someone out there was going to be caught up in her appalling obsession. She got through to him easily. That was a start. At least he was able to take Pete Holloway's wife's phone-call easily enough. Ms Ivanov might not even have got within half a dialling tone of his personal line. There were advantages to being the wife of a very best friend. Indeed, he sounded gratifyingly pleased to hear her request for a meeting. He'd always shown her that he liked her. She started off talking to him at great speed, virtually incoherent with nerves. He sounded quite a lot more than a little bit mystified. He obviously had to get over his basic initial instinct that little itty-bitty women should not need to meet men of his station to discuss 'business ideas'. But by the time she replaced the phone, she had hooked him. They were on their way, Natasha and she. And it had begun. At last.

He explained noisily that he was a member of this delightfully eccentric dining club, just round the back of the English National Opera, off St Martin's Lane. Tiny and not particularly fancy, but 'they did ever such good chow, you know', and had a perfectly phenomenal cellar for such a tiny place. He would see her there. He would clear a space in his diary, especially – 'What the damn Yanks unbelievably call "a window", what? How about tomorrow?' Harriet shuddered with fear and said quite gravely how much she was looking forward to it. And it had begun. She was off. Off the rails? Off her trolley? Offside? No, just off. Off and running.

She wasn't going to be able to involve Peter in this first precarious episode. This was going to have to be entirely private. But she had a first-class plan worked out. Over the third consecutive evening cauliflower cheese – greeted, now, with exceptional opposition by the assembled males at her less than groaning board, Harriet explained that tomorrow she was planning a really lengthy torture session down Greenwich way. She then played a trump card. She released a last fiver from her father's almost exhausted resources and suggested to her boys that they all three use it up on the Heath, at the Hare and Billet pub, tomorrow, where not only could beer, double Cokes and beer-nuts be consumed but the tatty family kite, wind-willing, could go on its annual flight. They could take Sam and Pippa from next door too. Give Marianne a break. In return for all those lunches she had given the boys.

Jonty and Timothy seemed pretty bright-eyed and bushy tailed at this idea and even Peter didn't appear too martyred. He would be able to have an afternoon when he need not pretend to be desperately busy and could slurp a lager, for once – just one tiny lager. With such modest briberies are the souls of the redundant penniless purchased.

The following day, Harriet hoovered the house like a woman possessed – which is what she was. She scrubbed her kitchen to within an inch of its life, scalded the cutlery in the cutlery drawer, and then, when she couldn't put it off any longer, she rode down to the Greenwich Leisure Centre for the briefest possible workout, with her handlebars hung about with a great multitude of plastic carrier-bags. After a veritable lick and a promise on the machines, she retired to the changing rooms to bring Natasha Ivanov to public life for the very first time. She would try to be Natasha in everything except voice, really. After all, her target, being her husband's best friend, while knowing her extremely well by sound and vision, probably hardly knew who she was, as a person, at all. So she would give him a first preview of Ms Ivanov, without the voice.

For it was Peter's oldest friend, Toby Lydell-Smith, who was about to be the very first to undergo the Ivanov experience.

She gave herself a good shower and then enough time to cool down. She was going to go as Chic, Demure Leg-over Executive Woman. Very, very, smart. She had brought out of her cupboard her most favourite pride and joy. It was the best cut little black suit that she had ever seen – Karl Lagerfeld. Two years before, she had saved up for what had seemed like forever to land it. It had a neat short cut-away jacket and while the skirt could hardly be called very short (although it flirted away well above the knee), it had been tailored by God. Under this she wore a taut little, scoop-neck, white body; best denier black legs and, what she might see now as, her working heels. Natasha would embody the great universal archetypical eighties icon. And she imagined Toby'd adore that. Remind him of being back in Thatcher's dream heaven when all was still right with the world.

Otherwise she wore her new, faintly over-the-top business-lunch slap – Dust-on Golden Copper Tinted Bronzing powder, True Black Spectacular Mascara, Raisin lip contour pencil. Really dandy. Bright, not caricatured. Quite big hair, pinned up on top. And then the giveaway – a veritable Ph.D. in earrings. Peter was fond of saying that there was always something good and tribal about earrings. It was true, they seemed to whisper 'chattel' ever so subliminally. They suggested gorgeous gift-wrapping: 'I am all dressed up as a special treat especially for you.' After all, earrings were about the only thing that a wearer would never be able to see and enjoy for herself. They seemed to exist purely to raise a wearer's mettle, and to twinkle all manner of potential promise to a companion.

As she left the Arches Leisure Centre, Harriet could almost hear the receptionist's astonished jaw hit the deck. The Arches had at least ten dozen Harriet Holloways turn up every week. It never saw a Natasha Ivanov stalk out.

Would Peter's best mate be equally gob-smacked? Could she do it anyway? Well, she would find out before tea-time came around, before kites were all folded away for the duration. This was make or break time. The sun shone down and gave her a short, and she hoped lithe, shadow. Up on the heath, her three boys were, no doubt, failing to raise the kite very far off the ground – and noisily accusing each other of incompetence. She was doing this for them. They would never know how much it was costing her.

Toby's dining club was at the end of a really noisome alleyway, close to the Colosseum. It was up a suspicious looking carpeted stairway, behind a completely anonymous smart front-door. Upstairs on the first floor of what was, in truth, a fairly modest little house, lurked the most urbane and civilised, panelled retreat. She arrived spot-on at twelve-thirty, out of breath – from the stairs or from her fear, she couldn't tell.

Toby was at a window table, with the sun flooding in behind him, from above Charing Cross Station in the Strand. He parked his large whisky on the spindly table and rose to meet her, surrounded by pieces of his collapsing *Daily Telegraph*. She saw his eye, for a fraction of a second unguarded, review the way she looked and assess the body beneath. For the very first time in her life, she was genuinely really pleased at his response, instead of the more usual feeling of being mildly irritated. After all, that was her whole point. For a brief second she felt almost as thrilled as when she had passed her driving-test. Perhaps there were some modest compensations about being a sex-object – you didn't need constantly to be bothered by how bloody sexist men were. Toby held her shoulders briefly and kissed the air around both ears – very European. She caught the tang of his cigar smoke. She sat to one side of his table, next to him. She moved the chair out carefully away from the table, so that he could see all of her, if he wanted. She could get good at this.

It was a nice place. The staff were genuinely friendly. The menu was stuffed full of surprises. Although her stomach had shrunk to the size of a pea, the idea of food was still amazingly provocative. Toby and she pondered the likely delights of the many proffered coulis and pennes and filos. At the same time, they ran through the usual dutiful conversational gambits that mutual friends have in order to fill the space between them. Finally, an order for food and wine and water was squared up and sent winging on its way. Then they talked, yet more, of this and that. They talked of the

Lives and Times of Pete Holloway – a little fancifully. They talked of rock climbs ascended – a little fancifully. They talked of the exploits of offspring sprung – a little fancifully. The usual things – modern fishermen's and fisherwomen's tales.

Trays and plates and bottles arrived. Harriet began to operate the first of Natasha's working principles: eat and drink nothing. Enthuse, admire, murmur appreciation, sip, slurp and worry everything edible with your trusty knife and fork, but consume the barest minimum. In that way, Natasha would always be able to monitor the tenor of the engagement. With virtually no alcohol in her bloodstream, she could smile and bob and offer sincerely listening eyes, parted, wondering lips. She could even glancingly finger a companion's wrist in conversation, without ever being unable to sit inside her head and gauge the warmth of the communication, how far they were along, and in which direction they were going now. And indeed, for the future, she presumably needed to remember that where rich food is concerned, there is absolutely nothing quite so excruciating as copulating on a full stomach.

Toby got slowly more expansive, and more noisy, if that was possible. The music, gently filling the air of the club, was the unearthly sound of Peruvian pan-pipes. The club filled up. Simon Callow edged by, looking abstracted. At one point, an acquaintance of Toby came by and Toby was more than ordinarily pleased to introduce 'this little lady' who obediently stood and grasped a hand, as the man, who was her own height, pretended that he wasn't looking at her bosom.

Harriet guessed the best business is done once the wine is consumed. So they left the business of the day entirely unspoken until the arrival of the *cafetière*. As soon as Toby had done the honours with the tiny cups and had offered the cream and they had agreed that only he should indulge in an elderly brandy, he began to cut his way into the round end of a suggestively thick new cigar. They had reached the dreaded: 'Any Other Business.' At last Toby asked the inevitable question: 'Well, what's all this about, then, my dear?'

'Not all that easy to say, Toby,' she said shyly. She was going to play it in 'thick-little-lady-with-naff-enthusiasm' mode. She wasn't proud of this, but it seemed to her to be an effective way of reaching out for Toby's particular kind of patrimony.

'Spit it out,' he said, happy to josh with her. He puffed billows of fairly satisfied smoke about the table.

'I'm looking for an investment. For a new business idea. That I want to develop myself. The difficulty is, Toby' [Use his name, it makes it feel more personal and intimate.], 'that I can't tell you very much about it. It's a new corporate entertainments idea. I want to run it from home. It's going to be called "Tricks & Treats".' This had been an inspired idea that came to her that very morning, on the train up to town. In the spring, she had taken the kids to see a Saturday morning children's show at the Blackheath concert halls, just around the corner from home. An old codger had done a kids' show which he had called 'Tricks & Treats with Sainsbury the Rabbit'. 'Tricks & Treats' sounded about right. Perfectly honest and straightforward for the Toby Lydell-Smiths of this world – and actually pretty accurate too.

'"Tricks & Treats", eh? Sounds very jolly. What sort of thing?'

'Special dinner parties for companies, for individuals, for any-body, really.'

'Is there an opening for this? Is there a market? I mean, isn't the world and his goddamned wife moving into this corporate entertainments business? I'd've thought it was a damn crowded field. Barbara's got some sort of directory full of, oh, I don't know, fun casinos, paint war-games and all that kind of nonsense. Have you done your research? Got any projections? Business plan?'

'No. That's why it's so difficult to present to you. I'm sure that it's going to work, Toby, but a lot of it is still in my head.'

'And a very pretty head it is too, if I might say so. But I'd need to see some figures, I'm afraid. And I'm not saying for a minute, my dear, that I can help. I'm pretty well fully extended just at the moment, in point of fact, this recession makes beggars of us all. What are we talking about here?'

'Five thousand pounds.'

'Five grand, eh?' He sat back in his chair and looked at her over the top of his glasses. For a long time. She sat there and looked back at him as coolly as she was able. Then she sipped her Perrier, smiled at him, crossed her legs as elaborately as she dared, and repeated her request. For Toby Lydell-Smith it was nothing, of that she was sure. 'Five thousand pounds, Toby, yes.'

'Well. Five thousand smackeroonies, eh, Harriet?'

'It's not very much.' She would need every penny.

'It may not seem very much to you, Harriet, but I don't throw money about without looking into it very carefully. You produce some figures and I can think about it.'

'I can't do that. I want to keep my ideas under wraps,' she said steadily. Her strategy was that the plan should seem so bold and so simple and so meagrely supported by the lack of any paperwork that Toby might perhaps be unsettled by it. She was beginning to head for the denouement. She felt very scared and yet strangely excited about it all at the same time. She fervently hoped that she hadn't misjudged him. She prayed she hadn't gone and misinterpreted years of fairly clear body-language and countless slightly obscure compliments.

Toby made his money by moving paper around in the City, but he had also a few company investments, salting away money in all manner of things – dead certainties as well as less likely but nonetheless lively ideas. He must have got used to people – men – coming to him with schemes, plans, ideas and possibilities, all of them worked out to the last decimal point, with graphic projections, pie-charts and appendices inches thick, on smart shiny paper, decently stitched together in laminated folders. It would surely be unique for him to find himself opposite a girl who held him with a steady brown eye and asked him, simply enough, for five grand, and not a single paper to be seen. The idea was that his brain would be switched to full-scale patronise mode and then she would turn the whole thing around with her ultimate play for him.

He was making such a big thing of sitting back, puffing and contemplating her question that it was now fairly apparent that he was indeed disturbed. She hoped she guessed right that you couldn't make such a business of looking unperturbed unless you were, a bit. With luck she'd got him. To him, she obviously appeared completely lacking in artifice and was financially pretty desperate. This was quite easy to portray as indeed it was precisely the case! She continued speaking to him gently, leaning close in to him so that he could hear her voice against the hubbub of the other diners in the room: 'You would have to trust me, I'm afraid. But I can absolutely guarantee, Toby, that you will get the fullest possible return on your investment. A far better return than on any five grand you've ever spent. I know I can promise you that.' Was she really that confident in her appeal? Apparently so.

'You can, can you, my dear?' He was grinning avuncularly at her, peering through his cloud of blue smoke as it caught the afternoon sunshine and made patterns between their heads. 'If this is such a dandy idea, from such a dandy lady, why, in heaven's name, doesn't young Peterkins put up the dough? He can afford it, for God's sake. He's loaded, isn't he?'

'This is between us, Toby, please.' She was speaking an octave down, holding his eye all the time. She quietly placed her forefinger on his knee for emphasis. And she kept it there. She was inviting his complicity in the earnest truth she was about to tell: 'This is a terrible thing, Toby, but Peter lost all the redundancy package. It was on Julian's business – my brother – which makes it so very much the worse. For us both. His fast-food franchising thing. Oh, and Peter had had a lot of debts too when he left *The Chronicle*. He got those paid off first. And anyway, Peter thought he had a bankable future – which he did have – but then the recession really began to bite. But that was later.' She had three finger-tips on his knee – perfectly manicured nails, pressing his knee – uppermost in his mind, she hoped.

Toby's face was successfully avoiding any reaction to her revelations, but she had an astonishing extra-sensory impression of his hidden secret pleasure at Peter's misfortune, tucked away within fulsome commiserations. She had always known that these two 'best of friends' were, at the same time, mortal combatants locked in some dread, mystic rivalry, but until that moment she had never realised how acute that competition might be. Toby Lydell-Smith was a prime example of how the upper echelons of the English education system, while producing vastly effective and justly famed effortless superiority, bred, at the same time, a wicked self-seeking autocracy as well. And Peter had imbued that culture too. From Toby, himself, as much as from anywhere. She suddenly sensed that these two men, who always claimed so to love one another, simultaneously hated one another with a like passion. If she was going to try to be in their two camps at one and the same time, she might very well be getting out of her depth.

She found she needed to defend Peter: 'Julian gave him the whole battle strategy, the projections, the business plan for the next three years. It looked really very good too.' Her voice caught and she cleared her throat – it wasn't acting. 'It was a pile of garbage, Toby – lies. He lied to us. Made it all up. Forged the accounts, the balance sheet, the state at the bank, everything. My own brother. The business had already gone right down the pan. I don't think Julian really thought it had. He was still trying to pay his way through to saving it. I don't think he's actually properly wicked – not really, he was just in such a hole. He must have been under enormous pressure. And he has always been hopelessly optimistic. Things had usually come right for him in the past. But some of it was real deceit. Peter's nest egg disappeared into a black hole, overnight.' She remembered ruefully: 'Between a Saturday and a Tuesday – gone. One minute we were at the NEC thinking about what new car we might buy, and the next, the bank was closing down our accounts without bothering to tell us. And Julian just disappeared. Took off. Ran. Never heard from him – oh, just a garbled message – just went. All he left us was an old bicycle! I'd always worshipped him as a girl. Ireland, I think, he's gone to. Maybe somewhere else. Christ knows where. Peru?' She laughed almost lightheartedly, thinking of the music that was eerily playing at them in the club. 'Of course we should have gone into it more intelligently, but with your own brother . . .'

'I'm so sorry. Poor dear Harriet.' He continued to sound genuinely sympathetic.

'Poor Peter and the boys. Poor Peter, he feels so stupid. As if it's all his fault. And of course it isn't.'

'Of course it isn't.' He agreed with her, lying. Then he did a little more dirt-digging: 'And so, has the jolly old work not exactly been rolling in?'

'For Peter? Not really, no. Keep this to yourself, Toby, please.'

'Of course, my dear. The tomb, the grave – silent as. Trust me.' And, theatrically, he put a big ringed third finger to his closed lips.

'So. Well.' Go for it, Natasha. Do-it-do-it-do-it! Now! 'Do you think you could possibly help me, Toby?'

'Well, well, well, well. Five thousand pounds is five thousand pounds.' He stubbed the cigar away into the glass ashtray. 'What do I get out of this?'

And she did it: 'Me,' she said firmly, looking straight into his cold grey eyes.

'How do you mean?' He knew – he was sufficiently sure of himself to know – but couldn't allow himself to believe it. He might just have got it wrong. He couldn't afford to look a fool. She helped him: 'You get me. Once a month for a year. All night long. Wherever you choose, whatever date suits.' She had learned that line, so it wasn't too hard to get out. And she looked at him really brazenly with Natasha's own special brand of cool limpid brown eyes. He had to look away. Her voice cooed breathily on: 'Good times. In bed. With me.' She could feel the blood running in her neck and the perspiration between her breasts. 'Simple as that.' And then, to make sure, and it wasn't anything like as easy as she thought it would be: 'I'd so like that too.' She felt better, and like dying, all at the same time. She couldn't believe herself! She'd done it.

'Good God!' He came back to earth with such a loud shout of laughter that for a moment the chatter in the room stilled and people glanced in their direction – they glanced at the big man over by the window who looked as if he had just won the pools. There he was, in a halo of summer cigar smoke, grinning at the raven-haired girl in the earrings, who was bending forward, her hand now gently cupping his thigh, not overly far from his crotch.

'Do you actually mean that?'

'Of course. One favour deserves another. A few others.' She could be quite sexy, if she wanted to be. It felt a bit powerful.

'Harriet?'

'I'm positive. I'd like it so much.'

'Does Peter know anything about this?'

'Of course not. Good God no. Toby, I couldn't tell him. He must never know. It would be our secret. Our very special, private secret.'

'Oh, right. Yes, of course, right. Well! Well I can't say that I'm not astonished. And delighted. Well, you're some girl, aren't you, Harriet Holloway? Well, I have to say – I've never – '

'– had such a good offer before, Toby?' she smiled at his confusion.

'You really want to do this? It's that important for you – this "Tricks and Sweets"?'

'"Tricks and Treats", Toby. Yes.' He made a determined effort to remain looking magisterial: 'Well, let me see. Um. When exactly would you see this, this, er, arrangement as starting?'

She'd got him! Her body sang with ecstasy. She almost threw up with the excitement of her success. Then and there. She'd stonking done it! She was in heaven. Or in hell. OK, she was going to have to take him in hand and bed the fella. She could do that all right. He wasn't such a bad old bloke. Well, one hurdle at a time, girl; at this precise moment she was flying high, up there in the sky. Her boys could eat. Peter and her sons could lift up their heads. She could set herself up. She would get Jonty his dreadful old Nintendo. She could do anything. She was alive. She was God.

But she didn't give a hint of her celebration, she didn't move a muscle. She didn't reveal a flicker of what she was feeling. She just quietly removed her hand from his body and said: 'We could start in four weeks' time. You'd just have to ring me. The ball would be in your court. As the saying goes.'

'What would you tell Peter? How would you manage it?'

'I'd sort it. He must never know. All I would just say is that I had persuaded you to invest in a good little number.'

'You have,' he said, 'you have.' He pushed his glasses up the bridge of his nose and fished in his inside pocket. He gave another short explosive laugh. 'You have. Indeed you have!' A Coutts cheque book was on the table between them. And a big black fountain-pen: 'Who do I make the cheque out to?'

'"Tricks & Treats" – well – "T & T Services", actually.' Her would-be customers would need to have a fairly anonymous reference on their credit-card accounts. Toby was writing. He stopped and looked at her again. He was still half in shock. But coping. He gave her another sharp look, over the top of his spectacles: 'That's just over four hundred quid a night, Harriet.'

'A bargain, Toby, my dear, you'll see, a bargain. You'll just love it. You're investing in paradise.'

Today we ate! Proper food! My significant other, my dearly beloved Harriet, smiling in that almost arrogant, individually wonky way that only she can essay, sashayed elegantly, nay sensuously, from the environs of her stove with astonishing, succulent, blood-bolstered, meaty steak! Well, in fact, steak for myself and the ever beauteous H. and fairly disgusting-looking veggiburgers for the offspring, as they are going through a Blue Peter-inspired infantile Animal Rights phase, just at the moment.

After the past few months the meal was such a distinctive pleasure. And there were chips. And mixed salad. And crusty old baguetty-type bread. And a pretty duff old Rioja. But a proper bottle of wine with an honest-to-goodness cork in the top. I don't think the kids can have seen me wield a corkscrew in living memory. I virtually had to explain what this wondrous apparatus was used for. As my son, swimmer J. Holloway, now honourable Penguin with the Greenwich Swimming Club, was heard to say before the little men in white coats came to take his jabbering father away: 'Well nice, Mum, the food!'

Yes, he and I had returned this afternoon from this new mega-enthusiasm of his – swimming. I spent a limp hour or so hanging about in their draughty poolside corridors while an obscenely bronzed, very short, wiry man called Gary Hope put all these pale, small, shivering boys and girls through various appalling timed routines. There is a very great deal of talk of breathing and of leg action and Mr Hope appears to be worshipped by his progeny who number some fifteen and now, somewhat astonishingly, seem to include my very own eldest son. Jonty quite definitely adores it.

I am marginally thunderstruck and cannot imagine where this talent has seeped into him from. I myself have only ever swum briefly from poolside ladder to poolside bar, there to refresh myself with additional multiple Pina Coladas. My mother, for example, cannot swim at all. As a kid I used to worry about it all the time – particularly on those very rare occasions when she would use the Woolwich Free Ferry – for fear it might go down, leaving her exposed in her ignorance, and me in an orphanage.

And now, by heavens, here I am, just a weeny bit pissed. So the day was stuffed full of unusual circumstance. Except, of course, for the habitual happenstance of England losing the Lord's Test by an innings. Some things do not change. Ever.

But steak? I tweaked an interrogatory eyebrow at H. And she trotted out the usual time-honoured cliché like: 'Yours not to query, yours not to reason why.' And side-tracking things like: 'Do you want me to get you a sharper steak knife?' She was very very hyped up and almost high-spirited. It was delightful. And she looked really great. There was a small moment when we were all digging into unlooked-for heaven in the shape of individual Disneyland yoghurts with black cherry, and when I looked about me we were all laughing. For the Holloway family at home, this was a first for a pretty good long while.

I can only imagine that the good Dr McGee has, once again, added to the Holloway Family Public Residual Borrowing Requirement. God knows how we will ever manage to pay them back. I suppose Alasdair and Deborah are so very very unhappy about Julian's disappearance that they are, I think, very kindly, trying to make things a mite better for their daughter by pushing much-needed funds in a Blackheath direction. I suppose it means Julian McGee's existence or, at least, ex-existence has, at last, to some degree, been of benefit to someone.

When the kids had been stowed, H. and I retired to almost our one remaining piece of furniture, the sofa. Here some television of no fixed worth was imbibed by the two of us in apparent harmony. In fact, as H.'s secret funding had allowed her to purchase this bottle of fairly drastic supermarket whisky, we undertook to imbibe just the minutest quantity between us. I must say that I rather thought that, given a bit of unusual male sensitivity, charm and a touch of dogged persistence, we could be in for a husband/wife bunk-up situation before the end of this extraordinary evening. But, of course, I thought too soon.

Harri zapped the screen into silence and began to ask me about my researches into the shadowy world of escort work. I suppose I had sort of hoped that she had forgotten all about that little wheeze. But no, she's still pretty focused on it. In fact she's like Starfire with a yogurt pot. We ummed and aahed our way around the subject for a while with H. getting steadily back into her more recent ball-breaking demeanour. This discussion (for want of a better word) finished up with H. slamming out, yelling: 'Well, at least you could have the balls to draw up a theoretical scheme, you stupid impotent bastard!' I remained (with the now severely depleted whisky bottle) on the now extremely depleted sofa, zapping from channel to channel, feeling very badly done by, like blokes do. Then J. came and looked anxiously about and said could Timmy have a glass of water, as he'd woken up.

I sat my man Jonty on the sofa and told him how impressed I was with his sonic-man swimming and then went in for some man-to-man male-bonding chat about how brilliant women could be if they liked – when they weren't being completely impossible, that is. 'Like Mum?' asked our wise little lad. And I told him that Harriet is just the tops in every way – which is a complete lie – no, which is totally and absolutely true. And I told him a little of the dreaded, wait-for-it, P.M.T. Not that she's suffering from that, at the moment. She's suffering from another kind of P.M.T. – the Poverty Meagreness Trap.

Then he poodled off with his glass of tap water. And I did some more channel-riding and whisky-tasting. So what did she mean by 'impotent', eh? I know we've not done much of that for an age, but I'd been banking on a bonk this very evening. I suppose she's right, we're not very sexy these days.

Actually, I have done a lot of thinking through the stuff I gathered from that Pamela. I finished a reasonably good piece which I'd hawked about a touch fruitlessly until Bernard on the *Statesman* vouchsafed an interest. It's with him now. He said, 'It might come in.' God, I hope so. Bernard will no doubt sub it about and I'll get fifteen hundred words in the *Staggers*, in an edition at the turn of the century, called immortally: 'Recession And The Sex Worker'. Well, we'll have to see.

So.

Anyway.

I'm sitting here tapping this out, on the hottest night of a pretty hot year (temperature-wise anyhow), avoiding trespass in or around the battle-zone (sorry, bedroom to you, friendly green screen). Perhaps I should tease out a few hypothetical notions? I suppose it is quite an interesting cerebral exercise. Well hardly cerebral. But if I can produce one of my world-famous schedules of useful points, that should please the damn woman and bring her down from the outer stratosphere, whence she seems to have repaired.

So, just supposing . . .

Oh, this is all nonsense, isn't it? I mean, can you really imagine it? In actuality? Anonymous guys fucking Harriet? For money? I'd rather die.

Anyway, as I said, just supposing:

OPERATION JEZEBEL

I will briefly cover
1. Finance.
2. Security, including communications.
3. Publicity and Marketing.
4. Product, including decor.
5. Cover.

1. *Finance*

We would need a product name and a building society account. I favour: *Favours* as a business title. We would also (OK, I'm going to phrase this a little less conditionally:) – We will need the facility to be able to take payment through all major credit cards.

2. *Security, etcetera*

We will need an account with a good reliable minicab firm. We will
need to operate the whole thing from a mobile telephone number. This
is a lifeline that the product (oh bugger the jargon, I mean Harriet,
dumbo) can have about her at all times so that she has ready access
to assistance if/when necessary (am I *really* writing this?). What else?
Oh, I can get a can or two of 'Mace' from someone coming back from
the States for her to carry, just in case. 'Just In Case – Mace!' Oh dear
I am really more than a tiny bit pissed. I've not drunk whisky for all
of fifty-nine days, until H. produced this shit called 'Old Grouse' or
'Merry Haggis' or something, a 'fun' whisky from Château Locost. It
rotteth the taste-buds but the corruption is sweet, my Lord.

3. *Publicity & Marketing*

Well, we would have to take out a regular discreet and sexy ad
in *What's On*. (It would take forever to get into *Yellow Pages*.
If we could, I rather fancy the notion of a *Yellow Pages* ad. with
the copy: 'Let her fingers do the wanking.') Anyway, we've got
to be up there in the market place with the others. She talked
about masquerading under the name 'Natasha' – Christ knows
why 'Natasha'. I mean, isn't that just such a cliché? I rather
fancy 'Tempestua', or 'Floribunda', or something really raunchy
like 'Mildred'. Anyway, from my extensive and absorbing study of
the literature, I notice that none of the present ads offer intelligence
at all, so, perhaps, something like this:

> NATASHA, extremely beautiful, articulate,
> intelligent young woman of style and sensitivity.
> A graceful companion for any event. Ring 0831 der-der-der.

And we would need some really discreetly tasteful business cards
with just her name and phone number on them – nothing more.
I mean, that's what would generate the business. There's nothing
better than word-of-mouth to get things rolling. It is just a matter
of anonymously distributing cards in the right quarters – people
like Francis Tanner at the Press Association, David Groombridge
at B.D.D.L., what's his name Tom? no – John? yes, John Carrick
in Brussels, at the European Parliament. People who are well known

to put it about a bit, and know others that do too. It would take a bit of time, but I reckon there's a well-established sleaze circuit and once you're on it – the whole thing could run along reasonably smoothly and fairly profitably. They're all men who have a deal of dosh that they like to spend on gratification. Funny, I'm quite getting into this. Anyway, as a theory.

4. *Product & Decor*

Well, I imagine we'd have to leave this to her nibs. She'd need to buy some gear. I can see a severe attack of shopping coming on. In fact I sometimes think that maybe the only reason why we're trundling through this farcical rigmarole is that Harriet is desperate to get into fast-forward shopping mode. I mean, for the best part of six months, she's been totally denied the orgasms of that three-in-one, that August Trinity of the Flexible Friend: the Kensington High, the New Bond and the Holy Sloane Streets. At the very least, this whole notion could be just a grand opportunity for a total virtual-reality fantasy shop! I can just see the delectable creature, on the pavement outside Peter Jones, drowning in a plethora of fifteen hundred individual designer-label carrier bags, and not a taxi for miles.

That's if we ever get to go ahead and could drum up some capital. Oh well, never mind.

H.'s Herculean fitness purdah has delivered electrifying results. I went down to the Arches in Greenwich again with Harriet and Jonti this morning to see what the big compulsion is. In all honesty, for a man of my bulk to have to acknowledge relationship to two such suddenly changed athletic personages was something of a turn-around. I mean, for years it used only to be me who would venture, say, on to the mountains. I was totally banjaxed by the sight of the girl in her leotard. I can't have looked at her properly in the last little while.

Back to business: well, truth to tell, we would have to have a proper sit down and have a real talk through this mad scheme of Harriet's – there are an awful lot of impossibly dreadful implications here. For fuck's sake, she's had such an incredibly sheltered life. And I couldn't handle it at all anyway. It's just absurd. I might not finish doing this. Go to bed. This is a waste of time.

But a halfway interesting hypothetical topic, too.

5. *Cover*

Harriet suddenly would have to get some night-time employment – as far as Blackheath neighbours are concerned. Say, a night shift at one of the reference/cuttings libraries at one of the newspaper publishers – or with Reuters – or with ITN or something. It would probably have to be some completely fictional outfit so that it couldn't be checked out. Yes, let us say: library assistant, late shift, for something like: Corporate Press and Electronic Media – C.P.E.M. for short. Sounds pretty good, doesn't it? She wouldn't need to do a big song and dance about it – just let it be taken as read. And any noticeable enhanced increase in our family income could be put down to my own, of-a-sudden, devastatingly successful career as columnist (ho-hum). That, and Harri's steady income for her work at C.P.E.M. Hmm, I'm almost beginning to believe that's a real organisation, already.

Then Harri would need a *pied-à-terre* in town somewhere – a bolt-hole. We'd need to rent a small space in town where she could kip down on a camp-bed if she needed to and, more particularly, a place where she can transmogrify from wife-and-mother into working-girl. This would mean she could go off into town and return in the sort of guise that would not create an overdue stir in the communal Blackheathan psyche – nor indeed require J. and T. to do any overburdensome analysis as to what their mother went out to do for a living.

I think that's it. Garbage idea, isn't it? Oh well. She must be asleep. I'll go and look. Drank nearly all the 'Heather Peril'. I will doubtless reap a just reward, *dans ma tête, sur le matin. Bon soir*, old screen. Nice talking to you. Pip-pip. Now, let's see if I can make the door in one, in a straight line.

DOING IT

The last twenty-four hours have been definitely the most unlikely of my life, of anybody's life for that matter. I am still in a state of terminal astonishment. What an extraordinarily bizarre frolic! It was unique. Gentle, ordinary, everyday, pretty, mother-of-two Harriet, my very own darling wife, produced such a multitude of the unexpected that I am still striving to recover from it.

It started modestly enough – I'll try and write a halfway decent account:

So, it's last Thursday evening and Harriet (Good God, Harriet, Harriet, Harriet, I still can't get my costive bloody brain properly around all of this) and I find ourselves, unusually, sharing the stone wall seat thing that we have, by the little lily pond in the back-garden. I had promised myself that I would cut the lawn and, indeed, after some days of petty prevarication, I had done it. Young H. came out, in her extremely fetching jeans and her skimpy 'Leaden Jury' singlet and diligently applied herself to clipping the edges. In fact, it looked bloody good when we'd finished it. It takes a long time, though.

Now, I realise, that H. manoeuvred us into this conversation. She was certainly fulsome in bringing forth two suddenly communicative mugs of tea. It being a peerless glorious evening, J. & T. were, of course, totally immersed in watching the box with the living-room curtains almost fully drawn. By that time, Timothy should have been setting off on the long long journey to beddibyes. The dog was eating H.'s Dr Scholl's in the kitchen. In fact, everything was much as usual, chez Holloway. Weatherwise, it was one of those great evenings, when you don't ever want it to be different. Apart from the money situation.

So, Harriet is sitting terribly quiet, beside me on the wall. I'm going on, I think, dead innocently, about a scheme that will help us protect the goldfish from the herons, or something. H. suddenly

89

interrupts me, in full flow. And she tells me very quietly that she thinks it would be wise for her to have a dress-rehearsal. A dress-rehearsal? I had no idea what she was on about. She says that she wants to have a dummy-run at the whole scheme. With a friendly subject. It took me considerably more than half a dozen astro-seconds to realise that she meant it. And she meant me.

To start with, I dug into my resources of humour and joked somewhat flippantly about it all, but then I could see her knuckles were taut and white, as she sat there hugging her untouched mug of Typhoo, so there was some sudden need for me to start taking the conversation seriously. What she was saying was costing her more than somewhat, and *it was for real*. This has been, all along I think, for her, a genuinely, actual, possible idea. She goes out there, does her stuff, whatever that means for Chrissakes, and some money is duly earned. And we, sort of – well, we survive. Or something. But survival on what sort of terms, eh?

She has this notion that she is now all prepared to go out and activate the 'scheme'. She's got enough dosh, from her father, I suppose, to set it up and actually to do it. And she wants to. Well, she certainly seemed to want to when we had this conversation. Just to keep us stabilised, I suppose until, well, until I'm earning properly again. Which will be soon, surely? She gabbled some typically half-learned Harriet-type notion about how all the world's women, to a large degree, exchange sexual favours for security, somewhere along the line. That's not how I've seen it. I thought love and fidelity and one-to-one relationships had a place in there somewhere – but, then, what do I know and, furthermore (honesty rearing its ugly and surprising head here), who am I to say?

So there we are, suddenly oblivious to the merry mayhem that Starfire is provoking in the unguarded kitchen, as H. informs me quite firmly that, in order to see what 'the life' might be like, she wants to have one go, first, within the safety of her own home. Well, not quite her own home actually. And with a soft target – me. To see if she could actually do it. Her plan is that she and I should go through the whole rigmarole. I would be the john. She would pretend to be this Natasha, this character she says she's invented as cover. I would have to ring her, make an appointment, dress and behave as little like P. Holloway Esquire as possible, meet with her, not know her from Eve, and 'proceed from there'. She would provide the funds. Harriet suddenly has funds. She suddenly seems like a pitiless bottom.

At first it was funny. And I found it quite hard to take seriously. But I did try very hard not to scoff. I couldn't help a certain rising risibility. Probably more out of a sense of defence than anything else. It isn't your normal run-of-the-mill, middle-class weekend outing though, is it? You don't usually find it in the weekend guide of activities for established married couples in the *Observer* – 'Art-deco Fairs, Boot Sales, Pick-your-own fruit, Bungee Jumping, Wife as Whore'. So I gave a sort of disbelieving grunt. She didn't sulk. I think she had guessed that this would be my first reaction. She just steam-rollered along explaining what she wanted us to do. We would pretend that 'Project Jezebel', or whatever I'd called the thing, was a going concern – but without having to invest in a vodophone. She would give me the wherewithal to check myself into a decent hotel (would that the good Dr McGee knew what his hard-won Health Service screw was subsidising). I'd ring her and we'd, um, go from there.

Well, as I say, I was initially fairly reluctant about the whole thing, when, suddenly, slightly surprisingly, it began to feel like a nicely sexy idea. I mean, to be honest, H. and I are the most kink-free people you've ever met. We've never felt a need to have to do it over the phone or with ropes or on the top of Primrose Hill. But the idea of doing a small piece of sexual role-playing, well, actually, the more I thought about it, sitting there, not watching the sun sinking behind next door's willow, the more I realised that I found the idea rather more than appealing. Pretending is always something of a turn-on, isn't it? And, if she did it even half well, it might be a little like slipping some stranger a sly one but without the attendant bolt-on factors of guilt and fear and subsequent self-loathing.

By the time this intriguing idea had lodged in the old grey-matter, I was sitting there with that nice and naughty glow about the crotch that heralds a good stiff hard-on. I hadn't had an erection just contemplating H. for, well, it might be years actually. It's OK in bed, of course, when in the throes, but not in your usual dreamy old contemplation. It was a pleasant surprise. And surprisingly pleasant. Sorry, but there it is. I began to feel genuinely enraptured by the idea. After all it's not illegal or anything – a married couple dressing up and pretending to be these two other people to have a good bang. Odd perhaps, but not wrong or even sick. Certainly kink-free.

So it was a nice and crazy idea. It wouldn't mean anything more than H. and I having a quick knee-trembler away-day. Nothing more, believe you me. It would certainly break up the monotony of this year's endlessly desperate times. H. seemed tolerably turned on about it too. She always gets a small pale in the smile-lines of her mouth when she's feeling randy. I think. Anyway, she was pale about the gills now. Oh, she's a funny old devil. As I say, what a woman!

It was going to mean a deal of proper self-discipline from yours truly. H. was very serious about it. I guessed that if I farted about, she would as good as kill me. I would have to act out this role of customer with a deal of earnest fervour. It would be important for me to try to summon up some of the frame-of-mind of this guy who had called this Natasha character and was about to spend his money on an evening with her. H. was going to give me the cash for this too – 'the money goes round and around and it comes out here!'

Harriet was on at me, immediately, about inventing some sort of name, scenario and background for myself. Well. In the end I said at least I'd get to come up with a name. I quite fancied 'Mervin Grope', but I reckoned she'd get furious and start pummelling me physically as well as mentally. As she's funding this whole malarkey, I thought I'd better do my stuff. When, on the day, I booked into the hotel, I plucked 'Roger Conway' right out of the air. I think there had been a furniture lorry heading towards Euston with that on the side. So I was 'Roger Conway' for fourteen hours. It was difficult to remember. I actually told the hotel clerk, the second time around, that I was called Roger Convoy!

Harriet wasn't going to take no for an answer anyway, and by this time my dirty old psyche was well and truly right into it. We fixed it for Saturday night. It seemed that she had already arranged for the stoical Marianne to let us stoic-pile the boys next door all that night. I was to go off Saturday morning, fill in the day becoming a stranger, and then go for the Olivier Award that evening.

God, it felt good and sexy, almost like I'd been smoking dope. I felt excited and somewhat apprehensive all at the same time. Exactly like when you're a kid and about to ring up some girl you fancy at school, to ask her out to the cinema. It was odd for someone my age to have that buzz again. A bit of a treat, really. So, at the end of this extraordinary discussion, I couldn't get up off the garden-wall without embarrassing myself. I had this very welcome, full-sized pre-stressed concrete dipstick on me. When H. went to do the good offices for young Tim with Pooh, Piglet and the other ratbags, I stole off to the garden-shed to put away the tools in every sense of the word. When I'd got myself together, I felt altogether brighter than I remember for a fair while. We remaining three had a very perky evening, guffawing at some laughable thriller starring Burt Reynolds' hairpiece. I can't remember us having such a friendly evening for a very long time. It was like this dodgy little plan was an unspoken bond, a secret language between H. and me – our very own bizarre shared madness. It was like I remember feeling when we were in love. We were both so good all evening with J. too. It was a proper sort of time for a lad and his parents – he even did his teeth without being nagged. Came and showed me them.

But we made sure that we didn't mention Saturday to each other after that. It was just sort of settled between us. We two, Harriet and Pete, hadn't got any particular plans for Saturday evening. That was for two other folks. So the topic, while no doubt shouting deafeningly into each of our separate brains, never lifted its surprisingly attractive looking head again, until Saturday at 2.45 p.m. when, at last, Roger Rabbit, in deepest London town, rang Natasha Fluffytale, at her warren, to make a date.

I went into town while she was at the gym, Saturday morning. Me and my wifely donated, absurdly welcome, wedge. I wore the summer cotton suit that I found in Lisboa three years ago and have hardly worn since. I bought a new tie and went to Arnaldo's in Curzon Street, and had him snip my hair. Hee couldn't entirely rescue H.'s grim efforts with the kitchen scissors over the past three months but it was a slight improvement. This 'Roger' character didn't look quite as much like me as he might have done.

Had a cappuccino and booked into the King's Hotel in Bloomsburyville. It's not too furiously expensive but feels as if it might be. Nice corner room on the second floor overlooking the end of Gordon Square. A thirties edifice, I think – parts of it spared by the Blitz. High plaster ceilings. It felt so bloody pleasant to hang your jacket in a sweet-smelling hotel wardrobe again and rip the paper seal off the loo. Big bed, biggish bathroom, a thousand fluffy white towels, a minibar and cable TV. What more could an out-of-town exec. require?

Companionship.

So I rang home E.T. (Extremely Tense). Yes, I actually noticed my pulse begin to race as I listened to the dialling tones at the other end. Funny to feel slightly breathless about ringing your own home telephone number. Finally the receiver was lifted. Silence.

'Hullo,' I said. Could I do this? Was it the right number? Had I misdialled? My mouth was quite dry. Astonishing.

'Hullo.' Harriet's voice. Well anyway I was pretty sure it was – but there was a startling amount of doubt in my mind. I had a big toe dipped into the beginning of a fantasy, and nothing was certain. 'Yes,' I said, unsure. 'Is that – Natasha?' I felt like a buffoon. I almost laughed. I could have blown the whole thing, then and there. I wondered if the boys were listening.

'Yes.' Her voice seemed deeper, quieter and was tinged, was it, with some touch of an accent. She didn't sound Scots at all. I stumbled on, having to lead the way: 'My name's Roger.' I actually said that – 'My name's Roger'! 'I'm in town for a day from – ' Where? '– Stoke-on-Trent and I was looking for someone to take to dinner. I saw your advertisement and I wondered if you might be free to spend a bit of time with me this evening?'

'Of course,' she said, 'I would love to meet you. You have such a nice voice. What time?' I was almost speechless. My wife said to a complete stranger who'd rung her up out of the blue, that he had 'such a nice voice'. She was gently, instantly, coming on to him, without so much as a mortal quiver. 'What about seven-thirty?' I managed to sound reasonably compos-mentis.

'That will be lovely. I charge one hundred pounds for my time with you up until eleven o'clock. Would you like to give me your credit card details and we can get that out of the way.' So, almost expiring, I did that – date of expiry, name on the card, all that. (Not, of course, that there's a smidgeon of credit there.) Then this mysterious voice said: 'Shall we meet in the Café Penguin? It's in St Martin's Lane almost opposite the Albery Theatre. I have dark brown hair and I'll be wearing a rose in it. Could you have a rolled-up copy of the *Financial Times* with you, please?' Still poised between a lethal fit of the giggles and early teenage shyness, I managed to tell the voice that I would be there and that I was looking forward to meeting her. And, thankfully, I rang off. I'd done it. But it had been surprisingly hard to insert myself into that scenario without any proper preparation, when all along my brain was screaming: 'It's only old Harri having a bit of a game.' I had set off thinking, well, it would be a laff, wouldn't it? Maybe even a little bit of an innocent enough kink. Sort of thing that old marrieds sometimes get up to, in order to perk up the old love-life, why not us? And it *was* so deeply satisfying to have some cash jingling about one's person, believe you me.

My initial plan had been to ring Ellen and fill in parts of the afternoon being a successful writer about town, catching up on the sleaze. I thought I would go and lavish a fair amount of alcohol on the little lady, but, do you know, I couldn't. Having rung H. (or N., I suppose that should be), I was completely obsessed by this play-acting, this meeting. What would it be like? Would we be able to manage it without eruption into the aforesaid fit of the giggles? Would it just be embarrassing? Would it, finally, be nothing special? And, folks, most important, would I get my insistent and all-important end away?

It was the morning after the night before. Harriet felt pretty tense as she waited for Peter to arrive back home. She decided to calm her nerves by cleaning out the Under-The-Kitchen-Sink-From-Hell. Before that, in the morning, she had purchased Timothy a beautiful wallet of luminous felt-tipped pens and he was in a four-year-old heaven. He sat with her, at the kitchen table, stockinged feet dangling, poring laboriously over his new colouring book, absentmindedly tattooing various parts of his body with indelible glowing colours. Harriet kept her head and her scrubbing-brush, for the most part, deep into the black dankness of that underworld of buckets and bleach that constituted 'under the sink'. Even so, she managed to dish out some appropriate colour co-ordinating advice to her son as they both went about their business. She was thinking mostly about her first trick.

It had been all right, last night. She had been much more tense than she would have liked and much too managing. But that had been self-preservation. She had been dealing with the potential problem of Peter breaking their cover, and their whole ridiculous artifice tumbling all of a heap. He had done really damn well and, until she had got his clothes off, she had been able to imagine him ever so easily as an anonymous punter. When he had been naked, he had become again so familiar to her that the idea of him being a stranger had ceased to exist.

She supposed that the idea of the event showing her if she could go off and do it with a stranger, had not quite worked. She knew that she might have seemed very much like someone new and different to him, but she had herself been able to rely upon the security of knowing, all the time, that he was only safe, dear, moderately surprised old Peter.

The most interesting thing about the experiment for her had been that she had been able to think of herself, genuinely, all the time, as a totally different person. And that, at least, would be even easier with a punter who didn't know her at all. All evening, Natasha had taken over. And she'd enjoyed that. Natasha had genuinely saved Harriet from any embarrassment about what kind of tricks she had got up to. It was astonishing how well protected and separate Harriet had believed herself to be.

At the end, true, she had felt terribly tired (and, actually, rather sore) when she left the hotel bedroom. That had been almost the most frightening part. In fact, she had walked out of the hotel very quickly and very easily. Hardly anyone had given her a second glance in the empty, darkened hotel lobby. She had hailed a black cab in Russell Square and taken it all the way home, all the way to Blackheath. After all, she had earned three hundred pounds, that night, hadn't she?

Harriet was shocked, afterwards, by how much she had enjoyed the show she had put on. Not just astonished, she had actually felt almost fulfilled by it. The game seemed to have dug up all manner of surprising sexuality within her that she had not realised lurked there. And, perhaps it had counted in a way, as Peter, that night, had felt pretty well like her first different man. A different man, and on entirely new terms. It had been incredibly liberating.

She had read in one of her magazines that for some people sex with a stranger was easier. It had seemed so for her. She was awfully surprised. She had to bear in mind that it had been sex with a stranger who was also her best friend. Even so, she seemed to have triggered off an appetite that she had not realised she possessed. Maybe that Dour Scots Presbyterian Upbringing, which she always claimed her parents had *not* given her, had indeed indoctrinated her, in spite of the pill, and in spite of the media, and in spite of the seminal sixties, still to be shy of expressing herself sexually. Probably, she guessed that Peter was right: he used to claim that the upbringing of any middle-class young British woman tended to condition an undemanding second-fiddledom when it came to fiddling about with men in bed. Harriet seemed to think that once you found the trigger release mechanism, the world might need to look out.

She had once read that this was precisely the problem at those swingers parties you sometimes used to read about – wives said that their husbands forced them to go along, mostly because the men wanted to get into a situation where they could have sex with other women with wifely permission. But, apparently, once there, once the brakes were, however reluctantly, released, it was the wives who found an unlooked–for promiscuous sexuality suddenly loosed for the very first time. From nowhere, they would find they wanted to get in there and screw every available able-bodied body. The husbands, it seemed, would get deeply miffed, furiously jealous and proceed to have to drag their now willing spouses unwillingly away. Well, that was what this magazine said anyway.

Maybe all her previous life, without ever acknowledging it, she had been scared of it, sex. She had always been sort of modest. She still had a clear memory of a feeling, just about the time when she was leaving the Guides – all these unlooked for bits had arrived: bosoms, elbows, a need to look at boys' flies, hormones – and no very clear idea what to do to get it all in order. That had been some fourteen years ago and only yesterday, doing what she had had to do with Peter in that anonymous hotel bedroom, she had felt, suddenly, somehow clear. If you're actually frightened of sex, it might be a real proper copper-bottomed joy to be able to be obliged, to do it as a job – a job that demanded you to be really up-front about desire, about function, about pleasuring. 'I don't necessarily want to do this but, heyho, I'm lumbered with it – it's my job. So I'd better get on with doing it, properly.'

And it wasn't as if it had been wildly pleasurable. She had been having to think too hard, work too hard. She had needed to get it right for him. But she'd felt reasonably turned on, and very happy to be there. She'd given him ever such a good performance of an orgasm. It made her grin just to think about it. But she hadn't, in fact, got anywhere near one herself – which was pretty usual for her, with penetration. Apart from the odd surprising twice-a-year freak, Harriet's Big O usually needed a friendly helping hand. But, golly, she had provided him with the most satisfactorily graphic simulation. She had come for him with such an explosion that it had felt like she had distributed herself all over the hotel's second floor. But she was going to have to think things like that through a little – she couldn't afford to get sore like this too often, if she was doing it a lot. And she had wrecked her throat a bit. She would have to watch that. You learn all the time. Like, for example, she now knew that sucking rubber latex was nothing like as pleasant as licking willy. But there was bound to be good and bad in every adventure.

Jonty came in demanding Coke and proceeded to lecture his brother on the realities of the colouring of locomotives. He managed to make Timothy cry in about two minutes flat. Almost a record. Not quite.

Four and a half hours is so long when you've not much to do. So short when you're on a deadline.

In the end, I didn't even try to ring Ellen. I took myself off, out of the hotel for a walk around bits of the West End. A proper tourist. I was actually almost nervous. Strolled down Neal Street and wanted to buy things in virtually every shop. Gave a quid to this black guy being very funny doing break-dancing for a big crowd of Japanese in a muggy Covent Garden. Watched the clock, with all those carved figures, strike three and play some incredibly endless tunes, very loudly, at the Swiss Centre in Leicester Square. The Swiss obviously like their clocks loud.

Felt a bit bored. Keyed up and bored all at the same time.

Decided to see a film. Oh, I loved having the money available, you see. I was so proud of not having spent anything in the shops. Usual intense internal debate as to whether to see some mindless piece of unchallenging entertainment-crap or a really first-rate piece of thought-provoking nineties-film-art. Went for the crap. As usual. It was colossally bad. Anyway I couldn't have concentrated on it, even if I'd wanted to. Though, as an actor, Patrick Swayze really does knock the spots off two planks of wood.

Then it was just an hour and a half to go. I took my exhausted Shanks's Pony back into Covent Garden where yet another black street performer was entertaining the (same ?) crowd by spinning around on his head in a kind of nineteen-thirties motorcycle helmet. The kind of things people are prepared to do to themselves for a living. Yes, well.

The hour had come. I went and ensconced myself behind a vast beaker of acidy white wine at the Café Penguin. I was about thirty-five minutes too early, of course. I spent the next three-quarters of an hour being unable to stop myself from scrutinising absolutely everyone who entered the place – my head constantly whipping around like it was on a magnet.

Finally I didn't recognise her! Not for at least thirty seconds. Mark you, she came in against the light from St Martin's Lane. It was so extraordinary – the first thing I thought when this woman came into the brasserie was 'Christ, there's a bloody tidy looking woman'. Then I saw this tiny red rose hidden in the curls of her hair. Only then did I see it was my wife. Then I realised it wasn't. It was this Natasha. I had my folded *Financial Times* on the table in front of me, like a good supportive bloke. So she recognised me.

I don't think I had ever seen the gear she had on – a sort of stretch wool gabardine jacket, hugging her, and a gold chain at her throat (which I did know about because I gave it to her), but with a tiny gold padlock hanging centre stage. Big collar but an incredible amount of tanned skin showing down the front, her cleavage caught together by a taut black zip. I'd never seen her in earrings like that. Legs, heels – she looked terrific. I was suddenly very pleased to have her sitting at the table with me. The waiter was more attentive than I've ever known them to be at Café Penguin – normally you can pass out from malnutrition and dehydration before they give you even a passing nod. But then they're mostly French.

We were both watching each other for evidence of the charade. Both of us busy doing ground-breaking chat in our newly invented roles while watching each other's eyes for any glimmering hints of communication. I wanted to say: 'Harriet, you look so absolutely fucking gorgeous, I didn't recognise you when you came in!' but instead I said mawkish stuff like: 'Have you come far?' But it was odd too, because with her surprisingly grave and positively deeper voice and the hair, the earrings and the outfit – I mean, for God's sake, she didn't even *smell* the same! – although clearly it was good old H. in there somewhere, Harriet had completely disappeared into this other, this foreign person. And I have to be honest with you, boring, bleeping little VDU screen, this other person was quite a turn-on, for an old fella.

We drank our bucket-sized glasses of tense white wine and then went through to the back for dinner. Sometimes there are chums of mine who eat at the Penguin and indeed on this very priceless day, there, at one of the first tables, was the vertically challenged Malcolm Nicholls and a couple of other guys from the Press Association. Each of them in his own edition, of course, of those dashing, vomit and blood-rag ties, they effect. I almost walked by, pretending not to notice, because Malcolm had met Harriet on a few occasions. In fact one Christmas party we went to last year, she had been able to squat down and have a good face-to-face chat with the little blighter. But I thought, what the hell, and stopped and exchanged merry newspaper banter. And then, deep breath, I briefly introduced them to my companion, Ms Ivanov. Yes, friendly screen, that's the extraordinary woman's chosen name. It was really extremely jolly to see them preening themselves, like hacks do, giving my delectable companion the twice-over. They all three watched her posterior every inch of the way to our table. When we sat down, I think I thought I saw a fraction of an acknowledging wifely glint in her eye saying: 'Well done.' I could be wrong. Anyway, I think she was enjoying herself.

So was I. We had our first restaurant meal together for months. She was great. I chuntered on about a version of myself. This Roger had much the same life, problems, family and concerns as one Peter Holloway, whom I know vaguely. For a while, it was difficult to stop myself from trying to make her laugh. On the whole I managed it. When I was modestly disparaging about the wife, Natasha didn't crack. She smiled and laughed and glittered at me and told me tales of her (completely fictitious) childhood. She had dreamt up this entirely worked-out life history which was absolutely fascinating – stories about some old Russian émigré tailor and a very fierce single-parent schoolmaster father. Maybe she should be the writer in the family. All the time I plied her with a now rather better wine and peered only comparatively occasionally down at the golden padlock which nestled modestly in that bravura display of pretty bosom.

We had a fairly extensive repast, although she ate very sparingly, I thought. And then it was time for action. I simulated taking a deep breath and asked her if she would like to come back to the hotel with me. She said she would like that very much but that it would be extra. It seemed like a good deal of coinage. We negotiated slightly around the price, in the middle of which she suddenly said: 'I think you'll find it's worth every penny. I promise you, you'll love it.' I came out in a thumping pulse and an almost instant sweat.

I said I'd give her the money in the taxi. So that's what happened – I gave her Harriet's notes while we cantered around Trafalgar Square in a black cab. One of the very nicest things that you can do in London is to snog a gorgeous young woman, up the Charing Cross Road, in the back of a taxi. Do whores kiss on the mouth? This one did. What an astonishing feeling of ownership there is, I discovered, in knowing that you have purchased the unalienable right to touch the nylon on the thigh, to gently cup the warm privacy of the breasts. And what a real pleasure it is to exchange tongues and the taste of lipstick and to inhale the scent of an eager woman who, quite suddenly, to your delighted surprise, places the length of her fingers on the thin material that hides your cock. To reach that point so very quickly with a stranger (well) from a position of zero knowledge is an exceptionally unusual experience. I couldn't remember feeling so hard for years. I could hardly manage myself at all when we got out of the cab.

It wasn't like making love to the same girl at all. She took on such a calmly, managing, leading role. She suggested she should run a bath and virtually undressed me with lots of affection, and modest, moist, schoolgirl kisses and a few soft teasing bites around my chin. She then put me into the tub with piles of bubbles and smells of every different kind. She had undressed me like a geisha, sort of admiringly – I'm not sure, in honest truth, that there's a lot to admire!

At one stage, as she unbuttoned the shirt, she whispered softly against the crashing of the tap water: 'I do so love a man with hair on his body. It really does turn a girl on. God, I'm looking forward to this,' and she put both hands on my extremely stiff appendage to make sure that I understood exactly to what she was referring. I seem to remember thinking, slightly pissed, that the line came from a Harrison Ford film – Greta Scacchi saying it as she laid him across some office desk.

And then suddenly I began to get desperately concerned that neither of us should break the spell of our two assumed personalities. I seemed to think that if Pete or Harriet should suddenly rear their mundane heads in that King's Hotel bedroom, all bets would be off and we would have to go home with our tails between our legs, and walk Starfire on the Heath or something equally unappealing. I got into the bath and felt happy to wait and see what happened next. I just lay there slopping around in the suds feeling slightly woozy and nursing those harder, more vertical parts of myself in my hands. It felt ever so nice. She went out into the bedroom and zapped the channels about on the TV until there was some music – desperately historical Fleetwood Mac, I think. And then

101

she came back into the bathroom and took off her clothes. It wasn't a strip-tease or anything, but it was nicely done and I could watch more and more of her familiar body revealed in the various walls of steamy mirror that lined the bathroom. She took her earrings off last. She looked gorgeous in only her earrings. She's a fine looking girl. Getting better all the time.

Yeah, I know – it was just like some typical unoriginal male fantasy, but that's what she did. And this strange, familiar woman was just so witchingly wonderful to gaze at – and this brilliantly knowledgeable girl did things that Harriet would never dream of doing – stroking, smoothing her hands over her beautiful breasts and touching the hair at her crotch, the top notch of her third finger kneading casually in there, at the top of her cunt. I mean, however lovely Harriet is, if she behaved like that, I would just be embarrassed for her, for us both, but this fictional woman could be as crude as she liked and your faithful ole chauvinist reporter here *adored* it.

Then, smiling her very special crooked, enigmatic smile, Natasha, bless her, climbed in the other end of the bath wearing just one small red rose and full mascara, like some Cadbury's Flake advert. It was fortunately a wondrous king-sized bath – with me in there already, it had to be. Hot water soaked the floor and ran out into the bedroom and spread like a map across the fitted carpet. She held on to me with both of her hands while I remembered how very lovely it was to massage her breasts with big fingers. Obviously we'd had baths together before often enough – but not in the last year or so. I'd forgotten that odd sensation of being hot and also parts of you being out of the water and cold, and the water being massively out of control and the taps biting into your shoulder blades.

I edged her towards me on to my thighs. I wanted her to ride on it now. I hadn't done it in the bath for, oh, forever. She kissed me with considerable concentration with a big wide open mouth and then, knock me down with a packet of Woodbines, she produced a bloody Mates from absolutely nowhere and lovingly rolled it down over the offending item. Only then did she lift her hips up out of the water and allow her cunt, very slowly, to enclose the thing. We held on there together, hot and cold and steamy and, with that blessed fantastic feeling of having reached home! She seemed to be having such a very good time. It felt genuinely heavenly. The water got agitated to a degree

102

that was just ridiculous. We were going to get complaints from the floor below.

We left the bath and almost got out of the bathroom. There on the damp carpet, on the hardness of the floor, with my cock still encased in its macintosh, I mounted the woman, her legs reaching their length either side of me to the ceiling and then binding me to her crotch. It was good to be on top, in charge, going at the kinds of speeds that I fancied, holding off the big one. She had her hands around my face and in my ears and in my mouth and, even, if I remember this right, up my bum. And she scratched me with hard nails. And I've never heard her make so much noise or talk so much. Such fabulously filthy talk. It was like she was having the fuck of her life. She groaned and roared and screamed such beautifully ugly things – filthy stuff that I'd never ever heard from Harriet's mouth before. She's always been what I have thought of as oddly Scottish about language. It was as if a dam had broken. I didn't know she knew all that. To start with I was genuinely shocked. And then, God, I adored it. It was glorious. I felt invincible. Pathetic really, but for a while, in that room, I felt happier than anyone has a right to be.

I'm getting hard now just remembering it all, typing it out. The one genuine souvenir of the evening that I will have for a while are the two inner sides of my knees, rubbed pink and raw on the carpet, with her clamped under me, eagerly asking for more.

Well, with Stevie Nicks panting appropriately in the background on MTV, we finally made it to the bed. And she finished on top of me shuddering and popping her lovely hips, like her life depended on it. I was getting pretty terminal by this stage and was leaving it to her now. I was just there for the ride.

She looked magnificent – her hair had all come down over her shoulders and was wet and shiny from the sweat of her body and from the bath. Her make-up had been licked away and her juddering nipples addressed themselves to the ceiling, hard and crinkly and brown like sun-dried tomatoes. I've never known any girl in my life come like she came. It was shocking in its intensity and extremely blatant. She howled like the wind and fetched up groans from the depths of her soul that must have been in danger of wrecking her vocal chords. It was so incredibly, delightfully, bestial. She was like some sort of fabulous possessed animal that had been let out of incarceration.

And then it was over. The storm was gone. The body stopped

shaking and she was soft as a kitten. She tumbled in a heap on my chest and almost seemed to be suckling her thumb. I slipped out of her and we giggled contentedly as she removed the rubber johnnie. Then we must have slept.

It was gone midnight when I opened an eye. The room was in absolute chaos. The telly had Jack Lemmon and Shirley MacLaine eternally together in that apartment of his, sieving spaghetti with a tennis racket. There was evidence of extreme physical exertion in every part of the bedroom. The earth woman had risen. She was standing beside the bed with her face, now, sorted out and her body tucked privately away, wrapped in a towel. She bent down and kissed my cheek: 'Thank you so much, Roger, that was so nice. I'm leaving my card on the table should you need to get in touch again,' she whispered gently. 'I'll run along now. Thank you so much. Don't disturb yourself. Have a nice sleep. Good luck in the morning, with your meeting. I hope it goes really well.'

'Harri,' I mumbled.

'Sssh sssh.' She stroked my head with her hand.

'Don't go, Harriet,' I said – I've always been a fool – could I play the whole thing out to the end? No.

'I don't know who this Harry is. I don't think you've been in bed with a bloke, Roger. No, this is Natasha. Natasha Ivanov.' And it was Natasha's voice. 'Go to sleep now.' And do you know, I did.

When I woke up, oh some hours later, to have a pee, she had disappeared. The TV was off but, apart from that, the room wasn't much tidier. You could still smell her perfume and the heavy fragrance of sex in the room, but otherwise there was no evidence of her at all apart from a big dark damp patch of carpet around the bathroom door. And her card on the dressing table which had the five words written on it: 'Fun, eh? See you tomorrow. x.' In Harriet's handwriting.

I padded around the still wet bathroom and had a shower. In the morning, I took charge of a King's Hotel full English breakfast – the works. Then I checked out and caught the train to Blackheath, wondering what I would find.

What I found was Harriet in jeans and sweatshirt, her hair all caught up anyhow in a yellow clip, scrubbing-brush in her hand, completely devoid of make-up. She was doing extraordinary in-depth cleansing and was appreciating some drawing of Timothy's all at the same time. She looked sweet. And as if she had slept rather well, all through a relaxing night. Spit-making.

'Hullo, lovely,' she said kissing me quickly on the cheek. We didn't seem to have any difficulty meeting each other's eye. 'Tell Timbo that it's perfectly all right for a train to be pink.'

'Timothy, your mother's right, as always, it would actually be a considerably better world if every single one of British Rail trains were pink, particularly on the dreaded Network South East. Hullo H., my darling, I thought you'd be at the gym.'

'No, I'm giving Aaron a miss today. It's a gorgeous day. Your oldest son is therefore, of course, in a darkened room watching some Spielberg epic. I thought we should walk the hound-from-hell.'

'OK. We could take him up on the Heath. With all those roads he might just run out under a bus.'

'Peter, you are a wee bit cruel about that dog!' she laughed.

'Of Starfire, there's naught crueller than thee, lass.'

'Yeah, I know, but I keep it to myself. He'll get a complex.'

'He's got a complex already. That's his trouble. He is an abjectly complex dawg. What else do you keep to yourself, Harri?' I asked her quietly.

'Not a lot,' she said. 'Anyway, a walk would be a good opportunity for a modest private debriefing. I'll go to get me notes.' And Harriet gave me a quick crooked sideways glance to see what clues I might be dishing out. Then, she pretended that she hadn't, and finished putting important things away in the cupboard under the draining board. Jonty came in to see who was there. I ripped into that morning's quota of envelopes full of double-double-red demand notices and promises to disembowel unless instant payment was received within the minute. I allowed myself to mutter privately to her: 'Oh, I love your private debriefings.'

'Shut your gob till we're on the Heath, Peterkins!'

'Don't they say that it is the lot of the Western Male for most wives to turn out to be a whore in the kitchen, a hostess in the bedroom and a chef in the living room. I'm glad, Harriet, you've got your rooms sorted out.'

'I thought the *Western Mail* was a kind of impotent suburban newspaper.'

'Ho ho, very satirical. Firing on both cylinders, I see.'

'What's a whore, Dad?'

'Er. Um.' I did a bit of quick thinking: 'A person of an enormous amount of energy, and of imagination and, well, love.'

'I'm a whore to you then, Dad.' And Jonty went out saying, 'So's Timothy. But he's a stupid whore because he thinks trains are pink.' As I think I noted a few days ago, we are going through a sort of familial surge-of-happiness stage. Nothing like weathering a long low depression of adversity to beef up the old togetherness stakes.

She and Peter didn't talk much, even after they had got their breath back, after climbing the hill out of the Village and up on to the Heath. She was roasting. The summer was continuing with such a vengeance. It was really hot up there on the brown grass, with a warm wind blowing. The Sunday lunchtime drinkers had spread themselves right across the Heath for miles from the Hare and Billet pub by the depleted pond with its willows and reeds. Starfire mooched raggedly around the crowd at its fringes, trying to steal crisps and sandwiches and the occasional small child. Harriet and Peter stolidly pretended that the dog had nothing to do with them. They walked their short midday shadows across towards the distant park. She smiled as she thought how good the two of them seemed to be at pretending things together.

Ever since Peter had returned, he had looked a little bit like Starfire after a really good refrigerator raid – the dog who had got the cream as well as the weekend bacon. He lightly took her hand as they strolled aimlessly along, heading vaguely towards Greenwich Park in the sunshine. The Heath was alive with tennis-ball cricket and multitudes of coloured kites plunging about against a blue sky. She felt ridiculously well. And Peter had done really OK the previous evening. She thought she ought to tell him. 'Thank you for last night,' she said, breaking their silence.

'Thank *me*?' he exclaimed. 'I had a wonderful time. You know.'

'Well, I hope so. After all, that was the idea. But I was aware that it wasn't easy for you to pretend not to know me and everything. You did it awfully well, for an old guy, Roger! There were times when I thought you were going to explode with laughter. I had had some time to prepare myself. You didn't.'

'Well, yes, I suppose, it was odd. Yes, it was very strange. But, in fact, I stopped thinking of her as you after a while. It was a bit like playing away from home, I imagine, without the danger. I liked it enormously. I've never had such a good time, for ages. Well, you know that. Can I book you again?'

'You've got my number. Just give me a call.' She laughed: 'Oh, Peterkins, I'm so pleased. Thank you. How brilliant.'

'I thought she was wonderful. I thought you were wonderful. My only thought now is that I'm suddenly just a little in awe of you. Walking along here doesn't feel like it would have done before yesterday. We've got this kind of secret between us, and it's a really nice feeling. But, also, you've suddenly got this, oh I don't know, this capacity, this power, this thing of yours. And I'm in awe of it. I've always found it difficult to adjust to performers when they're just being their dull, everyday, ordinary selves. The chemistry of performance is so – well – mystical and transforming. I think that's why people worship stars, you know, of the stage and screen and all that. It's not just the hype. Stars are able to metamorphose in some strange, unknown, black-magical way. We see them do it. And marvel. Hold our breath. One moment they're in their kitchens drying up lunch, leaving a note for the milkman, doing the usual stuff that we all do, the next, they can be holding the capacity of the Albert Hall spellbound, which none of us mortals will ever be able to do. Which one are they? Who is the real person?'

They stopped together and watched the traffic on the mainroad, waiting for a gap, in order to cross. Peter went on: 'I remember I once saw Madonna trotting along the front in Tel Aviv – training. She was doing a big concert there that night. Running along in her peaked cap, T-shirt, trainers – oh yeah, with a coach and a minder on a bicycle, of course – but no big deal, just a mundane, ordinary, slightly squat, very fit blonde. I was probably the only person who noticed her. That evening I saw her live on the telly, with the whole of the known world in the very palm of her hand. They could not possibly have been the same two people!'

'I'm very flattered, pet, but I'm no Madonna!'

'No, but what I mean is, it's weird, it's uncanny. I find it difficult to handle. And yet I could see myself worshipping it, easily. Performance and ordinary life – they're such poles apart. You know, I'll tell you something, I think I might suddenly be a little tiny bit afraid of you, H. Perhaps. Anyway, I thought you were thrilling. Better than Madonna. Because you, personally, actually fucked me. Instead of just miming it to a capacity-filled stadium.'

'Not me, actually.'

'No. Sorry. Natasha. Thanks, Natasha.' He kissed her on the nose.

And then they walked along some more.

Peter was being unexpectedly generous and open, she thought. Something had happened to them both. It was worthwhile exploring further. She had to ask him, it was important that she should know: 'Could you handle it, Peter? If that's what I did?' They sat down on the sunburnt dusty grass at the highest part of the Heath. Peter stared out across London town. He rubbed his face with his hand and ruffled his hair and took in great gulps of air, as he thought about it.

'Handle it? Oh God, I don't know.' A great orange kite rippled across the sky above their heads, rattling madly in the light wind. 'No, it's simple. The answer is "no". I'd be too jealous. I'd want to kill them. It's out of the question.' He sank his head down between his shoulders and made the ugliest face, as he thought about it. When he spoke, he spoke with his large hands almost covering his eyes and his mouth: 'No, oh dear God, no, it's so bloody awful but that's not entirely the case, if I'm really honest.' He stopped and groaned and then he went on: 'I've thought about it all morning. I'm pulled in two by it. I've thought about it and thought about it. I actually feel a bit unhinged, you know, about it.'

He lay back on the grass in the sun with Harriet sitting cross-legged at his side. And, as sometimes happened, Harriet was suddenly moved by his meaty vulnerability. Only she, in the whole wide world, knew how muddled and faulty was this big man, with his erstwhile confidence and clout and drive. What had happened in the last year had virtually crippled him inside. She did still love him, for all his past neglect of her. Peter spoke to the sky with his eyes firmly closed, feeling his way through what he was trying to say: 'I think I seem to have discovered a very unpleasant thing about myself. I suppose I've always vaguely guessed at it. But I've never really known. Don't think too badly of me, H.'

'I won't,' she told him quietly. 'Don't worry. We're both learning about ourselves.'

Peter said nothing. Then he exclaimed: 'Oh I can't say it!'

'I think I probably know. You can say it. Go on. I don't mind. Say what you like. It's OK. It's fine. Everything's fine.' It was. She thought she could handle anything that day.

'It's dreadful really, I feel so, so incredibly possessed, so appallingly, sickeningly, ashamedly, bloody-stupidly fucking randy because my wife put on this elaborate disguise and took herself off and went and had this excessive bonk, entirely with my knowledge and permission. She fucked all night – '

'Well – '

'And enjoyed it hugely. And, oh shit, Harriet, I loved the very idea of it. Of that. Not of me being there with you. Although that was great too. The idea of it. You doing it with a stranger. Oh, yes, of course, it actually was me and it wasn't really a strange man. But the idea – the idea overwhelms me.' He was silent. Then: 'I'm sorry. This is so sick. I feel so torn apart. I feel two completely opposed, desperately contradictory things. At one and the same time, I'm crazy, absolutely loopy, insanely jealous at the idea of you giving all that – that private, intimate magic – to some ghastly anonymous bastard who has to pay for it. Worse, perhaps, to someone who you really like, who, oh Jesus, oh Jesus, oh Jesus, perhaps even turns you on! On the other hand . . . Well, God knows, on the other hand, and I almost, almost can't say this out loud to you: I've got this great black shadow of evil sneaking delight lurking somewhere at the darkest vilest corner of my head. I'll tell you, there's something really mad inside me. I absolutely adore this secret between us, this plot, the idea of this wickedness. It feels like I've been introduced to the ultimate most attractive deadliest sin. *I – absolutely-adore – it.* We two are the only people in the entire universe who know what we know. That we, that you can break all the rules. You can do the forbidden things. And I would be the only man on your side, in your team, part of your cohort, our cohort. I seem to have this appalling lust that wants you to go out and, oh, I don't know – enrapture all these lecherous, faulty, dreadful old males.'

Peter looked wretchedly perplexed at what he seemed to have discovered about his own desires. He appeared almost not to be able to continue. Finally he did: 'Are you appalled by me?'

'No,' she said. And it had to be as resilient a 'no' as she could find. She couldn't allow even a smidgen of doubt to be heard in her voice. But she was taken aback. It was a new element. She was having a hard enough time trying to see if she could cope with what she was proposing for herself. Now, typical of the man, he had offered her an additional concern and one about his own psychological make-up. They're always moving the goal-posts, men, so that they become the focus again, themselves. Well done. Very clever.

Peter still had his eyes shut and his hands to his head. He whispered to her, quietly: 'It's so dreadful but I do fancy the weird idea of you coming back and telling me intimate secrets about their, oh, I don't know, eating out of your hand.' He was muttering almost to himself: 'Oh, my dear God, I'm turned on by the very idea of it, of you doing it, giving it to them, for money. Telling me. Me knowing. I must be crazy. I don't think I can even listen to what I'm saying. I can't bear it. Oh, I couldn't bear it. I'd want to kill them. Oh, Harriet!' It was a heart-rending sigh. 'I think I love it. I certainly love you, Harriet Holloway.'

'And I certainly love you too, Peter Holloway.' She didn't know what else to say. It had been an unexpectedly honest and naked confession, particularly from someone so usually personally guarded as Peter. It made her feel very warm towards him. Warm and confused, even frightened. But then she was frightened all the time these days, underneath. And with reason.

She thought that they felt very close, sitting there, high above London as it lapped below them in a great saucer, with Hampstead Heath looking across from the other side of that gigantic valley of the Thames, all those ten or so miles away.

Then they found they had nothing more that they needed to say to each other. Each of them, she thought, was considering their reaction to what they had done the night before. In a funny way, it was almost as if they had done something entirely new and illicit together, like snorting coke or swallowing a tab of LSD. Recovered but still rather mind-blown, they were now, in the cold light of day, having to think it all through.

After a little while, they got up to walk again and stood there, holding on to each other tight, her forehead familiarly, damply on his chin, looking out across the possibilities that the great City offered. And the dog came snuffling up to see if anything was going to happen. Starfire seemed to have been able to avoid instant demise by traffic, as usual.

Later, when they'd got back and before she had had to give the boys their tea, they lay on their bed very quietly together and held each other more comfortably than she remembered for a long time. She very carefully let him do it all – easing her jeans down over her bum, slipping her knickers aside, sliding it into her with such affection. Once there, they hardly moved for ages. 'Only ever you, without a condom,' she breathed in his ear.

'Two different women in twenty-four hours. Not bad, eh?' he whispered to her.

'That can't be a first, can it, Peterkins?' she dared herself to say.

'Harri!' he remonstrated with her but they were not into fighting at all that day, and she just laughed and kissed him on the nose. Later they heard *Eastenders* finishing downstairs. She opened her mouth and snogged him energetically. Then they bucked and squirmed together briefly, happily. She hurt her throat again. They expelled air and then they both groaned and she came too, which pleased her very much. For a short while they almost slept but then there was the noise of boys shouting about sliced bread getting stuck in the toaster.

So I've been and gone and done it. Set it all up. I can't believe it really. Felt half hyped up and sort of sexually excited and the other half just mindless, depressed and on automatic pilot. H. has opened herself a building society account. We're called 'T & T Services'. She dished out a load of legal tender and I put the whole of 'Project Sell The Wife' into effect. Cards being printed (very smart and discreet they're going to be – Panic Printers in the Village – buff card – chocolate lettering: Aldine Bembo Italic). Got a mobile phone line – a lovely compact folding Motorola. Archie Aitken, who was at school with me in Peckham and who is always in the States nowadays, says he'll bring some cans of Mace back for us. He says he does a bit of a number bringing them back across the pond for anxious husbands and fathers. Didn't mention anxious pimps. And finally, yes, I guessed right, Harriet's hit the town in Brobdingagian-shopping mode.

Arranging for the small-ad to appear made it suddenly feel very real. And hateful. What the hell are we doing? I'd purchased another half bottle of 'Hairy Sporran'. It made things easier. Nice to have the money. Timbo came up to kiss me goodnight. He sipped my whisky with much circumspection, professionally wrinkled nose and declared it tasted of pepper, and was unfit for human consumption. He is, of course, right.

Drank nearly all of it anyway, and spent a long time thinking about all this. Man spends most of his life training himself how not to be jealous. That, maybe, is what maturity, finally, is. He has to learn this skill, because his whole life is built around rivalry and competition – look at me and TLS, the greatest of good friends who would do each other down at the wink of an eye, at the first opportunity! – so to lessen the misery, man finds ways of conditioning himself to feel it less and less acutely. And it's all about power, isn't it? You lose the power to have control of things and, immediately, malevolent jealousy creeps into your soul and destroys your mind. If you're in charge, if you've given permission, if you know what's going on, if you set it up in the first place, you can deal with it all, quite easily, whatever happens.

Well. In theory.

I suppose that's why I've been so keen to do all the admin. with 'T & T' etcetera etcetera. And I think if she's prepared to keep me in the picture, dish the dirt, let me feel in charge, I can probably deal with this whole macabre thing perfectly OK. Well, I hope so. It may very well, probably most likely, not come to anything at all, anyway. And d'you know, actually there are genuinely times when I rather like the idea of it. After all, it's not infidelity, it's work.

She didn't go mad in South Molton Street. There wasn't enough cash. But she spent six very happy, exhausting hours being a clothes-horse in various drab changing rooms, pouting at herself suggestively in numerous mirrors, wearing some very costly and definitely not-at-all-drab outfits. A visibly walking wallet in the midst of a recessionary West End, she was plied exhaustively with every kind of herbal tea, coffee and extract of carrot juice. She was informed with every change of image that this was the one that really flattered her colouring, by smart and eager young women for whom the term 'commission' was not a dirty word.

The point of this exercise in mild shopaholicism was for her to find the things that would 'put-out but not off-put'. There was the most wonderful colourful single-breasted patchwork jacket from Dolce and Gabbana, with a matching waistcoat and a silk shirt. Harriet saw that she looked eatable in it and, at about a grand the lot, it was an outrageous buy, but not impossible. But it was wrong. Harriet might look groovy and fun and pretty-as-patchwork in it. But for Natasha it would just be too damned noticeable. So with a catch in her still sore throat, Harriet saw it returned to its padded hanger. And she promised herself a present of it in the future for when the times might be marginally rosier.

No, the private parade that she gave for Peter in their bedroom at the end of that long afternoon included only one really excellently gorgeous item – an asymmetrically cut, dark blue velour dress, very full, very short with long sleeves and a high neck from Romeo Gigli. Otherwise it was simple, straightforward stuff – a fantastically sweet, high pair of open-top mules with a brilliant wooden heel from Manolo Blahnik and a breathtaking full Sonia Rykiel sweater with cuffs and a neck trim that seemed to plunge for her navel. And for the current hot evenings, a pretty, simple, full-skirted cotton shirtwaister dress from Melvyn Rodeo which she instinctively knew would always look as if she had nothing on underneath. And a smart cotton pique shirt body from Jasper Conran to die for.

She wore this last to go down to Greenwich pools that evening. They all went together with Marianne and Sam and Pippa in the Webb BMW to see Jonty compete in the swimming club gala. Harriet seemed to be spending all her life in that red-bricked haven. Jonty won all the races in his age group – the breast-stroke particularly easily. There was a lot of frantic cheering and everyone inhaled the special pools atmosphere of neat chlorinic poisoning. Peter went around the corner for a quick one but got back in time to hear Gary Hope say that Jonty was a very good prospect indeed. The boy shone with unalloyed pleasure, which he then proceeded to hide behind an enormous bag of taco-crisps which Peter had brought back with him. It was very good for Peter to have the money to do that with. Harriet thought that having money was good fun. She wanted more. She so liked having money. Wasn't that terrible? She must be a very spoilt person.

But, God, she did so love buying things. It was like a weird curse. She felt it must be very like drug-addiction. You needed the anticipation, the toying with it, the final consummation as you passed the money from your hand to the hand of the smart girl at the till. It seemed that it wasn't just the basics of life that Harriet needed, she needed the luxurious hit of the plastic, the fashionable buzz of the credit-card, the sweet toke of the Switch-payment. And it appeared that she was prepared to do almost anything to get back on to that fix. Apparently she really didn't mind what she did to get that disgusting mind-expanding high. Funny, that. And she who came from such a modest family too. She and her brother? Did they both have some deep-seated insecurity they needed to assuage? Was it rebellion against the simple certainties of Mummy and Daddy? Presumably they had both been corrupted by the lure of urban glitter? She prayed she wouldn't self-destruct and disappear like her brother, poor Julian, had.

At the end of the gala, she stood looking down at the now empty pool, its waters settling down for the quiet of the night, around her the echoing noise of the girls and boys changing and shouting. She looked at Peter, up the other end, being fatherly, no doubt talking some rubbish to Timothy (it was well past his bedtime). She had spent days wondering what Peter really thought about all this. That evening she was suddenly surprised by the thought that she, Harriet, had never once wondered about her own relationship with her husband in this new and very unusual scenario. She had used Peter last Saturday night. And he had been pretty happy about being used. From now onwards it felt like they would be different with each other. But, she thought, he had probably used her pretty mercilessly during the last ten years. Swings and roundabouts.

Days in the life of a ponce. Well, truth to tell, there's not very much to report. Thank God, perhaps? Actually there's been so little response that I had to go out and buy *What's On* to see that it, actually, featured our advert. Harriet's special visiting cards were delivered – they look so sophisticated you could probably use them at a cashpoint machine.

We had to find H. a base from which to operate. Simon Baines, the son of the Village florist, is a bright young architect who basically does period house conversions – he did Marianne's new kitchen. Until last year, he used to have a small office in a place called Flitcroft Mews – just off the Charing Cross Road. There's a whole building run by a man called George Lipcombe. It's a maze of little serviced offices in a kind of converted, fine, Edwardian warehouse building, round the back of the Phoenix Theatre. We've taken the smallest, dankest, coal-cellar that they had to offer. It feels like a nuclear fall-out shelter. T & T Services, being an events co-ordinating business, operates odd hours, I explained. George seemed to buy that. I fixed it up with hanging rails, dressing table, dinky folding camp bed and a sleeping bag. We've got a rolling monthly contract. We can pull out quickly, if we need.

The Motorola phone doesn't work in the basement so I'm going to have to put a phone line in there too. We'll need it as a kind of modicum of 'business' cover anyway, although I imagine that George might twig what's up after a while – given H.'s presumed hours. But, as long as we keep the rent up-to-date, I don't think he's going to worry unduly. It's very private down there anyway. And only a place for her to get dressed and sleep.

So we are all set up. And I feel sick and frightened and sort of interested. I can't believe we're ever going to get our investment back. Harri's investment.

But nothing happened. Well, not entirely nothing – Harriet said there was one slightly embarrassed wrong number which could have been a potential client/booker/punter/john, whatever they're called, when she was jogging back across the park. And a couple of episodes of heavy breathing – so maybe people *do* read *What's On*. We're both fairly stressed out and, yes, scared and awkward with each other and we tend to shout at the kids more than usual. And at the dog. But then everybody always shouts at the dog. This is a tense house.

Finally, yesterday, I bit the bullet. Meat marketing. I did it without really thinking it through at all. I just did it. Sat there and did it. Didn't let myself think about what it was that I was doing. Just did it. I'm astonished. Yes, I did this big, sickening mail-out. Anonymous notes, with the business-cards, to about twenty possible characters scattered about the cities of Europe, London and the Home Counties recommending Ms Ivanov for pleasantly companionable ways of fending off bleak lonely evenings when in the Big Smoke. A good bit of copy, although I sez it, as shouldn't. I can't really believe it. It doesn't feel real. Here am I sorting out a quiet little sales campaign; basically, potentially, selling my wife's sexual favours! And what do I feel? Sort of nothing. Just putting it into effect, without thinking. Depressed. And oddly excited as well. You don't know what's going to happen next. Frightened too. For H. I suppose I keep telling myself, comforting myself with the fact that nothing will actually happen. Harriet won't actually go out and do this thing. So why am I going on with this myself? What a sick, muddled, unprincipled man I appear to be. There, that's a good let-out, isn't it? If you can confess to being sick, senseless and unprincipled, you can probably just get on with being exactly that. It's the self-deluded people who lie to themselves that you have to pity, eh? That you have to watch out for? They're the real sickos!

It came to me that I don't remember exactly when I made the decision to do this. I seem to have reached this moment by an unnoticeably gradual process of osmosis. I can remember a time when it was just an absurd joke, and I now know that we've got to a stage where it could possibly happen. I just can't remember the exact click of the switch when we made the decision from one state of mind to the other. I think H. made the decision and I just stumbled along after her. I think I might be completely morally bankrupt. Maybe we both are. We're certainly financially bankrupt again now that we've made all this ludicrous expenditure.

It's simple, really – it's all come out of there having been seven years of fat cows, eaten up in a twinkling by seven months of famine and neither of us being able to bear it. Other people seem to survive without going to this incredible extreme. Why not us? Had we just got too accustomed to being so very comfortably off? We're certainly hopeless at being poor. The poor seem to be so very much better at it. But then, the poor have had so much more practice.

I had said that I would go down to the station with her. She looked so determined, her face pale and closed down with her chin jutting. Jonty's looks exactly the same, I realised, when he's about to do one of his swimming races. She insisted on carrying her canvas hold-all on her shoulder, crammed full of mystically important bits and pieces. It felt as if she was off to sit an exam for which we had both been watching her prepare and revise. Normally so voluble, I couldn't think of a blind thing to say. Nothing. There aren't any useful hints as to what you say in these circumstances – husband saying farewell to loving wife who is going off to hawk her body. I felt as I imagine you might feel if you were a bomber going off to leave Semtex in a rubbish bin in a shopping-mall. All around you, life goes on its blithe sunny way much as usual. Only you know the dread secret. The rest of the world seems suddenly so goddamned innocent and easy and carefree. It was, anyway, what Dr Alasdair McGee would call 'ever such a bonny evening'. That unique beautiful liquid English summer light. Around us, people were cycling off to play tennis, wandering home early from the office with their fiancée and a cornet of Italian ice-cream. Flies were still buzzing in the wet fish-shop, kids were swooping down past the flower stall on their dangerous looking skateboards. Everything I thought to say seemed monumentally irrelevant and banal.

We went into Blackheath Station and stood and read the instructions on the automatic ticket machine as if our lives depended on it. Would a one-day travel-card serve for both today and tomorrow?

The instructions on the machine were incredibly unclear, they made me unreasonably angry. Could you use it over a twenty-four hour period or did it cease to be valid after midnight? Irritated, I clunked in the coins and the machine, unmoved, spat out the tickets.

Then we went down on to the platform together and stood there with the late afternoon commuters – people going up to town to work as usherettes, as firemen, as waiters, as office cleaners, as bar staff – fifth-form girls off to catch an early film with their very first boyfriends, gentlemen off to toddle into their Pall Mall clubs for an evening of gossip and *The Times* crossword. I stood there with my arm rather stiffly around her shoulders, as if I were protecting her from the cruel world. Huh! I wasn't, was I? I was guilty of helping to put her at such risk. If I were publicly to confess what I was doing, no one would be able to conceive of it ever being possible. No one but a complete louse would be party to selling their wife, would they? Then, all of a sudden, I realised that she was weeping, absolutely silently, but weeping nonetheless – tears tracking down both cheeks, her eyes full. I said: 'Listen, come on H., this is crazy. OK, OK. This is garbage. Come on, you don't have to do this.' She didn't say anything, she just cried, looking sightlessly up the track to where the train must come from. 'OK, come on, let's go,' I said. 'Let's go home. Forget it. This is all nonsense anyway. Come on, off we go. Game over.' Then she really cried and I hugged her heaving shoulders, shoulder-bag and all. She was sodden with tears now and sort of gasping with her crying. She nodded incoherently at me. The other waiting passengers looked on in that nonplussed, embarrassed way that only Londoners can, pretending it wasn't happening. I gave her another big squeeze and led her away from the platform, holding her damp hand in mine. We went back out of there, up the stairs towards the main street, the open air and freedom. It was over. Every step seemed almost impossible for her to make. It was as if she was ill or crippled.

I was just filled with the idea that we had been screamingly right round the bend. It had been a madcap, stupid, bloody, unhinged scheme and I couldn't, for the life of me, imagine how we had ever got so far down that particular manic track. It was as if we had existed in a kind of private fantasy land with no foundation in reality at all. I had this intense overwhelming feeling of relief and a sort of numbed surprise. I had been bracing myself for this appointment for more than four weeks and all of a sudden the pressure was gone. It wasn't going to happen.

Then there was the burst of the train noise as it arrived and roared out of the tunnel, and slid into the station below us. There was the familiar squeal of brakes as it shuddered to a halt. Doors opened and slammed.

Suddenly, without a word, Harriet tore her hand out of mine and launched herself down the stairs towards the platform, two at a time. I yelled at her 'No, H.!' or something equally banal. I galloped down the stairs after her, shouting. I got to the platform to see her ripping a carriage door open and throwing herself aboard. Almost simultaneously, the train began to move and it wasn't worth my while running any more. Harriet was on her way and, like it or not, I couldn't reach her. I stood on the platform staring at the back of the departing train in a kind of stupor. There was an old gentleman left on the platform too, who reckoned it had left before time.

I thought of catching the next train up to town. It would arrive in about twenty minutes. I could go up and seek her out at Flitcroft Mews, talk to her, bring her back. But the boys were on their own at home and I didn't have Marianne's number and, actually, I didn't have enough money for a ticket. And then I thought, if she was going to come back, she could just turn around, she knew that. And then I thought: what a pile of lame excuses. And then I thought: she only has to go and have a meal with the guy, that's all. And we did desperately need the money.

Not a very nice man.

Harriet sat in front of her big mirror in her tiny cell in Flitcroft Mews and spent five minutes on each eye. She could say everything she needed to say with two well-drawn eyes and the most carefully cantilevered mascara. And, of course, the totally over-the-top earrings. Although she had scrubbed away with endless cold water, she still had horrid piggy eyes from that pathetic crying. But, for her, sometimes, smaller eyes looked better. Relaxed, her eyes could often look like two mad exclamation marks going on holiday together.

It had taken her the whole of the train journey to recover. She had picked up a morning paper left in her carriage and hidden her face behind it. It was full of a story about some awful accident the night before; a minibus had come off the M2 near Canterbury with an army swimming team aboard. Three of those young boys had been killed. She had thought what the hell had she to complain about? In comparison to a tragedy like that? Those poor poor boys. Their parents, their friends. And she thought of her two lovely healthy boys, sitting up in their respective secure beds – no doubt, at that very moment, being read altogether too short a passage of the Mini-the-Minx Christmas album by their almost dutiful father.

And here she was, on a peerless summer's evening that those poor bloody soldiers would never see, dressing up in her best bib 'n' tucker to be taken out on the town. What's more, earning a living. Earning a living being taken out to Quaglino's! She was actually a lucky beggar. She was a petrified, bothered, wary, lucky beggar, who wanted, very badly, to throw up.

So the condemned woman consumed a hearty Nescaff. Harriet finished her face and took off her T-shirt and folded her jeans with extravagant care. She hung her clothes on a wire hanger in her cramped dungeon, putting her canvas loafers neatly side by side under the camp bed. She comforted her nervous fingers with the warmth of her mug of coffee. She wondered ruefully what shit was she going to have to cope with before it came time to tug those jeans back on again? She had, of course, given herself easily double as much time as she needed to get herself ready.

She did feel terribly alone now. She thought of getting the Motorola out and calling Peter, but she also thought that if she heard his voice, she wouldn't be able to go through with it. He would tell her to come home, and she would. She would funk it. And then she would never be able to live with herself.

Outside her little room, in the elderly warehouse building that was 12 Flitcroft Mews, there was a maze of small screened and now deserted offices. The architects and draughtsmen, the theatrical agents and the tiny PR companies had nearly all taken themselves off to the pub or to their homes for the evening. Now it was solely her shift that was about to begin. She, alone, remained in the white-washed brick-lined basement, locked in her cubby-hole with only the lad who did the cleaning, doing his rounds, collecting coffee cups, wiping desks and emptying wastepaper baskets. Harriet's cassette radio wheezed bits of news at her, and music, and advice about traffic jams. It helped to blot out the emptiness of the building.

It was as if the whole thing was some kind of drug-induced dream and she was about to step out on to the surface of the moon.

Although her hand had stopped shaking as she finished her lips, her stomach was still doing a whole gamut of sicky somersaults. Perhaps for the first and only time, or perhaps even for the first of many times, she carefully soaped off her wedding ring and tucked it away in her purse.

The man's voice on the phone had been gruff, but comfortably north country. He had called her 'love' in that gently forceful way that Mancunians have. It would be all right. She didn't have to do anything more than eat a meal with him, chat him up, make him feel special and take herself off. If she didn't want to, she didn't have to do anything else. She wouldn't. There, so that was settled.

Before she had left the house with Peter, he had said, falteringly, play the long game, not to do anything she didn't feel absolutely comfortable with. When she had finally run away from him at the station, he had just shouted at her that she was a fool. It wasn't surprising; it was pretty tough for him too. Tougher perhaps as he couldn't be around to control it. It was all up to her. He had never had to deal with that before. Even when she was in labour, he had kind of sorted it all out for her, or so it had seemed at the time.

It was funny, she seemed somehow closer to Peter now that she was, in theory, in charge of what she might be doing, completely separately from him. They felt strangely more intimate now that she might be going off to sleep with other men, than at any time since Timmy was born. They both knew she was on a crazy journey to another land and the fact that he couldn't be there, alongside her, to check her safety, was costing him a hell of a lot. Yes, it probably was worse for him, just sitting at home, not doing anything. Maybe not, actually.

She was finished. She stepped into the long pink cross-back velvet fitted dress that she seemed to have had all her life. Certainly it was such a treat to have the opportunity of wearing it. It had a shawl too. Quite dressy.

She called the cab firm, Taxi A Go Go, and checked herself for the last time in the mirror. She hadn't been able to wear the pink for years. Now it hugged her hips like massage-oil. And she was pleased, her underwear was suitably minimal and didn't affect the line of it at all. She felt better. If she ran into someone she knew, would they recognise her? If they did, they wouldn't know what she was up to. But, most probably, they wouldn't make the connection and would fail to recognise her. People always saw her as Peter's side-kick, not out on her own, in full rig-out, with heels like daggers. Anyway, just because you vaguely recognise someone decked out and having dinner doesn't mean you would ever immediately think 'oldest profession', does it?

Actually, she thought, probably the oldest profession must have been midwifery. Or being a witch-doctor.

She was ready. She said: 'Hullo, how do you do, I'm Natasha. You must be Mr Cunliffe,' twice out loud to herself in the mirror. She checked the contents of her handbag for the eightieth time, crossed herself, touched wood, switched off the light, left her sanctuary and locked the door behind her.

The guy cleaning the kitchen by the stairs whistled appreciatively and called out: 'Out on the town?' She laughed and used Natasha's voice, for the very first time in public, to say that she was. The sound of her voice made her feel suddenly a lot better. It was 'opening night'. She could do this.

The Taxi A Go Go driver was a thin black guy with a moustache and a great big floppy cap. Harriet asked him his name, again in Natasha's voice. He was surprised, but she reminded him that Ms Ivanov had an account. He fought his way through the Shaftesbury Avenue theatre traffic and said he was called Melvyn. He wanted to talk about his plans for the Carnival. She didn't want to talk very much at all.

Quaglino's was like a glamorous nineties art-deco aircraft hangar. Black-suited young men and women smiled welcoming smiles and gestured her through to the bar which hovered above the main restaurant area on a kind of mezzanine. She felt a little over-dressed really, but then, it was still early in the evening. She was thankful that the staff, at least, were dressed up to the nines. The place was buzzing with people – full of Gary Blokes and their womenfolk, clean-limbed middle-aged American couples with virile iron-grey hair and Imelda Marcos lookalikes with cantilevered shoulders, vying with each other about the talented brilliance of their respective, remarkable grandchildren. A black guy played a big white grand piano and sang 'Moon River' in an echoey kind of way.

In the bar area there was already a crowd of people and, among them, two different men who seemed to have the *Financial Times* about their persons. That was all a girl needed. There was a fair young boy reading it. Her heart skipped a beat as he was a tolerably scrumptious hunk of manhood, really – more pleasure than chore. Then she saw the other copy of the pink paper, rolled, unread and lying like a blushing slug on this man's table, placed there like a talisman. He was looking out for her as well and grinned a welcome. She smiled radiantly at him and walked over. As he stood to shake her by the hand, her heart had dropped to her boots. He was a small, thick-set, jowly man of about fifty or more, with odd dark eyes and with a few specks of dried food on the lapel of his black suit. She sat at his table and accepted a mineral water and took the guy in. The prospect was just appalling. He sat there like a toad, a great big fat square toad, with, yes, even slightly blood-shot eyes. He had those fleshy kind of lips that have spittle stretched between them when he spoke. He had a breathy grunty north-country voice and his name was Graham. When he had finished his whisky, they walked together down the glorious flight of stairs into the restaurant itself. In her heels, she was half a head taller than he was. Diners turned to take them in briefly as they went to their table. For a second, his thumb and forefinger held her elbow and guided her through the throng of tables. If she kissed him, would he perhaps turn into a prince? Her stomach turned over at the thought. As they sat, she could see how pleased he was at the public reaction. Perhaps she had done enough of her job already?

She would give him three damn good hours of chat and delight and then she would go home. Even assuming anything more was actually on offer.

And there was no reason to believe that it was on offer anyway. There was nothing at all lascivious about this Graham. He wasn't a very attractive prospect, but he had a pleasant enough smile and he chatted away amiably enough. His wife was dead (of course). He lived in Smithy Bridge, which was a place just outside Rochdale and he ran a printing company – 'food packaging and the like.' He came down to London twice a year for some kind of show at Olympia, no doubt about food packaging and the like. Harriet and he had nothing in common in the slightest. They knew completely different television, magazines, sport, culture, even politics, she guessed, if she could ever claim to know anything herself about politics. They might have been from different planets, so opposed were they in everything that they knew and admired. Harriet thanked God for her preparation. She sat there behind Natasha and heard that woman's mysterious cultured foreign voice giving Graham Cunliffe such a good time. Indeed, the story of Natasha's life and works filled up every tiny piece of space between making their order, celebrating its arrival, and appreciating it.

Harriet felt that she was doing quite well, all things considered, and she allowed herself a whole glass of wine. It was breaking one of her so recently established rules, but she felt she deserved an encouraging treat and she was going to be back in her sleeping-bag in Flitcroft Mews before midnight, wasn't she? A proper little Cinderella. But at least she had managed this much. And it hadn't been too bad.

But by the time they had come to the selection of the sweets, Harriet had begun a furious internal debate with herself. The guy was godawful, it was true, but she had always known that this was going to be the case. The world, doubtless, was full of godawful guys who thought that they might buy themselves an expensive bonk. And she had spent two whole solid months preparing herself for just such. Natasha had been invented to handle just about anything and now a tubby short piece of just-about-anything had turned up. Was she going to walk away from it. This was her job – you didn't walk away at the first smell of bad breath. He seemed a kindly enough little old guy. He laughed at her jokes. He did all the normal sidelong glancing at her breasts, but, in this profession, to be honest, that's presumably what her bosom was there, and all tricked out, for. He had said not one thing out of line. He was polite and interested in what Natasha had to tell him. And he had a vaguely beady humour about the goings-on of small-town life as seen by a printer of food packaging and the like. Most of all, he represented money, earnings, the beginnings of survival for the Holloway family. Fear fought with greed within her.

She excused herself and went to the Ladies' and peered at herself in the mirror. Had all this just been some pie-in-the-sky game? Was the whole thing, as Peter had said, a malevolently expensive idiotic wank? Had Peter been right when he had called her a fool? Was she now going to funk it? What would she say to Peter over breakfast? 'Sorry, Peter, he was small and ugly and wore nylon shirts.' She could see Peter being kind and understanding but with his famous 'told-you-so' face pervading his features, reminding her he was better than she was, all along. She could be braver than this. Natasha could do it. She had to. She had never said it was going to be easy. This was why people, in general, didn't do this sort of thing.

123

She got a grip on herself and decided to take Natasha back to their table. Be in charge, she told herself. She walked slowly back to him between the tables, breathing steadily and smiling calmly. He had ordered himself a brandy. Did she want one, lass? She declined and sat in the seat next to his and put her arm around the back of his chair. She could feel his warmth through the back of his jacket. She braced herself to be outrageous. He was stumbling through some clumsy compliments about the way she looked. He had become a little nervous. She guessed he was leading up to something, but it was going to take him some time to get there. He told her that his mother, now long passed away, bless her, had had a similarly grave and peaceful demeanour to her good self. Oh God, he wants to fuck his mother, she thought. He ploughed on: his mother had been psychic, had had second sight, or so some had thought. Was Natasha?

'I don't know, Graham, possibly. Yes, I do sometimes think that I can, at least, read minds. I suppose it's mostly a matter of accurate character analysis,' she said with her arch Russian vowels. 'I mean, let me try you, for example. Let me see if I can read your thoughts.' He looked so uncomfortable for a moment that Natasha felt almost buoyant. With mindless resolution, she took his fat earlobe affectionately between her finger and thumb, and murmured closely into his ear: 'Would I guess right, for example, Graham, if I said that, although we've shared the most delightful meal together, and it's been really interesting talking to you here, secretly, in your deepest heart of hearts, you'd prefer me back in your hotel bedroom with my kit off?'

Mr Graham Cunliffe's expression seemed to be caught for a fraction of a second between panic-stricken shock and intense relief. He said she was a girl after his own heart – which, of course, was right – indeed this was what she was trying to be. That is what he had bought. He instantly ordered the bill and knocked his wine glass over. She quietly told him her terms. He did not demur in the slightest. She felt as if she was on a kind of unfeeling conveyor-belt and although her pulse was pumping, the words came out reasonably intelligibly. Yes he had it in cash, and, yes, he would give her the notes in the taxi. She felt high at having actually managed to do it. God, all of a sudden she wanted that money really desperately! His money in her hand would make it all seem honest and sensible, would make her feel OK.

The restaurant ordered a cab and they were out of there. He
wanted to maul her about in the taxi and she heard Natasha, rather
more foreign than usual, telling him to wait until they got back to
base. Even so, he virtually sat on top of her and stroked his stubby
hand along the length of her suspender through the long pink velvet
of the gown. He did smell, of course, of tobacco and of living on
his own and of old suit. She had a sudden flash of memory of a
late teenage dance, being trapped in the back of some old parental
Vauxhall with a boy she had known ten minutes, who wanted above
all things to get her out of her bra, whether he undid it or no. She
had managed then. She would manage now. Everything comes to
an end, finally. Even the boredom of swimming forty lengths has
to finish after thirty-five minutes or so.

It was the Cornwallis Hotel just off Piccadilly. An enormous
place. A vast foyer full of newsagents and post card shops and
perfumeries. Rather tacky for a posh place. She waited on the
pavement, hiding her shoulders in her big shawl, while he paid the
cab. Then they walked in through the revolving doors and across
the acres of the foyer.

Honeymooners, Darby & Joans, exhausted American tourists –
they can, no doubt, all walk into hotel lobbies hand in hand or with
perhaps at least a mute finger dragging on a partner's hand. A whore
and her john, she thought wryly, presumably never hold hands, they
walk in like working colleagues, folk politely on first-name terms,
going to a business meeting together in an upstairs room – which,
of course, is exactly what they are about.

The Cornwallis was all wide, dark brown wood-lined corridors,
deep red carpets and a thousand doors. Graham Cunliffe had a room
on the fifth floor. Together they went up in the empty lift, standing
silently, shoulder to shoulder half a metre apart, They must make
an odd-looking couple, she inches taller and pretty stylishly turned
out, he rather crumpled and apparently so very much older.

The room had two single beds in it, one of which had his suitcase
open on it – white shirts and rolled-up socks. A ghastly brown and
beige room with a print of some nondescript pale pink roses above
the television. The long theatrical swags at the window were almost
closed and the place stank of tobacco smoke. He locked the door
and went into the en-suite bathroom. Her heart sank – he took his
rotten room key with him. She could hear him having a pee.

She switched off the bald overhead lighting and clicked on one of the bedside lamps. She went and edged one of the windows open. Then she stood there and waited and decided where she would put her clothes and, most important, where she would tuck her bag. She had just decided that it might be intelligent to get out of her clobber and into the bed, thus avoiding a lot of problems, when he flushed the loo and was back in the room.

He took his jacket off. She had a sudden thought that he seemed slightly different. More in charge. She had a sudden wild premonition that she might get hurt. She moved towards him, but he stopped her: 'No. Stay there by the door.' He stood there looking across the few yards between them and then he lit a cigarette. 'Let's have a good look at you, love,' he said, 'now I've got the chance. You're a bit of a looker, aren't you? My lucky day.' He coughed wheezily and then recovered. 'All right,' he said, 'all right.' He just looked at her. Rudely, up and down. She felt abused by the way he smiled at her. This wasn't how she had seen it at all. 'All right, my dear; now, take your clothes off. I just want to watch you.' He sat himself down in the chair by the window the other side of the room. 'This is very nice, lass. Favourite.' Although the room was now by no means well lit, she felt terribly daunted. She walked back to the door – striptease time. Oh God. Could she do this?

'No, don't start yet. Listen to me. Listen up, lass.' He was very sharp with her. 'When I say, I want you to take all your clothes off for me and then – then' – he coughed and spluttered on his damn fag again – 'then I want you to crawl, on your belly, lass, very slowly, all the way across here. Drag yourself on your elbows, inch by inch. Across to my feet. I want you to rub your dirty filthy hairy cunt all the way over to me, across the carpet, and all the way over to me, love, I want you to beg me for it, beg me for it, moan for it, all the fucking way.' The words seemed to knock Natasha stone cold dead. She felt utterly disgusted by him. It was such a change-around. This wasn't sex, this was degradation. She turned and looked at him, with dead eyes. So, he was into humiliation and there was no way that she could cope with that, even if it was some kind of sick game. Not first time out. She needed to hold on to her power and to the tattered flag of her self-respect. She couldn't do this one. She would have to get out.

'I won't do that,' she said simply.

'You will, my lass.'

'Let's just go to bed. You'll like that. I'll give you such a very good time.' It was an extremely hard thing to say.

'Do it! Fucking do it. I've paid you for it.'

'I'm sorry, I'm not prepared to be humiliated by you, Graham. I came here to fuck you, yes. I'll play games. Good games. I'll give you such a very good time. But you'll only have a good time if I feel OK about what I'm doing. I need to feel friends with you. And I won't feel good doing – that. You've got the wrong girl.'

'You bloody will, girl! It's what I want.'

'Sorry.' So demure, so very polite! She was in the wrong business.

'Bitch, bitch. Fucking do it, bitch.' He was suddenly wildly overwrought and snarling at her, red-faced: 'I've paid you, bitch,' he roared at her. 'That's what I want!'

'Well, you'd better have your money back.' She was soaked in sweat down her back and front.

He got up. Was he going to hit her? He was. 'Do it, cunt! Fucking do it! I've paid.' His hand walloped against her cheek and she lost an earring. Her head swam. Momentarily they stood a foot apart, breathing heavily. She almost clipped him one back, but that was asking to be killed.

Then she was off. She was going to have to get the key out of the bathroom, for God's sake. 'Fuck off, you beast. I'm getting out of here.' What else could she do? She tore her way across into the bathroom. For the briefest second her heart sank as she couldn't see where he had put it. It must be in his pocket. Then she saw it on the edge of the bath. She grabbed the big metal fob and then realised that he was trying to pull the door closed on her from the outside. She was going to be trapped! She found a sudden superhuman strength and wrenched the door open, back into the bathroom. Then she was heading for the exit door. The man grabbed at her and brought her down in a sort of stumbling rugby tackle. For a moment they lay on the floor together in a bizarre embrace. She fought to make him let go of her, wriggling her way out of his grasp, thumping his head with her fists, bashing him with the key. The top of her dress tore. Then she realised that the man with his arms clamped so firmly around her waist with his face buried in her belly was shaking with sobbing. She stopped pummelling his greasy head with her fists. He was crying and saying things that she couldn't make out at all. For a moment she lay there and listened. Between gasps and the lurches of his lungs he was saying over and over again that he was sorry, how he was so ashamed.

'Fucking sorry you should be.' She was astonished that it was still resolutely Natasha's voice. 'You fucking hit me, you sick bastard. I'm out of here. Let me go.'

'No, please, I'm sorry.' He had let her go. They were both still on the carpet. Her hair had come down and her cheek tingled. 'Stay here,' he said. 'Please, please stay. You must, I've paid you a lot of money.'

'You've got your money's worth, mister. You hit me. All bets are off.' She scrabbled away from him across the floor in her tight skirt. She had got her handbag, she would leave the earring. She had trouble getting up in the dress. He was up first and he came at her again. His main thought seemed to be that she wasn't going to give him what he had paid for. She was almost upright when he pinned her against the wall by the door. He tried to fasten his evil, wet, open mouth to her face. Wine glasses tumbled on to the carpet from the table. She dragged her skirt up around her hips and kneed him hard in the crotch. She was completely astonished by how very effective it was. He fell away from her and half sat on his suitcase on the bed, which tipped its belongings all over the floor. She turned to the door and it seemed to take forever to insert the key.

She ran down the empty corridor. She ran as fast as her dress would let her, right, left, left and right again. Through various heavy fire-break doors and then she was lost. He did not seem to have followed her. She couldn't think where the lifts were.

She found a Ladies' toilet and went in. She locked herself in a cubicle and sat down on the loo seat. She sat there for a long time. Her mind didn't seem to be functioning any more. All she knew was that it had been far far worse than she could ever have imagined. Now she felt strangely tired and numb. It was just unbelievable – one minute her life, while financially dire, had been quite ordinary, dull even; the next, there she was, rolling on the floor in her very best dress, with some dangerous perverted anonymous bastard. And now, on top of all that, here she was, locked in a loo in the Cornwallis, wondering if she could get out of the hotel alive. Perhaps he was wandering the corridors outside, at this very moment, searching for her, looking for his pounds of flesh?

*   *   *

From the moment I got back to the house, I couldn't stop pacing about the place. I tried sitting down, but it was pointless – the inside of my head was shrieking like a siren and I found I couldn't breathe. I kept on having to gulp down great mouthfuls of air. I must have looked like a stranded bloody goldfish. I must do something about those herons. And my old ticker was pumping away in double time. I could hear it in my ears.

And when I wasn't charging up and down, like an expectant father denied the labour-ward, I was into good works. Well, I thought it might be best to do things to take my mind off the broad spectrum of what might be going on. So to curry favour with the gods, I did stuff that H. would really have approved of. I was like a man possessed. I thrashed up and down the lawn with the Off-with-your-toe-mo and even trimmed the godforsaken edges in a manic action-painting kind of a way. All helped by the hound sniffing about, trying to turn it into an Off-with-yer-dog's-nose-mo. After this, I had conjured up a feast and a quarter for the garrison. No microwave chips for his progeny from this father. Oh dear no. I'd filched my mother's chip pan from her kitchen a couple of years ago. Of course, we never got round to using it. Not till today anyway. J. & T. were, rightly, tickled pink by this sudden jump into the culinary unknown. Yeah, all right, I know it was just packet batter but you have to assess the right quantity of milk and mix it all up properly yourself – it was almost cooking. I got fairly hysterically into the challenge of it and the benighted mess that you could make of the kitchen when dipping the cod. The batter, when cooked, turned out a bit like armour-plated tarmacadam but it was something of a first, at number 17. They looked at their father with new eyes. So did I.

But you can only do so much displacement therapy can't you? I also had to retire to the privacy of the back loo, at times, and take enormous deep breaths and press my fingers into my eyes until they hurt. It stopped me from crying. The boys didn't notice anything.

Then I read them their bedtime story. The turgid adventures of that fascist and his queen, Babar the Heffalump. No sign of any democracy in jolly old Celesteville, as far as I could see. A world of bovine, kowtowing, smiling, exploited working elephants. This Babar, and his equally tyrannical missus, ran the outfit like a malevolent dictatorship, basically dishing out good intentions and martial law. That monkey's a dead ringer for Goebbels too. Smelled all too familiarly like Chile for comfort, I thought. Is this what we should be providing for our children as role-models in the 1990s? Nevertheless I did all the voices – BAFTA award-winning stuff, I thought – though young J. opined that 'Mum does a better "little old lady".' The jury's out on that one. They just love hearing the same old stories – familiarity breeds content.

After kissing them on their respective noses, I had nothing to do but this endless pacing. Up and down the living room, in and out the kitchen, that's the way the worry goes, pop goes the weasel. I couldn't face watching the telly. I couldn't face doing anything. I felt sick. I just kept wondering what was happening. What a bloody stupid awful thing this is.

After a long time, Harriet got herself out of the loo and addressed her appearance in the mirror over the sink. Her face was quite pink where the man had hit her. She took off her remaining earring and pinned her hair back into place. She re-did her lips and tackled her cheek. It wasn't all that bad. Mostly, she supposed, she was pissed off about her dress. The seam at the right side of the bodice was badly torn and it would be very difficult to fix perfectly. And the thing had cost hundreds of pounds, even in the mid-eighties. It was easy enough to hide the damage under her shawl, though. It wasn't as if she was going to tumble out of it or anything.

She tucked her make-up back into her bag and wondered if she should ring Peter and tell him about it. Tell him she was all right. Then she saw Cunliffe's great wad of twenty-pound notes folded up, next to her Motorola. She grinned bitterly at her reflection in the mirror. In the end, he hadn't really got very much for his money, had he? Serve him right, the sick shit. But she was grimly amused by a carping fair-minded middle-class voice in the back of her mind that told her she had been wrong to rip him off. Then she thought what an idiotic fool she was even to begin to think that. She was dealing with a fool here!

There was no one at all in the dreary corridor when she got the courage together to leave the sanctuary of the loo. Where the hell had they hidden the lifts? She turned the corner and gave a start. There was a wiry man in a slightly shiny grey suit, standing, waiting. She was very surprised to see him there. It felt as if he had been there for a while. She walked past him without a glance, praying that the lifts were, in fact, down that end of the corridor.

'Can I help you, madam?' She hadn't heard him. She kept going. She had already had enough for one night.

'Can I help you, madam?' Much louder now. If she was an innocent guest, she would never have been able to pretend she hadn't heard him.

She stopped and looked at him: 'Sorry?' she said. 'Me?' she asked.

'Yes, you,' he said with an almost invisible touch of insolence. 'Are you a guest?'

'Yes. No. I'm just visiting.' He had some sort of plastic card in a leather wallet that he was brandishing at her. He was security or something. 'I've been to the theatre with my uncle,' she said, improvising wildly, hoping she wasn't constructing a blind alley for herself. Were West End theatre shows over by now? What time was it anyway?

'Which room is your uncle staying in, madam?'

'I can't remember. I've got a bit lost. He's just up there.' A scenario formed in her mind in which this pompous little weasel of a man delivered her back to her persecutor, the mad Cunliffe. Her stomach shrank at the thought. She should have stayed much longer in the loo.

'His name, your uncle?'

'Listen, what's all this about? I've got to go home now.'

'Just security, madam. We try to avoid too many strangers wandering around in the hotel.'

'Well, thank you, that's just fine. Are the lifts down this way?'

'Would you come with me, madam, and we can give your uncle a ring. Just for safety. I'm sure you understand. We are obliged to take great care. For your own safety as well as others. What did you say his name was?' She had no wish to be in contact with bloody Cunliffe again: 'Roger Conway,' she said. 'But I think he's booked in under the name of his company.' This was probably absurd and they both knew it. The man walked with her to the lift. Once again she rode the Cornwallis lift with a strange man and knew not what the outcome would be. It felt just as grim as before. She felt very frightened. Supposing he looked in her bag and saw all the money tucked in there? She folded the shawl and her arms across her damaged dress and awaited the worst. She made herself the most solemn promise: if she ever got out of this in one piece, she vowed that she would stop this whole madness once and for all, forever. They got out at the first floor and walked to a room which the man unlocked with a great clattering bunch of keys.

'In here please, madam.' Her heart fell. It was another of the Cornwallis's dire beige bedrooms. But it was clearly also an office. There was a desk and papers scattered over it and a Sasco wall-chart on the wall. Three short-wave radios were flashing silently on the dressing table, recharging their little lives. She couldn't bear it, this evening was beginning to become the longest in her life. The man invited her to sit down and picked up the phone. 'Sorry,' he said, 'what did you say his name was, again?'

She would have to go in a new direction. 'I'm sorry, I can't tell you.'

'Why, don't you know it?'

'Of course I know it. But I can't tell it to you.'

'Why not?'

'Well – well, I don't see why I should have to tell you, but he's my boss. We're, er, having, he's married, and we're having – well, you know – do I have to spell it out to you?'

'Why did you say you were visiting your uncle?'

'I was embarrassed. In fact I still am. Why are you doing this to me?'

'Well, madam, we have to check these things out, don't we? Actually I think you're not being straight with me, er, what is your name?'

'Marina Farnsworth.' Well, why not? She'd lost Natasha in the loo. She was talking in her own frightened Scottish tones now.

'All right Ms, er, Farnsworth. Is there any way I can check your story? Someone to whom I can give a quick call – for your own, and the hotel's, security?'

'No, I don't want you to call anybody, thank you.'

'Well, that's very difficult. You see my alternative is to call Savile Row Police Station and ask them to come around and have a word with you.' He made more play with the telephone. This was all just so awful. What, in heaven's name, should she do? Ring Peter and ask him to come and get her out of there? The man went on: 'You see, Ms' – he referred to his note – 'Farnsworth, we have a number of sneak thieves who operate in our hotels at times and of course I'm sure you know, ladies of, let us say, temporary virtue, who also trade on our premises. Of course, I'm not suggesting, for one minute – but we have a responsibility to keep our guests safe. These things are crimes. People sometimes go to prison thanks to our vigilance. So I need to rule you out of the equation, if you see what I mean.'

'I'm sorry. I'm in a difficult situation – '

'Yes, I think you are,' he interrupted.

She went on inventing, without much idea of a plan: 'Owing to my personal situation, I can't ring anyone at home. You'll have to understand that I'm not meant to be here. It would destroy everything if my husband knew I was here. Please let me go. I'll just go. You can see I haven't stolen anything.' She smiled as winsomely at him as her painful face would allow. And thought of the wad of money in her bag.

'Most nights, this hotel has its fair share of couples, where one or other of them, or both, are somewhere where they shouldn't be, as it were. The striking thing, on the whole, is that they tend to remain together, to have tender breakfasts together at the end of their stay. It's early, Ms Farnsworth, to be going, isn't it?'

'That is really nothing to do with you.' She was looking around for a big bluff: 'I think I had better see the manager.'

'You think so, do you? You see, I tend to think you may have something to hide. I think it could be that you were here for purposes of trade.'

'That's ridiculous. What an outrageous thing to say. I will have to see the manager now, please.'

He began to dial on his outside line: 'Outrageous or not, I will just have to see what The William have to say about it. I'll give them a call. If I'm wrong then you will have my and the hotel's thousand apologies. You understand, I've got a job to do here.' But then he had a change of tack. He stopped in mid-dial and looked at her through the top part of his spectacles. Then, quite slowly he replaced the phone on its cradle. He got up and went across to fill his coffee percolator with water from the bathroom. As he came back to switch it on, he said: 'I'll let you think about it. Have a cup of coffee and think about it. No need to rush into things, is there? After all, there is probably a perfectly easy way out of all this, wouldn't you say?' He began to slice into a foil packet of Sainsbury's ground coffee with a pair of nail-scissors. 'I mean, I'm happy to leave things much as they are. You could just go on your way. If I felt somehow recompensed for my time, and my, er, blind eye. I am, to some small degree, my own boss here, you see.' He looked at her quizzically, almost kindly. 'The good thing about this particular hotel security position is that I have a most comfortable billet. Private. I sleep here when on duty too, you understand. No one in till 7.30 a.m. That's when Jason comes to relieve me. Lots of time. And I won't have to do too many rounds tonight, his nibs being away in Australia for his daughter's wedding.'

This was intolerable. What a frantically grim night it had turned out to be. She would get out, tear off her battered dress and forget all about this dreadful pathetic humiliating scheme. She must have been mad. The man filled the filter paper with the coffee. 'You can be friendly to me and take yourself off, or you can be stupidly trying and then you will have to deal with the boys in blue. I know what you are, my dear. New to it, but nonetheless I've been in this business for thirteen years. I've seen every kind of human behaviour. So I know what I'm talking about. We'll have a nice cup of coffee. Then I'll lock the door. You can call me Philip.'

Harriet's brain was in free-fall and she seemed to be feeling both hot and cold all at the same time. The guy had switched on his smug plastic coffee machine. He removed his tie, sliding the knot down. In a moment he would have locked the door. Could she fuck him and then get out? She was hating all this.

She had an idea. She reached into her handbag. He looked at her startled, as if she was going to bring out a gun. She flipped open the flap on her phone and saw thankfully that she had a line in there, even in the hotel room. She dialled a number and held it to her ear. The man watched her astonished, with his glass jug of water halfway to its little hot-plate. She didn't get through to anyone.

'Hullo,' she said. 'Thank you. Yes, thank you. Is Chief Inspector Doubleday there? Yes, can I speak to him for a moment please. He's my brother. My name's Mrs Farnsworth. I need to report something. Thank you. I'll wait.' She sat there with the dead phone pressed to her ear.

The man was spilling his water on the carpet. 'Go,' he said. 'Just go.' He came across towards her and tried to take the phone from her, tried to close the flap and cut off the line. They wrestled mutely for a moment but not with any great force. She stood up holding the phone in front of her like an amulet.

'I'll escort you to the front door,' he said.

She wasn't going to be marched out of the hotel! Something seemed to snap in her head: 'You'll escort me no fucking where. You just watch your fucking step or I'll fucking report you for propositioning me and I'll get you sacked. I'll have you out on your ear!' she screamed at him. 'How dare you!' And, holding the phone to her ear, she turned and left the room, slamming the door behind her.

Now, she had to get herself out of this awful hotel as quickly as possible. She ran down the corridor following the signs to the exit. Get out, get out, get out! And then she was overcome with an incredible nausea, food rushed to her throat and burnt it. She was going to throw up all over the Cornwallis' ghastly beige carpets. There was another Ladies' up by the lifts. She ran to it and almost immediately found herself offloading a digested Quaglino's dinner into the lavatory pan. When that was over, she mopped herself up with the loo paper and sat in the cubicle to collect herself for her final exit. In a moment or so, she would walk her way out of the Cornwallis and out of her one-night stand as a working girl, forever.

She had been in her cubicle with her head in her hands for what must have been just a few minutes when she heard a woman come into the loo. Harriet froze as she listened to the rustle of this newcomer moving about outside by the wash basins. Then the woman went into the cubicle next to Harriet's and there was a long silence. Harriet decided to use the moment to escape. She was just going to have to gather her courage together and leave the safety of the Ladies' and brave the inhospitable outside world of the hotel corridors once again.

She slid the lock back and stepped outside. She crossed to the mirrors and examined her face. She sighed. Her eye was looking puffy.

'You all right?' The words gave Harriet such a start. She turned to see the woman sitting on the lavatory pedestal with her cubicle door wide open, looking at her interestedly. She had her handbag on her lap and was putting her hand mirror away. Her voice was almost public school with a touch of London twang – Camden rather than Hampstead. The woman stood up and joined Harriet. She was very short but slim with blonde curls and a smart straight black dress, fitted. They stood next to each other at the sinks. The woman padded at her lips with a tissue and sniffed massively. She smiled at Harriet. 'Sorry if I gave you a start. You OK?'

'I'm all right. Yes, thanks, I'm all right.'

'You're not. Someone's biffed you. Haven't they?'

'Oh God, is it so obvious?' She turned to the woman and looked at her for the first time. She had pretty blue eyes and nice smiley lines at their corners. She must have been thirty-two or so. She smelled gorgeous. The woman said: 'Let's have a look. Oh Gawd. No, I think it's just your cheek, I don't think you'll have a black eye.' She turned back to regarding her own make-up in the glass: 'Was it a punter?'

'How do you know?'

'Single woman in the full gear, this time at night, in hotel public loos, stands to reason, got to be a brass. You get to know these things.' She snapped her make-up bag back into the handbag. 'No, actually, I saw you in the foyer earlier, when you came in. Stood out a mile.'

'I couldn't believe I was that obvious. The security guy knew too.'

'Well, they do. That's their job. This is a filthy mansion anyway. I wouldn't be here if it wasn't for having to pay the school fees at the end of the month.'

'You too?'

The woman took Harriet's make-up from her and skillfully padded at her puffy damaged cheekbone. 'You look fine now. You been doing this long?'

'No. Not very long. No, not very long at all.'

'You going home? So am I. We'll trot out together. They won't bother us then. What's your name?' She gave the woman one of her splendid cards. 'Natasha, eh? I call myself Louise. My real name's Daisy. He give you a bad time, darling?'

'I wouldn't do what he wanted. He got angry.'

'They do, they do. They can be so pathetic. You question their particular little foibles and they go raving mad. You've torn your dress.'

'I know. Isn't it awful? I love this dress too.'

'Listen, love, don't get me wrong, and it's not really my place to say but you're a little bit over-dressed for it. That's why security picked you up. You've got to be smart, pretty even, but not too striking or they notice you too much. And don't come here, this is a shitty dump. Always ask the punters which mansion they're at. Skip the Hilton, Browns, Penningtons and the Regent International. The staff are all grief there. Listen, you want any advice, ring me – Daisy – I'll give you my number.' Then she asked, 'You got kids? I've got twins. Thirteen-year-olds. Cost me an arm and a leg. Lovely kids though. My reason for living.'

'I've got two, too. Jonty's eight, Timothy's four.'

'They cost even more in their teens. Bloody hard on a single mum. No one has any idea. My fella died. Cancer of the colon. Had to do something, didn't I?'

'Can I ask you something? With the, um, work, do you get a lot of trouble?'

'No. Well, sometimes. But, really not a lot. With some of them, there's such a lot of anger. They seem out for revenge or something. Mostly they're pussycats. I get better at choosing. If in doubt, go home.'

'I suppose I was in doubt, really.'

'Did he pay you?'

'Oh yes.'

'And did you fuck him?'

'No.'

'Best of all possible worlds.' And she laughed uproariously. 'Makes a change to get one up on the likes of them, eh? Business-men, they're all bloody crooks, love. Makes me laugh. Not like us at all. You know what they say – when a businessman pays a whore for sex, you can be sure that there's at least one honest party to the deal!' Daisy's laugh echoed embarrassingly loud in the little lavatory. She had bright brittle eyes. Harriet guessed that the woman had been doing some coke when she had emerged from her loo sniffing so painfully.

'What else can I tell you? From my vast fund of experience? Eight years I've been at it. I don't know. Yes, I do: don't use KY, it gets like glue, I reckon, unless you lubricate like a wet Wednesday anyway. And it smells of Vim. And Johnsons is no good, it gives you this funny kind of warm feeling. You know what I use? – Soltan Aftasun. Yes. You wouldn't believe it. Absolutely ideal. Soft and easy and no smell. You have to decant it into one of those small Bodyshop plastic pots though, or they look at you like you've gone out. Don't use baby-oil or oil-based lipstick with a condom. They split.'

They left the sanctuary of the loo and walked down the stairs together. Daisy took her arm. They spun out through the revolving doors of the hotel without anyone giving them a second glance. Like sisters. It was two in the morning.

'I'm going to get a cab,' said Daisy. 'Listen, keep in touch. If anyone ever wants a double, you and me could handle that. Lots of money in doubles.'

'What do you mean?'

Daisy looked at her surprised and then smiled at her. 'This is new for you, isn't it? You get stag nights. I sometimes get a call. Of course you have to fuck the groom. But best of all they like to see a couple of working girls doing it together. They pay really well, doubles. I'm no dyke, darling, but sometimes it's preferable – pleasant even, almost comforting. Well, see you. You'll do fine. Just dress down a little. Here – ' The woman pulled a roll of adhesive labels out of her handbag, with the name 'Louise' printed on each, together with her phone number in flamboyant italics. She tore off two and gave them to Harriet. 'Give me a ring if you've got a problem.' And there on the deserted pavement of Sackville Street, she reached up, kissed Harriet firmly on the mouth and trotted in the direction of Piccadilly in her tight black skirt and heels.

Harriet walked up Shaftesbury Avenue past all the empty theatres. She would go and take her bruised cheek off to sleep, as planned, in her cell in Flitcroft Mews and think about it all in the morning. Being London, the place was already pretty deserted. One of the greatest cities in the world, with the night-life of East Grinstead. What was it Peter used to say? – 'London after midnight? – the dead centre of the universe'. She walked quickly along the southern fringe of Soho. Doubles, eh? It was all very well fantasising about it, but however posh the hotel, however lavish the meal, the whole business was much closer to the street than she had ever thought. And that was terrifying.

I did finally manage to make myself sit down and watch the telly. Didn't take in a thing, of course. Late-night telly is a bit like tinned minestrone – funny lumps, pallid tastes and the very occasional odd sharp chewy bit – endless taped laughter, noisy music, no one listening to what anyone else is saying and no sentences longer than six words. I couldn't bear it.

I went out into the garden. It was virtually dark. I walked extremely slowly down to the very end. It's only about fifty yards but it took me all of half an hour. Filling in time. The trees still smelled of the heat of the day, all those hours ago – and the scent of roses in the dark was overwhelming. And the rosemary and the lavender. H.'s and my garden. It's where we've always been at our most comfortable together. And I wanted to take a chain saw to the lot. She's up there in some place banging some bastard who has to pay for it – 'Give it to me, give it to me, oh yes! Oh I do so love it with you!' Death death death death death death. I wanted to die. But all I could do was wrench wretched, dry tears out of my eyes. Pathetic really.

The filthy misery of all this is that, at bottom, it's my spectacular lack of achievement in the last twelve months that has brought this shit upon us – upon her – upon me. Oh yes, of course I blame Julian like it's bloody going out of fashion, but, truthfully, that's only part of the story, isn't it? That's mostly just a weary, face-saving excuse, when you get down to it. What about my own contribution? Or lack of it. Right, yes, *mea culpa*, *mea maxima* bloody *culpa*. But, OK, what else was I going to try to do – apart from taking myself off to try to be one of Rupert's little helpers? But, truth is, even if I could have borne it, I doubt if I could ever have got Murdoch's people to take me on, given my patchy record at *The Chron*. The thing is and, do you know, this even astonishes me, but, by the end, on *The Chronicle*, I had got really totally fatigued by it all – with the leaden dross of it – the knicker-sniffing, the pandering, the door-stepping, the conveyor-belt trivia that, it seemed, we had to be party to, day after day, night after night, until hell froze over. And I suppose being given totally the wrong guidance about something like Dorcas Leaftree didn't exactly make me feel I had to stay with the tabloids forever anyway. Yep, I know the broadsheets aren't much to write home about either – but I had got together this mad, unhinged, 1950s-type Attlee Government fantasy of a little decency somewhere – coming gently out of left-field.

But like every crazy little dream, it led me stunningly astray. Dumped us all in the doggie-poo.

There's a narrow alleyway just beyond the wall at the bottom of the property. Between our garden and the old garages in Pond Road. I went through the door in our wall, by the compost heap, and stood there for a long time in the dark between the constricting brick sides of the passageway. The walls are all every which-way there, black and bent and old, with Dickensian shadows from this great big moon. Starfire came and had a look at me, but decided I wasn't very interesting and he went away again to harry the goldfish. Thinks he's a heron, that one. Lots of stars, for London. The walls along there have glass embedded in cement along the top – bits of broken milk bottles and old Victorian beer glasses. I reached up and tapped them experimentally with the flat of my palm to see how sharp they felt. They were easy to reach. And they were sharp. I kept tapping away, almost without thinking what I was doing, banging my hand harder and harder on to the glass until it hurt a great deal and I had punctured my skin and there was blood all over the place. It seemed to help.

I did stop myself finally, as it was a pointless, stupid thing to do. By that time, I had done quite a lot of damage. I came back to the kitchen and cleaned up and wrapped my hand in acres of Elastoplast. Now that's a slightly difficult thing to do when you're on your own, and one-handed. Nutty bugger.

At half past two, I lay on our bed and I supposed that by now she must be in some fucking bath with him. Or groaning lasciviously on some sopping carpet. I found it almost impossible to breathe, I was so tensed up and in such turmoil. How the fuck have we got to this? Drank the remainder of the Glen Vomit and felt sick as a dog and frightened, but, you know, I had a little bit of an erection. I think I must be pretty nauseating.

Then she rang me from the command bunker. She was fine. It hadn't taken long. She would see me in the morning and tell me all about it. It had been a doddle. She had earned a great wad of the folding stuff – yeah! – mixing business with treasure. She sounded well bushed. I came up here and exhaustedly tapped this out and I will now crash.

She lay in her truckle bed, in her grim brick-lined designer cell and was unable to sleep. She turned restlessly in the constriction of the sleeping-bag, the zip catching at her throat. Oh to be at home in her familiar, cool, safe bedroom with Peter rhythmically grunting away, sleeping, as ever, like concrete beside her.

Was this what life was going to be like? Facing dreadful cretins in the no-man's-land of anonymous hotel rooms and returning to sleep by herself in a coal cellar. It wasn't a job, it wasn't a life, it was sheer unadulterated shit. What a stupid idiotic cow she had been – what a brainless, middle-class romantic fool. She had been kidding herself if she thought that there was some high-class velvet-lined upper-stratum of whoredom. There was just one scenario – penurious women getting money off men for fucking. You could be in the Hilton or the Cornwallis or on stinking York Way at King's Cross in a six-inch zip and a gram of coke up your nose, it was all the same rotten business.

Well, at least she had managed to learn that without getting her face cut.

But, like people say, it did look astonishingly different in the morning.

Perspectives seem so altered in the warm light of day. Particularly if you've got three hundred smackers in your pocket. And you're alive.

It was the kind of clear sparkling spring-like day that you reckoned you would not see again in mid-summer. The air felt crystal fresh and the sun played with the shadows among the leaves in the plane-trees around the National Portrait Gallery. She walked, at what felt like the crack of dawn, to Charing Cross Station through a West End alive with colour and good smells. A West End that was still struggling to wake up. Pakistani newsagents and Turkish café owners smiled at her as they began to open up their little shops and splash soapy water on their portions of pavement. Tables and chairs began to be assembled on the narrowest of pavements. Boring old London was changing – it was almost beginning to look European.

She took an empty train in the opposite direction to the earliest commuter horde, bought a paper and some warm croissants in the Village and walked up the hill, past the red-brick concert halls and into her home. In her handbag was a carefully counted thick cluster of twenty-pound notes. Her cheek hurt but it looked all right. Her lovely house and garden were going to remain their own. They would be able to begin to pay off a few bills, even her father's loan. She might, in the long run, even be able to put down a deposit on a car for Peter. Things looked different in the morning. Was she fickle? She was professional at it.

It was completely unbearable. I really needed to know. It was breakfast. Old H. was dishing out deeply unexpected manna from heaven in the form of individually boxed breakfast cereals to a pair of eager sons. Her face was just deadpan – pleasant, smiling, but private. She must have known that she had a fairly eager husband as well. Of course, with the boys all about the place, there was no way I could ask any specific questions. So I asked her trite little husbandly queries like: 'How was your first day at the office then, dear?' and 'Any complications?' and 'You managed everything all right, did you?'

She didn't give me so much as half a private glance. She just said: 'Yeah it was all OK' and 'Fine' and 'No prob.' and busied herself about the kitchen with her percolators and her cartons of orange juice. She didn't even ask me about my hand.

I was just about to get round to demanding that we go up to the bedroom and have a proper private chat when Harriet waves her hand and leaps on the bloody bike and chases off to the gym. I didn't think she'd go today. In fact, she looked a bit puffy-eyed and tired. Up all night, I should think. And she didn't think to take the dog.

I was so pissed off. But I had to keep it to myself as the boys were bashing about making a tree-house under the dining-room table – demanding supplies and equipment, and requiring me to be 'the enemy'. I couldn't co-operate. To escape I went and sat in the loo and did ten minutes' deep breathing. I imagine it's just a stage, but I did feel we were going to share all this. I mean, I know it must be a very big thing for her to have to handle – it's way outside anything that we could ever have known. And yet, I really do loathe being excluded by her. I enjoyed that dread black secret we had together. And I had spent the night scared witless for her. I think I deserve a touch more generous treatment, I suppose. Yeah, I know – self, self, self. But I just need to feel the power of being part of it all, in order to avoid the legions of little green devils doing in my head with jealousy. And, to be honest, at the moment, I do seem to be doing nearly all the bloody parenting.

And most of the bloody cooking too. It turns out the pressure-cooker has this instruction manual – well, a recipe book, I suppose. I'm doing kedgeree for tonight. I don't think we've ever had kedgeree chez Holloway before. Very Scots, that. Might cheer the Ice Maiden up a touch. 'Ice Maiden' can't be the right term technically, can it? – perhaps 'Ice Courtesan'. If she rates the cooking, perhaps she'll spill the beans.

But yes, it wasn't all gloom and doom. It was a good news day for Pete Holloway too – the *Statesman* is going to use that thing I did about recessionary vice. Perhaps my little life has turned a raddled corner. This could be the hinge. Maybe the recession is over. I was so inordinately thrilled it was really shameful. Mark you, one meagre acceptance doth not a summer make. I succeeded in being really ice cool on the phone. I gave the impression that I was totally submerged in projects. Well I was, I had the rice on.

But I couldn't concentrate. I mooched about the house, sitting in all sorts of places where I don't usually sit, thinking about what my wife had got up to the night before. It seemed as if I, too, was out there, with all the rest of the pathetic johns. My brain triggered off this constantly repeated memory of her coming so exuberantly with me in that hotel bed in Bloomsbury. At the same time, I had this endless, insane image of her having an even better time with some (oh, I don't know, hunky, blond?) guy in the infinite luxury of the best suite at the Cornwallis. It got to be almost unbearable. I found myself wanting to cry. I had to know. She had to tell me. I wanted it so much. It was only fair.

Harri came back and then she volunteered to go out again and do some much needed shopping. And so she did, indeed, disappear once more. Although, true, she said how pleased she was to hear the news about my piece for the *Statesman*. She had had no calls on her pocket-sized hot line. Well, if the writing takes off we can forget all about her joining the ranks of the clitorati.

Eventually, and only after another sodding bedtime exploration of the wacky world of Alison Uttley's Little G. Rabbit (those stories are so dauntingly *long*!), did I finally grab H. on the stairs and bundle her into our bedroom to have a decent, face-to-face, fact-finding chat. I was still hurt and angry, but I managed to keep it to myself. Just.

'I don't really want to talk about it.' She sat on the bed and looked uncomfortable, nothing more. I told her that we'd agreed that she'd keep me informed, let me in on how it was, how she felt about it.

'Yes, well I will. But I can't yet. It's all a wee bit more of a moral culture shock than I thought. I'm OK. I'm OK. It's just that I've got to get used to it. Peter, I mind that you need to know. I mind that's what we said we'd do. But you're going to have to make some allowances. Some of it I'm going to have to keep to myself. Look, I promise, some of it I'll happily tell you. I'm sure it'll get easier. It's just not easy at the moment.'

'But you were all right about it?'

'Yes. Yes, it was fine. It was OK, Peter. Strange, but OK. And I've started earning. We got the money. That was the best bit. It made it all feel worth while. That was good, wasn't it?'

'What did you say his name was?'

'I didn't.'

'Well, what was it?'

'Oh. Well his name was Graham.'

'Nice?'

'Peter.'

'Sorry.'

It was at exactly that moment that her phone went off in her bag. She took the bag and went with it and sat in the bathroom. I could hear her talking quietly. She talked quite a long time – Natasha's voice seeping unintelligibly through the bathroom wall at me. And she laughed – Natasha's deep-throated chuckle. Then she stopped talking and after a while she came back into the bedroom again. She had washed her face. 'Sorry,' she said, 'I can't do her yet in front of you, to order. Tuesday. Tuesday night. I'm meeting him at the Penguin. German, I think. I think I'm getting better at it already.'

But I reckoned she looked pretty doubtful. I thought: Oh shit, we're in so deep here and I'm beginning to feel like a complete gobshite. Then H. seemed to pull herself together and she went to her big cupboard and took off her eternal grubby tracksuit and tugged a big golden coloured sweater over her bra and pants. It has this great big open top, at the collar. I like it, it slops about on her body and you can see right down the front of her, if you want to. 'I'm sorry, Peterkins,' she said quietly and she came and lay by where I was sitting on the bed and gave me a hug. She felt warm and firm and strong. 'It's early days,' she said and she sighed massively, 'It's very early days. It's going to take me some time to be able to handle it easily. It was all right, but it was more difficult than I thought. I know what you must be feeling. I must try and help you. After all, it's a lot for a nice guy like you to put up with.' She lay there with her head cradled in the pool of her hair in the gathering dusk. One of her cheeks looked red. Apparently she had taken a tumble on a machine at the gym. She said I was sweet to notice. And then she kissed me and I felt an awful lot better. 'Funny old Peter. You're so transparent!' she said, 'All right. OK. So you really do want to know what happened, do you?'

'You know I do, Trinket. I'd die for it.'

'Blow for blow?' She didn't mean it rudely, but I tickled her anyway and she squalked and curled up defensively. It felt better between us again. She put her head on my chest and ran her fingers over my tummy. She's so tiny wrapped up against me. Then, quietly and refectively, she told me about it.

He was called Graham, some printer from 'oop-north', nice enough guy, apparently. Not much in common. They'd fed at Quaglino's and then she gave him the come-on and they'd gone

144

back to the Cornwallis after he'd given her the dosh. I was quite dry-mouthed by this time. I suppose everyone wants to know what sex is like with other people. No one ever dares ask. And so no one ever tells. All those millions of people out there doing it every day, and never ever talking very much about it to anyone else. Not even to the person with whom they've done it with. Except for the odd quick joke. So the soft-porn trade flourishes. That's why there is so much sex in the press. There's this deep-rooted massive lust for surrogate sex. Everywhere – the yellow press, the broadsheets and as for the women's magazines – if they can't get the word 'penis' twice on their front cover they sack the editor. I reckon we're all insatiable would-be voyeurs, but only I am brave enough to admit it – and then only to this very limited audience of one. Fortunately, it just so happens that yours truly has his own personal lust-line reporter and it was snuggling warmly up against him, punctuating communication with the occasional quick dry kiss. God, I felt a lot more robust. We were getting closer together again spiritually. Physically too. Suddenly I didn't seem to mind it any more. I was her fella and jealousy had flown out the window. I didn't even know what it felt like any more.

She grimaced for a bit deciding how much she could be brave enough to tell me. She said he was old but reasonably tender and attractive. She said that although it was very bizarre fucking someone she hardly knew at all, it wasn't any worse than those fumbling teenage knee-tremblers that everybody gets up to when they're young. She paused and ummed and aahed and said she couldn't say any more. And I bullied her good-naturedly. There were so many questions that I was trembling to ask her. She could feel my heart pumping away and finally she laughed at me and said she was sorry. So I got my bottle up sufficiently to ask them. I whispered them in her ear, feeling humiliated and absolutely thrilled by it: Did you like it? Go on, did you have a good time? Did you suck his cock? Was he well hung? And, oh god, oh god, oh god did you come?

'Peter, you are an absolute disgrace. You're as bent as a wire coathanger,' she muttered and she grinned at me ruefully as her hand sought out my tediously concrete cock. Then she laughed dryly and answered: 'Yes – yes – no and no, in that order!'

'You didn't come?'

'No, I said not.'

'But did you like him in there?'

'He didn't put it in there.'

'He didn't?'

'He didn't. There was no need, Mr Nosy. It didn't last all that long. He wasn't like you, Mr Holloway, always endlessly standing to attention.' She made me feel so really really great. When she concentrates, Harriet has always known precisely how to sort me out. And she was concentrating today. It was so lovely. She went on, in rhythm with her wrist movement: 'I must have been just much too sexy for him. Too-sexy-for-his-hat. Too-sexy-for-his-shirt. It came away in my hand, Mr Holloway, quite early on. Then he fell asleep which was very sensible of him and I trotted off like the good wee girl I am, to languish in my solitary pit.' She pushed her warm body as close to mine as possible and laid her thigh over my spreadeagled legs. 'With all that lovely money, money, money, money!' she breathed. Then, as she whispered to me about what she had been up to, she stuck her tongue in my ear and kept her hand at work. 'Money, money, money, money, money, money,' she kept on whispering breathily, like a mantra. We kissed and enjoyed the ten-year familiarity of our tongues together. That wicked anxiously seeking tongue of hers that had spent hours of last night presumably flicking this anonymous Graham into early capitulation. As far as I knew it was the first time she had ever had carnal information with anyone other than myself since we were married. I told myself that she must have loved it. God, she must really have loved it. And I loved her more than ever before. Oh dear God, I loved it! And then, very specifically under her thumb, I shot warmly, palely into the palm of her hand. She rubbed the sperm into the hair on my head murmuring: 'There, that'll make your hair curl.'

'You make my hair curl,' I murmured. At least that's what I think I murmured, because, by that time I was virtually asleep. I like to think that my last thought could have been that I was the luckiest man in all the world. It was astonishing to be able to share such private innermost secrets, so honestly and so truthfully.

Harriet found that it was very difficult indeed having to tell Peter all about what happened; on that first morning and on all the mornings that were to follow. It made her feel even more grubby, if that was possible. But that was the deal that had been struck between them. He said he would be able to handle what he called 'the pain of sharing her', if she came back and gave him the lowdown. Not, of course,

146

that he was sharing her at all. As she said countless times: it was work not infidelity. And what about *her* pain, damn you, Peter, she would think furiously? What about *her* everyday excruciating palpitating fear that it might get out, that the world might discover what she was doing? What about that? What about the fact that every time she went out on a gig she was almost disabled by fear, had the most gritted teeth and a painfully clenched stomach – every single solitary time. It wasn't fun at all, she would whisper to Peter, in her bed, on those afternoons when she had to buckle down to calming his own rotten jealousies.

Just very occasionally, her claim that the whole operation was hugely less than fun would be a slightly whitish lie. Like the German on the Tuesday after the awful Graham Cunliffe. If he had not turned out to be such a gentleman, she guessed that she would not have persevered and that would have been that. But after the Cornwallis Hotel experience, he had been *ausgezeichnet* – the German word he had used to describe her – 'excellent'. What a godsend that had been. Or what a disaster, as sorting him out rather effectively in his narrow double bed that evening had meant that she had found the resolution to keep on with the business.

He had been a doddle. She had been dead lucky. He had been so kind and charming over the dinner-table. He was a very distinguished-looking, grey-haired, bearded family man from Düsseldorf. He had been living in London for about six months, a 'fixer' for Nord Deutsche Rundfunk, the television company. She had been pretty frightened, for a while, that he might know Peter, but in fact he didn't seem to know too many newspaper people. He wasn't really lonely as there was quite a busy German media social scene, but there wasn't any sex involved as everyone was so settled. His own family had stayed in Germany with his wife, because they were all at crucial stages with their schooling. She came over every six weeks or so and he said he missed her.

He spoke perfect, very grammatical English. He showed her pictures of his three grown-up rather punk-looking children and asked her with such appealing diffidence if she would like to come back to have an aperitif with him at his flat in Barton Street. He had a small semi-basement flat tucked just behind Westminster Abbey.

They sat either side of his dark Victorian fireplace with the gas-effect flames flickering on their faces, sipping their drinks, talking about his children's achievements at tennis and their liking for strange noisy music. If he noticed she had the trace of a foreign accent, he didn't query where she came from. Anyway, she toned it down a fair bit for the evening. He didn't ask her very much about herself at all. He didn't seem to want to know. There were some long silences but, on the whole, they had felt moderately easy together.

When Big Ben struck midnight it sounded as if it was in his living room with them.

'You are such an attractive young woman, I am honoured to have spent such a delightful evening with you,' Dieter said. 'Would you do me the honour of sleeping with me?'

'Of course. I'd like to do that very much,' she replied, not showing a flicker of nerves.

'Let me just sort out some money, put out the cat and put on the electric blanket,' he said quietly, and he did. When they had finished their drinks, they went into the bedroom at the back and they quietly and almost formally undressed one another and got under his duvet. He was surprised that she kissed him on the mouth; he said normally they didn't. She thought she preferred it, really, where the fella was nice enough. It went fine. She was so relieved by how OK it was that she was able to do quite a big number for him. To her total astonishment, this exercise resulted in her actually climaxing herself. She was extremely shocked by this. Later, she supposed that in a funny way she was also fairly pleased. It was definitely a bonus. A gratuity. It seemed to have just been a matter of properly getting into it. She remembered that she always used to reckon she could actually get very wet just cuddling a pillow, if she allowed herself to.

And so from that night on, Natasha began her career as a working girl.

Of course trade came and went. Sometimes nothing happened for a few days and then, in the space of half an hour, she would get three calls for the same Saturday. Every gig she did made her dreadfully wary, but she also felt a deal of satisfaction in earning her menfolk some more ready cash. Throughout a gig she would find it impossible to relax. All night long, her heart would be in her mouth – quite apart from the other things that had to be placed there in the course of her duties. She got to learn a hell of a lot about men and sex, very quickly. How, very often, they matched her in their fear. How much good-old-fashioned chauvinism, how much bravura, how much cruelty needed to be catered for. What astonished her particularly was how much infantilism and regression lurked behind those apparently unflappable elderly male exteriors. It was a wonder how many of them finally confessed that, most of all in the world, they wanted to be ordered about and slapped like babies. And allowed to suck a teat.

While she began to be able to manage some aspects of it with reasonable aplomb, she was always much more frightened than she could ever confess to Peter. Certain things made even a tough little cookie like Natasha quake inside. She always experienced the keenest, most desperate vulnerability every time she found herself completely naked on her back, on some mattress, with her legs enfolding some new, complete stranger's, embrace. She would feel that her very core, her soul was being invaded and opened up for inspection. It was the one part of it that she always really loathed. And tried to avoid. She discovered, early on, that with a pile of flattery, some filthy-minded chat and quick fingers, she could do one heck of a lot with a guy without getting into any of that.

It was actually often devastatingly quick – the fella would have been getting steamed up, ready to come with her all evening long. At work, Natasha would think of herself as 'going to market' from the moment she met the john. For Harriet, this would mean the vivacious Ms Ivanov at her most flirtatious and intimately arousing. She would let the hip motion flow, look them deeply in the eyes, dispense some more of their wine for them, pout them a mute kiss across the table, place their fingers on her thigh – gross stuff, but it paid dividends in the sex stakes afterwards. Later, all she had to do was hit the right buttons and allow it to happen. That was always the safest and easiest gig. There was never too much fuss once they'd come. And no one could argue that she hadn't done a good job. They would both have the evidence.

It often felt rather like therapy. Harriet thought she could enlist as a kind of sexual social worker, on the State. The boss of a Midlands travel firm, with whom she lunched meagrely at Carlengio's in Bond Street before he knocked her off on the floor of his father's bathroom one hot afternoon in Islington, told her he would never dream of going out with anyone except escorts. After a fairly taciturn afternoon, once he'd shot his load, he got astonishingly talkative. He tucked himself into a dressing gown, allowed her to shower in the same recently very noisy bathroom, and diligently made her a post-coital pot of herbal tea. He claimed he was a widower. He was most anxious not to get emotionally entangled 'with any young lady'.

He told her that it was such an astonishing release for him, 'in this day and age', to be able to express his lust for a sexy girl without forever looking over his shoulder wondering if anyone was going to call him a sexist shit, or summon him to arbitration for harassment. 'It's not as easy as it was, being a man. So I just buy into knowing exactly where I stand.' And he laughed pleasantly, happily watching her towelling herself in the wreckage of his bathroom.

Occasionally she didn't get anywhere near the sex. Some of them were oafs, just plain vulgar, or pathetically bad-mannered. She quickly realised that if she was, let's say, with a john who needed to talk about what he called her 'minge' at the dinner table, he would, like as hell, have no judgment or manners when it came to bedtime either. So she would go home. There would always be someone else in a day or two's time, so why worry? If there was the tiniest sniff of uncertainty, or the smallest suspicion of danger by the time they had got to the profiteroles, she would sling her hook after the three hours purchased and go back to Blackheath on the train – to have an early night in her own, not too complicated, bed.

In the main, it was bearable if she kept her wits about her all the time. She watched the ways that doors were fastened, she always knew exactly where she had placed her clothes, and in what order.

Harriet's Natasha found that she was able to tell each and every john that he, and he alone, was something really special. She even amused herself by repeating the precise self-same words, evening after evening. It was a little private joke. Something to amuse herself with during the long watches of the evening. And she would receive such simple happiness in response. She knew it was fairly cynical of her but it gave her a subtext that helped pass the time. And, after all, the punters were getting their valued reassurance. How badly they all needed to hear it. How easily they believed it. And how well they paid her for it.

Gig after gig, Natasha would interrupt serious concentrated bonking to gasp breathlessly, with a look of sheer delight on her face: 'Christ, Bernard, but you are really something special, you know that? With you it's just so really special. God you're good. So big! I knew you'd be special. And I'm not speaking entirely without experience!' And they swallowed the line, rod and all. They adored knowing that they and they alone were somehow different, that for her this moment with them was somehow spectacular. That for her and with her, they surmounted all others. All she had to do the following night, to maintain her own private underlying entertainment, was slot the name 'Eddie' (or whatever), into precisely the same enthusiastic encouragement instead of the previous night's 'Bernard'.

It was difficult not to get a little cynical as you discovered how similar everybody was in thought and deed and in what they wanted. Nightly, the conversations with the johns swung unerringly along the same old grooves. They all wanted to ask the universal question: 'Wot's-a-nice-girl-like-you-doing-etcetera-etcetera-etcetera?' And Natasha would grin frankly and tell them that she needed the money for her dream cottage on the Backs at Cambridge. And she would tell them how much she loved the sex. They all simply doted on that. Laid them to waste. Easy.

She didn't love it. It was wearisome and endless and frightening. If anyone goes out with someone for the first time, it's pretty hard work if you don't really hit it off. Natasha went out with everyone for the first and, very often, for the only time. And if it had been Harriet at the table, she wouldn't have hit it off. Their attitudes, their philosophies of life and their aspirations all stank. Not that Harriet herself really had a philosophy of life. But if you'd been conditioned by the patented Pete Holloway Peckham-born outlook on the world, for all of ten years, you knew well enough that theirs stank.

To start with, she grabbed every call that came along. After the first three months, she began to ration herself, refusing to work on some Mondays and Tuesdays and she would take some five days off during the time of her period. It was hard work. When she went out, it was a ten-hour day. She would start by going to the gym at four in the afternoon and usually finish by tumbling into her sleeping-bag at Flitcroft Mews at about two in the morning. And every minute, in between those hours, was filled with watchful sensitive accommodating activity. There were still men that she needed to suss out and decline in good time, who would have wanted to kill their wives, or tear the face off their mothers, by hurting and humiliating her. Then there were taciturn factory owners who wanted to suck her knickers, professional cricketers who wanted to lick chocolate-spread out of her fanny. There was the nice elderly Coventry optician who laid out stockings, padded bra and suspenders on his bed – for himself to wear. She could still hear Natasha saying to him, delighted, after he had put them on – 'Paul, you look adorable.'

151

And there were guys who just wanted to talk. Men who wanted to moan about their lot, their wives, their kids, the boss, the system, their first headmaster and the fact that their car needed a service. Blokes who weren't sure if they might be gay. Blokes who needed to go off and ring their wives twice in mid-session. The tiny man who claimed that he was a Pakistani prince and who insisted she insert her high heel into her vagina while he, incredibly, gave himself fellatio – doubling up in a ball on the floor to suck his own cock.

She would get home for a late breakfast. She would spend the day doing housewifely, motherly stuff in her jeans and sweatshirt with her hair anyhow, together with her lovely boys and with Peter, if they could prise him away from his word-processor. Then, if she had a booking, after the gym and the pool she would hit the trail to town. She would try to meet the guy at eight, normally in one of the more salubrious wine-bars, thus avoiding running the gamut of a mansion. Eight o'clock allowed her time to get into the war-paint, don the gear, deduct the wedding ring, insert the cap and summon Ms Ivanov. Her three-hour official slot would then finish at 11 p.m. That meant that if nothing else was on the cards, she could catch a last evening train back to Blackheath. If more was on offer, she could usually reckon to get away with a discreet exit at something like 2 p.m. to the waiting Taxi A Go Go, usually with the trusty Melvyn, who would arrive in the nick of time, comically panting at the wheel.

And Melvyn was a godsend. He would come and pick her up from the weirdest of addresses. And he never showed any surprise or made any comment on her activities. She would make middle-of-the-night exits from the crash doors at the back of the Esplanade Hotel in Tutton Street, or pop up from among the laurels in the front-garden of a house in Potters Bar, or appear from the shadows of a skip in Queens Gate and he would say 'Evenin', Natasha.' And not another word, if it seemed that she didn't want to talk. Or he would tell her about Millwall Football Club. At length.

And then there were those nights when the complications of her escape from the mansion-in-question, when the thought of her depressing white-washed accommodation off the Charing Cross Road, or when the john himself was pleasant enough, meant she would fail to get out of bed at all. At seven in the morning she would wake to find herself still warmly kipping away next to someone whose name now escaped her. It was much more difficult to be Natasha when she was waking up in the morning. She would usually have to pay the forfeit of having to do a number with the guy, before she could go off for breakfast, but that was often easier than leaving him at one in the morning. And very occasionally a good bit nicer. Quite apart from additionally earning herself something more than extra pin-money.

She certainly couldn't tell Peter everything. A lot of it she needed to keep to herself. Sometimes, anyway, he didn't ask for a few days. But then he would get devilishly inquisitive again, his eyes would take on a wicked gleam and he would sit on the edge of her bath and press her for details.

And she would tell him, because Peter seemed to need it so very much, but she did occasionally find herself despising him for his hunger for dirty secrets. Even so, there were moments when his roguish good humour got the better of her, and she could quite enjoy teasing his wicked tubby libido with a little light-hearted fantasy, or even, very occasionally, with a goodly version of the truth. She was shocked by her enjoyment of her power over him. Maybe this is what they had been drawn together for, all those years ago? Maybe they had been uniquely selected to fit together by the Devil Himself, because they were so intriguingly and ideally suited? Even so it was very exposing because it was Harriet, in the daytime, who would have to tell him about the messy, embarrassing, pathetic and extravagant things that Natasha would find herself having to do in the night. He could never seem to understand her very real need to keep that vital separation. And, of course, she could never ever allow him to know the truth about those very occasional times when Natasha seemed to enjoy herself more than she should.

She discovered that it was perfectly possible for her, on occasion, to reach a decent enough orgasm if she allowed herself to. And that was often the only way to manage what would otherwise be incredibly dull and unattractive prospects. She would fill her head with very rude images of Jimmy Nail and Liam Neeson and Micky Rourke and she would moan and squeal and gasp and swear and sweat and bounce and, lo and behold and astonishing to relate – bingo! Mostly, of course, there was nothing doing. She was much too tired or bored, or sexually closed down. But there were, amazingly, a few times when it worked. Then it seemed like a fair exchange for the ever-present dread – getting really high on herself. And it helped to pass the time. It was something to do while you were hanging around.

Neighbours in Blackheath were fascinated by the fact that she had this night-time job. She found she was forever in the greengrocer's queue, explaining to people like Mrs Stoner the range and importance of her night-time librarian's work with – what was it? – C.P.E.M. And the kids seemed to be fixated on this new element in their lives – 'Mum having a job'. Jonty, particularly, was always keen to hear further tales of office culture – it's humour and tragedy. One morning she had quickly invented Penny and Janet and Max with whom she worked – and, randomly, Penny's unhappiness with her live-in boyfriend. From there on in, Jonty was always coming up, over the cornflakes, with questions like: 'How's Lazlo getting on with Penny now?' And she had to remember where they had got to in her ever more complex fictitious office soap-opera. She reckoned she really ought to start a notebook in order to help get the facts right, and keep their stories on course.

'I thought you said she was dark-haired, like you, Mum,' he would say, bemused. And Harriet would have to give a long account of Penny's mismanagement of hair-colouring systems.

'Why don't you ask them over to supper one weekend?' Jonty would ask of Penny and her fella, ever hopeful of being a kind of little boy Good Fairy and helping to cement their rocky relationship more firmly. Somewhat foolishly she said she would see if she could. She was getting into deep play-acting waters here. She could see herself having to ask Daisy or someone to impersonate these figments of her imagination and turn up for supper one night. What a tangled web we weave.

Complicated though it might be, she found she didn't mind lying to the boys like this. In fact the more she did so, the more complex her invention, the more she felt that her work at C.P.E.M. was almost a reality. In the comfort and security of her Blackheath kitchen, mixing batter for waffles or planning the weekend's activities for young lads, she needed to feel a hundred miles away from Natasha. Harriet Holloway worked for C.P.E.M. It was someone else, someone called Natasha Ivanov, who groaned lasciviously underneath naked motor show executives.

On the whole, the constant pressure of her work meant that she and Peter, as a number, began to take a bit of a back-seat. If your job consists of endless, meaningless chat, dealing with man's self-delusion and deceit, accommodating the gamut of human foibles, and fucking, there is only so much the human mind and constitution can manage. And she couldn't bear to get to a stage where she had to grit her teeth to have an encounter with her own husband, so most of the time she relied on a certain friendly affection to carry them through.

Actually, as long as she told Peter intimately enough that she loved him and took a reasonable amount of time to jerk him off, he didn't seem too bothered by their lack of congress. There were the odd really puzzling times when she couldn't make the separation and he seemed more like a john than she cared to let on even to herself. But he never knew.

They were just beginning to be able to pay their way. Peter had had a piece published for the first time in yonks. Jonty broke the swimming club's long-standing under-eleven breast-stroke record at the September gala. And the summer sun was going to go on forever. It was just so wonderful that, at last, they could almost begin to enjoy it a bit. Yet, of course, it wasn't by any means brilliant all the time. There were days when she had no calls at all and thought she would never hear her phone ring again. And there were days when she wished to God she didn't have to do this, when every prospective evening had the tension of a West End press night but with the additional frisson of actual potential danger.

And there were astonishing things at home, like her eldest brimming over with tears at breakfast when she told him at last that thanks to her Trojan efforts, he could go back to Goldings after all. Please please please could he not go to Goldings, he cried. He wanted to go to Darren's school. Please please please. Darren, the captain of his junior swimming team at Greenwich baths, was Jonty's summer role-model. She and Peter calmed the boy down and said maybe. They would go and look at it anyway – James Brookfields School. That might be one problem out of the way. At least, Harriet's bank manager thought it was OK, didn't she?

And, on top of all this, she hadn't forgotten that she still had a private arrangement outstanding with Peter's best friend. He had been summer-holidaying – sailing off St Lucia with friends and his two sons – so he would, no doubt, reckon he had two months' credit to come, now he was back. She would have to deal with all that as well. Oh God.

*   *   *

Wednesday, 1 September.

Ellen rang. I was mightily surprised. And inordinately pleased. And fairly fed up with myself for being so inordinately pleased. She had seen my thing in the *Statesman*. Ellen said she 'wanted to pick my brains'. I said I could try and fit her in, on the morrow, between my many high-flown assignments (Tescos and discovering what it is that we suspect Starfire has hidden in the cellar). So I hit the Land of Gridlock early yesterday morning.

Ellen suggested we meet in Battersea, in the Stalker's Hide, a somewhat world-weary pub just opposite the Arts Centre and miles from her usual spheres of influence. And ridiculously tricky to reach from tubeless South-East London. She said she had a meeting there before lunch. So anyway, I trotted off, all chuffed and obedient-like, and reasonably uncomplaining. I was really absurdly interested in wanting to see her again.

Seemed to me that it was actually her day off, as she was dressed right down in jeans and sweater and a dashing little suede waistcoat – quite a tasty looking lady, nevertheless. I splashed ten-pound notes about in the old style and did the honours. God, it made me feel so much better than that awful previous time when all my pockets contained was pocket.

We chatted away about what a summer it was being – little does she know. And then she began to give me the eighth degree about my sources for the vice piece. She wouldn't really say what it was for, so I was pretty cagey. She went on and on about how many women I'd talked to, and pimps and so on. Well it was slightly difficult to be terribly expansive as I'd only really talked to that Pamela and to my good wife. We fenced about. She was so eager, that for a moment I had this manic vision that she was thinking of going on the game herself. It felt like she had some sort of hidden agenda and for a while I couldn't make out what it was.

Then it all came a lot clearer. We risked some of the pub's shepherd's pie. And then, suddenly, Mrs Herbert looked as though she was going to blub. I was terribly reassuring and fatherly and rushed off to get some more comforting alcohol to pour down her sweet little throat.

And it all comes tumbling out. She's stopped screwing Michael Stainton. He's gone back to his rotten old family (anyway he was impotent, she said – and, well, what a delightfully heart-warming piece of news that was), but, what was a great deal worse, she and hubby Andrew Herbert have fallen out – I think only temporarily, actually. An archetypal run-o'-the-mill media mess. Anyway she's moved out and is living, at the moment, in a flat that belongs to her sister (who's in the States) *just around the corner* (exclamation marks to the power of ten!!!!!!!). And so, all of a sudden, a brilliant clarity shone upon the scene. And, naturally enough, we repaired to inspect her temporary accommodation. To have a spot of coffee. Of course.

And then her motivation got rather more obscure again, as Ellen got pretty agitated, asking about H. Maybe it was I who got agitated. Whichever, I was plied with a hefty interrogation as to what my wife was doing dressed up to the nines, some ten days ago in the foyer of the New London Theatre (is it? Anyway, that dreadful lecture hall that masquerades as a theatre) going to see *Cats*. Harriet was espied by Ellen Herbert herself, accompanying Ron Easterbrook, the vice-president of the print union UPGA. 'Looking absolutely scrumptious too, curse her. You're a lucky man, Peter. I'm surprised you should need to put yourself about at quite the rate you do.' I ignored this. Of course, Harriet hadn't told me that she had had to pay the penance of a Lloyd–Webber – is there no sacrifice H. will not undertake? We didn't solve the equally absorbing topic as to what Ellen herself was doing mixing with the plebs and the Japs there either. I said Ron Easterbrook was Harriet's uncle. It did the trick.

Ellen's sister's flat was a tiny box of a space with a nice bay window and a lot of that plain black-shelves-and-grey-walls decoration that made it look like the waiting room of a small up-and-coming PR company. I guessed that some up-and-coming was reckoned to be on the agenda for that afternoon's plenary. There was that smoke-screen rattle of coffee cups and the determined crushing of the coffee bean that attends these post-prandial rituals. And Ellen is such a honey and I couldn't help remembering that she gives as good as she gets. She's got eyes to die for and breasts like half-bricks tucked away under the gentle exuberance of her Tibetan sweater.

I guessed that she had decided that she needed a decent reaffirmation of her desirability and some overall general comforting. And I had been resurrected as the man best suited to fulfil this mission.

I am astonished to say, in spite of the fact that it was all there for the asking, poured out in a coffee mug as it were, I couldn't lap it up! Truthfully, for once it needn't have been a grim and dirty secret either. After all, there's my wife screwing strangers some three or four nights or so a week – she couldn't very easily have got very stroppy about a tipsy moment with an old friend from the office, could she?

But it was not on. I'm not quite sure I understand why, either. We juggled coffee cups and sugar spoons and then we got into a little mutual mouth-to-mouth resuscitation. But I just didn't have the will to take it any further. Perhaps this truly is my middle-aged menopause in reverse. She sniffled and her shoulders heaved. I held on to her firmly and stroked her head and said things like: 'Dear Ellen. Sweet, dear Ellen.' She felt warm and moist and larger than I remembered. I suppose the only woman I've held on to recently has been H. and she feels taut as a coiled whipped steel and now makes the very word 'slim' seem fat. You can wrap your arms four times round H. and have wrists to spare. So I took the po-faced way out, saying garbage like: 'Look, my darling, you're upset and this isn't a good idea for you just at the moment.' She said: 'Yes, it is. It's what I want. I've so missed you, Peter.' And that was just a killer. I mean how can you resist that? But I did. I fucking did! And after a while, E. began to realise that I wasn't going to come across and she began to unpick herself from my person and refreshed our damned boring coffee mugs yet again and we finished up sitting at the extreme opposite ends of the sofa being ever-such-good-old-friends.

Why?

I didn't know at the time. But it's because of H. I think. For all her adult life – after all, I virtually plucked her out of nursery school – dear trusty old H. has always been there. She was my right-hand woman, for God's sake. Trust her with your life. All of a sudden, she has this other extraordinary life. She has found the bottle to do these astonishing things – I mean, I couldn't have done any of that. And, worst of all, I detect in her a kind of mysterious Mona Lisa smile. Harriet seems, in the last two months, to have become the mistress of a wry shrewdness that I don't recognise in her at all. And I sometimes feel so excluded by it. I'm scared that I'm getting very slightly obsessed by her. Because, all of a sudden, she seems as if she could just float off out of my reach. She has these hidden secret places that I know next to nothing about. And it means that she is beginning to fascinate me in a way that I think I might regret. And for once in my life I didn't think I wanted to risk a flutter. Funny, eh?

So Ellen and I slurped yet more Kenyan breakfast beans instead. Then, as she began, to summon up a fair bit of loathing for P. Holloway Esquire, a touch more subtext arrived:

'What do you know of a Ms South, Peter?' she asked archly (I think 'archly' rather than 'acidly', at this stage – it got to 'acidly' later on. It even just about touched on: 'barbed'!).

'South? Dunno. Never heard of her. Don't think so. Who she?'

It appears that a Ms South had turned up at *The Chronicle* building asking for a Deputy Editor by the name of Holloway. She had been fobbed off by Security who said I was yesterday's man and that I didn't work there any more, hadn't for decades. Well, blow me down, this Ms South reckoned that this Holloway character owed her money, had bounced a cheque on her. Christ. She left a card with reception. And E. had it. She gave it to me. It was my own old *Chron.* card. On the back in neat green ink capitals were the words: 'You owe me, fuck you, Holloway! Pay up or I'll spill the beans about your drugs, vice and currency laundering rings!' It was signed 'Pamela' and there was her phone number.

'No idea,' I said unconvincingly. 'Some crackpot.' Had Ellen rung the number? I pocketed the card. 'Who knows?' I muttered.

'She on the game, Peter?' Ellen asked. Had she rung her? God knows.

'I've no idea who she is.' I would ring Pamela and say how sorry I was and ask her if Ellen had rung her.

I was bloody confused by then as to who knew how much about what. So as soon as it was reasonably feasible, I took myself off – a chastened and, indeed, a seriously surprised man.

I sat on the train and thought it all through on the way back to Blackheath. I came to the conclusion, in the end, that no one could know very much, could they? The fact that I'd interviewed Pamela was a given, considering the *Statesman* piece. You could interview a whore without it ever suggesting you were about to put your wife on the game, couldn't you? I didn't need to worry.

I continued to debate with myself, as the train hesitated its way above the black back-gardens of New Cross, as to why I had inexplicably declined the suddenly available Mrs Herbert. It's to do with this awful thing between me and H. That's all I can guess at. I'm entirely in its grip – this impossibly dirty frightening secret the two of us have from the world. Now, today, if ever I need her to, Harriet is prepared to fill my sodding voyeuristic brain with pulsating pictures of such sick delight. It appears that I don't want to sully that with anything else with anybody else, however potentially sexy that might just turn out to be. I may be mad. Yes, I think I am mad. I certainly may have made an enemy in Ellen.

Got home. And there, would you believe, is TLS vaulting down our stairs. He'd lost his way to our loo. He was in Blackheath picking up a case of vino from Casements in the Village. He gave us a couple of bottles too. Very jolly to see him. H. made us all tea in the kitchen. She looked scrummy in her black tights. The boys had got 'Ninja Turtles – The Wilderness Years' or something from the video shop. A little panic-striken moment when Harri's Motorola phone decided to ring with Toby looking on in an interested way. She had to swan off out of the French windows and down the lawn to talk without being overheard. It would seem to appear that, these days, Harriet gives great phone but needs a modicum of privacy in which to do it. I covered this incident by noisily getting the ancient croquet set out and challenging TLS to a grudge match.

We had a tenner on it. H. and Toby versus me and Jonty. Timothy, furious at being left out, had a really big shout. Balmy evening but no contest, I fear. Jonty really can't play, so however hard I worked at it, we finished up five hoops down. It took forever. J. may swim like a nine-year-old Duncan Goodhew but he's lousy with a ruddy mallet. I got a tad pissed off and TLS was well amused. Anyway I paid them a fiver each – Toby saying: 'Nice to have at least that little something over you, Pete, old man.'

Toby and I talked about our annual climbing weekend, before Christmas. For seventeen years now, he and I have escaped to the hills, most years, at the end of the Michaelmas term. So that when the shops and media are all Wenceslassing their way unerringly towards the Big Yule, we can turn a blind eye for three days. Thank God, that in spite of everything and to my epic astonishment, I'm going to be able to go to Wales again this December, after all.

Actually TLS hung around forever. Which was useful, in point of fact, as there was swimming for J. at the Greenwich Swimming Club and Toby took all of us there and back, squeezed into his ancient C-type Jag with the lid off. Bit of a treat as it very rarely comes out of its garage. H. wasn't very well in the evening. She left the pools and had to go and sit in the car until J. had finished.

Didn't tell her about Pamela. I'll keep it to myself and send the woman a really big fat cheque. That should keep her trap shut.

*   *   *

For Harriet, the previous day had begun with something of a shock. They had all been in the kitchen having breakfast when the house phone had rung.

'Harriet, my darling.' It was Toby's voice growling at her intimately from the earpiece. She pressed it firmly as possible into her ear to avoid the sound of his voice leaking into the room.

'Hullo, Mummy.' She squeaked brightly, quaking inside.

'Is he there? Brilliant. Well, Harriet, you owe me, my dear. What are you going to do about it?'

'How's Daddy?'

'Well done, little Harriet, can we make a date? I'd quite enjoy setting something up with dear old Peterkins actually sitting there alongside you, all uncomprehending.'

'Listen, this line is just terrible, Mum. Can I ring you back in a wee while?'

'All right, coward, ring me back. Ring me at the office. But do it before lunch, lovey. Pete has got the number. You'll have to sneak a clandestine peek at his phone book, won't you?' And he rang off. Harriet then continued to improvise some moderately effusive dialogue about a neighbour of her parents in Edinburgh, who was recovering from some non-specific illness or other. Finally, she rang off, promising the silent phone that she would ring back 'when Daddy's got back'. She was sure that she was blushing to the roots of her hair. Her trio of menfolk did not seem to notice her confusion at all. Well, at least she hadn't spoken broad Ivanov-speak. That would have confused absolutely everyone, including herself. It would have been a possibility; after all, Toby was just a john.

But a complicated and difficult john. Later, when Peter had gone off to meet with 'that Ellen' who had called and wanted him to do lunch with her, Harriet had called Toby at his fearsome offices.

There were a thousand minions and haughty secretaries to plough through before you got to speak to the great white chief himself. Why couldn't he fuck one of them, she had thought to herself irritatedly, instead of wanting action with her? Because none of them had asked him for a cool five grand, she reminded herself, as she waited.

'Harriet.'

'I'm sorry, Toby, I couldn't really talk to you before. I was surrounded by my menfolk. I'm on my own now.'

'Is he away all day?'

'Yes.'

'I'll come over.'

'Toby, you can't come over here. I've got the boys here. Anyway, I don't want to do it here.'

'Listen to me, my dear Harriet. We did a deal. I seem to remember we shook on it. You said once a month, anywhere, any time. I promised I wouldn't bother you for a while. But then I would call. Well that was me, calling. I want it now. And I really want it there. Stash the boys somewhere, there's a love. You want to be a business woman of note, I'm sure you wouldn't let such a minute thing stand in your way. I'm sure I don't need to tell someone as bright as you that you have to look after your major investors. Your only investor, I would imagine.'

'Toby, listen, my dear, we could go to a hotel. It's always so marvellously sexy in a hotel, don't you think? And I haven't had a good raunchy time in a hotel for years. That would be such a turn-on, wouldn't it? A really good hotel. Oh yeah – M.T.V., acres of white bath towel, king-sized bed, lashings of room service. God, yes, that would be really such good fun. I bet. I can't wait.' She was blathering, dreadfully.

'Harriet, my dear, don't you dare sell me short. There could be trouble. I know absolutely precisely what I bought. I bought Peterkin's wife. I bought Peterkin's wife, exactly when and where I want her. Available to me, any time. And I want it now. I want her in Peterkin's bed. Today.' He was speaking very quietly and firmly. 'I hope you're not going to mess me about, Harriet. As I expect you can imagine, Harriet, I've an aversion to being messed about. I could get angry. I wouldn't like that. And, I'm afraid, neither would you.'

'OK.' She could put the boys next door with Marianne. 'OK, what time?' Peter was bound to be away until about four at the earliest.

'I'll be there at one-thirty. Don't change the sheets.' And he'd put the phone down. She was once more alone in her kitchen. He was hateful. When he was Peter's avuncular toffee-nosed affable friend from decorous Dulwich, he had been just about bearable. He was quite, quite different now she was trying to work this out with him. It was horrid. She was going to hate all this. He was worse than the johns, because he was reaching out and touching her family.

Appallingly, Marianne turned out not to be at home. Harriet hared down to the Village and got the kids a video from the Blackheath video emporium and secretly checked the locking mechanism and the availability of the key for the living-room door. She did change the sheets. She felt a lot better for having disobeyed him.

At quarter past one, she started the film off for the two boys, prettied herself up – wise-dazzling-house-wife-and-mother image – and had a stiff vodka and orange. He finally arrived at ten past two, the sod.

She surreptitiously locked the boys into the living room and took him and his proffered champagne up to the bedroom. She'd guessed he'd be rough and of course he stank of cigars – well his clothes did. There really wasn't time enough for her to go through a nervous-house-wife-who-has-never-done-anything-like-this-before rigmarole. So she tackled him a bit like an ordinary john. Not absolutely as up-front and dirty, and without the accent of course, but it cut corners and took less time. She knew he was somewhat surprised. At one stage he growled, 'I can see you've done this before, you delightfully filthy little scamp.' He wanted to damage her clothes and she had to do everything in her power to avoid him hurting her with his big hands. She compromised by letting him tear and rip off her knickers. Oh yes, he thought that was just the business – loved it! Well, they do – the Life was costing her a fortune in underwear. Thank God for Knickerbox.

'I'm not wearing that,' he said when she produced the condom. She laughed and said: 'Oh yes you are, Mr Man!'

'I'm much too big for one of those.' And he was a very big boy.

'Now don't be naughty. You've no idea where I've been, Toby. Be sensible. No condom, no cunt. And you'll love my wet little pussy. It's aching for it.' She said all the usual malarkey. She put it on quite quickly after that.

He came, seconds after he was in her, shouting 'Oh, God, yes. Right up her. Having Peterkin's little wife! Peterkin's cunt! In Peterkin's bed! Right up!' God knows if the kids heard. The whole thing, start to finish, had taken some thirteen minutes. She had absolutely loathed, detested, doing it in her bed. Throughout the business, she had watched Pete's clock-radio resolutely, continually calming herself with the thought that Peter couldn't be back in the next quarter of an hour, surely, could he?

He was pathetic, was Toby. And he was going to be Big Trouble. She mopped up and dressed and left him snoozing with his size thirteen feet sticking out of the end of the bed from under the duvet. The boys hadn't stirred, they were completely transfixed by the film's closing moments of mayhem and destruction, with the sound, which she had cranked up good and proper, still at ear-drum piercing level.

It was a damned close run thing. She was only able to check the bedroom and re-make the bed after Peter had actually returned home and was guffawing with his best chum, over some wine in the kitchen.

She rather thought that Peter would probably guess something, but he never mentioned anything. He got everyone playing croquet out on the lawn and then got miffed because his side lost badly. Toby, who was her partner in the game, insisted on helping her running her hoops with the mallet, by putting his great arms around her from behind, in front of Pete. She could feel him gently pressing his cock at her bum. What a bastard!

Later, Peter said that it was odd that Toby had bothered to go with all of them to the Arches to watch Jonty swim. Harriet knew perfectly well that the man was just getting off on being around his 'best friend', having had knowledge, that very afternoon, of his best friend's wife in Peter's own marital bed. For thirteen titchy little minutes. In their heads, men really are all such tiny little boys.

At the pools, one of the parents from the rival Bromley Swimming Club gave her such a stare. She suddenly realised that she thought he might just have been a punter, a john that she had seen very early on, in a penthouse flat in the Barbican. She wasn't quite sure. But it was possible, and he went on looking at her. She arranged for a quick migraine to come on, and went and sat in the car till the whole thing had splashed itself to an end.

Earlier in the evening, before all this, before they had all roared across the Heath in the Lydell–Smith show-off-type Jag, Harriet had had a call from Daisy, of all people, on her Motorola. Would Harriet possibly be interested in one of those celebrated 'doubles'? 'This evening – well, one in the morning – Pimlico?' Daisy laughed. 'Rich Egyptians. A load of spondulicks, darling.' She went on: 'Enough for a couple of trips to the Caribbean. What do you think? It's a dead easy way of making a load of coin. And quite friendly.'

Harriet stood in the dying light, on the now almost autumnal lawn of her garden where she had trotted out to take the call privately, away from the men. She couldn't see herself doing it. 'Not doubles.

Sorry. I don't think I'm up to that yet,' she squeaked, ashamed at her lack of bottle.

She realised that Toby had strolled across the grass towards where she was. He seemed to like hanging around her. Harriet wished Daisy well in her search for a cohort and quickly rang off.

'Doubles?' Toby asked.

'Yes,' she said. 'Tennis. On Sunday. Greenwich Park.'

REAPING IT

Harriet looked perversely clear-eyed and innocent in that great white shirt of mine this afternoon. Nowadays, people turn and look at her all the time: in the Village, out shopping, waiting outside Jonty's school, on the train to town. Men and women as well – I watch them looking at her with what I see as covert admiration. Well, the men look at her with thinly disguised lust, actually. And she's *my* wife. I think it's thrilling. She has this astonishing beautiful dignity. It genuinely made my heart flutter to see her picking up the early fall of chestnuts on the lawn – baggy blue jeans, with her hair piled up like a chocolate-coloured sand castle.

J. insisted, of course, that we had to roast them on the barbecue, so we tipped it up and poured all the water away into the goldfish pond. He and Timothy made a great pile of firelighters in it. They love playing with matches. Oh God, we all do. There were more noxious chemicals and methylated spirits than fire and the burst chestnuts tasted as much of petrol as of anything. But the boys thought it was a great adventure and turned to trying to poison the dog with their cooking, but he wouldn't eat it. He's a survivor, that one.

I watched Harriet in the garden, almost secretly, as she moved about in the blue smoke with the sepia autumn sunlight catching her hair. There she was, a wise, warm, wholesome, pretty mum, telling her boys about the history and traditions of the horse-chestnut. And what had I forced her to tell me about last night? This fresh-faced, beautiful, clean-limbed young woman? I had got her to tell me the history and traditions of last Thursday night at the Connaught Hotel. 'A piece of my clothing for every inch of your zip, Patrick,' she had told the guy. 'Well,' she had murmured provocatively, 'he was into games and challenges. I looked him dead in the eyes and rotated my hips and said disgusting macho competitive things. I suppose I sometimes get a bit of a buzz out of how disgusting I can dare myself to be. Oh, God, they think it's so groovy, getting smut in an educated foreign accent.'

'Like what, like what?' Desperate fevered questions in the tense darkness of our bedroom.

She sighed. 'Oh, I don't know. Tired stuff, I suppose. Oh God, I can't say it in cold blood. It's mortifying stuff to talk about. Filthy chat whispered into big Arab ears, Peter. You can imagine it. It was the usual.'

'Like?'

'Peter! As I say, the usual. About how wonderful they are. How sexy. How strong. And about size. And virility. And how much she loves it – Natasha. How she wants it to go on all night. Basic garbage really, Peter. Big dirty lies to get me out of there and back here. Nothing special, I'm afraid. I'm not always wildly imaginative. You don't really want to hear all this? Isn't this all a bit too much, even for you, Peterkins?'

'No, no,' I said and I was sweating. 'Do you ever think of me? Do you ever think of me. You know, when you're –?'

'No. No, I don't think of anyone. What do I think about when I'm doing it? Oh I don't know. Nothing much – I worry about whether the condom's going to split. All that. I think about, you know, things like Timothy liking playgroup. Whether we've remembered to pay the electricity. I worry about putting on as horny a show as I can. I just want to earn my money as well and as quickly as I can. Mostly it's terribly boring. I think it must be a bit like when people used to play Agatha Christie in weekly rep. – they'd have the devil's own problem getting the lines to sound as if they're anywhere near convincing; it's crashingly dull to play, but it had to be done really professionally or else they didn't get cast again the following week. And, funnily enough, in both cases, the audience always seems to adore it.'

And I sat on the garden wall-seat in the cool sun with them all and watched her cutting the slits in our thin little chestnuts with the old kitchen knife, and I wanted to die. I wanted to keel over and fucking die. What the hell is it with me? Why do I have such a raddled, corrupted, septic brain? There's this pretty, stylish, loving, dedicated young mum, my wife, for God's sake, and I spend my waking hours imagining her in congress, rutting with some fat old git in the honeymoon suite of the Connaught. I invent the idea of her gasping sweatily at him things like: 'Give it to me, give it to me! I so love it!' And I toy with those thoughts endlessly, picking at the scabs of those ideas obsessively, like some deranged perverted masochist. There are times when I can't shift the images out of my brain at all. I want her to do it and I hate her, loathe her, detest her doing it. I want it never to have happened. I can't bloody bear it. I bloody can't bear me. I'm beginning to feel almost suicidal at times. This is almost worse than being broke. But I smile and I'm cool and I carry on and love them all and – and – and – oh Jesus, I want her to tell me more tonight, tonight in bed. If she will. Or not. Probably not. Oh, but yes, I do need to hear more. I want to die. I found myself jabbing the kitchen knife into the side of my leg. Bloody unhinged.

'Who's Sir George Harcourt?' Harriet asked Peter from behind the big rhododendron. They were tidying up the lawn together. Scrape, scrape, scrape went his lawn rake painstakingly across the dark grass. It was sweaty work. Peter was being pretty stalwart, she thought. The autumn leaves were going into big black plastic bags. The Blackheath Drive garden – apart from the boys, it was their best bit. They probably liked the communal husbandry of doing the garden together almost more than they actually liked one another, sometimes. It was good to see Starfire being really helpful as usual – pooing on those parts of the lawn they had finished.

'George Harcourt? Why?'

'I don't know. It was just a name I saw. I've done a couple of gigs with this guy who's got a big house by the river at Maidenhead. I think he's a kind of Sir Harold Appleby fella. You know – like they have in "Yes, Minister"?'

'"Humphrey Appleby".'

'All right, clever dick. Anyway, he's a civil servant, is what I mean. He took me to the opera. *Philip Glass*. Hell's teeth, it was boring. I think he just went there to nod at people in the Crush Bar. All very proper. I just had to be attentive, look adoringly at him and wear the backless-from-hell. Anyway, he takes me back to where he lives. With his mother, I think, but she's never there.'

'Surprise me.'

'Anyway, last time – I've been there twice – he looks like he's going to be a regular. It's absolutely bleeding miles – depths of rural England – thank God, he slips me money for the taxi back too. We'd just got back, and he was plying me with this important ancient brandy he was so dead chuffed about. Which I had to dump in his rubber-plants. And he was feeding his cats – clearing the decks, getting ready for action – typical civil servant this, gets his priorities spot-on – so I had a bit of a read of the letters on his desk. Nothing very top secret, I'm afraid. But there was one – from this mate of his: Sir George Harcourt, like I said, complaining that he'd lost out in a battle to secure the services of someone called "Bunter" to edit some new thing he's going to bring out. A publication – *Eleventh Hour*, I think it was called. Who's Sir George Harcourt?'

'Owns Hartbeck Publishing. It's a special interest magazine house – you know, judo, train-spotting, military memorabilia, antiques, sheep-stealing, cunnilingus, the usual things.'

She laughed. 'Ah, you see, I just knew my media-sussed husband would have a handle on it. What's *Eleventh Hour* when it's at home?'

'No idea.'

'Ah, not so media-sussed, after all, eh? Well, there's a thing! Losing your touch eh, Peterkins!' And she yelped and ran off down the lawn as her husband threw half a wheel-barrow load of leaves at her. And fell over the dog.

So H. is jumping famed Sir Walter Burton, eh? God, we're moving up in the world. First it's anonymous insurance executives and public school sports coaches and now it's folk with access to Number Ten! And I always thought he was thought to be a shirt-lifter. Maybe he is and displaying my wife's bosoms to the gentry at the Garden is his bid to prove otherwise. I must ask her whether he was of any significance in bed.

Even so, wonders will never cease. It is absolutely incredible where a determinedly pretty girl with loose knickers can find herself. The Cabinet Office, eh! I just told her to keep her ears open when next she is losing her maidenhood in Maidenhead. Trouble is, with H., she's so unaware of what is useful info and what isn't. She just insisted on passing on to me a lot of guff about the two big ginger cats he's got there, one of whom has the flu at the moment. Not exactly information destined to bring down H.M.G.

I'll ring Hartbeck and see if I can corner George Harcourt – it might be a useful move.

That was such a stupid episode. Last Wednesday evening.

I don't know how much it was my intention to do what I did. I definitely had a perfectly genuine reason for being in town. I had decided to chase up some background on Hartbeck Publishing. H. had a working evening, so we got Helen from round the corner to babysit the progeny. Like all eighteen-year-old kids she's heavily into D. H. Lawrence at the moment but she's got nice hair and the boys like her.

I suppose the notion of what finally happened had been lurking about in my head for a little while. God knows why. Pure purience? Or evidence of my own special, very personal madness.

Anyway, I trotted into Gray's Inn Road to seek out Patrick who used to work at London Bridge, for Hartbeck. We had tea together in his canteen. He was pretty cogent about Sir George, who turns out to be not such a bad old buffer to work for. Which is different to what I had heard.

Then, feeling a decided degree of self-contempt and loathing, I took myself, almost against my will, over to the Charing Cross Road where I squeezed myself into a little table in the window of Valoti's, the Italian café opposite the entrance to Flitcroft Mews. By then it was just past six o'clock. I played around with a couple of cappucinos and kept on telling myself to go home.

But I didn't. As expected, H. came along at about the appointed time – jeans, sweatshirt, sweater knotted around her waist, little rucksack. You wouldn't particularly distinguish her from the rest of the hordes in the Charing Cross Road, except she is surprisingly tall. She was swinging along, relaxed, cool, and protected from the outside world by her personal stereo. Paul Weller, I think, at the moment.

I sat inside the steamy front window of Valoti's and felt execrable. And tense and bothered. And excited. I know my pulse was running. By that time, the staff must have been somewhat puzzled by my monotonous caffeine intake and my strangely solitary vigil.

After about fifty minutes or so, there she was again, turning the corner and heading for Cambridge Circus. A different person. Well, of course she was. And the entirely ghastly thing about it is that I don't know which I like the better – the steady, tomboyish, good chum that I live with in Blackheath or the voraciously sexual vision that had now taken shape and had apparently decided to dispense with the services of a taxi. The first is a proper, lovely, muddled, irritating human being – a companion and a friend. The second is a well-honed product of the male imagination that makes me sweat with a terrible excitement and which I instantly want to possess. And yet I don't possess her. It's dear old Harriet who's my wife. Not Natasha.

It was quite a balmy evening for the time of year. This object of desire – slinky silky Natasha stalked off south, down towards the river. Under the streets lights, with her head held erect, her hair piled high, her heels pricking the pavement, it seemed to me she turned every masculine head all the way down St Martin's Lane. Not cool now – watchful, energised, at work.

She was wearing a light plum-coloured satin trouser suit which entirely failed to hide the delectable shape of her bum, the slant of her thighs and, presumably, if I'd been in front of her, the invitation of her boobs. She had told me about the outfit – Benny Ong, I think. It was a recent buy. I'd never seen it.

I had to assume this was going to be a trick with someone that she had seen before. I think she normally makes it a rule to wear a skirt on a first gig.

I had left Valoti's in something of a lather, holding well back, wondering why I was doing this at all. I had no trouble in following her. She seemed to cause a light ripple of attention all the way along, as she crossed the Strand and walked down to the Savoy Hotel. It certainly wasn't the anonymous, low-profile image that she usually reckoned was favourite for the task in hand.

And that was why I was there, I suppose. All I knew about Natasha is what Harriet allowed herself to tell me. Since that extraordinary night when I had been Roger Conway, I had been obliged to share Harriet's working life only via the over-workings of my imagination and her all too occasional and probably censored reports. And I think I must just have got impatient. I found that I wanted to see Natasha for myself. Again.

I slowed up in the street that runs down to the Savoy. It always reminds me of my dad. He used to tell me countless times that it is the only street in Britain where it is legal for the traffic to drive on the right. He must have told me this over a hundred times in the years before he died. I believe it's so that customers for the hotel can disembark from the right-hand side of their cars.

H. went in through the revolving doors and I hung about in the shadows outside the Savoy Theatre on the right hand side, under the canopy. Looking through the glass at the entrance to the hotel,

I saw a dumb-show of Natasha Ivanov being greeted by a tall, crusty-looking, white-haired man with a moustache who rose from one of the big armchairs in the foyer. She clasped his hand, rose on tip-toe, and kissed him neatly on the cheek. For a moment I could see his big hand silhouetted against the silk of her jacket, holding the small of her back, pulling her body into him. They looked rather elegant together.

They were immediately on the move and disappeared into one of the art-deco lifts. The lift-doors closed.

I knew it was a big mistake to have been there. It would be so much healthier to keep out of this. Put it right to the back of my mind. Tell myself that she just does an office job. C.P.E.M – night shift. I felt great swamping surges of emotion, some of them total wild, physical jealousy and others, well, not good even to write down privately.

I decided I'd better get off and go home. But found I had wandered down the back, behind the hotel in the streets between the Strand and the river – Savoy Hill, I think. The back of the hotel is a thousand windows facing the river, through the trees – reception rooms, kitchens, laundry rooms and bedrooms, bedrooms, bedrooms. A thousand lighted windows ablaze in the dark. It was useless and stupid for me to stand there in the middle of the narrow empty street, wondering behind which of those windows was my wife strutting her stuff. In a minute it would begin to rain and I would become the most pathetic specimen in the whole of London. Talk about: 'Husband To Watch'! Ugh.

So I went and caught the train.

I mustn't do that again. It was a serious mistake.

Interview with Sir George Harcourt at their London Bridge office 11.30 a.m. on Thursday next. He seemed interested. No time to write more here now. I have a stack of research and reading to do. Feeling much better.

Harriet and Peter found themselves making love, that Sunday morning – about a quarter of an hour into the Archers – like thousands of other British couples with children who have been up for hours but who still seem to be nicely hooked on some morning TV cartoon downstairs. It was very nice and relaxed and friendly. Harriet said something encouraging to him. It probably came out a bit pat, but she had meant it – she *was* enjoying it going in and out of her pussy. And so she had said so, without thinking.

'That sounds like I'm a john.'

'Stop it, stupid,' and she kissed him solidly.

'It's the sort of thing you say to a john, isn't it?'

'I say a million things.'

'Well, there you are.'

'Are we doing this, or have we stopped?'

'I'm no more than a john to you.'

'That is so ridiculous. I said it because I meant it. I was enjoying it and I wanted to tell you. I say things to johns because that's my job – nothing more, nothing less. You know perfectly well it's quite different, Peterkins.' He had pulled away from her and was lying with both his hands behind him, grasping the metal of the bed-head, gazing at the ceiling. Sweat had begun to cool on her body. She had better go and have a bath before she got angry.

'I'll pop through and have a wee shower before the boys start dashing about.'

'They're up already. Can't you hear? They've had the box on forever downstairs.'

It was an accusation of poor motherhood. She had better sort this out: 'Listen, my darling, you know what I say to johns doesn't matter. It's not me anyway, it's Natasha, and she is obliged to give them a good time whether she likes it or not. She has to say those things. I don't.'

'Natasha! So she likes it sometimes, does she?'

'That's just a phrase, Peter, you know that.'

'Well?'

'Oh God, man. I think she finds it more bearable on some occasions than on others.'

'God you get off on it, don't you!'

That was enough. Harriet jumped out of bed and struggled to get into her bathrobe – the sleeves of which, of course, were inside out: 'I thought we'd sorted all this out ages ago. Either you want to know about it and can cope with me telling you, or you don't and I'll keep mum and we'll never talk about it. Which is it to be? Come on, Peter, tell me.'

'It kills me, H. It fucking kills me. Every day, my mind swarms with the idea of their hands all over your body, up your body. Quite honestly you've no need to tell me anything any more. I know it all. My mind seethes with it. All the time. I can see it all – you, doing it. My mind teems with pictures of their hands up your skirt in the Dorchester grill, their humping you in the back of their bloody Rollers. I've got a constant sickening bloody video-loop playback in my head of you on your knees in their fucking showers with them. I can't stand it! I just can't stand it. It makes me die. Every minute of every day.'

'Well, you shouldn't have asked, should you!' she screamed at him. 'You said you adored hearing about it. You kept on and on about it. Never stopped. I hated telling you all that stuff, but you begged me to. You said it turned you on so very much. And it did! What was I supposed to do? If I'd said I wouldn't talk to you about it, you'd have said I was keeping it all secret from you, excluding you, not allowing you to be part of me – all that!'

'I know, I know, I did want to know. The idea of wanting to know was exciting for me, desperately important. I thought we would feel like two people against the world, together, you and me. But it's been and gone and done my head in. I now feel that it's you and the johns, sniggering away, against me, the universal cuckold! I just can't bear it. We've got to stop now, before I go completely stark raving round the bend. You mustn't do this stuff any more. Pack it in, love. This is wrong. It's killing me, H.' And he began quietly to cry, muffled, his head buried in the pillow. She knelt back on the bed, near to him, uncertain as to what to say. The Archers prattled on about someone who had fallen off a horse. She put her hand limply on his damp head.

'What are we going to do?' he mumbled. He got to be tragic sometimes. A big, sad, pathetic man, hiding away in a lot of noise. She could hardly recognise him as Peter Holloway at all when he was like this. 'I love you so very much, H. I love you so very much. You are so bloody special and I am so very proud of you – your courage, the way you look, the way you are – I just find it impossible to know that there are piles of other shits who know you and have you, and laugh with you, just like I do.'

'But they don't, pet. They're not important. They don't mean a thing, love. They're just another payment on the car. You're worth thousands and thousands of them.' She was talking very slowly and carefully. 'I've said to you, heaps of times before, Natasha says lines – like in a play – like in an extemporised play. If you're playing Lady Macbeth, you say: "infirm of purpose, give me the daggers" and then you go and smear the grooms' faces with blood in the same bedroom as the murdered king – but you're an actress – you pretend it all. You don't have to be able to be a murderer's accomplice in reality or anything. You just have to act it – really well, so that people think it's true and believe it and feel moved by it. But it isn't true. It's the same with Natasha – she says dirty sexy things to play her role with. If you say something really obscenely filthy, you can normally be out of there in about another half-hour. It doesn't mean more than that.' He had rolled away from her but was listening again. 'I sometimes find myself in there doing stuff with them, thinking really methodically: "in about half a minute I'll say such and such or do such and such and that should finish him off and I could just about get out and catch the last train home – or get Melvyn to pick me up and I can be back here with you lot in Blackheath, instead of in the cell from hell."'

'What sort of "such and such"?'

'Oh, Peter! Just stop it.'

'Well?'

'I'm not saying. This is just so stupid. It doesn't help you any, at all.'

'I want to know.'

'Well, you can't.'

'You have such a dirty mind, Harriet. Where did it all come from? Where did you get this filthy mind?' He was looking almost cheerful again. With Peter, these storms came and went quickly. With her they stuck around, eating deep into her heart.

'I haven't really got a dirty mind at all, actually.' She laughed bitterly. 'I'm a properly brought-up Bonnyrigg High School girl. But I'm just decently prepared and well work-shopped for a job that I need to do as brilliantly as I can. That's all. I have a "come" trigger phrase for every occasion. But I have to have, or I'd be there till breakfast time and,' she grinned, 'I'm the only one of us who ever remembers when Jonty needs a packed lunch or anything, so I have to get back, don't I, dumbo?'

As if on cue, the bedroom door suddenly clicked and swung majestically back to reveal, theatrically, a dishevelled Timothy looking balefully at them from the corridor, his mouth full of the dreadfully ancient towel that he still sucked on every night, when he was asleep.

'Hullo, Timbo,' she said. 'Do you want breakfast?' The boy was completely silent because his mouth was so full of soggy cloth. He stomped noisily across the room in his bare feet, and dived on to the middle of their bed. He scrambled up towards the bedhead and took up position between the two of them, sitting on her pillow, evil smelly cloth and all.

'Hullo, old man. What's with you?' Peter shook his head massively as if to clear their conversation out of it, and mopped his face with the sheet. 'Sorry, H.,' he said, 'I get in such a completely ridiculous muddle about it sometimes. My head gets completely paranoid. I go nuts. And yet I'm afraid, if we're going to go on with this, you're going to have to continue saying things to me about it. Sorry. I need to know. If you stop, I'll die at the secrecy of it. At the exclusion.'

'But you die when I tell you, as well.'

'Yes. But I think I prefer it. Just. And I sometimes like it too.'

'Yes. You do.'

'I'm a bit of a bugger, aren't I?' Timothy removed his disgusting mouth blockage to ask, cheerfully enough: 'Who's dying?'

'No one,' she replied firmly.

'Well, I am,' he went on, 'cos there's no cornflakes left! Not even yucky Allbran!'

And it made them laugh.

Success. I start with Hartbeck on the 21st. We can stop all this madness now.

Well, my gob is well and truly smacked! What a turnaround – a job, folding stuff, the potential opprobrium of the Groucho Club, possible Olympic offspring, wife about to retire, what more could any man ask?

Gary Hope has taken Jonty permanently under his wing. He gives the boy a full hour's special tute, after school, four days a week! For J. there is no life without Hope, but the Greenwich fetch-and-carry logistics are an absolute nightmare. But who's to say the lad is not thriving on the attention? You can actually see him imperceptibly (is that a "Colemanballs"?) broadening at the shoulders. Gary pads his bare feet up and down the poolside in his white Nike shorts (and these are wicked, windswept autumnal days for Chrissakes!) throwing out what seem to me totally incomprehensible gestures at my son, who, in his rubber head-condom and goggles, looks like some kind of anonymous biped fish. During the hour, very little of Jonty ever seems to come to the surface. Apart, that is, from those moments when he stops thrashing like a knife up and down the pool and he screws up his earnest little face, to listen to the great white Hope and consider the implications of the man's ever-faithful Mickey Mouse stopwatch.

There's a thing – what about that, eh? – I covered the boy's adventures first, didn't I? In this first entry here for days I could so easily have waxed lyrical about the glories of potential full-time employment.

Yes, Sir George Harcourt, he of Hartbeck Publishing, followed up our interview by insisting on a series of what my father-in-law would call bonny lunches at the Gay Hussar where he introduced me to a whole tranche of his people. Hartbeck made their fortune with a spectrum of puzzle magazines with which the desperate disenfranchised are encouraged to fill in spare parts of their waking hours. They also handle a great pile of specialist titles.

George is desperate to push his lumbering empire up-market with a high-profile ombudsperson-like weekly (or fortnightly) to be called (yep) *Eleventh Hour*. Well, that's nothing that can't be fixed. Somewhat like Footy's pages at the back of the *Eye*, or what his column in the *Mirror* used to be – but a whole journal. Quite courageous, really. George went on at length about his perception of there being a need for more responsible popular journalism – information for the people, all that. It was probably just the claret speaking. He even quoted Baldwin on the power of Press Barons: 'Power without responsibility, the prerogative of the harlot throughout the ages.' It struck me as pretty damn true. But not necessarily about Press Barons . . .

The final upshot is that I am to be given command as Editor-designate. A small team to start with – two researchers and a junior and a young administrator from the *Spectator* who's already started: June Southern – who brings a good reputation and who seemed bright as a button. We start publishing in the very late spring of next year. So we're in a desperate hurry.

George made an offer that I couldn't refuse – particularly so, once we're publishing. Any offer would have done, but he wasn't to know I'd've done it for two Kitkats and a packet of crisps.

Anyway, it'll pull H. off the streets, won't it? Exit the strumpet voluntary. Thank God for that. She's going to be so relieved.

*   *   *

Harriet strode away from the hubbub of Piccadilly and into the court-yard of the Royal Academy. It was a beautifully crisp, autumnal London midday. She was going to the Royal Academy where a man who said he was called Jack Robinson had suggested they should meet.

It struck her that it was not the most obvious time of day nor even a very usual location for the potential initiation of impromptu sexual shenanigans. Indeed, so exceptional was the circumstance of the gig that Harriet had been hard pressed to know what best to wear. She had finally plumped for a businesslike suit, in black. To set this off, more as a joke for herself than anything, she wore a large pair of black horn-rimmed spectacles – with plain glass in them so that she wouldn't blunder into things. She would see if art-lovers made passes at lassies in glasses.

The security man checking the contents of visitors' handbags as she went up into the palatial entrance of the Royal Academy, might have been somewhat astonished by the fact that her little shoulder-bag contained nothing but a wealth of ludicrously varied condoms, but if he was, he certainly kept it to himself.

The 'Jack Robinson' person was inside the big hallway at the bottom of a columned sweep of stairs, among a busy crowd of oldish arts *aficionados*. He was so thin he was positively gaunt, with skin stretched tautly over his cheekbones below spindly glasses. He wore jeans and a denim jacket with a red-knotted cotton scarf at his neck. He had dark, short brown hair, nicely gelled, and good full lips and a frightened smile.

His appearance was, of course, a bit of a surprise because Harriet was used, on the whole, to attending upon men in their fifties or more. That was usually the generation that could afford her. Furthermore, she tended to see gentlemen who, to a man, never sallied forth unless decently attired in a proper suit-type jacket. Indeed, it was even the general rule for that generation of gentlemen, when removing such apparel, later on, to get more comfortable, invariably to offer murmured apologies for this wicked act of disrobing. This was, of course, at a stage considerably before she got to help them out of their trousers, by which time they were, as a general rule, well past apologies.

This Jack Robinson found it difficult to look her in the eye. His head jerked away to take in the useful cloakroom facilities as he thrust a single small white envelope into her hand. 'Here,' he gulped, 'you'll find it's right.' He was so shy, Harriet was for once almost reluctant to take the money. The package seemed to have the right sort of thickness. She put the envelope away in her bag without further ado.

The time of day, the youth of the man and the hushed, almost holy activity in the entrance hall to the galleries made the whole thing seem so much more like some kind of date. Her accustomed meeting routine usually had her fetching up in some leeringly up-market drinking-hole just as dusk was falling sexily and clouds of rampant starlings were screaming their way into the West End to roost. A Friday afternoon seemed much more like a time for meeting maiden-aunts, for taking children to Madame Tussaud's or walking around the Round Pond in Kensington Gardens.

The guy muttered that perhaps she would like to take in one of the exhibitions. The posters advertised Picasso drawings. The two of them walked slowly and rather separately around the three or four galleries. On all sides there were these countless vibrant, almost animated drawings of horses and satyrs romping about, and buxom maidens and cows apparently laughing at some quite good jokes. Harriet felt as if she was attending a noisy party, although the sound in the rooms never lifted above an educated murmur. It felt more like a cerebral school visit to the National Library of Scotland than a prelude to commercial lustfulness.

At the end of their silent trawl around the exhibition, the man said, 'Shall we have some coffee now?' There was not a little evasion going on here, Natasha thought, but she actually said out loud how nice that would be.

They had tea, in point of fact. In the Fountain restaurant of Fortnum and Mason's, across Piccadilly from the Academy. It was early, so they got a table as soon as they arrived. Gentility reigned supreme and black and white uniformed tea waitresses scurried about, delivering pots of Earl Grey and thinly sliced tradition-encrusted cucumber sandwiches. Jack Robinson filled in time passing sugar and trying to press toasted tea-cakes on her. Harriet thought she had better get on and find out a little more about the guy. All she knew so far was that he had a charming stutter, a neat little bum and a tendency to wander off at exhibitions.

He was a graphic designer. He produced company logos, and theatre print and album covers for CD's of pop bands. He had a daughter aged four who was cared for by his mother. His wife had been killed in a car crash two years previously.

The conversation was already winding down. Harriet liked him and felt sad for him too. Since they had left the exhibition, all his energy seemed to have evaporated. They sometimes did need so much help, these men. Harriet braced herself and got on with it. Natasha asked him: 'So, you are looking for some company?' There was a long reflective silence. He took a deep breath and, at last, fastened grey eyes on her. 'I'm sorry, I'm not very good at this. I've never done anything like this before. I don't know the rules. I don't know how it works.' He drank some of his tea. Natasha waited. She found that an awful lot of her job was waiting. And listening. He went on quietly: 'I don't want there to be anyone else. Ever. My wife, Rachel, will always be there in my life.' His eyes were damp. 'Even so, I thought – well, I thought it would be nice to spend some time with someone who didn't matter to me in the slightest.' He was almost shocked by what he had said to her. 'I'm sorry.'

'Don't be. It's fine. I spend most of my evenings with people to whom I don't matter in the slightest. And most of my nights,' she added helpfully.

'Yes.' He paused and then he went on slowly: 'I don't want to go out with anyone, have a relationship, I mean.'

'But you thought you might be able to do something impersonal?'

'Yes, I suppose I did.'

'In that case I'd so like to be able to help.' Nurse Natasha to the fore once again. 'Dead impersonally, of course. For a consideration.' Oh God, she was never backward in coming forward, was Ms Ivanov.

'All right.' Well, his agreement wasn't fulsome but it was a start. She waited. Nothing. He gulped massively again at his cup of tea. Then: 'I'm sorry, I don't know how it goes from here. How does it work?' he said. 'You'll have to tell me.'

'It's simplicity itself,' Natasha said, 'if you're quite sure this is a good idea for you.' He seemed to assent. Natasha slowly removed her horn-rimmed specs and gave him a slow burn without the benefit of the glass lenses. After all, she had to earn some money here. The monthly mortgage payment fell due on Thursday next. She murmured softly: 'There's nothing to it, Jack. You pay me money. We go to a hotel. I fuck your brains out. It's nothing personal. You feel better.'

'Golly.' He was looking out of the window at the sunlight on the building across the street. 'Golly,' he said again. Then he collected himself. 'OK. Where do we go? Um, how much is it?'

She told him. He looked startled, but seemed to think it might still be worthwhile. There was a small discreet hotel in St James's Square which was only just around the corner. Arthur Marquesons, the City finance people, used it for overseas business visitors all the time. She knew it well. She had suggested a very reasonable deal to this Jack Robinson. Well, she could be nicely home by the early evening, at this rate. The man seemed bothered about booking into the hotel. 'We haven't got any luggage,' he said.

'There's no law that says you have to have luggage, Jack. It's not obligatory. Give me your credit card, I'll handle it.' And he did. Natasha could be as assertive as merry hell when she wanted to be. And she liked that a lot.

She got them a very good 'saver' deal for an entire damn suite at the rear of the building, which the man at reception said was remarkably quiet. As she trotted around the rooms switching on table-lamps, adjusting the heating, summoning up some music from the telly and selecting a groovy location for the expected congress, Harriet was pleased to see that the windows of the accommodation were double-glazed. It kept noises out. And in. A few minutes later, without the double-glazing, they might have been able to hear her vocal performance in Jermyn Street. And it wasn't all pretend. She never usually got to sleep with people younger than herself. She was startled by how difficult it was to make herself get out of bed and leave.

Jack Robinson came down with her to help her find a taxi. He was so sweet you wanted to take him home with you. They stood on the corner of St James's Square looking out for empty taxis.

Then she saw Peter.

She reckoned Peter saw that she had seen him but he appeared to pretend that he had not seen her. He ducked around the corner into Ackerman Street. The last she saw of him, as she got into a cab, was his big raincoat flapping as he turned into the Haymarket and hurried away.

Eleventh Hour is on the third floor of the Hartbeck Building, just south of London Bridge Station. Most of the staff tend to think it's the most obscure place on earth but it's convenience publishing if you live in Blackheath. It's not the most luxurious suite in the cosmos, but it's early days yet. It must be one of the last examples of Thatcherite Smoked Glass Finance House Chic. The interior designer, no doubt, thought it shit-hot. It's actually Motorway Service-station Gents Loo Post-Modern. I've got a large room overlooking this great grey elephant's backside which is the roof of the station. It's like having your own toy-train set to watch. Thomas-the-Tank-engine time. I feel wonderful – it's so good to be the 'Fat Controller' again.

Oh, I'm as happy as a pig in muck.

Of course, Harriet thought afterwards, what a complete fool she was to try to tackle Peter in the checkout queue at Sainsbury's.

'Peter, have you been following me?'

He didn't reply. He was flicking through the free shopping magazine that they had stacked in a rack at the entrance to the checkout. It was a busy Saturday morning in Sainsbury's. She and Peter were in quite a formidable queue. At the head of it, a young woman was manoeuvring packages into plastic bags and trying to organise her frail-looking father all at the same time. It wasn't easy and she was being slow.

'Peter?'

'What?' He said it sharply, almost as if annoyed at being dragged away from his desperately enthralling shopping magazine.

'Were you following me? Yesterday? St James's Square?'

''Course not.'

'Well, what were you doing there?' she hissed.

'London Library. I'd been to the London Library. Checking some stuff for work.'

'At the London Library?' She didn't believe it.

'Yep.'

The young woman and her father moved off and the otherwise silent queue shuffled obediently forward, pushing their loaded trolleys towards the bleeping cash machines. Harriet would have to leave it at that. It was always possible that Peter had gone to the London Library. It was there in the corner of St James's Square. But she didn't feel that his story rang very true.

Peter didn't seem to think so either because he appeared to need to justify himself: 'Why should I follow you?'

'I don't know. It just seemed so odd you being there.' She was trying to speak as privately as she could to him. There was a lot of noise in the store but she wished Peter would come and stand a bit closer to her, then it wouldn't be quite so embarrassing. She shouldn't have begun this limp confrontation. A young, almost student-looking girl behind them, who had a toddler with her, sitting in her trolley, seemed to Harriet to have taken a definite interest in their muted conversation.

'Sheer fluke,' Peter said and he returned his thin magazine to the rack. She would probably have thankfully left it at that had he not pressed on, under his breath: 'Who was the john? He looked pretty tasty. Fourteen, was he?'

'Ssssh,' she grimaced at him.

'What's to sssh?' Peter was being horridly ratty throughout the exchange. His attitude towards her was one of guilt. She knew him too well. He had been following her all right.

'It felt as if you were spying on me. I hated it. You of all people. You know that I tell you what happens. What's the deal about being there?' she muttered. The student woman was riveted. She rammed half a bar of chocolate into her child's mouth to keep him quiet and decided to tidy up the shopping in her trolley. This strategy meant that she could inadvertently edge nearer to the two of them. Harriet turned away from the girl and took his arm. Peter wouldn't look at her. She spoke to his ear: 'Don't do it, Peter. Please. I can't bear to think of you lurking around like that.'

'I wasn't. I told you. It was just happenstance, H. Why should I trail around after you? As you say, as you so cogently say, I know exactly what you bloody do. You've told me. Well, some of it, I suppose.' His face was grey. He spoke with his face still turned away from her, looking out across the busy, occupied shoppers as they went about their allotted tasks of filling their wire baskets. He was failing to keep his voice down. The student woman had pretty well stopped the pretence of hiding that she was eavesdropping. Her face was a picture of rapt fascination.

'I didn't know you got to jump guys who looked so bloody hunky, H.?' He was trying to make it sound teasing and light-hearted but he wasn't being successful.

'I don't.' She was being so quiet Peter would hardly be able to hear her voice at all. 'He was a very unique gig, that's all.'

'Nothing can be "very unique". It can either be "unique" or not.'

She ignored his sudden irrelevant bout of semantics: 'Oh God,

Peter, you know the kind of pathetic blokes they usually are. Crusty, deadbeat, rich, grey, balding, impotent, boring, sick.'

'But this one was scrummy, was he?'

'Shove it, Peter. It's all quite bad enough without all of this.' The young woman was watching Harriet's face transfixed with interest and pretending to be in another world all at the same time. Her little boy's mouth was a Jackson Pollock in chocolate brown.

'Well, you won't have to do it any more now, will you?'

'How do you mean?' she asked, knowing perfectly well.

'It's over. You've got to stop now. Thank God you've survived this far. But it's over now, H. Over. End of story. I'm earning at last.'

They had reached their turn at the till. They stood shoulder to shoulder, ready to receive their long pile of two weeks' worth of shopping and tuck it into pristine white plastic bags. So ordinary – just like every other mundane family in the whole of the western world. Nothing strange or kinky about the Holloways.

Peter had his Switch Card in his hand. He had plastic again. She knew he felt so much better now that he had his credit card back.

Their cashier was a young boy in spectacles. He began to weigh their vegetables and bleep their groceries through. There was an awful lot of liquor, Harriet thought.

'We still owe a fortune,' she said to Peter.

'Over, Harriet, over.' He was almost spitting the words at her.

'We still owe a fortune.'

'God, you love it, don't you?'

'Fuck off, Peter,' she whispered.

'Language,' he muttered. 'God, this really has twisted you, hasn't it?'

'Yes, I expect so. Be surprising if it hadn't,' she said.

The groceries and bottles flowed inexorably down the counter towards them. They had to keep busy not to let the items pile up. They liberated yet more carrier-bags and stuffed them full with a haphazard but goodly selection of household goods, food and drink and dog food.

The boy in the glasses smiled at them and said: 'A hundred and twelve pounds, sixty.' She reckoned that he had been concentrating much too hard to have heard any of what they had said. As opposed to the student mum who was now staring at her unashamedly.

'Jesus Christ,' said Peter startled by how much they seemed to have spent.

'You see?' Harriet said meaningfully.

'Even so, even so,' he said as he gave the boy his bank card.

'Let me be the judge of that.' She could be vehemence personified if she wanted. She picked up four of their filled carriers, two to each hand, and set off for the car park, leaving him to sign the chit. But, truth to tell, he was paying for their shopping with her money.

Harriet stood in the dull functional shed that called itself Terminal Four, Heathrow Airport, and waited for this Frank. She was feeling pretty grumpy and Terminal Four wasn't helping very much. With its slowly gyrating roof fans and its ugly exposed trunking, it looked more like an empty cash 'n' carry warehouse than a place to return to, from Paris. Frank Pickard, the john in question, was flexing his Hertz gold card in order that he drop her off in the West End before driving back to Doreen and Ray and Angela at the family home in Northampton. All around her, waiting relatives and friends practised their smiles and waited patiently for loved-ones to be delivered unto them by British Airways.

It had not been a scintillating weekend. True, they had flown via Paris but then had been obliged to speed immediately on to Tours where Pickard's weekend conference had its annual frolic. For all his trendy floral ties and camp leather shoulder-bag, Pickard had turned out to be a thumping humping bore, and her lengthy solitary hours in Tours even more so. In London, during the autumn, Frank Pickard had become a nice enough regular little earner – a simple enough, no-nonsense trick. During this much vaunted weekend, he had proved himself about as deft a companion as Starfire and twice as yawn-making. He was manic about types and makes of cars, a passion which had always left Harriet pretty far behind, even when he told her in the midst of rather unfit congress that she reminded him of a Lamborghini. He also had taken the opportunity of displaying a depth of petty prejudice, which startled her. He had, for example, a deep dislike of the Northampton Asian shopkeeper, which she found positively alarming. And he truly believed that any embryo suspected of the slightest blemish or disablement should be excoriated. Harriet found it very difficult to hold Natasha's tongue.

It was also very dull being at a conference, if you aren't actually at the conference. Frank had required her to be banked for the bulk of the time at La Touraine Hotel, only cashing her in for the black-tie reception on the Saturday night, which was held in the old town at Place Plumereau by the Loire. There, although glowing with sexual possession, he had preened comparatively tactfully and called her his 'amanuensis', which sounded dirty and was most definitely a first. The usual term her clients tended to employ was: 'my PA' or in more rarefied Whitehall circles: 'my researcher'.

Harriet guessed that the delegates had all known precisely what she was. She was much better dressed than anybody else to start with and, at (um) twenty-three, half their age. The men had stared at her unabashed and their wives had stared at her abashed. Harriet had got the distinct impression that this Frank probably took a different girl to Tours every year. He certainly seemed to run all his personal sexual relationships from his wallet, using a multitude of working girls by way of a multitude of credit cards.

It was so odd to feel irritated about three nights in reasonable luxury in a busy French town, for which chore she was earning a great deal of money. Really her only duty was to appear in public for the one evening, looking a million dollars in her Helmut Lang without the benefit of her knickers. Yes, of course, she had had to do the usual for the guy each night, but that, thank God, hadn't been over-burdensome. But Tours as a town didn't seem to her to be a thrill a minute. Once she had walked by herself along the dirty brown Loire from Pont Napoléon to the Pont Wilson, and once she had drifted around the St Gatien Cathedral staring at the glass and the guttering, yellow candle flames, she had got so pissed off with the unwelcome attentions of every available Frenchman, old and young, that she had returned to the hotel and spent the rest of her time sitting on the bed, zapping between five or six meaningless French TV stations, like a bored heroine in a French movie.

She had sat, tucked up there, missing the boys, worrying that Frank might glimpse her real name on her passport and feeling panic-stricken about the frightening news that her friend Daisy had suddenly revealed to her just before she had left London. At the same time she found that she was inexplicably churned up about Peter's new job. She was being emotionally besieged and catatonically bored all at the same time.

And on top of all that, there was the whole appalling problem about what to do with the dreaded Toby Lydell–Smith and his increasingly bizarre requirements. Things, this autumn, were not working out very smoothly for Mrs Harriet Holloway and her good friend Natasha Ivanov. On all fronts, she was facing intractable difficulties and she didn't know how best to handle them. True, she and Peter were, to some degree, climbing out of the ghastly financial hole from where they had started this whole thing, but she was paying for it by getting her head into severe dislocation. And 17 Blackheath Drive still didn't have all that many pieces of furniture.

The week before, Daisy had rung Harriet about a friend called Ingrid. It had been a kind of girls' warning. This Ingrid was a brass who had been left for dead by some punter at her flat in Swiss Cottage. It seemed as if Ingrid was going to be all right but the guy, some German or Belgian businessman, had taken a blade to her and Daisy was in a terrible, terrible state about it. It still made Harriet's heart pound just to think of it. A Stanley-knife. He must have taken it along on purpose. Oh God, it had brought Harriet up short with such a vengeance.

So far she had made herself shut her mind to the dangers. She wouldn't even allow herself to consider them. It was like motorway driving – if you thought about an eighty mile an hour pile-up all the time, you would probably have to stop being a driver. It was quite bad enough at times, thank you very much, having to deal with that queue of evenings with tubby, unfit, grey-bodied, old men. Sometimes, when Natasha's confidence was at a low point in the month, the work almost made her gag. There were days when she thought that if she saw another anonymous, wrinkled, oblique, blue-veined cock creeping slowly and inexorably aloft, she would scream. But the money was really so very very seductive. She would say to herself – she would even murmur it out loud to the john: 'Trick and treat, trick and treat,' and that would usually carry her over the worst times. However, Daisy's lurid description of her friend Ingrid's face had made Harriet vomit with fear. This was not a pretty business. Ye gods, she earned every single penny, each and every desperate night.

Then there was Peter and this job of his and how to manage the boys now that he was commuting. It was so great he had got the thing, but she couldn't ask Marianne to cope with the boys forever. And Marianne, she thought, was beginning to give Harriet questioning looks anyway. And would Peter continue with his demands that she should stop? He was well and truly in macho, breadwinning action again. It had been a desperate lengthy episode, but now as far as he was concerned it must come to an end.

As far as the work was concerned, Harriet continued to be totally ambivalent about it. There were countless days when she abominated it. Days when her bum clenched up at the very thought of it. Those endless, endless days of feeling a constant undercurrent of tension because, that very evening, she had a gig on.

But then, as well, yes – and it continued to shock her very much – there were times when she almost liked it.

It was odd, wasn't it, but it did seem that, in a number of very funny ways, she and Peter had similar psychological make-ups. They were manacled together in a macabre dance of the appetites – a mirror image of one another. They both of them seemed to need to go in two diametrically opposed emotional directions, at one and the same time. Peter loathed her doing the work and wanted her to do it more. She abhorred it and didn't want it to stop. After all, there were parts of it she actually felt drawn to – the power, the money, the freedom to come and go and to choose, even one or two of the blokes.

Yes, she was in a hole. She was lying altogether too much to Peter about her work and about Toby. That wasn't how she used to run her part of their marriage. Peter lied of course, but then he was a bloke and it came with the instruction booklet. Harriet, for example, was totally incapable of telling Peter about something like Ingrid. He would just self-destruct with his fear for her. Secondly, she couldn't confess to him about the impossible situation with the appalling Toby. Her relationship with his best mate would always have to be top secret.

All told, she was learning to live a life of deceit. Out of control. Lost in an immoral morass.

For a number of weeks, Harriet had happily not heard from Mr Lydell–Smith and she had allowed herself to hope, in a vague way, that he might have got bored with the idea of their deal. Then she heard the rumour that he and Barbara were in Australia. This proved to be the case. The very minute he returned, Toby had rung her again. Harriet's heart sank. But he only suggested a meal at Le Gavroche. Well, a girl couldn't, very lightly, turn down the kind offer of a sophisticated evening sampling Mr Roux's skills, could she? Harriet put on her new and demure little black thing from Ralph Lauren and took herself off to Mayfair, like all the best hookers do.

It was a surprisingly pleasant meal. The atmosphere purred with well-lined civility, the service was firm, discreet and charming. Gentle lesser-known Chopin calmed the stress of the day. Toby was in expansive and not too noisy form, mellow from successes Down Under. Harriet made do with a soufflé Suissesse and slightly more of her share of a bottle of Côte de Beaune Blanc than she would normally have allowed herself to consume on a gig. But it felt so unlike a gig with Ms Ivanov not being very much in evidence. They talked about their families, the mundane achievements of their respective children and Toby's wife's notorious ambitions in the world of charity. And they talked a lot about her husband, Peter, and the potential of his new job. Toby obviously loved keeping Peter in the forefront of his conversation with her.

But nothing untoward was said between them until they reached the danger zone of brandies and cigar. They were both smiling inanely about some touching recent invention of her son Timothy, when he crashed into her reverie with: 'I have to tell you, my dear, I just so love being able to roger Peterkins's sexy little wife whenever I want to. I love it. I think about it all the time, every day. I thought about it throughout our trip to Oz – every rock-hard night. Even in Darwin, which must, surely, be the very least sexy place in the whole wide world. Perked up our love-life more than somewhat, I can tell you. Babs was somewhat disconcerted by my attentions. But she's a game girl. And she wasn't to know that, in my head, I was poking your very good self. I hope you're flattered. You should be. It is an extraordinary real delight for me that, any time that I want it, all I have to do is set it up. Topping, my dear, absolutely topping!'

It felt to Harriet as if he must be talking about some hazily known, mutual acquaintance. And it wasn't true either – he wasn't in a position to do it whenever he wanted. But Toby was soldiering on, totally regardless of such niceties. In the middle of the most carefully crafted Upper Brook Street propriety, Toby Lydell–Smith was saying slightly too loudly: 'You were right, my darling Harriet, in what you said, at the very beginning of all this, it was the very best deal I could ever have lighted upon. I know what I think we must do now. Can we go back to your delightful marital bedroom, just as soon as I have finished this slightly less than superior old Havana?'

'Absolutely not,' she said quietly, her voice lost in the polite buzz of background conversation. 'No, we certainly can't.' She was surprised at the speedy firmness with which she said it. 'We're not doing that again. It wasn't really part of the arrangement at all.'

'I don't seem to remember any particular terms to the contract.'

'You know and I know what I'm talking about. Come on, Toby, don't give me a hard time.'

'My dear, it's you who give me the hard time. All the time. All over Australia, I'm glad to say. What power you have over me – thousands of miles away!' She could cope with this from a john. That was all part of the game. But with Toby it was different, it made her feel sick. It made her feel obscene. Then he relented and became old-world charm again: 'You're right, Harriet, my dear. I'm sorry. Of course these things take organising, don't they? Let us organise it. Together.'

'When I made an agreement with you, I meant to honour it, Toby. And I am doing so. But I assumed we'd find ourselves in reasonably neutral territory. I said I'd sleep with you, but in sensible places. If it's whatever you say goes, you could have me doing it in the fountains in Trafalgar Square!'

'And very jolly that might be too. Chilly. And we could all finish up with Legionnaire's Disease. No, I am happy enough as it is. Just organise it. We don't have to alter our present delightful strategy. In fact, dear darling Harriet, the next time we get together, I would rather like you to organise a little extra touch of magic for me. Would you? I am sure you will, there's a dear. In the last month, I have been totally obsessed with a gleeful and totally wicked fantasy. And I want it. You'd organise it for me, wouldn't you? If it was important for me?' The charm dried up and his face looked cold and older. He was a man used to getting his own way. She couldn't even begin to be a match for him. 'Would you sort out my unusually bizarre fantasy for me, Mrs Peter Holloway?'

'I can but try. What is it?' she said warily. Already she could see herself down at an Anne Summers shop picking out some ghastly tacky all-rubber nurse's outfit, or something.

'It's simple enough. I want to have you while he's in the house.'
'What?'
'I want to have you while he's in the house. At the same time. I want us to fuck, in your bed, while he's in the house. Simple. He mustn't know, of course. Mustn't ever guess, that's the beauty of it – the secret between us. I so adored our last tryst. Your boys sitting watching telly, two doors between us and them. Hearing our noises.

Wondering. I loved it. Heavenly. Then later that evening hovering around that grimy little civic swimming-pool with your talented progeny, mixing with the populace. And Peter being the keen father incarnate, and you and I nursing between us the intensely delightful secret that we had been at it for hours in his very own bedroom. It made me want to shout for the delight of it, my dear. You, looking stunningly cool and collected, and me with my hands still reeking of you. I really adored that. Oh yes!' And he laughed one of his hideous great shouts of laughter.

Harriet thought wryly how quickly a few moments of unappealing anxious squelching could lengthen, in the imagination, to hours and hours. The male mind was a truly wondrous self-deluding thing.

'Well, it's not on, I'm afraid. I've said that that was never part of the arrangement. I'm sorry, Toby, you can just forget about it. I said we would go to bed, nicely, enjoyably, twelve times, once a month for a year, in order for you to get paid for your investment. There was never any question of any kinky stuff about you getting yourself off on me cheating on Peter.'

'That was the whole point for us both, wasn't it? You wanted the money. You wanted me. And you knew what I wanted. I badly wanted to know what having Peter's buttoned-up teenage lady wife was like.'

'This is all so wrong, Toby. This was not what it was about.'

'Are you disgusted?'

'I am a bit, yes.' And she was. Which was odd because every week in the past couple of months, Harriet, as Natasha, had put up with infinitely more potentially mind-broadening activity in her work than anything staid old Toby could think up. But that other stuff never could reach the soul of Harriet Holloway. The separation nearly always worked a treat. But what Toby was suggesting certainly reached out and touched defenceless, shockable Harriet. 'Listen,' she said, after a while, 'my business is doing OK. It seems to me that our "arrangement" probably isn't going to work, I'm afraid. Let me pay you the money back. I can probably afford it now. Over a period of time, anyway.'

'No, no, no. I'm not interested in my money back. You offered me a good game and now it seems to me you've got squeamish about the rules. I think that's a touch pathetic, Harriet my dear. No spunk, my girl. I'm surprised at you. I would have thought, having had some intimate knowledge of you now, that you had rather more balls. I have to say to you that I am decidedly disappointed. It's simple enough. We've both been liberated enough to put our cards on the table. That's rare where sex is concerned. Let's take advantage of it. We both stand to be winners. I promise you, Harriet, you and I will continue to have an excellent and quirkily enjoyable time together. But you have to do what I say, I'm afraid. Tough that, but business is business, and business is, regrettably, sometimes tough. There are them as screw and them as gets screwed, as my dour old father used to say. In this case, totally appositely! No, you can't pay me my money back. You, my dear delectable creature, have to deliver! Tough shit.' He laughed mirthlessly again. 'Sorry, Harriet.'

He was actually pretty fed up. He was pink about his upper cheeks where hair grew on his face at a point above where he shaved. His big nose seemed to quiver with irritation as he paid an impossible amount of money for their meal. He had stopped looking at her. He looked pretty grim – what Harriet's father called 'lemon-faced'. She was frightened. Where did this stalemate leave her?

They left the restaurant in silence and walked together down the street towards Grosvenor Square. Harriet assumed they were looking for a taxi, as Toby strode his big strides alongside, but completely separate to, her. The streets were already pretty deserted and the buildings echoed to the clack of her high heels. It seemed that there was unspoken business between them that hadn't been settled.

He stopped and looked down at her. 'Well, Harriet,' he said brusquely, 'we need to sort out September's little instalment, don't we, before we worry about jolly old October and November, eh?' And he flashed a big false grin at her. His eyes continued to look bloody dangerous. He seemed more tense than usual. As if he had something on his mind. And he had stopped trying to pretend not to look frankly at her body enclosed in the tiny black dress. If this is what it was like with a family friend, give her a john any day. You always knew pretty well where you were with a punter.

'Down here,' he said suddenly. There was the narrowest of alleyways, hardly as wide as a person, running between two high buildings. It smelled of urine and litter and was pitch dark. He pushed her roughly down the passageway ahead of him. When they were about five yards in, away from the pavement, and up against a stinking Paladin bin, he let go of her shoulder and stopped. She already knew what was happening. But couldn't believe it.

'Here'll do. This'll have to do. Serves you right, bonny Mrs H!'
He was growling fiercely at her: 'You could have had the luxury
of a double-bed but oh no, oh bloody hell no, we had scruples,
eh? Well, this is where scruples get you, my girl. Fucking down a
fucking alleyway, girlie. That suit you?' He was already wrenching at
his trouser zip, leaning up against her, his heavy weight crushing her
against the side wall. He was drunk. 'And let's see you sodding enjoy
it, Harriet, my darling – "Trinket", isn't that what old Peterkins calls
you? He's nowhere as big as I am, is he darling?' He grabbed her
skirt with both hands and wrenched it up hard, around her bum.
His fleshy mouth encompassed hers and she could taste the drink,
the meal and his cigar. He continued to push her firmly against
the red brickwork. She felt the sudden chill about her backside
and she peered anxiously over his big shoulders, in the dark, to
see if there was anybody out there in the street, watching. Her
shoulder-bag fell between their feet and one of her shoes came
off as they shuffled it about on the ground between them. She
felt so desperately humiliated and very very shocked. His big hand
pushed between her legs. She was frightened that she was going to
get hurt, although she thought that he was actually trying, in spite
of everything, to be reasonably gentle. She felt totally invaded and
abused but she thought it might be better if she resigned herself
to it. She began to pretend to kiss him back. It was horrible but
seemed safer and quicker. She put her arms up around his neck and
hauled herself right off the ground. She wrapped her legs around the
bastard. She could hear him breathing hard and grunting from the
sex and from her weight. His hands were fumbling at her stomach.
She held him away from her as long as possible trying to get herself
out of her state of shock and into some semblance of control. She
just wanted to get it over with as quickly as possible, and as quietly.
If he made much more noise, the police would come around shining
torches at them.

He never got into her. He was pushing her pants aside and they
were hurting her bum, when with an almost comically loud groan he
seemed to come. She felt the affirmation of the warmth of his semen
running down the upper part of her leg. He stood there, breathing
throatily, holding on to her. She was still wrapped around him, with
nearly all her clothes in place. Her hair was still up. Her first thought
was that she hoped she wouldn't get semen stains on her dress.

Then, after a while, they disengaged. They stood next to each other, sideways on to the dustbin, in the passageway. He was breathing heavily. With any luck he might have a heart-attack and die. She scrabbled around and found her bag and picked it up. She felt hurt in every possible way. They silently, carefully, adjusted their dress. He cleared his throat a number of times, but they had nothing to say to each other. Harriet supposed that it had been a quick, if far from painless, monthly reckoning.

Another five minutes or so and they emerged into North Audley Street. Harriet felt numb and sick but, even so, was able to feel sardonic at how well turned out they were when they reappeared. Anyone passing them would think they were the smartest of couples out for a stroll in the smartest, most decorous part of London, not, an instant before, a couple of dogs fornicating in a stinking alleyway. As far as she could see, she hadn't even laddered a stocking. The man hailed a cab for her. She didn't say a word to him as she got in.

'Think about it,' was all he said to her by way of farewell. It sounded to her awfully like a threat.

I've heard it said that the less secure you feel about the one you love, the more urgent, in an almost direct inverse proportion, becomes your love for them. And that it's when people are just beginning to disappear on you, that you realise just how essential they are. I can't say that I go along with any of that. I suppose the only time when I thought of it as true was of my sex-life in my twenties. During those periods when sex was readily available in an easily accessible flip-top packet, it didn't much bother me, either way. Yeah, it was there, and very pleasant too, but I couldn't really say it was a very big deal. But the very moment access was denied and there was some uncertainty as to whether I would ever suck sweat again, it instantly became a mindless, overweening, frantic obsession that filled every cranny of my waking hours, and some of my sleeping ones as well.

Thank God this doesn't seem to be true about middle-aged emotions. Not that I think that H. and I are going through any sort of crisis anyway, but I do seem to see her so bloody rarely. I mean, it's extraordinary; getting to bed with her these days is like bloody carnival day. She's *always* working. I see that bloody Rover mini-cab with our cool dude friend Melvyn in the driving seat, man, virtually every day — yet again whipping her off somewhere to boost our bubbling liquidity. I just don't think about any of that any more. I have almost found a way of convincing myself that she works shifts for C.P.E.M., with the endlessly fascinating and totally fictitious Max and Penny and Janet and the rest. She and I hardly refer to her work now. Well, I don't think we do, though H. gets irritated and claims that I pester her about it more. I think she's got that wrong.

I sometimes think I preferred being totally bankrupt and knowing exactly where she was. The only difference is that I certainly fancy her much more of the time these days. Love her, even. Good laugh, eh? – 'Want to jazz up your marriage? Put your woman on the game!' If I don't watch myself I can get quite misty-eyed about her tight little bum and her throaty rasping in my ear and the sharpness of her tits and the damp on her belly. And, yes, of course, I suppose I get kind of moody about Harriet out of bed as well – her laughter around the kitchen table, the fucking obstinacy of her chin, the look in her cuckoo eyes when she's quietly watching the boys, her overwhelming smile – stuff like that.

She's a workaholic and the only way that I can begin to compete is to paddle up the same creek. So I'm throwing myself into this Hartbeck thing. It is, mercifully, very absorbing and time-consuming. I've got my hands full and what H. gets up to doesn't really bother me.

After all, I've no reason to whinge. The woman has just bought me a Porsche, for God's sake. What more could a man ask? Mark you, it's a very very old Porsche.

Now here's something pretty damn extraordinary. When I went into my room this morning, at Hartbeck, the Statex was on, and there in the centre of the screen, blocked in red, was the word 'PIMP'! Just the one word – caps, in blue. On its own. Christ. I sat down and looked at it for a long while and wondered about it. There was a sender reference-index BG3.1. We're all networked to the computer that services the whole of Hartbeck Publishing, the entire building, so it's not impossible to post something on to someone else's screen, but you always get a sender-reference index. I rang the network supervisor, a boffin called Fiske, who couldn't make out what I was on about – of course. He finally got the picture and I idly asked him who this character BG3.1 was. He said it didn't exist on the network and couldn't have been slotted on to my screen with that code at all. So there we are – it hadn't happened. Well, that's all right then. And yet, there it was, looking at me from my screen, large as life and twice as natural, smug and red and blue and deeply worrying. So I left Fiske to whatever he fills his day with.

I suppose I assumed, therefore, that someone must have strolled into my office at crack of sparrows and tapped it in. He'd have to have been bloody sharpish as spunky, busy June Southern trots in, with her squash bag, needlessly early herself. I wondered if it could have been her. And, anyway, did it mean what I thought it meant? Perhaps I put it up there myself when doodling last night? No. No, I switch off like a good well-trained housewife each evening, and perch the keyboard and the mouse on top of the screen, so that the cleaners can flick the casual duster around, when they come in at seven.

So I wiped it, and strolled into June who lives in a slightly lesser room (filled to the gunwales with Triffid-like rubber android plants she brought in from her mother's place, just after I started). 'Anyone been around? In my room?' I say, dead relaxed. 'No, why?' she asks. 'Nothing,' I say, 'just some stuff's been shifted about, and it's irritating.' 'That's the bloody cleaners,' she says, reaching for the phone. Could it be the cleaners, I thought? No. Then I had the first of a series of meetings and I almost forgot about it. No that's a goddamn lie; I thought about it every minute of the day, but I did manage to keep half an eye on the job in hand as well.

It frightens the shit out of me, but I suppose it's nothing. All I know is, however adamant Harriet is, we're going to have to knock her evil entrepreneurial activities on the head good and proper at last. Thank God nothing awful has happened to her. We can afford it, too, now the bank's being fed intravenously by Hartbeck.

Harriet lay on the sun-bed. She was in a state of shock.

She loathed her time on the sun-bed, but with winter virtually about to mothball London for the next five months, there were things that a woman of her cloth had to put up with. Though for how much longer, she couldn't begin to guess. She lay motionless, her bum tacky on the plastic, beneath the dreaded lights, and she considered their options.

Today's news had been pretty bloody awful. What were they going to do?

Since the Sainsbury's debate, Peter had had her under constant pressure, even before this godawful news had turned up. Sometimes by just hinting, at other times in full-scale shouting mode – she ought to give it a rest, call it a day and come back into the fold as full-time wife and mother. 'Take back the baton,' he said. Not that she reckoned he had been gripping hold of the parental baton all that strongly himself more recently. Thus far she had managed to avoid a lot of this talk by sliding stealthily off to work or to the gym at those choice moments when he seemed to have cornered her. And, to be honest, she was seeing him comparatively rarely just at the moment because their hours had begun to clash so badly.

Even so, there were still occasions when the so-called adults of the family did find themselves, together and alone, odd nights when they were not both instantly comatose because of their combined total exhaustions. It would be then that Peter would begin to lay down a few principal guide-lines about their futures.

And all this was happening already, well before today's news had come along.

Before today, when Peter had started to get heavy, Harriet would steel herself to undertake creepy diversionary activity. She was getting to loathe it, but she was still, at least, able to derail Peter with her somewhat sordid strategy. She would simply distract her husband with imagined tales of bizarre bedroom misdemeanours. They had to involve convoluted embroidery, as the reality was usually so very mundane. She would brace herself, close down her brain and put a wet tongue in Peter's ear and whisper: 'God, Peterkins, he was so stonking big, he made me scream absolutely all night!' The result would be that her husband came and went, and she got some sleep, and none of his immediate demands had to be considered.

But this was all before today. Today, immediate demands could not be avoided, because, that very morning, Peter had stayed home and told her that he was being blackmailed. Somebody knew. Somebody knew in detail. Somebody was demanding money.

Peter was receiving anonymous electronic notes at work. It started just with hints and words, half sentences. Peter had tried to have the message maker traced. He obviously couldn't tell his network supervisor exactly what was being sent. Various checks were made. Some doubt was expressed about whether or not it could possibly be internal. As the man in question, someone called Andy, couldn't be told what the messages said, he was not terribly energetic about sorting it out. He showed a basic academic interest in the possibility that someone had somehow hacked into the Hartbeck Statex system. But he couldn't get anywhere near solving the problem as to who it might be. And, truth to tell, he wasn't really all that concerned.

A week later, in the middle of November, the dreadful hints and clues and accumulating threats came to an end. The blackmailer delivered his full demand. Peter had taken a copy and then deleted the words from his screen. That evening they sat together in Peter's office at home and reviewed an appalling situation.

The final message read: 'Dear Pete Holloway, As you will have gathered by now, I have information, nay, proof that, for periods of the past year you have taken on the role of professional pimp, hawking your wife's favours as prostitute. Clearly this is an illegal activity and, at the same time, an absolutely delectable media story, even for a man of your modest profile and reputation. It is rich, indeed, for someone whose intended role is editor of a whistle-blowing publication. Unfortunately for you, knowledge is power, and I propose to wield this authority for the greater good of mankind by levying a monthly emolument from your illicit earnings.

'Should you fail to fulfil the following procedure, or decide to go to the police (and I can't really, in all conscience, see you doing that) I will make my information (and photographs – oh, yes) available to a newspaper of the tabloid variety with the word "sun" in the title. So, to avoid this, please contribute one thousand pounds each month, forever, in your name to The Imperial Cancer Research Fund, 44, Lincoln's Inn Fields, WC2A 3PF. You should, of course, make sure that you receive a receipt for your donation and then I would like you to prove your charitable urges by arranging to display a photocopy of this receipt each month in the window of the Epic Newsagents, proprietor: B. Patel, Queensway, London, W2 (directly opposite the post office on Queensway). This receipt must be in the window by the last day of each month, starting with the current month of November. So you'll have to get on, won't you? Simple enough little ruse, isn't it? My thanks on behalf of all those whose suffering your donations will help to alleviate. Best wishes, A FRIEND. (I like that, it's so traditional!)'

'Jesus Christ!' said Harriet.

'If it does get out, we're fucking done for. The police will come sniffing around. All manner of hell. And Hartbeck would have to push me out. Have to. George would have no choice. Just as I'm getting to grips with it too. Sorting out the team. Getting June

Southern in order. God, H., you know how much I need this job –
the challenge of it, my career on its way again. Oh God, dear God.
What the hell do we do? Christ knows. I feel completely stymied.
Just as we'd got started again too. Properly. You know how much
we need young Juno and the pay-cheque.'

'And I could go to jail.'

'God, no, you won't go to jail. It's impossible to prove anything,
photos or no photos. None of your clients are going to stand up in
front of their families and say "Yes, it was me, I pay for sex", are
they? There won't be any hard evidence. They can't prove anything.
So you don't have to worry, lovely. But, even so, if it gets out, we
would be pretty well fucked. Who the hell can it possibly be?'

'It must be someone close enough to know.'

'Someone who's computer literate. Someone who can hack in to
the Hartbeck system. Someone in the Hartbeck Building?'

'Who could know?'

Harriet was thinking that it could easily be the emetic Ellen
Herbert. Peter had let slip that the evil dwarf woman had been
exceptionally interested in what it was that Harriet was 'up to'. And
it seemed linked in Ellen's head somehow with the *New Statesman*
vice piece that Peter had written. Ellen had apparently questioned
him very closely about his sources. And Peter reckoned that she
had probably met up at some stage with the Pamela woman that
he had interviewed. Harriet guessed that horrid Mrs Herbert could
well possess a multitude of unimaginable reasons for having it in
for Peter.

Her husband, meanwhile, was ploughing on regardless, spraying
suspicion all around: 'Marianne's been looking pretty cold-eyed at
us recently.'

'Oh, come on, Peter. Do you see Marianne Webb hacking into a
computer system in some tower block in Waterloo? She can't even
set a video machine.'

'Can anyone?'

'It could always be a john. Or the police. Or one of the mansion
managers. I've always thought that it would be a doddle to be set
up by, say, someone like that. I mean, if they did it right, it's a nice
little earner for them. And they're all broke, the police. Or it could
just be a john who'd found out who I was, in some way, and made
the link with you. Getting his own back. Oh Christ.'

Harriet was thinking, of course, that it could be Toby. And, oh

200

God, it could even be the Jack Robinson guy. It had turned out that that actually was his name. She had seen him a couple of times now. And liked him and had stupidly allowed herself to get a bit tiddily one evening and let slip a few intimate details that she later regretted. It was hardly as if she had told him very much. But she knew it had been enough information for him probably to be able to seek out the rest if he had wanted. He certainly knew her real Christian name. And by all accounts he was a wonder with computers. Well, as far as graphic design went.

'How would a punter guess?' Peter asked, almost as if he knew what she was thinking.

'There was the guy who stared at me that one time at the swimming baths when Jonti was swimming against Bromley. Do you remember? He could have put two and two together. Or there may be guys who could have seen us together at some newspaper junket and subsequently recognised me. This could be one of them. I don't know. There've been people in government, industry, civil servants – '

'Yeah, I know, supermarket managers, Boy Scout troop leaders, travel agents, yeah, all the most influential people in the world!' he sneered.

'Don't be a manky bastard, Peter. I'm just thinking, that's all.'

'Bully for you!'

'Perhaps it could be Daisy. I think she knows where I live. No. I'd've thought she was pretty unlikely.'

'All right. Sorry. Let's go from first principles. What do we know? We know that they have apparently got the complete, well pretty nearly the complete, picture about us. So they must have been told, or guessed, or somehow found out. They've presumably followed you about. Do you remember seeing anyone odd hanging about? Even taking photos of you, apparently, for fuck's sake. I mean, have you done any kinky pictures with anyone? You never ever told me anything like that, Harri. You been doing kinky photo games?'

'Shut up, Peter, for God's sake. 'Course I haven't.'

'All right, all right, but what do they mean, "photos"? And this is a major clue, they know your connection with me. And where I work. And they've got some kind of electronic access to the Statex at Hartbeck. And this is the giveaway: they've got this kind of arcane sense of humour – all that stuff about the *Sun* – the whole ironic tenor of the thing. All those sneery snide phrases like "Good ruse, eh?" This is ghastly, isn't it? I feel like shit.'

'Well, I don't feel all that bloody wonderful, either, actually.' And she couldn't help it but she began quietly to cry, tears running softly down both cheeks. Peter turned the page over in his hands as if there might be something on the back. '"A friend"' he read once again, '"A friend" – I like that, it's so traditional. It's that awful arch sense of humour.'

'They could have just decided to assume that kind of tone of voice.'

'No, I don't think it's assumed. That's too subtle. After all, they don't have to hide – we haven't a clue.'

'They're into Cancer Research.'

'Yeah.' Peter rubbed his nose as he sat in his office chair and gazed at his green cursor flashing impotently on the screen in front of him. His face was pale with worry. 'Yes, I suppose that's true. Cancer Research, Cancer Research. They're into Cancer Research rather than into it for themselves, for the money.'

'And it's dead safe, for them, like that. No one could ever reach them through the business of delivering the money.'

'Well, we're not going to deliver the money anyway. They can whistle for it.'

'Perhaps,' said Harriet uncertainly. 'Right, they're either really charitably inclined or they're filthy rich. Or both.' To her it sounded awfully like a rich punter getting his own back on her for some reason. They had batteries of surveillance equipment, those people, bugging equipment, secret cameras, all kinds of know-how. When she was working, she'd never looked round for security cameras, bugs and things. It wouldn't have crossed her mind. God, she was so naive. She wouldn't have the first notion what to look for. And she had always reckoned her cover was pretty opaque. How wrong could you be? But how would they connect her with Peter? Through Flitcroft Mews? George, the manager there, must have guessed what she did for a living by now, really. And Peter Holloway was the name on the leasing agreement.

And then, to be honest, it could be any of a dozen or so grave and grey, late middle-aged men with thick wallets, she thought. One of them, having invested in the comfortable copper-bottomed certainty of not having to face sexual rejection, could easily have found himself, to his astonishment, being agreeably jerked off by someone whose face he recognised only too well. It had always been a risk they had run.

'All we really know is that they've got us,' said Peter.

'What are we going to do?'

'You're going to have to pack it in. Thank God. It's time. I told you you had to stop. I wish you'd done so already. Then we might not be in this hole.'

'And then?'

'Find out who it is.'

'We're going to have to pay.'

'Find out who it is and – and – I don't know – fucking kill them.'

The idea of it all coming out in public made Harriet's blood freeze, but even so, if she was going to have to put a stop to it all, she would prefer to pick the time of her own choosing. The job had changed her, and some of it had been for the good. Not that she thought that her job was very laudable, but then what job was? But it had settled down. And the pickings continued to be tolerably substantial. She knew a lot more about it. On the whole, she had started to see a small number of what she called her regulars and she more often than not refused a lot of new contacts, passing them on to Daisy and to another working girl she'd met called Caroline, who lived with a musician in Streatham.

The job did offer her a kind of freedom, it offered her a funny sort of strength, it offered lashings of dosh, and an important, if sick, purpose. And not a little admiration.

As far as the work was concerned, she was into a second, more manageable stage now. She had culminated that original honeymoon period of her 'career', when it was come-one-come-all, with a mind-boggling week in which she had seen *Phantom of the Opera* twice, attended a big charity ball at the L.S.E., spent two hours being shown around the library of The Reform Club, examining a first folio of William Shakespeare with a member of the African National Congress who had shamelessly fondled her backside. She attended a very grand dinner at the Royal Albert Hall addressed by the Prince of Wales, graced a reception for Leon Brittan at the Duchy of Lancaster and while there met, very briefly, Lady Antonia Fraser. It was a name-dropper's paradise. And an 'Eternity' paradise too as, at each event, astonishingly enough, just about every woman present would be using the self-same fragrance.

And in the course of her duties during that same week, she had totally laid to waste seven different men, plus her husband. And made an enormous amount of money. And finished up positively catatonic with exhaustion. And slightly over-fed. Harriet began to be pleased with the number of punters who wanted to skip the dinner part of the deal, and get straight on to the main course of what they were paying for. Enthusiastic anticipation could make for trouble-free time-keeping.

But the converse to all this was that Harriet knew perfectly well that her luck would probably not hold out and that she was a serious assault just waiting to happen. She was a gambler who was risking her very life, or certainly her face. So far she had been obscenely fortunate. There had been that first awful night at the Cornwallis, there had been some young guy, later on, who had drunkenly slapped her about in a room at a mansion off Lancaster Gate. Perhaps the worst night had been when some john had presented her with the exterior of a really flea-bitten, greasy-looking guest house off the Gray's Inn Road, just south of King's Cross, at about one in the morning. One look, and she had decided that it definitely wasn't for her and that she should go home. He had wrestled with her in the road, and she had run off into those cold grim back streets near the Euston Road. The phone battery had gone down and she'd been unable to raise a cab.

For about forty grim minutes, she had felt like she was really on the streets. It had scared her terribly. No policeman, no security officer nor anybody official was ever going to be on her side. There was only her lonely, inadequate self and her tense, watchful body to sort out awful situations like that. She had felt there was no one on earth that she could appeal to. It was always the same, she was forever out there on her own. On that cold night, she had felt that if she made even one tiny mistake, she could end up dead. Stanley-knife blades are available on every street corner. She had been terrified. It wasn't worth it.

So it would be sensible to stop. Peter was right, her family didn't depend upon just her any more. And the problem of the boys was a constant nightmare. There was such a lot of complicated time-tabling and endless fetching and carrying and regular feeding to be seen to. Marianne Webb continued to be a star as far as boy-care went, but for how long could you depend on a neighbour? Gary Hope became Jonty's regular taxi service to his swimming training sessions. Jonty was, from every report, quite clearly going to be the natural born swimming genius of the 2008 Olympics. But, on the whole, for the four of them, it didn't work. You can't run a family on the basis of notes pinned up on the kitchen notice board. And the dog pined. And ate her favourite pair of trainers.

She should pack it in while she was ahead.

We are neither of us able to sleep much, tossing around, riddled with suspicions. Ten days, we've got, before I invest with Mr Patel in Queensway and advertise the first donation to bloody old Cancer Research – well I'm quite sure it's a first-rate and exemplary charity, doing great works, but I'd prefer to put a grand into the collecting-box of my own choosing and of my own free will. Well not a grand, perhaps a bunch of tenners.

Suddenly we may need for H. to continue, just in order to pay the blackmail. Is it illegal for a National Charity to live off immoral earnings? If it isn't, shouldn't it be?

Rang my main suspect, E., and arranged to have a drink with her. Spent another morning with Andrew Fiske in his lair in the basement at Hartbeck talking about the likely originality of famous sender index code: BG3.1. Well, you can't really call it 'talking' with Andy, as he is mostly silent. Occasionally he rubs a finger over an eye behind his glasses and his Adam's apple, which is decidedly scraggy and pronounced, goes up and down like a manic lift on acid. I hate him. Is he our quarry? Probably not, but it doesn't give him any excuse to begin every sentence with a pause.

The whole conversation with Fiske was deeply tricky as I had to invent this obscene stream of disgusting abuse which some anonymous git had apparently dumped on to my screen. Fiske, in among his many and varied silences, seemed privately to surmise that I had written the bloody thing myself. Which was really ironic, wasn't it, because of course I had. All in all, we got nowhere. Bugger. When Fiske does manage to summon a partial communication, he just mumbles obscure technical jargon at me. His conclusion was, again, that it isn't really possible to do what has, in fact, been done. He may have to go.

Had this bizarre notion on the train home, that it might just be H. herself. You know, in a funny kind of way, however horrific,

I think there may be a tiny part of her that is seduced by the whole unsavoury business of her work. She's certainly hooked on the income. She loves having the money and, I think, really likes some of the favoured swanning about she gets to do. I mean, she spent a jolly weekend in France a couple of weeks ago. All paid for, and then all paid for. It just struck me that this could be her dick-headed way of ensuring the continuation of her sexploits. It would be just like H. to think she could make it moral, at the same time, by funding a charity. It's a wicked, evil, blood-red monster when it gets its teeth into you – suspicion.

Harriet hacking into a Statex system? I must be mental!

Ellen was not a happy bunny. She is still in solitary, camping in Battersea, and last month our abortive 'coffee' together there had not helped the old Holloway approval rating at all. She genuinely didn't seem to know much about my job at Hartbeck. I gave her a good few shrewd looks and talked philosophically about the ethics of blackmail – she must have thought me considerably more unbalanced than usual. She's either a bloody good actress or she knows fuck all about BG3.1.

LATER: I wondered about TLS too. H. mentioned him as having asked her about what she was up to. She told him the cover story about being library assistant at C.P.E.M. He could have gone off and checked on that, I suppose. She went over to Dulwich last week to bring back a whole pile of apples from his garden. I'd wondered at the time why this sudden interest in giving the Holloway family stewed-apple collywobbles and I said as much to H. She said that while she was there he had pressed her somewhat about her life and times and the price of eggs, but she had deflected the conversation and they finished up talking about his boys and the problems of the late teenager in love.

She spent ages over there. Ran out of petrol on the way back, apparently, and had to walk for miles with the can. She was away forever. Before this, he gave her a hell of a scrumptious tea. What the devil's he after? Yes, it could be TLS, I suppose. It's certainly got his sense of humour, if you can call it that.

I've never seen so many hard green battered apples. Can you die of Bramley apple poisoning? Why am I trying (half-heartedly) to joke at a time like this? All we'll ever know for certain is that Timothy had the most dreadful stomach ache – I expect TLS sprays his trees with chemicals and stuff? He would, he's a great control freak, TLS, like clipping the ducks' wings on his pond to keep them from flying away. Yes, it could just be TLS. If he wasn't my best mate.

Harriet was back once more in her hateful camp bed in Flitcroft Mews. That evening, she had had a spiritually bruising encounter with a refrigeration engineer. He had wanted to truss her up with garden wire. 'Just the wrists,' he had pleaded. A complete madman. She hadn't hung around to find out more. She had left a lot of her clothing behind but, thank God, it was colder now and she had taken her Armani coat along on the gig. She had escaped with it covering her modesty via a fire exit into a deserted and freezing Upper Cheyne Row.

It was so much tougher, now that there was a real pressure, once more, to earn the money. She would not find it easy to say to Peter, in the morning, that she had walked out on this one tonight. Peter had looked so relieved when the thick bastard had made the call and booked her. She had got used, in the last little while, to being able to pick and choose. She had felt very much more in control when she had been able to play God with their unsatisfactory needs and desires.

More and more, she found she was learning to dislike men. But her work often seemed like a useful therapy for her antipathy. Watching that queue of fellas working off their petty climaxes often disgusted her, but it also made her feel ever so masterful and superior. Mistressful. And since she'd left Arts Ed. she didn't think she had ever felt all that superior about anything. Her way of life and Peter's success had never allowed it. The work had begun to stem her natural automatic affection for men. But she found that she could deal with it all perfectly well if she remained in charge. When the men were at her beck and call, and her servicing of them was primarily in her gift, she could deal with them very well indeed.

The blackmail was beginning to deny her that strength.

Whoever it was communicated with Peter's office Statex once again. This time with a full-dress mock-up of a newspaper column – headline, column, the lot.

Harriet never saw it, of course, and Peter deleted it pretty speedily. But what he told her was enough to make her hair stand on end. They got themselves into another flat-spin of the wildest suspicions. Peter had even taken to suspecting June Southern, his administrator at Hartbeck, because it was so odd that on neither occasion when the blackmailer had communicated had it appeared that she had witnessed the message. But then if he could suspect Marianne from next door, he could suspect anybody.

This latest awfulness on Peter's screen had featured a tabloid page mock-up with the headline: 'NEWSPAPER MAN'S WIFE A HOOKER' and '*Chronicle* Ex-Editor Pete (buy-my-wife) Holloway puts more than the paper to bed each night', etcetera etcetera. Peter said he reckoned the lawyers could never have passed the story as it stood – it was stuffed full of libels, but you got the idea. It certainly wasn't a real piece of professional popular journalism either – so that tended to rule out the odious Ellen Herbert.

This dummy column announced that Harriet had been thus employed for a year which, of course, was not true. Most interesting of all was that there had been a photograph alongside the story on the screen. She could remember it being taken. She had gone to a charity film première at the Odeon Leicester Square, late October, with a man from Elstree who was called Kevin Barker or Barber or something. There had been a bunch of press photographers standing on their little step-ladders, waiting for Princess Anne. They would photograph anything female with legs and as she had attended wearing this microscopic virtual promise of a skirt from Jigsaw, they all flashed away at a moment of involuntary immodesty. The slightly fuzzy picture had her apparently alighting from this Kevin Baker's Merc. – legs for miles. Peter said you could see right up to Hackney Marshes. Ugh. Served her right. That's what you get, Ms Ivanov, if you affect the wearing of such brazen attire.

There was a note on the screen which summed up the whole horrible mock-cutting with one word: 'Pretty?' and then it just said: 'But fortunately you know how you can avoid any public embarrassment, don't you? Don't delay, pay today!' That was all.

So once again, good intentions or no, Harriet was back on the treadmill, whether she liked it or not. The Holloways needed the dough almost more than ever.

It couldn't be Peter, making up these blackmail tales, could it, in order to keep her earning? No, how stupid, he hated her doing it, loathed her doing it. Except for those squelchy times when he insisted she delve into her store of dirty bedtime stories.

Harriet knew it was one of those occasional nights when she didn't think she was going to sleep. It was cold in her bunker at night these days. She turned in the cramped constriction of the sleeping-bag.

She watched the light from her fragrance candle flicker on the white-washed brick walls. It was a prison cell and she felt terribly lonely in it. If she didn't have the candlelight, it became a totally pitch black cell and she knew she would cry there in the dark. She couldn't bear to cry just at the moment. What kind of an awful life was this? She hardly saw the boys, particularly now they were at school in the daytime. She was having to spend endless evenings feeling decidedly unsexy with men whose only assumption was that she was a positively insatiable wanton sex machine.

Peter seemed to have disappeared into the world of his work all over again. There had been a time when he was house-husbanding, and learning to cook by the seat of his pants, and being really good with the boys, when she had almost remembered what loving him was like. Now they seemed to be back at square one on the Snakes & Ladders board.

But if she and Peter didn't pay this incredible blackmail, it was possible that absolutely everyone in the world might discover what she was and what she had been up to. And that everyone-in-the-world would include her dear, innocent, trusting, admiring, puritan old parentals, her lovely, dashing sons, their, no doubt, clean-living teachers, their toffy-nosed school-friends, Peter's colleagues, Wendy, Marianne, Toby and Barbara, Aaron, people she had been at Arts Ed. with – Oh, it just didn't bear thinking about.

God, if it came out, she would kill herself. Yes, she would. No. No, she wouldn't. But she would want to die.

Well, they would just have to pay it. That's all there was to it. It would be all right then. And they would have to pay it forever and ever. There was no alternative. And she, Harriet, would slowly go mad down here, night after night, doing tricks, finishing up in her hateful solitary cell. She felt awful. Adrift, puzzled, panicked, in hell. She missed reading Timothy his bedtime story, arguing with Jonty about the telly. She missed Peter. She missed 'Top of the Pops', 'Blind Date', and even, God rot his socks, the hound from hell. She missed them all.

Her period was due, probably. Since she had come off the pill it had remained stubbornly fickle about timing. Yes, that was probably it.

The payment to Cancer Research might, at least, help to save a few lives – that was a mercy. It almost comforted her. She fell asleep with the image of the man in the bedroom at the Royal Chelsea, with his naked legs beneath his long white shirt tails, still wearing his polka-dot bow tie, waving a coil of green garden-wire at her, pleading: 'Only the wrists. Only the wrists, my dear. The wire's plastic-coated! It's just garden-wire!' It was a gruesome business.

I paid it. I don't know where we go from here. Yesterday, Saturday. Got the receipt. Did the business. We should be all right. If this guy is serious about his charitable works, he won't blow the whistle. They're going to be fairly intrigued at Lincoln's Inn Fields, me popping in with a grand at the end of each month. Let alone, tiny wizened Mr Patel in his shop. Jesus!

This morning – Sunday morning – I find myself in bed with Mrs H. – she was stood up by some punter last night and came home. Well, that was different.

She is very very tired. Dreadfully tired really. And a bit down. This whole blackmail scenario has really got to her, poor thing. Got to us both. But we felt quite warm and communicative together. We talked of family matters – my reprehensibly delayed duty to call in on my mother, what we should do Re Christmas-And-The-Parental-Call-From-Auld-Reekie.

And we talked of swimming. Apparently Hope springs paternal! Gary Hope and his Missus are having their third baby just at the same time as the Bromley swimming gala and he can't be around to do his worst with the Council minibus transport. H. has gone and offered our services to cart the team to Bromley and back. She asked TLS, of all people, to bring his Roller over to assist us too, as they won't, of course, all fit in the Porsche. Toby must have died of apoplexy, but as he sort of fancies H., he complied. Harri thought the kids'd all get a kick poncing about in his wanky old Rolls-Royce. And I don't escape. I have to do fathering. She wants me to video the whole bang shoot and bring all the would-be Duncan Goodhews back here to screen their competitive splishes and splashes. With crisps and Coke. This is next Wednesday evening. Yuk.

It was such a very risky strategy that she had conjured up, shot through with every kind of potential disaster. It was as leaky as a colander. She probably wasn't very good at this – a Bear of Extremely Little Brain. But she had to do something. Toby went on and on about it, in his most offensively unpleasant demanding way. Not actually making out-and-out categorical threats, but they were there, in the wind, in the drift of what he was saying. He was pretty sick, was Toby. But then, probably, so was she. As she was beginning to realise.

She had put his ghastly scenario off for one whole month by going to see him in Dulwich and doing a number in their hideous bedroom, while his wife, Barbara, was away at a conference in Cheltenham. Natasha had twanged her suspenders and thwacked his bum and did what was necessary, all the while marvelling at the designer-riot of manic drapery in peach and purple and wondering if she had left the car lights on in the drive. She had got home frantically late, bearing a gift of two hundred-weight of dodgy apples from his garden. The kids had got the collywobbles from them the following day. But it had been enough to shut him up for three weeks. Now the demands were escalating again. Thick and fast, they were escalating. And very specific they were too. She was getting embarrassed by the number of calls she was getting from Toby.

It would be entirely within Toby's character suddenly to tell Peter what his wife Harriet had secretly contracted herself to do with him. The deceit of it would presumably blow their marriage right out of the water. And although that was already sometimes a pretty dodgy item, she needed to be able to make her own choices about it.

So she thought she had better try to pull something out of the bag. It would no doubt be very tricky, but it might just be possible. Risky and difficult and very scary.

It was an appalling truth, but Harriet had found herself living by the nostrums of the Cult Of Recklessness in the past half year. And she had survived. In fact she had often felt more alive than she ever remembered. She found she was excited by 'scary'. It made her shake but it also turned her on. It seemed to her that she had recently stumbled upon a strange unlooked-for part of her psychological make-up. She was perhaps a tiny bit kinky after all. She couldn't imagine why she should be like this. Was it some kind of a revolt? Some kind of rebellion, in her old age, against the safe precision and innate sureness of the McGee family childhood? It didn't seem all that credible. Surely all those years in the secure embrace of that sensible upbringing, among those broad comforting Edinburgh streets, those staid yellow-stone buildings, and the constant love of two nice enough parents should have made for a solid no-nonsense security? But there seemed to be something odd that ran in the junior McGee genes – you only had to look at Julian. Did she need fear to make her feel properly alive? He had. Did she, too, need to try to risk all, in order to make her feel that something, at least, was actually really happening? When she went out to meet a john, when she took her tightly corked bottle of fear into Café Fish or Café Penguin or Doddington's Wine Bar or whatever anonymous hostelry she had selected, however much she strutted her stuff and hid inside ballsy old Natasha, Harriet was always dry-mouthed with anticipatory funk. She hated it, and she adored it, all at the same time. She was hooked on fear. An adrenalin junkie. And afterwards, when she had faced it, done it and had got out the other side unscathed, the exultation, the adrenalin-filled rush of self-esteem was like the very best kind of drug. And the high she got was seriously incredible. And there were times when she knew that she did actually live part of her life for the buzz that came from the triumph of her will over adversity. Was she totally bonkers?

Planning this present enterprise made her pulse run slightly faster all the time. The game plan was to accommodate Toby's most recent madness, for her to pay off her debt with another episode and for no one, apart from the two of them, to be any the wiser. No hurt. No distress. Just private personal humiliation for her. And she was gold medal standard at dealing with that.

Her instruments for this ridiculous exercise were to be plates of sandwiches and the family video camera. She commenced the scam by preparing a great pile of cheese-and-pickle rolls and a decent stack of bacon, lettuce and tomato sandwiches laid out on three of her largest plates. She covered them with cling-film and hid them in the saucepan cupboard together with two large plastic bottles of Coke.

The second inspiration about the video camera had come to her while jogging on her daily pilgrimage through Greenwich park to the gym. At the tourist-ridden Royal Observatory, there were the usual weekend crowds and she found herself thinking wryly how typical it was that the fellas always did the videoing. With every couple, where they owned a camcorder, it was always the wretched bloke had his finger on the go-button. There it would be, slung like a dead crow round his neck – never ever on the woman – heaven forbid. The truth was that, however much the world might ostensibly have changed, it was still men who drove camcorders, in the same way that they always drove cars and dominated restaurant menus, and thirteen-amp electric-plugs, and corkscrews, and Black and Decker drills, and airline tickets, and barbecues, and cricket teams, and religions, and governments and the United Nations and wars.

For a moment, there in the park, Harriet felt, for once, vaguely politically agitated and then it was swept from her mind by this simple, brilliantly wicked idea: 'Bingo! Yes. Video! That might do the trick – Peter, the video recorder and the Greenwich Swimming Club.'

So, with her heart pumping, and her rafts of sandwiches prepared and the obnoxious Toby apprised and vaguely cued, she triggered her shameful strategy. She suggested to Peter that when they took the swimming team over to Bromley Pools, he should video the races and bring everyone back home to Blackheath Drive to view the result.

So on the Wednesday evening, they picked up the juniors at what Gary was fond of calling the mustering point – the Arches Leisure Centre. She doubted if any local swimming team had ever travelled in quite such outrageously showy opulence – a silver Porsche (however elderly) and a Rolls-Royce! The team voted it 'wicked' and made an astonishing amount of noise.

Even so, Greenwich lost the match and Jonty was beaten by very good times put in by these hulking great eleven-year-olds on steroids and cocaine that the devious opposition produced. Even so, Jonty beat one minute, forty seconds for the first time for his hundred metre breast-stroke. Not bad for the youngest member of the team.

Harriet and Toby watched from the balcony and hardly spoke. He sat a couple of seats away from her and could have been asleep he was so inanimate. Peter spent the evening padding massively up and down the poolside in his bare feet, with the video-camera jammed to his eye, imagining he was John Boorman or Martin Scorsese. With a specific role to play, he seemed to enjoy himself enormously.

Bromley had gathered massed vocal support and had a triumphant evening all round. It seemed likely, Harriet thought, in those few rare moments when she could put the arrangements for the evening ahead out of her mind, that Greenwich Swimming Club tended to miss Gary's tactical poolside mutterings to his team.

Then, all of a sudden, going to the loo, in the corridor outside the main pool area, Harriet saw the man who had stared at her all those months ago, when she had attended the earlier fixture against

213

Bromley Swimming Club, but at Greenwich Arches Leisure Centre – the day she had had to invent an instant migraine. It was one of those extraordinary coincidences that she had often dreaded. This time, however, he didn't seem to notice her at all. But there was no question in her mind, some time back in August or whenever it had been, he had been a john. He was obviously a Bromley Swimming Club parent. She could remember nothing about him – name, work, where she had been with him – all blank. No, it had been in a flat at the Barbican, in the City. And he had been a john, of that she was absolutely positive. Had he now become a blackmailer?

And then, later, this odd thing happened. It was outside, at the end, when they were all trying to fit into the two cars, dropping towels and shouting and mislaying members of the team and generally carrying on. From out of the main entrance, into the cold of the evening, came this same guy, this time with, presumably, his wife and a child, a boy. The man's wife said: 'Goodnight, Mr Lydell–Smith.'

When she and Toby and some of the kids were driving in the Rolls-Royce back home to Blackheath Drive, through darkest suburbia, she asked him: 'Who was that – just now outside? Do you know the opposition, Toby?'

'Brian Taylor and his wife. I think she's called Dora or something. He's in my office.'

And everything fell into place. She guessed it all in one. The bastard blackmailer was Toby. This Brian man must have told him, after he spotted his boss with her that first time at the swimming pool.

Then they were home. The dread anticipation of potential embarrassment and disaster completely gripped Harriet's heart. She loathed it. And this latest piece of news had made her brain sick with anger. In the stark reality of the evening, the bizarre scheme that she had planned, seemed considerably more than lunatic, but she ploughed on, with her mind closed down, as if proceeding solely by numbers.

She fetched Timothy from next door, pushed nine damp-haired, chlorine-reeking kids into the front room with Peter and his video masterpiece and announced that she would go and make them all some sandwiches. Toby came up with his allotted cue line about walking off down into Blackheath Village to get them all some Coke to drink. This was greeted by suitable cheers from the young people, their recent defeat now satisfactorily forgotten. Once they were settled around the TV screen, Harriet tore into the kitchen and got the ready-prepared sandwiches out from their hiding place, removed their cling-film protection and scattered crumbs and knives about her working surfaces. She had been right, would-be Spielbergs adore having their work viewed by appreciative subjects. Looking in on the living room, she saw her husband, pretending not to love it, surrounded by shrieking, chortling young swimmers, cheering their successes and groaning at their failures, with Timmy sitting on his lap, looking grumpy, with his fingers pressed firmly in each ear.

She met Toby in the hall. He had gone noisily out of the front door and then had come straight back in. He headed for the stairs.

'Oh no you don't,' she hissed, grabbing his arm.

'What do you mean?' he said. 'It's got to be your bedroom.'

'No way. This is tough enough as it is, you sod, Toby. Come on, it's the back loo for us!' and she pushed him, protesting but almost silent, towards the garden door. It was as pathetic and as ridiculous and as awful as anything she could have imagined. There was hardly any room for the two of them in there, particularly when trying to close and lock the door. Toby seemed double his size in the tiny back loo. What a dump for sex. It would have to do and there was an end to it. Harriet had to climb up on to the seat. It was awful. Then, hauling a Durex from her back pocket, and accompanied by the only too omnipresent noise of the young people reliving their evening, she set about getting the bastard into some sort of adequate shape.

He began to make his grunting and groaning noises. 'Shut it,' she snapped, holding his face into her breasts and manipulating her one spare hand like a road drill and about as tenderly. 'Don't make a single sound, you sod.' But he liked her calling him names, so he didn't recognise her rage. He quietened down, his hands in the back of her knickers, stroking her backside. Her main attention was not with them, in the lavatory, at all. It was with her ears straining to listen for the slightest change of activity in the rest of the house.

She hadn't much time. From her stance on the loo seat, her head knocking the shade of the hanging lamp, she wriggled one leg out of her jogging trousers. She had to bend almost double to help prise her foot out of the elasticated ankle. Finally, thankfully, she mounted the rat – or the part of the rat stuck out from his unzipped fly. He was now mercifully silent; she guessed he was probably concentrating on not coming too quickly. She thought angrily, her legs locked around his hips, that she did more of it with this bugger standing up than you could ever begin to imagine. Get it over, get it over, get it over. It was just petrifying – there was no sense of achievement or thrill. She wanted it just to be quick and over and for her to be out. It felt as if she was on one of the machines in the gym – how many press-ups to go before she had done her quota? There was just the noise of two people breathing energetically and the cold of her sweat and the sound of her son Jonty, in the living room, shouting above the others: 'Yeah!' Obscene, disgusting dry humping with an out-and-out sod.

She was so incensed by this man. She loathed him so very much. This act of love was one of pure unadulterated hatred. Well, she knew all about his games now. It was a funny thing about secrets: once you knew, you knew that you had always known. She turned her hatred to her advantage, muttering: 'You slimy, fucking sod, I'll give it to you, you sick cunt!' All the worst words she could muster. And she bit his lip hard and put her finger and thumb deep into his mouth and pinched at the flesh of his cheek with her hard sharp thumb and finger-nails. She had his red blood smearing her hand. She hurt him and he kept quiet. He must have thought it the ultimate cruel sexual turn-on because, thank the Lord, it made him dump his load. What a relief.

The man allowed himself his usual wracking groan. He'd lasted longer than he usually managed. He was pathetic really. She heard him say one single word when he came: 'Pete!' She climbed off him. Hot and cold and sweaty and pissed-off.

Just at that very moment she heard her husband, from the direction of the kitchen, shouting very loud: 'Bugger!'

'Stay here. Don't come out until I say,' she ordered. She yanked her trousers back on and left him there, faintly hearing him lock the door again behind her. She sprinted for the kitchen, tucking her sweaty hair behind her ears, wiping her mouth clean of him with her sleeve. Peter was standing in the middle of the kitchen surrounded by devastated and scattered sandwiches, half-empty plates and no sign of Starfire whatsoever.

'Oh,' she groaned.

'Why did you have to leave them?'

'I had to go to the loo.'

'Couldn't you wait? Ye gods. Look at this mess, H. You're all hot, have you been running? Some of them are salvageable, just about,' he said.

'I can make some more. I've got some more of the cheese,' she lied. Her main thought was that Peter might suddenly want to go and have a pee himself. It was the one and only thought that entirely consumed her head. Supposing he goes to the loo? And Toby comes out of it? He turned to go, leaving her to resurrect the feast. He was at the door about to rejoin the kids when she had this grim vision of him meeting Toby coming from where she had, herself, just emerged. At this precise moment, she needed a full-scale evacuation of the hall.

'Come with me,' she said urgently, 'I've got something really important to tell you.' And she dragged him by the hand up the stairs and into their bedroom and away from the scene of the crime.

'What?' he asked, following, very puzzled.

'It's Toby,' she whispered breathlessly. 'The blackmailer. I'm sure of it. Don't say anything. But he has a guy works in his office – Brian someone. He's a Bromley parent. He was there today – at the swimming-baths. This guy, he saw me before, that other time, you remember, when I had to go and hide in the car, and pretend I had a migraine. He was a john. I did him once, I think, in August some time, at the Barbican. He and Toby must have compared notes. Toby was there, at the baths, that other time too. Definitely. I suddenly remembered. Stands to reason it must be Toby. Stands out a mile. The man must have told him something. It makes so much sense. I'm sure of it. Toby could probably manage the hacking in some way. It's certainly his sense of humour, we'd already said that.'

'Toby! Bloody Toby! Grrrreat! Yeah, I expect the Cancer Research thing is one of Barbara's bloody charities. Good God. I'll kill him,' said Peter.

'Say nothing. Let's think it through, Peterkins. Please. Be good. Please. Keep it to yourself.' And, shortly, they went downstairs. Toby was just coming in through the front door, looking bright-eyed and cold, with two big plastic bottles of Coke. Harriet was very happy to see that he had an inflamed and bruised cheek.

The evening finished with a lot of exhausted young people eating the annihilated sandwiches, and thankfully slurping Coke. Then arrangements were made between the two drivers to drop children all over the neighbourhood. The cars drove off leaving Harriet

217

shivering on the front drive, waving cheery goodbyes, with the deepest loathing for yet another man tattooed on her heart. Peter avoided saying goodnight to him altogether. But Toby was so full of kindly and solicitous words to them both that he certainly didn't notice. Greenwich Swimming Club may have lost the annual gala against Bromley but Toby Lydell–Smith seemed cock-a-hoop at the jollity of the occasion.

All right, let's get sensible about this. I mean, we are living in the real world here. Not some kind of soft Schwarzenegger wankerama. As Denis Healey said: 'If you're in a hole, the first thing to do is to stop digging.' But can we? I mean, what the shit can we do? Right, I've just paid the November 'emolument'. Yes, that's a TLS word if ever there was one – clear as a bell. This was as a result of more instalments of dangerously public pressure at Hartbeck from (presumably) my oldest and best friend. Just making damned sure that I didn't forget. He seems to get such enormous pleasure from laughing at our discomfiture. 'I'm so very sorry,' he said on this latest message, 'but I've got you and your wife absolutely all ways up, I fear! How difficult for you.' The man's clearly off his head.

I don't think we can run our lives around a twelve grand per annum hand-out to charity. And what I hate about it is the duress. No, what I hate about it is dishing out the money.

But supposing I confront TLS with it? Tell him I know it's him. I can't do anything more about it than that. He's still laughing. He can say, yes, you're right, it is me. What are you going to do about it? I've still got the info and I'm afraid that if you don't keep up the jolly old payments, I will unfortunately have to make use of it, willy-nilly. He obviously thinks it's ever such a good game. And when he gets bored with the status quo, he can move the goal posts. Why not – suddenly – five grand a month? Ten? We couldn't do anything about it. There's nowhere to appeal, apart from his good nature.

OK, I suspect the case against us might be difficult to prove. One photo of H., demonstrating the astonishingly inviting length of her thigh bones, is not exactly incriminating. However, once the story's out, the waters would be good and muddied, and some of the dirt would be bound to stick. It always does. The jackal fraternity'd be camping around our doorstep with their tape-recorders and cameras for months. It's too good a story to give up on. And the Met. would be round too. That's the problem. They could find out a hell of a lot very easily – Flitcroft Mews and H.'s fake job and all.

This is just what I don't need at the moment. In the last month, the market research johnnies at Hartbeck have been sounding suspiciously negative about the market share for *Eleventh Hour*. George has spent the last three meetings pressing me into lightening up the whole profile of the publication considerably – moving into *Private Eye*'s territory. It seems to me a pointless direction to go in, so I'm resisting it. But his initial enthusiasm has waned. The whole notion of the magazine stemmed, it now seems, from some clash he had at the Garrick, one evening back in the spring, with Lord Buttermere. Since his Lordship went and suffered a massive stroke in November, the bloody thing has gone marginally off the boil, for George at any rate.

So all we need now is a breath of even a second-rate scandal. I think George might be only too glad to find a reason to knock the whole operation on the head. I think he thought the recession was as good as over, but, it appears, advertising revenue is still bumping along the bottom much as before. To get the thing launched – and I really do believe the idea has legs – I will need every piece of ingenuity that I can muster. And a very very clean nose.

So what to do?

I've been going on pathetically about killing the bastard. And I half believe that I could. I had such a fearful shout with H. about all this. She was saying that she thinks we've completely lost all touch with reality. And, of course, she's right. We've been making up our own rules as we go along for almost a year. Since this whole business with H. started, it has felt totally unreal nearly all the time. This strange clandestine operation did, rather appallingly, have a kind of electricity for me. That is, when I wasn't chewing the bedhead with the thought of H. in filthy congress with some anonymous gunk. The idea of these shits possessing my wife stopped my heart. But there was also a lunatic buzzy feeling of power in it too. There were times when I felt as if we could do just about anything. Get away with everything. As if the normal rules didn't apply to us two. Particularly when I got the Hartbeck job as well. It's a bit like doing coke, you feel utterly invincible.

I sit on the train each morning and I look at the office workers and the students and the salesmen and the housewives and the executives and I want to scream at them: 'You poor bloody stupid stuck-in-the-groove dying people! What are you living for? Where are you going? What's it all about? Throw it all up. Pack in convention. Make your own rules. Do what you have to do. This isn't some kind of dry run, you know!' Stupid, actually, but it's what I've felt like.

And when I'm in that mode, I think I could actually do him in. I could do it – kill him. But how? And how to do it safely, so that we didn't get caught? How could one do it so that no one would ever guess? There must be a fair number of murders that no one ever knows anything about. And where the murderer gets off scot-free.

Where the hell *is* Charles Bronson when you need him?

Actually I think I know just how to do it. And get away with it.

H. says I'm mad. I may be. She says: 'Yeah all right, we're in trouble. But we can earn the money in the meantime. Pay it. Eventually tackle him. Sort it out. You can't really mean that you can truthfully allow yourself to think about murder? Are you really talking about killing someone, Peter, really truly and honestly? Grow up,' she says. 'You're talking about someone with kids, and a wife, and a bloke who, whatever he may or may not have done, was meant to be your friend? It's absolute garbage,' she says. 'We may have gone off the edge but we're not quite that far off the edge!'

But I think we are off the edge. I think we have been, ever since that night Harri and I spent together in Bloomsbury. Nothing has been completely sane since then. And do you know, in spite of this insanity, I can still legitimately contemplate it? Really. And I said so. H. has now stopped talking to me. She said that she's disgusted by me. We talk via the kids. And via notes – handwritten notes. So I don't mention doing TLS in any more.

She's pissed-off too because I've said, absolutely categorically, that she's got to end it now. She says we can't afford to stop, she's got to earn the money. Which is so much crap. We don't need it all now. We can draw in our horns. She's been seduced by the money. She's become such a tough little cookie. She's not the person she was. It's a severely corrupting business – this peddling something as intimate and personal as the very secret of your body. She seemed to think she could skate above it all, make it impersonal, pretend it was all happening to that idiotic *doppel-gänger* of hers, Natasha. Well, you can't, can you? And I always thought as much.

She has become so awfully knowing about the male psyche and

the masculine foible she frightens me – she's so wilful and knowing. It's not pleasant to be so sussed about humankind – well, anyway, about human mankind. And she's not got all that much time for me, it seems. Or any men for that matter. So we don't talk much, we just stutter along. And I feel ridiculously sad about it.

I need her back. So I've got to rid ourselves of the blackmail, and then I must, carefully, bring us all back down to calm, sensible reality and decency.

And I think that I know how to do the first, and no one ever need know that it was anything other than an accident.

Harriet sat in Emma Leo's in South Moulton Street and waited for John, her hairdresser, to come and finish her off. She sipped her coffee, idly flipped through her magazine while listening to 'Simply Red' and looked as crisp and as cool as a countess. John had done beautiful new hair. It would look great for Christmas. And for work after the holiday period when all those men had been released from their family firesides and were looking to reassert their youths all over again in her capable world-weary hands.

But, truthfully, of course, her appearance belied everything. Harriet was about as far from cool as it was possible for a person to be. Their life might be tough and sick and difficult, but firmly, somewhere in the back of her head, she knew for certain that, whatever the cause, you just didn't kill. No matter what had happened. You might just screw and lie and steal and betray and deceive and destroy and toy with your own safety and health, and other people's, in order to try to keep your frenzied life together – perhaps. But you did not kill.

Peter had never mentioned it again, but she felt it was still there, somewhere in the air between them. So she would have to do something. What she had learned above all in the last year was that you had to be proactive. You had to make the first move. Get in, do it, and do it immediately. Before they get in and do it to you first. No matter how nasty.

The magazine she was leafing through was *Marie–Claire*. It had a typical come-on article about the present trend in nineties cinema for 'luscious lesbians'. Hollywood trying to have it both ways – pretending to boldly go where no woman has gone before, while continuing to trudge faithfully along its usual, traditional rut, pulling its punches all the while. If the studio bosses reckoned they could pull the worldwide heterosexual audience into the cinemas with fantasies about what glamour pussies might get up to together in bed, then that's what they would dish up next – for a while. Lesbian sex, the safest in the world. And a hell of a turn-on for blokes, it seemed.

And then and there, without warning, what should pop into her unsuspecting head but the brightest, most wicked, brilliant idea. A honeypot of an idea. A honeypot that might very well trap a wasp. A double honeypot.

I've always known how to kill someone and get away with it. On the mountains. And the real joke about it is that TLS and I have spent days and days on the mountains together. Even now, we have a sort of weekend earmarked, as usual, for the weekend prior to Christmas.

And I've always known how easy it would be. You're crossing some needle-sharp mountain ridge, a thousand feet above a sheer drop, carefully placing your boots on the slippery wet rock, moving smoothly from handhold to handhold, scrambling together on some granite tight-rope, isolated from the world by the fluctuating mists. You both stop to catch your breath and listen to the wind and glimpse the sheep moving slowly in the cwm, way way below you. You stand there poised above the deep, like Gods on a high niche of stone. No one would be prepared, forewarned, forearmed. One quick, hard shove and your companion would be no more. Simple. A terrible, sad, mountaineering accident. The rock was so treacherously slippery that day.

I could do it.

I can. And I will too. I'm going to have to.

Harriet was terrified about the next three days. Peter was determined to go on his annual boys' outing with Toby to climb hills and dangerous bits of rock in Wales. She was petrified about what might happen. Not that they would fall off or anything – she had inured herself to those dangers, years and years ago. And now, thank goodness, she didn't believe that Peter would take the opportunity of being alone with their presumed persecutor to attack him with a poisoned crampon or something. In the last couple of weeks, since their big row, her husband had hardly mentioned that lunatic idea again. It had obviously just been a touch of 3 a.m., middle-of-the-night madness.

What frightened her was that the two men might use the occasion together to have a whisky-generated heart-to-heart about what appeared to have blown up between them. Cornered, she could just imagine the evil Toby producing, like some sadistic ace from up his sleeve, the fact of their secret deal together. For some twisted reason, he obviously adored knowing that he was darkly humiliating Peter. And that she, Peter's wife, was his cherished instrument. Maybe this had been what he had had in mind in the first place. Maybe he had always been building up to a terrible climax when he could utterly annihilate Peter with the truth of what had been going on. After all, if he could torment them so cruelly with his blackmail scam, he was capable of doing anything.

And these two were meant to be friends. Between them, Harriet and Toby had made Peter such an innocent. He would absolutely loathe that. And it was all her fault. She could so easily see Toby telling her husband the things that she had allowed him to do to her – the things she had allowed herself to do to him. And where, and when. There were times when it felt to Harriet that it would be even worse than her detailed history coming out in a welter of tabloid publicity.

Harriet already knew that she was probably holding her relationship with Peter together on the flimsiest ground. What they had allowed themselves to do in the last six months had always been based upon the tacit understanding that she was honest with him about everything. And, of course, she hadn't been. She had found a kind of independence, in the same way that she knew men did, by being deceitful. Deceitful about Toby, deceitful about, say, her liking for people like Jack Robinson, deceitful about where she was and what she was doing. She was beginning to loathe that part of herself when she really thought about it properly.

She had a feeling that living in this miserable tangle of duplicity was the lot of a large number of apparently honourable men. Her work confirmed this for her, time and time again. And indeed, these days, she herself often felt really more like a man than a woman, in choices she made, the way she behaved, the lack of emotion she seemed to feel and display. Had the working life completely corrupted her humanity and dehumanised her?

If Peter were to find out how false she had become, and even if he only half believed some of what Toby might tell him, his anger and unhappiness would do them all in. And surely the whole point of what she had been doing had been, willy-nilly, to try to hold them all together. And pay their way. She might not be all that easy or happy with Peter all the time, but at least now he seemed to think of her, care for her, protect her and even, sometimes vaguely to love her. And they both seemed, on the whole, surprisingly happy parents with their boys. Jonty and Timothy had come along leaps and bounds during that never-to-be-forgotten, long, hot and desperate summer.

Their desperate times had unerringly thrown the two of them together. Before this, Harriet had frequently not been all that confident that she had a proper relationship with Peter at all. Harriet often used to think that the most Peter wanted in life was a series of one-night stands but with the same person.

Even so, could you say that people hanging on to the same piece of wreckage have a relationship? Just because you are in a lifeboat with someone, in a raging threatening sea, doesn't necessarily mean that once you're in port the same intensity of feeling remains.

But Harriet knew that she would probably continue to try to hang on to the wreckage with Peter. It was probably not a very good reason, but she had been conditioned to it – marriage. All her life. It was for better or worse, wasn't it? After all, her parents' buoyantly happy marriage had been such an extraordinarily seductive role-model. She had never been able to think how it could be otherwise. And then there were the boys, the boys, the boys. Peter and her boys. Her three lads. Like it or not, Harriet always assumed that she was stuck with them. And she probably was. So she had better get on with the archetype as best she could. And give up The Life.

And that, at least, would be a good thing, surely?

Well. She was bothered. Bothered by a nagging apprehension of a special kind of culture. The all-enveloping coils of young motherdom. It was a culture into which she could once more disappear and be entirely swallowed up. The exclusive female-only circle of children's car seats, of coffee mornings for African famine relief, of rain dripping off the front of anorak hoods on wet afternoons, outside school gates, of 'if-you're-happy-and-you-know-it-clap-your-hands' at six-year-old birthday parties in the plastic heaven of McDonalds. The enclosed women's world of shared P.M.T., of being the ever-dependable tooth-fairy, of the eternal weekly checkout queue, of children's sudden passion for Sunday school, of piano practice, of getting them to Cubs on time, of watching under-elevens rugby on Saturday mornings, of the bedtime story, of the woman-dominated step-class, of persuading sons that little girls in their best party dresses are not disgusting, of wondering where the men are and what they are up to. A Blackheath mum.

But whatever she might want for her future, Wales could smash it all up. One cosy, mean-minded, drunken conversation in the brain-softening heat of the open fire at Hafody Fach in which Toby spilled the sickening beans about Harriet and he to a bewildered Peter would wreak infinite carnage. And there was nothing that she could do about it. She would just have to stay in London, in a state of extreme tension, waiting to see what happened.

We went to Wales. This is what happened.

The cottage, Hafody Fach, is at the back end of a field just at the top of the village of Nant Peris, deep in the dark cleft of the Llanberis Pass. The heart of Snowdonia. The sun doesn't reach the cottage very much in the summer, let alone in December and it's still pretty dark around that little meadow at eight in the morning. But although we had only arrived at half past midnight, TLS was stamping around shouting about cornflakes at that godforsaken hour. He and I have gone through those early-morning rituals for about twenty years – me groaning and declaring that the mountains would still all be there the following day, TLS bellowing about the shortness of the daylight hours and how we'd have to be coming off the hill by three in the afternoon. Which was true.

There were moments when it almost seemed like old times. Not blokes between whom unspoken things had occurred. Funny how men can lie to themselves and to each other. Were we unchanged? No, not really. I seemed to think he and I were subtly different with each other. More careful and polite, more aware of each other's space. For me, from the time we had got on to the M1, my heart had been drumming at the prospect of what I was going to have to do. It was all I could do to keep up a flow of mundane conversations with the guy.

The morning revealed, a thousand feet above us on the side of Y Garn, a good patch of sunlight and, because it was obviously windy up there, the cloud was quite high. In theory, it would be a good day for it.

Most years, when we've been to the cottage together, to relive old days on the hills, to sink catatonic in front of the log fire, to drink far too much whisky and poison each other with vile cooking, we would 'do the Horseshoe'. And today we were going to do it again. The Horseshoe must be one of the most wonderful ridge walks in the country. It's shaped like its name and has four great mountains strung along its wonderfully varied, nicely challenging (well, anyway, in winter) bread-knife of a ridge. Actually it's not quite as awe-inspiring as that – some of the Horseshoe has all the excitement and size of the roof of London Bridge Station – but Crib Goch is the crux. It's a ridge and a half. There's nothing like it in the United Kingdom outside of the Cuillins in Skye. They talk about your Striding Edge in the Lake District – that's like trying to compare supermarket Glen Scrotum Scotch with the heaven of Talisker malt.

If you stand by the door of TLS's outside loo and look up into Cwm Glas, to the south of the pass, you can see this incredible line of glistening brown cliffs falling more than a thousand feet in a great curtain with these castles of towering rock on the crest, half a mile along to the right. That's Crib Goch. I first walked along it when I was thirteen – twenty-seven years ago, almost. On a clear day, from below in the valley, you can see little Lowry matchstick people in silhouette, walking along the absolute top of the skyline. You know that, up there, they have a neat two-foot wide, polished, rock pavement to twinkle their toes along. Sometimes when you're feeling good, you can stroll virtually the length of it with your hands in your pockets. Another time, when morale is low, you can find yourself holding on to every stick of rock with both hands, your teeth and all of your knees. You could push someone off and they'd be killed. And no one would be any the wiser. I've always thought that. People fall off it most years at some time or other – even on the most gorgeous, balmy, summer day.

TLS is a great apple man. He thinks that's all you need for a mountain lunch, even in winter. He's pretty keen on dark green mottled sour old Bramleys – cookers. So before I had a chance to bring out battered much-travelled pasties and chocolate digestives, we were on our way, striding up the pass to the turning-off place. There's a stone bridge over the river at the milestone, two miles before you reach the top of the pass. We were going to skirt around south, to the left of the huge sombre crag of Dinas Mot and head for what they call the Parson's Nose – another cliff that they reckon

226

was first ascended by some mad cleric. It's an hour and a half of trudging up over coarse long grass and heather, very steep. For two less-than-fit desk-bound old gentlemen, neither of whom was prepared to admit their feebleness, something of a heart-tester.

We were both in a lather by the time we'd conned each other into stopping by the Llyn in the emptiness of Cwm Glas. We stood well apart so that the other could not hear one's own lungs gasping for oxygen. We're all getting older. And I'm seventeen times the weight I should be.

It always feels as if it's one of the most deserted places on earth, that high hanging valley, the rocks all of a tumble down to the lake, just wheatears and pippits and the occasional offended pregnant sheep. We saw no one, in spite of it being a Saturday. A few spots of rain and, although we were sweating and hot in our anoraks, quite cold.

You feel you're so on your own up there. For a while you can't even see the dinky-toy traffic pulling its way along the thin grey ribbon of road up the pass, way below us. Then, reluctantly, you have to start off once more. You wheel to the left again, around the dull grey ruffled waters of the Llyn and begin to fight your lungs up this steep gradient of shale and stone, towards the north ridge which provides access to the tiny picnic-table sized summit that is Crib Goch itself. Going up that thin scree is usually the only really horrible part of the day's expedition – real toil.

'Two and a quarter hours' was all the man said, when he reached the top about ten strides ahead of me. He needs to win, does TLS. He looked pale from the effort. We had both been more taciturn than usual. We'd not stopped much to talk on the way up. Too little breath and too little to say. Now we sat on this first summit of the Horseshoe, hip to hip, with our boots among the few bits of orange peel that always tend to grace those holy blocks that form the end of the Crib Goch ridge.

Again, no one about. It was like the stage had been set. I had a feeling that we both knew there was some uncomfortable subtext going on. TLS was so quiet. He normally roars along on some damn topic or other. I could feel his warmth on my arm even through the thickness of his sleeves. It began to drizzle. The rocks would be slippery underfoot for our rubber soles as we threaded our way along the ridge. We ate his sour old apples, crunching them noisily next to each other. With a sudden movement, TLS bunged his core out towards the Glyders, a mile away across the other side of the valley, and towards the ever-hopeful seagulls whose constant duty it is to monitor The Picnic Eaters Of Crib Goch.

The wind was up and the rain certainly made it much too chilly to sit there too long. We had to get on. Behind our backs, as we sat, and away from the pass, our route – the knife edge of the ridge, a shiny irregular path in the sky – snaked off towards the Pinnacles and then on to the elephant back of Crib Y Ddysgl (almost as high as Snowdon – only fifty feet or so in it) and then, a mile further on, the summit pyramid of Yr Wyddfa, the big boss herself – all of two hours away. We could reach the cairn there by a quarter to two, with a bit of luck and hard work. Would it still be the two of us? Could it be just me alone? Myself, alone, secure and safe?

'All right?' said TLS brusquely. He got up and brushed his hands on the seat of his trousers, steadying himself with a knee braced against the very top rock of the peak where we had been sitting. Then, quietly and methodically, like thousands before him, he began his slow, careful progress along the top of the ridge, stooping occasionally to place a steadying hand on the rock at knee height. The wind blew the rain into our faces and I followed him closely. Mist climbed up and sped across the mountain ahead of us like special effects in a film. I had been right. No one would be able to see what was happening up here. It seemed as if there was not a soul apart from us on the mountain. Looking both right and left, the drop was almost vertical. A body would bump and roll and fall and could not possibly stop its descent for fifteen hundred feet of acceleration.

I would only have to reach out, stumble, bump him. A simple error. A hand in the small of his back. A good shove. A hand trying to save and steady myself. I could do it now. Easy. It was almost impossible not to. Our boots and our panting and the wind were the only noises as we worked our way steadily along, concentrating, a couple of feet apart. He himself would hardly know that I had done it on purpose. There would be one brief moment of shock and surprise and it would be all over. No threat. No danger. All our problems gone in one quick tiny push. Then there would be the dash down the mountain. The desperate call to the Mountain Rescue. The interview with the police. The inquest. The funeral.

The guilt.

TLS's broad damp back strained on, his hands reaching and

pulling and his wet boots placed with quick and studied care as he made each step. He was so close to me that I could hear his every rasping breath. This was an evil, devious, snobbish, Tory, rich bastard. He would screw his best mate's wife for the fun of it. He would terrify a family just because he thought that he could. He had only ever really been friends with me, I think, because I was somehow useful to him, occasionally. And perhaps because he had a bit of an unsatisfied yen for H. Yes, that was probably it.

But.

Yes, but.

He was a living being. A puffing, sweating, grunting, flawed, product of his privilege. A fart with too much power and not very happy. As Harriet had said, he was a father just the same, a father of two young sons who presumably loved him a little. And a wife, who, at least, had stuck around. And my friend too, for so many years. My friend that, I suppose, I had never really liked very much. And I suspect he had probably never liked me all that much either. The usual blokish stuff. But even so, even so . . .

Finally, at heart, I am such an old coward. You probably have to be very angry indeed to kill. Or properly insane. And while I was sickened by him, I couldn't summon up real black depths of hatred. This cold-blooded stuff, that I'd believed I'd honestly thought through, well, I probably hadn't. Harri was, no doubt, right. She often is. And, after all, it could go wrong. His anorak might catch on something. Trying to save himself, he could grab me and take me over too. Excuses.

As the rain closed in, I clumped grimly along, not so tired now that we were up level on the ridge, climbing over the steps, the little towers, the age-old problems the mountain always throws up. I was pretty sick at myself – at my prevarication. I'd braced myself to do this. Lied to myself that I could, that I would. I wonder how much I have always kidded myself about how things are? Lots I think.

We then reached the pinnacles and the opportunity was gone. The ridge was wide from here on in. Just a funk, really, me.

The rain eased as we got to the trig point on Crib Y Ddysgl. We squatted at its concrete base. The view had completely disappeared in cloud. We were tired now. First day out. Unfit, over-weight, urban beings. We'd go up on to the top of Snowdon, stand on the cairn there and then retrace our steps and pop down the Pyg Track to the Pen Y Gwryd Hotel for damp, sweaty pints in the Everest

Room. It was too late in the day and we'd been too slow to do the whole round.

'Good-game-good-game,' he said, still breathing heavily. We both silently reviewed the last quarter of an hour of effort. I'll try to reproduce the dialogue as best I remember it:

He repeated the catchphrase: 'Good-game – good-game.'

'And you like good games, don't you?' The tone of my voice probably told him everything.

'What's up, Pete, old cock?'

'You know.'

'You've got me there, old kid.'

'Blackmail.'

'You all right, Pete? What's all this about? Here am I trotting around the Horseshoe, feeling severely unfit, gasping for breath, but damn jolly and, blow me, there's something else bleeding going on. What's this all about?'

I sat and watched the view going in and out behind the mist. Scowling. Looking meaningful. Uncertain as to how to progress. Had I got this wrong? He carried on: 'For Christ's sake, Pete, you can tell me. I'm your oldest friend.'

'Oldest friend!' I snorted.

And he turned to look at me. Quizzically – almost as if he had his half-moon specs on. I didn't know what else to say. He waited and waited. And I just looked glum. After a while, he shrugged and ripped open the Velcro on his anorak pocket and produced his ever-faithful metal hipflask. It had been a Christmas present to him from H. about seven or eight years ago. It was a bit battered now but still contained a good slurp or two of some excellent malt whisky. He unscrewed the little cap and gulped at it.

Maybe H. was wrong. Maybe we'd been barking up the wrong goddamn tree. I felt very confused. He seemed so dead calm and absolutely not bothered. More just idly intrigued by what I was getting at than anything else. But then that would have to be the best way to play it, wouldn't it? It was he who spoke first: 'You OK, Pete? I've thought you've been pretty damn silent since we left London actually. OK are you? Normally you chat away ninety to the dozen, and I usually want to fucking crown you. You've been positively monosyllabic. It's been a bit of a treat! What's up, old cock?'

'Christ knows, Toby. I don't know.' I took the whisky from

the bastard and poured some of it down my throat. It seemed to burn the inside of my neck. It felt pretty cold up there now. We ought to get on. There weren't hours and hours of daylight left. The wind was sharp, and the mist that had drifted up over the ridge continued to engulf us clammily. I had a very limp last try: 'I have a friend. Who's done something he shouldn't have.'

'What's he done, eh?'

'It's not significant really. Something he shouldn't have done. Something illegal.'

'Who's this? Do I know the fella?'

'Never mind. That's not the point.'

'No, but you know I do like a good bit of gossip.'

'No. I'm not saying. Just a friend and he thinks a very close colleague of his is blackmailing him. Because of it. Getting him to pay money. Because of what he's done.'

'What's he done, eh? Come on! Who is this? Is it Derek Yates? I heard some story about insider trading. Is that it?'

'God no. It's not Derek. It doesn't matter who it is. But he wants to fucking kill this guy.'

'Not surprised. If it was me, I guess I'm sure I'd want to top him. His best friend, eh? That's not what friends are for, is it? Not bloody likely.'

He sounded so very innocent. And not even terribly interested. TLS began to struggle with the straps of his rucksack and he finally produced a plastic bag with more of his sodding apples in it. He offered one to me. We both chomped silently away. TLS continued in a kind of ruminative vein: 'Incredible this – tell you something, Pete, I actually know a guy who is in contact with people who whack people! Isn't that extraordinary! You wouldn't really credit it, but apparently it does happen. People know people who top people that they don't want to have around. It's another world, isn't it? Can't believe it can you? But it's as true as I stand here – sit here!'

'Yes, I suppose people like us, though, wouldn't really, finally, ever do anything quite so melodramatic, would they?'

'Shouldn't think so, old boy. I should rather think not.'

We both thought about getting up and getting on. Then Toby turned to me and said, suddenly confidential: 'Is this you, old boy? Are you talking about yourself here, Pete?'

The fool that I am, I stumbled apologetically into blind motor-speak: 'No. No, of course not. Good God, no. What made you think that?'

'Just wondered. Well, best thing to do is – well, best thing to do is to confront the guy, isn't it? Have it out with him. Just best to make sure your friend's got the right jolly old chap. Doesn't want to make a fool of himself. That'd be all the worse. Doesn't need that, does he?'

'Yes, it's difficult. My colleague doesn't want to go and make a mistake. But he really needs it to stop.'

'He would do, wouldn't he? He would do. Grim stuff, kiddo, grim stuff. You don't have to tell me. Poor bloody blighter, eh? Rather him than me though, eh?'

TLS discarded his apple core. It shot in a fine, long arc out across the damp scree and into the gully below. 'Tell you something,' and TLS turned to me with a grin. 'It's sometimes useful to get a supernumerary to tackle these little problems. Tell you what, I could go and have a chat with the blackmail guy – for your colleague. Shake him up a bit – you know. I can be pretty persuasive. Or pretty bloody offensive, if you like. You can take your choice! You pays your money and you takes your choice. Actually, in this case, you don't pay your money. I'd do it as a favour for a chum. You give me the facts, the dates, times and places and so-called misdemeanours and I could go and sort it for your friend.'

Oh, I don't know. It was all so persuasive that I almost believed that we were talking about a real colleague of mine. I restricted myself to: 'I don't know. I'm not sure that I want to get that closely involved.'

'It's what best friends are for, Peterkins.' And he began to shrug on his rucksack again. It couldn't be Toby, could it? H. must have made one hell of a mistake. And I could have fucking killed the bloke. Good God, trust not in women's judgment!

'Shall we get on down?' he asked.

'Yep,' I said getting up into the wind.

'OK then.' And he set off. 'You'd tell me, wouldn't you, if I can do anything? To help?'

'Yes, you bet,' I said.

'Attaboy!' he chortled and he swung a light and affectionate cuff at the crown of my head with the flat of his palm, before setting off ahead of me again, through the mist for the summit of Snowdon.

And I had almost killed him, an hour before!

Harriet negotiated a sort of moratorium with Peter over Christmas. She played wife and mother the whole holiday. Extremely well. She cooked a less rubbery turkey than usual, talked too long to her parents on the phone and dished out brightly wrapped and amusingly educational presents to her children. Peter's mum came over for the day and insisted on them all watching the Queen's Christmas broadcast which was also less rubbery than usual. Jonty and Tim ran from their house to the Webbs next door almost incessantly the whole time – somewhat agog that Sam and Pippa's father, who was an airline pilot and who usually lived with a detested girlfriend in West Wycombe was over for the two days (and, mangled report had it, stayed the night in Marianne's bedroom – 'this sex stuff, it gets everywhere,' Harriet said to Peter's mum, who didn't quite seem to take it on board). No one walked the dog, and he seemed rather the better for it.

The evening after Boxing Day, Harriet did too much post-celebration, in-depth house-tidying and, once the boys had finally been cajoled into a bath together, drank a little too much Christmas present Chardonnay. This meant that when the Motorola rang with a regular but extremely voluble, slightly squiffy, executive from Aiwa who wanted to see her on New Year's Eve, although she put him off, she was altogether too public about it. The sound of Natasha's voice reached the jealous ears of one Mr Holloway.

When she had finished dealing with Mr Keiko, Peter joined her in the sitting room. The moratorium was obviously over. He looked grimly determined. 'This is not going to go on into the new year, H. It's got to stop. I've told you again and again. It's over. It was always a mad scheme. We don't need it any more. We're lucky you didn't get hurt. We're in enough trouble as it is, without you getting cut up. Or arrested.'

'Actually, we aren't in any trouble. I've sorted it, Peter. It's over. I'm sorry, I thought I'd leave it till after Christmas to tell you.' She paused and then, taking a deep breath, she told him: 'I've talked to Toby.'

'You've bloody what!' he roared. 'What the hell do you mean: "talked to Toby" – "talked to Toby"? What, in God's name did you say, woman? When did you do it?'

233

'Christmas Eve. When you'd both got back from yomping in Wales. I took him and Barbara some books over for the boys. Bearded him in his den. Denned him in his beard.' Yes, she was a bit pissed. 'We had an extremely educational tea together. I told him that we knew it was him.'

'And he denied it? What did he say?'

'He said, um, "oh" and "ah".'

'Oh for Christ's sake, Harri!'

'Sorry. No, well, it finished up all right. He said it had been a stupid game. Said he was very sorry. Said it had got out of hand.'

'So he confessed it?'

'Oh yes, it was him all right.'

'The bastard, the fucking bloody bastard!'

'He said it would stop.'

'He said it would stop? Just like that? I don't believe you. You haven't talked to him!'

'If you don't believe me, who can you believe, Peter?'

'No, all right, I mean I don't believe *him*. Why the hell should he give it up? He's got nothing to lose.'

'Our friendship.'

'Oh, yeah. Of course. Our friendship. Grrreat. Brilliant. Well done, Harri!'

'Shut up, Peter, don't give me this grief. I've told you – it's over. It's OK. I told him what he was doing was shameful. That it had gone far enough. I made him see sense.'

'And he believed you, did he? Fell on his knees? Begged for forgiveness? Went along with it, did he?'

'You are so hateful, Peter. Yes.'

'Oh, well, bully for you! Pull the other one, H.! He was just fobbing you off, darling.'

'You're just so supercilious, aren't you? Never give me any credit. He wasn't "just fobbing me off". I know he wasn't. It's over. That's it. That's something I know, as well as I'll ever know anything. I can guarantee it.'

'He'd tell you anything. You don't know men like Toby. They'll say anything. He's in just as strong a position as before. It's another part of his game – telling his gullible woman friend it's over and then jumping on me, on us, from a great height with more and more demands. That's just so like his sense of humour. He'd think that such a great gas. He must have been killing himself.'

'Peter, shut up.' She said it very calmly. 'I do know men like Toby. In fact they're one of the things that I've really become something of an expert in – tough, no compromise, egotistical, cruel, endless, eternal Public School boys, like Toby, like you too, actually, Peter. Like all of them. I've got my Masters in it.'

'Oh, right. You think because you've jumped into bed with a few, you know their games, you can counter their ploys, you can sense their limits?'

'"Jumped into bed with a few?" A few, Peter? That's a laugh. I've spent more hours in skin-to-skin stonking contact with more so-called power-brokers, more intimate tête-à-tête dining hours with alcohol-warmed men, pouring out their sodding, misogynist, fearful, self-seeking hearts than ICI send Christmas cards. A few! I *know* these men, Peter. I've serviced their weary lusts and celebrated their minuscule company victories and shored up their flagging self-esteems. I know what I'm talking about, Peter – I've got my Ph.D. in it – the psyche of the Enterprise Culturist, the world of the white-collar criminal. Listen to me, you can forget all about Toby Lydell-Smith, the blackmail, everything. It's all over. Period. I promise you, on my honour as the original golden-hearted whore, that as far as Toby is concerned, that whole business is history. We will never have to face any of that again.' Peter didn't believe her. 'Good eh?' she finished flippantly.

'He's a john then, is he? Is that what it is? He's just another of them. Who haven't you fucked? You're insatiable, you are. What's happened to you, girl? Can't you leave a single pair of trousers unzipped?'

'You are so bloody disgusting, foul and beastly, Peter. Of course he's not a john. You are so stupid. But I just know the type. He's one of a whole bunch of blokes who fit a pattern. And when I know something about them, I really do know something about them and their lives and their times. I know how they tick. You know them too, in your heart of hearts. You could almost have been one of them, God forbid. You know – women as part of the perks – above all, screw the opposition – brave, loyal, little wife and children back home asking no questions – high-class tarts like me around to remind themselves that they're still as good as they were when they were thirty – better even, because now they can afford a bit of class like Natasha.'

'How can you be so sure, Trinket?' He was almost wheedling now, trying to curry favour. 'What is it? Have you made some kind of deal? Are you going to pay him the dosh instead of me doing it? Or have you got some other way of paying him?'

'We're not going to pay him anything any more, at all, ever. Up till now, it was me paying him the money anyway. Who posts the certificate in the window in Queensway is neither here nor there, Peterkins. Is it? Actually?'

'All right, all right, yes.' He was humouring her now. He could patronise at thirty paces. 'Listen, lovely, he wouldn't just stop. You must have promised him something.'

'I didn't promise him a blind thing. I promise you this, Peter, as we go forward through the years, I will never ever sleep with your friend Toby. That's the honest truth, so help me God. Listen to me, Peter. This is Harriet speaking. Remember Harriet, your wife? The one who tells you the truth. Tells you the dirty secrets. Hullo? Is there anyone in there? It's over. He's had his game and he won't be playing it any more.'

Peter didn't say anything. She managed to grin at him and nudged him in the ribs with an elbow almost good-humouredly. 'Are you going to say thank you?' she said. Peter continued to look grumpy. 'Go on, say what you have to say,' she said. 'Don't clam up on me.'

He finally muttered: 'It'll have to stop.'

'Yes, I know. Yes, I know it will. But not yet. Let me be the judge of when. It's my life too. I'm happy to quieten down. I'll pick and choose. I may well stop. In the long run. But it'll be me who chooses when I'm going to do so. I'm not going to stop because you tell me to. The trouble is, Peterkins, you're a nice enough chap. I'm so very happy we've got the kids. I think you're bloody clever and I'm glad you've got this break at Hartbeck – you deserve it. But I've fallen in love with someone. And I'm not prepared to give them up.'

'Who?'

'You must have realised I've fallen in love with Natasha. I don't want her to go away. I love her too much. I love her bottle, and her masculinity, and her – what do they call it? – *chutzpah* and her incredible not-giving-a-damn. I'm sorry, I love her to bits. She thrills me. So, Peterkins, either we stick around together and do the *Hello Magazine* family thing, in happy-go-lucky Blackheath Drive, but with Natasha well and truly, but privately, in the picture, or she and I have to go off and um, sort out our relationship together somewhere else on our own. Sorry, Peter, it's going to be you who has to do the choosing. That's what you men do, isn't it? The decision makers of the world?' She slid her back towards him across the sofa and leaned her head warmly against his shoulder 'Dear God, I think I'd like you to want us to stay.'

'You're nuts, H. Always have been.' Peter sighed massively and went to get the boys out of the bath before they completely dissolved in the hot water.

Very shortly, two warm, inexpertly towelled sons joined her on the sofa from their bath and demanded that she read them: 'one of dad's verses'. She began the time-honoured one that started: 'Timmy, four, and Jonty, eight, get their dad in such a bate – '

Their dad went off to make them all a cup of tea. She caught sight of his broad back disappearing into the kitchen. It looked dejected.

Back at work. H. could just be right. Day after the New Year's bank holiday. Hartbeck. My terminal switched on yet again. Screen completely chocka with the repeated message (each in its own neat purple box): 'GAME OVER' – endlessly endlessly repeated. And the usual code number: BG3.1. If it is TLS, how the hell does he do it?

And yet. Oh, I don't know what to do. I can't believe he'd stop so easily. I mean, it was only old Harri chatting him up over tea or something. Unless she did some sort of trade! Oh, bloody hell, no. She wouldn't. She couldn't. Could she?

Two weeks previously, Harriet had arranged her vitally important, carefully prepared monthly date with Toby Lydell-Smith. It was Christmas Eve. The town was full of traffic and people being caught slightly out of kilter by the dash of last-minute shopping, children's excitement and the prospect of a holiday.

Toby and she had met together on the fringe of Clapham Common, at 'Teatime', a pretty little tea shop just off the Pavement. There they had sat together and shared a pot of Darjeeling and Toby had eaten a piece of lemon meringue pie, in enormous forkfuls.

Harriet was about to try to effect another of her crazy strategies.

Around them sat the mid-twenties executive class of South-West London, already on holiday, challenging Toby's guffaws with the loudness of their laughter, as they quaffed their Earl Grey. They flicked the crumbs of their toasted tea-cakes and pastries from the pages of their *Telegraphs* and their *Independents* and passed each other glossily wrapped presents before they all dashed off, that evening, to places like Norfolk and the Forest of Dean, for family Christmases.

Harriet had prepared herself, for the afternoon, at her most covered up and hidden away, indeed at her most masculine. She thought that if she was not obviously 'putting-out' at all, it might well be that for Toby she would seem the greater challenge. She needed him to want it now. In some way, she instinctively felt that if she started out by looking an impossibility, or perhaps like a bit of a dare, he might stumble along towards her all the more readily. She need not have worried. He seemed to be lapping her up – the high white collar at her throat, her businesswoman's pin-stripe suit, with the enormous trouser turn-ups discreetly hiding her spiky heels. Under his usual cover of urbane sophisticated *savoir faire*, Toby could not stop his vagrant eye from checking the pile of cunning ringlets that John had created for her or from cruising the starched white cotton man's shirt and the Old Westminster School tie that hid the rest of her. She reckoned she probably looked a bit dykey too.

He presented her with the most heavenly diamond dusted bracelet as a Christmas present. She was genuinely surprised and very impressed when she opened the presentation box. It must have cost a king's ransom, or at the very least, a monthly subscription to Cancer Research. It wasn't difficult to be enthusiastic.

'And I've got a very special pressie for you too, Tobias Riddle-me-ree. A Christmas Eve present,' she said when she had finished bubbling away about the bracelet. 'It's not very tangible. But that means that it won't be a difficult thing to explain away. There's nothing so awful as a gift that you have to keep tucked away in a drawer under your socks, is there?' Lydell-Smith looked suitably anticipatory. Harriet checked the time. She had ten minutes still to wait. She left him in what she hoped was high suspense and took herself off to the loo.

When she returned with her make-up in apple-pie order, he had finished with his tea and lit a cigar. Amid the tinkle of crockery and the gentle hubbub of polite conversation from the tables packed all around them, she took a seat right next to him and placed a masculine arm around his wide shoulders. She kissed him dryly on his whiskery ear. 'Toby,' she said, 'Toby. Toby. This is my intriguing and unusual Chrimbo present for you. A unique gift. No one has ever been given anything like this, Toby. It will be entirely unique. Listen.' She murmured in his receptive, excited ear, 'Toby, have you ever thought about – have you ever imagined – have you ever fantasised about the idea of women making love to each other? Have you never ever wondered what that might be like?' She stopped and cocked an arched eyebrow and gazed closely into his bespectacled eyes. She stuck out a long tongue and caressed his ear-lobe with it with a gentle throaty murmur of appreciation before she breathed her questions: 'Women fucking? Do you like the idea of it? Turn you on, does it?'

'How do you mean?' He was rewardingly gruff-voiced.

'I just wondered if that might be on your list of things you'd like to see. You know, before you die? Before that final bottom line? Women having sex together? You know what I'm talking about, darling. I mean you and I know that you're a man of the world. I'm sure you've seen and done most things. You're someone who wouldn't be shocked by something like that, aren't you? You've had a fairly adventurous, liberated life, haven't you? I do know about you, Toby, don't I? Your secret things. I know quite a lot about your mind, Toby. Your interesting mind. Does it appeal to you? Women? Double honeypot time?'

'I don't know.' He smiled calmly at her and crushed her hand firmly in his, her rings hurting her fingers.

She went on. She hadn't much time. Daisy would be with them in a moment or two: 'Attractive idea, is it?'

'I don't know what you mean. Orgies, is it?'

'No, not orgies. Gentle, loving, lascivious women. Nothing to do with orgies. Would you find it an idea to warm your old cockles?'

'I suppose it does. Yes, I suppose so. What are you up to, lovely Harriet?'

'Well, Toby, this may come as a tiny bit of a surprise to you. I know you think of me as a staid enough married lady.'

'I don't think you're staid at all, Harriet. Quite the reverse, my dear little thing. Good God, no. The last thing I'd ever call you is a staid married lady. Thank the Lord.'

'Well, you are about to meet a very special friend of mine. And you will be surprised by my friend. A very dear, very special, very important friend of mine.' And, once again, she was doing the whispering-in-the-ear thing. Had she no originality? But it always seemed to work. And she had to get on. Daisy would be with them almost immediately. It was a one-shot attempt and she needed it to work. It was the only way Harriet could get what she wanted from TLS. So she ploughed on regardless – oh God: 'A very sexy friend of mine. She really turns me on.' It was pathetic how bad she was acting this out. But she persevered. He seemed to accept it: 'She's called Louise. We were at school together. The same dorm. I expect you can imagine fervent pubescent girls in their dorms, Toby.' This was so gross! 'I've always loved it with her. My very first sexual experience, you see.' That bit was pretty imaginative, she thought. 'Very occasionally, particularly at festive times, well we – modesty forbids me to say what we do but – anyway – well, it's like this – my friend Louise, well, Louise has her very own special kink. She likes to have someone watching – a man watching. And I thought that – if you and I – went over to her place – with her, I could arrange for you both to have a very fleeting – intangible – and very original Christmas present cum celebration.' She liked that – that 'Christmas present cum celebration'! 'Two birds with one stone in more ways than one.' She was actually getting witty. And all this on Darjeeling alone. 'What do you think?'

At that very stage, while Toby was summoning up a circumspect approval for her scheme, Daisy entered and joined them. She looked neat and small and was dressed in a dour little black number – jacket and skirt. She looked like a trim and attractive off-duty air-hostess. Harriet introduced her to Toby who half stood and towered over her but could find very little to say. He seemed disorientated by the turn of events.

Then they were off. Toby paid the bill and settled them into his Rolls. Harriet directed him across Battersea Bridge towards Hammersmith. It seemed to take forever. There were traffic jams all over West London. Under stolid local authority seasonal street decorations, they seemed to stretch for miles. Some forty minutes later, with Harriet wracked with stage fright, they were parking outside Mary Varnals's house just off Hammersmith Grove.

Mary Varnals had been at Arts Ed. with Harriet and had been her closest friend at college and in the years afterwards. She was small and bubbly and had the most incredibly curly hair and she positively exuded energy and light. She had become a reasonably successful actress and had had minor credits in films with Ken Loach and Mike Leigh and been a regular in *Casualty* for two years, as an ever-pressed and, indeed, shortest doctor at Holby General. Mary and her husband and her two-year-old daughter Gemma had taken themselves off for Christmas to visit her mother in Wolverhampton. Harriet had shyly borrowed the key of their empty basement flat – 'for a nervous Christmas liaison of an illicit extra-marital nature'. Well, it had been the truth. Mary had giggled dirtily, said: 'good on her', and told her to strip the bed afterwards.

So that very morning, Melvyn had Taxi A Go Goed Harriet across to the flat, to check out the location. It had felt like unseemly trespass to stand there alone in the silence of that neat pot-pourried, empty cleanliness. Harriet's peace of mind had not been greatly helped by Melvyn deciding to use the journey to explain the off-side rule to her. He was very good on the off-side rule, was Melvyn. And incredibly painstaking.

Harriet let the three of them into the deserted, over-warm bed-sitting room. She flicked on some lights, switched on the tape she had bought along and made Toby open the bottle of Moët & Chandon that was already lodged waiting in the fridge. Daisy picked up and leafed idly through a copy of the *Lady Magazine* and read out small-ads for uniformed nannies with a tone that made them sound slightly rude.

'Right,' said Harriet and drew the thick curtains closed, shutting out the dark of the afternoon. Mary's 'granny-flat' was so very pretty-please, so deeply conservative, so glass-ornament ordered, that it made what was about to happen seem all the more outrageously wicked.

Harriet had talked on the phone to Daisy about it but had absolutely no idea how it might feel to embrace a woman, with intent. She never had, and had never really wanted to. Well, not very seriously. Daisy said it was easy. You just had to pretend a lot. It was like having a john but kinder. Daisy said that Harriet shouldn't be surprised if Daisy, herself, seemed really to be getting off on it – it would mostly be performance. 'Although, it's nice enough,' she had said to her, laughing. 'You might as well enjoy it, dear. Throw down a barrel-load of liquor and let yourself go with the flow, go with Flo, lazy with Daisy, easy with Louise-y.'

Indeed it wasn't difficult to do. As Daisy said, once you've had sex with various men who don't appeal to you in the slightest, pretending to have sex with a pretty, nice-smelling, clean young woman, whom you quite like anyway, is easi-peasy. They sat Toby in Mary's husband's big armchair, made him take his shoes off, loosened his tie, massaged his feet, poured him a great vat of champagne, lit his filthy old cigar and then left him to it. Daisy trotted into the bathroom and did various fiddlesome things with white powders and her nasal passages. Harriet threw down a triple gin and tonic in three seconds flat. It was Christmas. She completely forgot about Toby after about five minutes.

And she couldn't see how it wasn't going to work.

To start with, at any rate, it was difficult not to giggle. She and Daisy stood together on the hearth-rug in front of the real-flame gasfire with its flickering red hot coals and did some passionate staring into each other's eyes. Daisy was much shorter than Harriet, but had the nicest, warmest eyes, with gentle smiley lines crinkling up at the corners. They held moist hands and Harriet watched the blood clicking rhythmically away in Daisy's neck. Finally Harriet broke the ice and opened her mouth. She and Daisy had a good old-fashioned teenage snog together. She tasted nice, did Daisy. And her tongue was small and inquiring and she made delightful quiet welcoming noises with her throat. Harriet had never kissed anyone who was wearing lipstick before. Daisy was such a change after all those faintly whiffy men in their end-of-the-day shirts.

Then, very solemnly, they slowly took each other's clothes off. It was quite difficult to do decoratively but it was pleasant to tackle clothes that both parties understood so well. No incompetent strugglings with bra fastenings and suspenders here. These two were experts and could, after a little, even do it with some style. Actually it was easy, once she had started – even though Daisy was so tiny – to embrace her and stroke her backside and her shoulders and all the way down the smooth steps of her spine. Harriet found she really liked to feel the warm sleek certainty of their breasts sinking closely together. She just had to remember to call Daisy, Louise; although this wasn't a big problem, as her mouth was full of Daisy's tongue and her own hair, most of the time. Whatever the sex, she thought, she always finished up with hair in her mouth.

They finally made it, not too awkwardly, to the bed. Harriet remembered hearing once that Noël Coward, asked if he had ever been to bed with a woman, had replied: 'Yes, my dear boy. Didn't like it. It was rather like being in bed with a seal!' Harriet found she quite liked being in bed with a seal. It didn't feel as if there was anything that you had to prove. Most men turned out to be total ego, enclosed in skin, setting out goals and tests and temptations.

Women, or, well, this woman, didn't feel like a challenge or a threat. Harriet began to think that she might as well join with Daisy and give herself up to it. The whole thing felt like being gently at home with something and someone that she knew almost as well as she knew herself. Daisy felt like a blessed relief. After all the wiry-haired, muscular hardness she had dealt with for the last third of her life, she just had to marvel, her breath taken away by the silky almost invisible down on Daisy's upper breasts and on her shoulders and on her belly and flecking her inner thigh. She was beautiful and soft and warm and loving. And sexy. Harriet could see why men might find her attractive and want to do things to her.

Harriet's hair had, as ever, come all unpinned. She found herself naked and poised above Daisy on all fours, on the double-bed, with her hair hanging down brushing the woman's breasts. Daisy had her arms enfolded about Harriet's neck so gently, so generously, so comfortingly. Harriet sucked her own fingers and traced the form of the woman's body and then bent her head low and sucked her breasts, enjoying the hard sentinels that her nipples had become. You never get reactions like that from men, except from their ever preening, ever anxiously reaching cocks. Harriet reached down between Daisy's comfortably spread thighs. She felt she knew exactly what her finger on Daisy's clitoris felt like. So much so, she could almost feel it herself. She was rewarded by Daisy thrusting her hips up towards her hand to swamp Harriet's three fingers within the tangle of her pussy. And oh the exquisite pleasure of not having to break off and make jokes to cover ripping into another cold packet of Mates! Maybe there was more to this same-sex stuff than met the eye. She was beginning to revel in it, her mouth tracing a line of spittle down Daisy's tummy until, a hand on each of Daisy's knees, she was able to sink her gentle nipping teeth and her alert and knowing tongue into the wet nest of Daisy's fanny. This is what it felt like, being a man. She now began to understand why they were so keen to get in there and do it. It was just great. To be in charge, to listen to the noise you could provoke, to feel the thrust of the pelvis that you had stimulated and that you invited, but, above all, to be in charge. She was a bloke really. The pin-stripe suit had been right. On that bed, in that room, on that occasion, Harriet loved ravishing women.

She had thankfully totally forgotten that there were three of them there. It certainly wasn't of particular interest or excitement that

Toby was sitting two or three yards off, watching. Occasionally she had to remind herself that she was putting on a show. That was the whole idea.

There is a lot you can do with a ruffled duvet, and a fine old scenario you can whip up with the right amount of groaning and heavy breathing. She and Daisy were, anyway, expert at acting their way through an orgasm or two without any trouble. For a while, they lay together in a tight embrace, cupping pointed breasts and licking away sweat and tears of laughter and jigging about on the bed making it squeak in that delightful insistent way that beds, the world over, have. They lay there with their legs dovetailed and their hands working away on their own and each other's vital parts, conscious of the blood pounding in both their heads. Harriet felt suddenly extremely sexy.

Eventually, she thought they might have done enough. She was going to tell him that it was perfectly all right for him to play with himself but raising her head with an elbow, and squinting in his direction, she realised that such advice was surplus to requirements. Toby was still in his chair, his champagne glass on its side on the floor, his thick trousered thighs akimbo and his big hand down the waistband of his trousers. He disgusted her. Here we go, she thought grimly – stage two: 'Is this fun, Toby, my pet? We're having such a nice time. We always do.'

'That's right,' sighed Daisy.

'Come and join us, Toby,' Harriet said. 'We'd like that.'

He got up, an erection not hidden by his clothes. He dragged his trousers off and padded across to the bed in his shirt and socks. They had got him! The two women welcomed him and embraced him from either side and enfolded him between them. It was funny how an erect cock just gets in the way. Toby was doing his usual groaning stuff. He never lasted long. Harriet would have to move quickly. She had one more allotted task.

'I'll be back in a minute,' Harriet whispered and she quietly left them to it. She went to the bathroom, rubbed some of Daisy's residue of white powder around her gums with her forefinger, like they do in the movies, and then went back into the room. She stood just inside the tiny kitchen, separated from the main room by a Perspex screen.

It was no fun to watch. In fact, it felt really a little bit obscene to see those other two going about it. The beast with two backs wasn't a lot of delight to witness once you'd cooled down in both emotion and temperature. It was about as riveting as watching Starfire moult. She stood there with a bath towel wrapped around her shoulders. She had seen countless men in the throes, but then she had always been fairly adjacent to them. She had never watched a woman. It was interesting, but that was all.

If anything, it was Daisy that appealed to her. She could really admire the skill with which Daisy dealt with him. God, she thought, I hope I'm even half as good as that. And Daisy still had her heels on! Two rocking naked bodies and one pair of patent leather thin black heels. The shoes looked so absurd, surrounded by so much nudity. They must be part of some sort of erotic code which Harriet still needed to learn. There was so much that still eluded her – 'Golden Showers' and 'Going Round the World', she knew about now – but 'Heels in Bed' was a new one. She was still so naive.

The two of them on the bed, one so tiny and one so huge, moved swiftly from loving, friendly stroking, with Daisy babying him like he was a tiny child, to out-and-out frantic sexual activity, locked on for culmination, like a primed rocket. Daisy was suddenly on her back being vocally encouraging and the man was edging his big tilted cock haphazardly at her vagina.

Harriet watched fairly disengagedly. You never see this in films. It wasn't attractive. It was just mindlessly needful; well, certainly from Toby's point of view. He had lost it completely, his great square bum shuddering up and down, his girth wobbling between the two of them. He was just heading for home as quickly as possible. Men! That's what they do. Daisy, bless her, began to say his name fervently, and good and loud, and Toby went. The groaning and the bouncing rhythm echoed around the blind room. He was always the same, exactly the same. Then it was over, as ever, in a trice. What a lot of fuss about nothing.

They both looked dead on the bed. The Ella Fitzgerald seemed suddenly very loud. Harriet bustled into the kitchen and put on the kettle. Time for a cuppa.

Much later, well, about ten-thirty that evening, Toby parked his car up the leafy end of Blackheath Drive, ready to drop Harriet off, well away from their house and hidden under the shadows of a tree. He switched off the engine, unclipped his seat belt and leaned across towards her.

'No.'

'What do you mean "no"? Just a little Christmassy kiss, Harriet. I'm not going to see you until January, now.' He was a bit tipsy. He shouldn't really be driving.

'You often really surprise me, Toby.'

'I hope so. The feeling's mutual, I'm glad to say. You really quite surprise me, Harriet, my darling. Delightfully so, my dear.' He was slurring his words. She suddenly thought she might be going to enjoy this next bit: 'You appear so really well sussed, Toby. Smart, wised-up, almost street-wise. And yet you aren't. Are you? At all?'

'How do you mean?' Already he seemed slightly crestfallen.

'Lots of things you miss. Things I'd've thought people like you would catch hold of. Be on top of.'

'Oh? Like what?'

'Like, that this is all over.'

'Over? It's only just beginning, my darling.'

'You think so? Well, that's as maybe. You could well be wrong.'

'I don't think it's worth arguing about. It's Christmas Eve, for God's sake. Peace and goodwill. Come here, you gorgeous sexy woman, I want to give my tongue its Christmas present.' And he reached across the car for her again.

'No. God, Toby, you're not so very quick, are you? It's over. We're quits.'

'What do you mean "its over"?' Could he only repeat what she said? 'We've only just begun, my dear.' He said it again.

'No, I mean what I say, Toby, I'm afraid. This is the end. Sorry. You blew it. The deal's off. You've had your last moment with me this afternoon. You'll get nothing more. Not even one, last, wet, Christmas kiss. Bad luck.' She moved to get out of the car.

He was extremely angry, very quickly. 'What the hell do you mean? We've got a lot of business outstanding. You owe me. You know that.'

'No, I don't reckon so. We've done all we're ever going to do. And I can't say I'm sorry.'

'Don't give me that, madam. We've got another half year of our special relationship. I'm sorry, my dear, lousy or no, you're stuck with me. Bad luck.'

'No, I'm not. Listen, Toby Lydell–Smith, I know perfectly well what you've been up to. I know it's you. I reckon a dirty trick like that breaks our agreement. You've behaved like a shit to Peter. And he's meant to be your best friend. This what you do to best friends, is it? You are so sick, Toby. And anyway we've paid thousands to Cancer Research, on your behalf. The agreement's over, dead, terminado. Bad luck, Toby. You blew it.'

'I have no idea what you're talking about, dear dear Harriet. What's this about Cancer Research?'

'Pull the other one, Toby.' It was such a gamble that she was, in fact, right about it. She felt a shocking cold blast of doubt. 'We know it's you. And we're not paying any more. You crummy bloody blackmailer. It's so pathetically squalid.'

'More squalid than being on the game?' Got him, got him, got him, got him, got him!

'Fuck off and die, Toby.'

'I don't think you know the score, my darling,' he said very confidently. 'I've still got a sizable upper hand, dearest Harriet. Peter couldn't afford the scandal, neither could you, you dirty little whore, you filthy prostitute. I've seen what you're like tonight, my darling. You were really wild for it tonight, weren't you? Obsessed. So. You jump out of line, my dear and I'll empty such a pile of excrement over you and all your delightful family. Your boys would like that, would they? The big swimmer and little Timothy? – "Your mum's a hooker, a tart, a rampant prossie!" How do you think that would grab them? Make for happy hours in the school playground, would it? Oh no, Harriet, my dear, you've got me for keeps, like it or not.'

'You really are such a disgusting hateful shit, Toby. Why do you hate Peter so much?'

'I don't. I just adore having it away with his wife. You're a very very attractive girl and you bang like a shit-house door, Harriet. I'm not giving up my right to that.'

'Well you are, actually. And thanks for the extraordinarily attractive description. Goodbye.'

'What is all this?'

'What do you think this afternoon was all about?'

'What?'

'Anonymous room, anonymous woman. You doing your little number, in there? In good lighting?'

'What?' He'd guessed already.

'Sex, truths and videotape, Toby.' She so enjoyed saying that carefully prepared phrase. And it was so lovely because she could see he knew most of it immediately.

'What do you mean?' he asked.

'You ever do anything to damage me or my family or any of our reputations – if I even half believe for one tiny moment that you might, in the long run, be responsible for leaking the slightest rumour, I will have to release the tapes that we secured this afternoon – from two excellent and different camera angles – of you and your tediously fevered possession of my friend Louise.' There was a long silence. Rain spattered on the long bonnet of the car.

'Oh.'

'"Oh", indeed. Yep. They'll be in a bank vault, safe and sound, the day after Boxing Day. They'll only come out if you give me, or any of my lot, trouble. See? Barbara would get them first and your sons, then a couple of tapes to your board and then to one of the tabloids. One with the word "sun" in the title?'

'How do I know you've got anything incriminating?'

'You don't. That's the really rather kinky joy of it all. I may have nothing at all. I may very well not have had any video cameras hidden away there. But you can't afford to risk that. It's much too much of a gamble. It's what they call the deterrent. You just went mindlessly for the honeypot, the double honeypot, and never gave it a thought. Not very sussed. Not exactly street-wise.' She clicked open the car door. 'So goodbye, Toby. We won't be seeing so much of each other, except socially. And if you ever dare to put even as much as the tip of a forefinger upon my person, I will – what was it you said? – "empty such a pile of excrement on your head" that you won't be able to breathe. Oh, yes, and I will require you, Toby, to get BG3 thingummy thingummy or whatever you call yourself, to send a message to Peter releasing him from any further obligations, at the very first opportunity, which will be January the second, won't it? Or else. Do I make myself clear? And I really really really mean it,' she said in her coldest tones. 'I'm not soft-hearted at all, particularly where a shit like you is concerned. But then, that comes with the territory.' She got out of the car and was about to close the door on him. 'Oh, and Happy Christmas. Thank you so much for the heavenly bracelet. It really is much too generous. I don't deserve it.'

She walked off down the street, in the drizzle, towards her home, evilly giving him a good bit of Natasha's liquid hip movement for good measure. She felt so incredibly triumphant. Then she remembered one more thing that she needed to say to him. It was probably stupid and pathetic and mean-minded but a girl's got to do what a girl's got to do.

She took a deep breath and turned and walked, collectedly, back to the stationary car where the man remained sitting. She had a feeling that he was almost expecting her to say: 'Sorry, that was a joke, I'll see you after Christmas as usual.' She opened the big car door and half popped her head into the Rolls-Royce. She held his startled gaze for a brief minute. 'Toby,' she said softly, 'I think it's only fair that I should tell you, and, as you know, I speak with some experience, you are one hell of a lousy lay.'

She was so frightened that he might get out of the car and hurt her that she almost ran her way down the road towards number seventeen. It didn't give her exit all that much class. She was getting to be a heartless little bitch. She must watch that.

She heard his car start up and drive angrily away.

She pulled out her front door keys. With any luck, she would be back in time to help Peter fill the boys' Christmas stockings. She was going to have a happy Christmas and a prosperous new year.

If her luck held out.